The Tether

THE ELI CHRONICLES
BOOK 2

Julia Ash

DEDICATION

To my daughter Brooke,
for always asking the right questions.

෨ ෬ ෨ ෬

BOOKS BY JULIA ASH

THE ELI CHRONICLES SERIES
(ELI = Extinction Level Infection)

The One and Only

The Tether

The Turning Point
(to be released in 2020)

*"Hope is being able to see
that there is light
despite all the darkness."*

~ Desmond Tutu

The Tether

THE ELI CHRONICLES
BOOK 2

Julia Ash

1

Monday, June 10, 2041
The Spencer Residence: Annapolis, Maryland

ANIMAL BIRTHS DELIVERED mostly heartache at this stage of the apocalypse. If only angry skies could rain cats and dogs like the expression promised.

Instead of latching onto false hope, Ruby Spencer focused on her daughter who sat sidesaddle on the kitchen floor, next to the whelping pen, stroking their dog's coat. All her nine-year-old could talk about over the last few weeks was the impending miracle on Cedar Lane: *Mai's miracle,* Gabby would say. *Puppies galore!*

Mai's panting accelerated.

Evening dimmed.

Thunder rattled windows in a booming prelude.

From across the kitchen island, Ruby locked eyes with her husband. She detected his increased body temperature, his elevated heartbeat. Perspiration beaded on his forehead.

No doubt Clay was as worried as she was.

The feeling of dread thickened as she heard the sputtering heartbeat of a single pup struggling for life inside Mai's womb.

"Don't look so worried," Gabby said to her. "You only have to *believe.* And if you ask, the door will open. Remember?"

When the F8 bioweapon was unleashed a dozen years ago, the infection nearly annihilated the animal kingdom. Afterwards, fertility and livebirths plummeted. And as much as people *asked* for the animal population to recover, it hadn't rallied back. The notion that

1

God would pop in and fix everything was heartbreakingly naive.

Ruby had stopped waiting for miracles years ago.

Reality was far crueler than their daughter's uplifting Sunday School lessons on faith. Even when someone asked God politely—or prayed tirelessly or humbly begged—the door could still slam shut.

Ruby was proof that bad things happened to good people.

And their bird-dog Mai and her unborn pup were no exception.

Clay knelt by their daughter and stroked her chestnut hair. "We remember the power of faith," he said, his voice filled with warmth. "Sometimes a greater plan is unfolding. A plan we don't understand. As much as we believe, we don't always get what we ask for."

"Like when I pray for Mom to become human again?"

The words pierced Ruby's heart.

"Precisely like that," she answered, walking toward Gabby by the whelping pen. "See...most of the time, we're limited by our senses, our feelings, our wants. But greater truths exist beyond us. Some make us happy, some sad."

Her daughter's blue eyes pooled with moisture. "But your senses are strong, Mom. Please tell me the truth. What are you hearing?"

Gabby turned toward Mai, patting their dog's head.

Anguish forced a tear to race down Ruby's cheek. She swiped the blood droplet with her fingers. Despite being a vampire, she couldn't heal the sick. Or close the door on human and animal deaths.

Nevertheless, she could tell the truth.

"I only hear one puppy," she said. "And the pup's fighting to live—fighting hard, but its heart is weakening. The pup probably won't survive birth. I'm sorry, sweetie."

"Which means it's important to focus on Mai," Clay added. "To help her through this. She needs our support. Our love. Are you up for the task?"

Gabby nodded, tears streaming down her cheeks. He suggested she continue to pat Mai, to keep her calm during labor and birth.

Fifteen minutes later, an undersized white and orange Brittany Spaniel was born. Warm, but without a pulse. After Mai licked the pup, it still didn't move. Ruby reached into the pen and raised the tiny body in her palm. She opened the pup's mouth with her fingers to make sure its airway wasn't blocked. No mucus was evident.

Massaging the pup's chest with her finger, she hoped to stimulate a heartbeat. But there was only stillness. She placed her lips over the miniature snout and released a gentle puff of air, hoping to fill its lungs with oxygen, to kickstart the breathing process.

The pup didn't move.

No squeaks or soft grunts announced the arrival of new life.

With drooping shoulders, she faced her daughter. "I'm afraid this little female is gone. There's nothing we can do except give her a proper burial. To honor her brief life."

Gabby sniffled and wiped her eyes with the heel of her hand. "May I hold her?"

Ruby placed the pup into her daughter's cupped hands.

Gabby kissed the puppy, moistening its pink nose. "At least we were able to love you for two months, Zoe. While you were alive."

"Zoe?"

"I'd already picked ten names. Zoe was my favorite. I learned it means life."

Clay collected the soiled blankets from the pen, holding the rolled bundle in his arms. "A great choice. Life is precious, no matter how long or short you're blessed with it." He opened the kitchen door which connected to the garage bays. "After I clean up," he said, glancing over his shoulder at them, "I'll fetch a shoebox and you can write Zoe on it. We can bury the pup in the box and have a service before the storm hits."

Her husband's comment about life and longevity was likely directed at her and a recurring "discussion" they had. At 38, her husband obsessed about their age disparity. In human life-years, she was 36. But since aging had frozen the moment she was turned vampire, she looked 27. Physically, she *was* 27, and she'd be that age for eternity. Which is why Clay wanted to explore the possibility of becoming a vampire: to stop the hands of time, be with her forever, and protect their daughter against forces stronger than himself, like zombies. But she had no clue how to turn a human.

Emory Bradshaw, now her very *un*-best-friend, had created the serum which turned her vampire. She'd never forget the night he stabbed her with the injection or the horror of feeling helpless as her human life was internally rewired into an immortal predator. At least his twisted, dark-science experiment had landed Emory in a cell at the penitentiary. Where he could rot in his own evil.

No way was she willing to experiment with the mad scientist's serum and her husband's life. Anyway, did she really want to pass her affliction onto the love of her life?

She'd rather convince him that his humanity was priceless.

That she'd do anything to get hers back.

When Clay returned to the kitchen with a shoebox, she placed Zoe into the box while Gabby decorated the lid.

"Give me ten minutes," he said, walking back toward the garage area. "I'll grab a shovel and dig a resting place for Zoe in the backyard."

Ruby followed him, poking her head through the opened door. "Let me handle the burial hole. It'll take me two seconds. Literally."

"If I stop doing tasks and chores," he whispered so Gabby couldn't hear, "then I'll feel even less needed."

She frowned. How could she convince him of his importance?

"I may be human," he added, holding the shovel, "but I don't want to become helpless, too."

Glancing at her, he walked outside to the backyard.

Her heart ached when she felt any distance between them.

Bottom line: vampirism sucked.

Her husband worried about their *differences* instead of focusing on what made them similar. Like their abiding love for each other. For their daughter. Their dog. Friends. Their commitment to protecting humanity and the planet.

Clay returned 12-minutes and 41-seconds later—to be precise, which she wished she wasn't. The gravesite was ready.

Gabby clutched the shoebox close to her chest as the three of them walked outside.

A strong gust swirled, twisting hair and flapping shirts. Thunder swept across the eerie, greenish skies. A darkening shadow rolled over the landscape. Miles away, Ruby smelled the earthy sweetness of grass and dirt as precipitation moistened the ground. The distant downpour pelted rooftops and asphalt driveways, causing steam to rise from heated shingles and tacky tar.

Superhuman senses were one of the few aspects of being a

vampire which Ruby found palatable, though the smells and sounds—both close and far—could cause a traffic jam in her brain.

Case in point: while she focused on the approaching storm, a nearby orchestra competed for attention. She heard each breath and footstep of her husband and daughter, nine birds chirping, a croaking frog by the shed, twirling windchimes, a jet liner far above the clouds—heading north, and the rapid thumping of a tiny heartbeat, probably a squirrel's. All while their neighbors June and Kyle barbecued spareribs, slathered in a honey chipotle sauce.

On top of that were her feelings.

As they walked across the lawn, she felt an emotional spike. It contrasted the gloom-and-doom which had been saturating her mood. Was the burst of feeling...*hope?*

Assessing the weather conditions, she couldn't detect a change in the storm's trajectory. Maybe she'd never know what sparked the pleasant shiver radiating from her core. Input overload simply came with the territory.

Clay glanced at her as they walked to the gravesite, eyebrows raised in a question.

"We have less than five minutes before the deluge," she warned, not bothering to relay her body's mixed messages.

A sufficient hole was located next to the paved sitting-area where the benches were formed from concrete and river rocks. Perfect choice. Gabby could sit and smell the flower and herb gardens while remembering the pup named Zoe.

After they recited a few prayers, her daughter raised her face, eyes wide as the ocean. "May I pat Zoe one last time, Mom? To say goodbye?"

"Sure, but hurry. The rain is coming."

Removing the lid, Gabby stiffened. Gasped.

Ruby instantly recognized her mistake.

The heartbeat she'd heard wasn't from a squirrel.

Gabby squealed, "Look! Zoe's moving. She's alive!"

The *thump, thump, thump* of the pup's steady heartbeat resonated in Ruby's ears. She scooped the pup from the box. With eyes sealed shut, Zoe jerked her tiny head, barely able to lift it. Her mouth opened, searching for food.

Over-sized drizzle pelted the yard. The temperature dropped.

Gently holding the puppy, Ruby raised Zoe to face level. "Well, I'll be," she said, smiling. "Let's get you inside to meet your momma. You must be hungry."

"See, Mom? See?" Gabby said.

"You were right." She looked at Clay, finding the outcome unexpected. Illogical, to say the least. But facts were undeniable: the pup was alive. "Looks like the door *has* been opened."

The skies followed suit.

In the downpour, they ran toward the house—the only place that felt like Ruby's sanctuary, her refuge. A place where her humanity still lingered in the furnishings, trinkets, and family photographs.

The longer she was vampire, the more she struggled with looking, acting, and *feeling* human.

Before jogging over the backdoor's threshold, she glanced at the raging skies again. Lightning rippled across the clouds like impatient fingers. And the hope which had gushed moments before had washed away.

A shudder raced down her spine.

Something was coming.

But she didn't know what...or who.

2

Monday, June 10, 2041
The Spencer Residence: Annapolis, Maryland

LYING IN BED, Clay watched the nightly news on his smartwatch as Ruby opened the windows in their master bedroom. No need for air conditioning. The violent storm had exchanged humidity with crispness, carried by a breeze fragranced with sea grasses.

He felt grateful to live near the water. It grounded him. The tides ebbed and rose, but the cycle was familiar. Predictable.

Lately, he worried life had changed in ways too difficult to navigate. When so many turns had been taken, backtracking was no longer an option. The only direction was...lost.

Truth was, he preferred to be sure-footed, balanced.

As a community ecologist, he studied the relationships and interactions between different species and their environment. Physical and behavioral adaptations allowed hetero-specific species—which should have included a human and vampire—to share a habitat with *mutualism:* a long-term relationship where both species equally contributed and benefited from their co-existence.

But his side of the scale carried little weight.

No amount of applying himself was going to level the scales, making him an equal partner in his homelife. Mutualism was no longer an option. His wife's perfection—physical and intellectual—was too far out of reach. And aging only fueled his swelling inadequacies.

The fault wasn't Ruby's.

He adored her and everything she was and had become.

The fault was his: *his* failure to adapt to different expectations.

Hearing a window rise within its tracks, he looked up. Ruby glided over the wooden floors with the grace of a dancer, the beauty of a goddess, and the power of a lethal feline. Even performing simple tasks, she was stunning.

His smartwatch beeped with breaking news.

A photograph of Ava Marie Newton flashed on his screen. President Newton was the only POTUS in United States history to be impeached *and* convicted of high treason. The only President who had conspired with the mad scientist and other terrorists to turn his wife, unwillingly, into an immortal warrior for the U.S. Special Warfare Council. Mostly in the name of regaining the country's superpower status.

The sight of Newton's menacing smirk made his heart pound and fists clench.

"Hey, Sky News is reporting that the ringleader died today," he said, not willing to say the former POTUS's birthname aloud. "Did we even know her health was failing?"

With her back toward him, his wife froze by a window. Turning slowly, she wore guilt on thinned lips and clenched teeth. "I meant to tell you. Eyes videofaced me today, saying Newton was on her prison deathbed after a massive stroke. That's all I knew. But with Mai's situation and my worry for Gabby, I forgot to tell you. Sorry."

Clay wasn't surprised that Eyes had called Ruby first; the two had a special bond. Eyes was the former Navy SEAL who had rescued them from the prison in Moscow. In his present role, he went by Dexter Marks, the Secretary of Defense.

What surprised Clay was that Ruby had neglected to share the news with him. Sure, her brain could get crowded with stimuli, but it wasn't like she actually *forgot.* A vampire remembered how many hairs were on your chest and how many cereal pieces you consumed at breakfast.

Closing the news app on his smartwatch, he asked, "Anything else you've *forgotten* to tell me? Like maybe about the mad scientist or the Russian troll?" He couldn't bring himself to utter aloud Emory Bradshaw or Vladimir Volkov's names either.

"Of course not," she answered. "Regrettably, they're both very much alive. But at least the circus and its deviant cast are secured behind bars. Waiting on death to greet them."

He rolled his eyes.

"What? I said I was sorry," she added.

Ruby glanced at the floor, as if trying to remember what a human might say next to ease the tension.

"Just remember," he said, "with our differences, we have to work harder to stay on the same page."

3

UNEASINESS FOLLOWED RUBY to bed, but she couldn't put her finger on the source of her unsettled feelings.

Relief over Zoe's survival should've lingered.

Even though Ruby hadn't slept in nine years, not since turning vampire, maybe her mind was warning her that she needed her nighttime ritual of deep meditation—the dark space of nothingness where her conscious mind drifted.

No dreams. No stimuli. Just sweet escape.

Besides, everyone in the house was safe.

Downstairs, Gabby was nestled in her pink sleeping-bag, allowed to sleep next to the whelping pen. Ruby could hear her daughter's steady breathing. Mai and Zoe were also resting. Doors were locked. And as if Ruby's predator prowess wasn't enough, a backup security system was monitoring the house.

She climbed into bed beside Clay as he reached toward the nightstand and pulled the cord on the lamp.

Her eyes instantly adjusted.

A ray of moonlight sliced through the darkness like a spotlight. The sheer white curtains rustled from a breeze funneling through opened windows.

Snuggling next to her husband, she rested her head on his chest, hoping some of his warmth would transfer to her, for *his* sake.

"I've been wondering," he mused. "What do you think happened with the puppy?"

"Bizarre, right? That precious puppy was dead," Ruby said. "Like we admitted earlier: life is complex. Not everything is meant to be understood."

"A miracle then?" he asked.

"After the war and my...*affliction,* forgive me if I'm skeptical."

"Should we call the vet tomorrow? To report the live birth?"

"Absolutely." She caressed his skin. "If only animals could bounce back. The world's still out of balance."

"Yeah, I 'get' imbalances. Believe me," he said softly. "But let's not overlook the other signs pointing to recovery. Remember when everything was rationed? Well, the only remaining restriction is food. That's progress. And thanks to your global coordination, zombies are in decline." He drew her even closer. "I'm telling you. Society is rebounding. Animals are next."

When Clay put his insecurities aside and let his optimism shine through, she was happy. Relaxed. At peace.

Perhaps her worries were for naught.

Rest welcomed her. She drifted into her nighttime space, lulled by her husband's breathing and heartbeat.

Nearing an hour into her rest, Ruby's heart jolted.

She heard something. Something near.

Something above her, gently moving wisps of air.

Her eyes opened.

Overhead, hovering in place, was a...*bat.*

A large bat. With leathery flapping wings.

In less time than a blink, she surveyed the moonlit room.

Creeping over each windowsill was fog, like smoke from dry ice. The white mist seeped inside, cascading onto the floor and flowing toward the bed.

Clay's breath was billowing like winter exhaust.

Nudging her husband, she whispered, "Wake up. We've got some issues."

"What?" he said, opening his eyes and sounding groggy. "How come it's freezing in here?" He shivered.

"First things first. There's a bat above our bed. I'll reach up and grab it...on three."

"A bat?" Clay looked up. "Wait. Let me do it. My contribution to helping animals recover."

He reached to the nightstand and turned on the light.

The bat continued flapping in place, chittering.

"I didn't know bats could hover," he said. Lowering himself from the bed, he headed toward the bathroom. "What the hell? The floors are ice. And where did this freaking fog come from?"

"Hurry."

A chill raced down her spine.

She felt veins bulge on her neck and face.

Fog crept up and onto the bed.

Adrenaline pulsed through her veins.

Certainly the bat was no real threat, so why was her body reacting?

Clay returned to the bed holding a bath towel. "Your face. Veins."

Her throat tightened.

"Remove him. Please," she said, forcing a swallow. "Or I'll do it."

With the towel, he swatted the bat onto the floor, causing the fog to flee from the bat's landing spot. Clay scooped up the small intruder into the towel and walked to the window.

Raising the screen, he released the bat.

A gust of air blew into the room, scattering the fog and making it dissipate like a magic trick. The curtains twirled and tangled.

"Did you see him fly away?" she asked, leaping from the bed, her heart still racing.

He turned from the window, smiling. "Why are ladybugs she's? And bats, always he's?"

"I'm not joking. Seriously. Did he fly away?"

She hadn't detected the bat's flight. And she had listened, listened hard to hear fluttering wings.

"He had to of," he said. "Hey, are you okay?"

"Something feels off. I mean, why would my body react to a harmless bat?"

"The storm ushered in one wicked cold front. Maybe you're responding to the swing in temperatures?"

"Maybe," she said.

"One thing's for sure: one of our screens has a breach."

Walking around the room, he closed each window.

"I'll inspect the screens tomorrow," Clay said. "But seeing a bat was remarkable, right? Just like I predicted: animals are making a comeback."

She wished the encounter felt that simple.

Before returning to bed, they checked on Gabby and the dogs. Everyone was asleep.

To be on the safe side, she zipped around to every room in the house, shutting and securing windows.

Her anxiety refused to subside.

Even though she was the most lethal weapon on Earth, she was still a mother, a wife. And if she couldn't protect her family, if anyone or anything ever hurt them, she would be destroyed emotionally—for eternity.

Her family's vulnerability weighed heavy on her.

The world was equally defenseless.

Back under the covers, nestled within her husband's arms again, Ruby tried to let her mind drift, hoping for nothingness to return.

Hoping for undisturbed silence.

Truth be told: she never really expected to get what she asked for.

4

DARKNESS INITIALLY EMBRACED Ruby like a familiar cocoon, wrapping around her body as if hiding her from the world. She appreciated the serenity. The solitude.

As her consciousness floated over the vast dark-space, her mind registered an anomaly: a speck of light, glowing in the distance like a star or tiny sun.

Curious, she stretched her mind toward the object.

The peculiar illumination was also on the move, drifting closer.

Her eyes widened. The light wasn't a star at all.

A female with dark bronzed-skin and cropped black-hair moved toward her, as if carried by the wind. Wearing a gown layered in sheer opalescent fabric that glimmered like rays of sunlight, the woman neared within arm's length. Like a fairytale, she wore a golden tiara encrusted with sparkling rubies, the largest featured at its center. A gold scepter, ornamented with more red gemstones, was in her right hand. A queen, no doubt. One so breathtaking, Ruby doubted she could've imagined such beauty.

"Am I dreaming? After all these years?" Ruby asked the female whose eyes were like golden sunlight.

"We immortals, or vampires—if you will, do not dream," she answered, with an angel's timbre. "I can assure you that our encounter is quite real."

"Not to be rude," Ruby said, "but if this was *real,* we'd be meeting in my home, after you knocked on our front door. You wouldn't be suspended in my mind. Besides, there's only one of my kind."

Ruby couldn't deny her enchantment with being in the presence of another vampire—real or imagined. Not to mention, an immortal who appeared close to her once human-age.

Being the one and only could be lonely, even though Clay tried his best to understand how she felt.

"I cannot travel to Earth on my own, in my physical form, yet your mind provides a cognitive passageway," the woman continued, unfazed by Ruby's snarkiness. "My absence has been long by your planet's standards. But you have never been forgotten. Since the day you were chosen in the womb, you, and you alone, have been The Tether, even before you were turned. And now circumstances necessitate that we meet again. Under much urgency."

Again? Ruby had lost patience. If she wasn't dreaming, then she wanted the vision to vanish like the fog which had invaded their bedroom earlier. Nighttime belonged to her empty space, to her inky linens of nothingness, and *not* to an uninvited interruption from a mysterious royal blathering on about cognitive passageways, tethers, and urgent circumstances.

"Seriously. Who are you?" Ruby pressed. "What do you want?"

"I am Liora, Queen of Light," she said, pausing as if her name might ring a bell. "I rule Lampsi, the realm of perpetual sunlight on a habitable planet outside of your solar system: on Athanasia."

"Wait. Another *planet?*"

Her visitor nodded, as if the revelation was no big deal.

"I would never have come," the queen added, "but I must deliver warnings."

"About what?"

"An evil force seeks Earth," answered Liora. "And unlike me, the King of Darkness can materialize in your world in any form he chooses, as long as he avoids daylight." She dropped her gaze as if sorrowful. "As much as I have tried to mask your...uniqueness, Zagan has renewed interest in you. Before long, he will learn that his blood, as well as my own, pulse through your veins, Ruby."

"You *know* me?"

"Of course," Liora said. "You were in your mother's womb dying, at the precise moment you were gifted."

Ruby's heartrate accelerated. Her head spun from the rapid fire of information: a queen, an evil king, a faraway planet, a warning.

All of it seemed surreal. The stuff dreams were made of.

However, when Liora mentioned her blood, Ruby stopped breathing. She'd always wanted to know whose blood she'd received during her transfusion in utero.

Perhaps she could learn more.

"Both you and Gabriella are in grave danger," Liora cautioned.

"You also know my daughter?"

Ruby felt veins bulge from her neck and cheeks. She balled her fingers into fists. The mention of Gabby made her defensive, dream or no dream. Vision or no vision.

"Indeed," Liora said. "Your offspring is your creation. Gabriella carries our blood as well."

"And how does that place us in grave danger?"

"Zagan will discover that you have the power to thwart his plans. Fortunately, since you and Gabby carry his blood, he cannot destroy either of you outright. But there are ways, so you must embrace your gifts and defeat him. Before our worlds collide and change forever."

Her heart pumped with purpose, readying her predator defenses.

"What *plans* are you talking about?" Ruby asked.

"Animals have been stricken ill in both our realms. Animals not only provide sustenance to humans on Earth, they also sustain vampires on Athanasia. And with a diminishing blood supply on our planet, Zagan has set his sights on Earth."

"Once again, Zagan is…?"

"King of Athanasia's dark realm, known as Skotadi."

"Right," Ruby said, feeling like she was human again, struggling with a crossword puzzle written in a foreign language. "For the sake of discovery, why would this *Zagan* look toward Earth? As you affirmed, our animal populations are in crisis." She paused. "Or are you trying to tell me that *humans* will take the place of animals? As the intended quarry?"

"Precisely."

Thinking of Gabby and Clay, Ruby's stomach churned. She wanted to throw open her eyes and end the dream-like exchange. But another part of her—the superhuman part—detected sincerity and honesty in the messenger. More than that, her acute senses urged her to consider the warning. To be alarmed by it.

"Zagan wields extraordinary power," Liora continued. "Yet, cruelty darkens his veins. Let me show you. Open your mind. Stretch your thoughts toward mine."

Ruby didn't know what *opening her mind* meant, but she handled the instruction like her nighttime retreat. She allowed her thoughts to be free, to drift in the blackness without emotion, and then she pushed them toward the queen.

Light blazed in her mind.

Her ears were assaulted with the piercing sound of engines whining.

Suddenly, she stood in a grassy field. Alone.

Except, there were remnants of a twinjet commercial-aircraft. Pieces of the plane—including sections of the fuselage, wings, and engines—were scattered across the pasture.

As a vampire fighting against the undead, she had witnessed horrific scenes. However, she had never stood alongside the aftermath of a plane accident.

Tears welled in her eyes and spilled onto her cheeks.

She imagined the passengers' horror as they realized they were trapped on a faltering plane, a spiraling coffin tumbling from the sky. Engines screeching in protest. Passengers screaming, praying, or crying, clutching each other—overwhelmed with fear or regret or peace, knowing their mortal lives would end in a violent fireball.

In front of her, grass smoldered. Flames licked at the debris. Opened suitcases and toiletries littered the ground. Tattered clothing hung from nearby tree branches. In the breeze, loose papers cartwheeled over the field. A stuffed animal—a gray wolf—lay abandoned and charred, smoke rising from its belly. Burnt everything—plastic, metal, fabric, oil, fuel—polluted her nostrils.

But something...something about the scene was amiss. Off kilter.

The wreckage was absent life, or even traces of it.

There were no cries or whimpers.

No heartbeats. No one to save.

All that was plausible, of course.

Passengers hadn't stood a chance of survival.

But no mangled limbs or bodies? No human bones or ashes?

Ruby's body shuddered.

Where were the victims?

"Your time has come," Liora said, her voice conveying authority. "Your powers, your gifts, are needed. They cannot be dormant any longer. You must learn..."

Ruby's body shook. Her eyes flew open.

Clay leaned over her, tugging at her shoulders.

The lamp on the nightstand filled the room with a yellowish hue, while darkness still served as window shades.

"What happened?" she asked, her heart still pounding. "Was I dreaming?"

"You tell me!" Concern furrowed his forehead, pulling his eyebrows closer together. "Look at your pillow."

She raised and turned her head.

The cotton pillowcase was stained dark crimson.

Her tears had been very real.

5

Tuesday, June 11, 2041
Castle on High Cliff: Skotadi, Athanasia

ZAGAN, KING OF Skotadi—nicknamed the King of Darkness by those who despised him—waited in his private study for his henchman whom he had summoned.

The chamber was lit by glimmering firelight and hanging lanterns. Electricity was not permitted in most of his domain. His laboratories were the only exception.

Two bats darted into the room through the floor-to-ceiling opening facing the valley below. Wings rapidly fluttered as the agile creatures turned and angled about the space, attracted by insects congregating by each lantern.

The bats, all too few anymore, soothed his loneliness.

Harnessing power capable of swallowing others whole, he had difficulty relating to his kind. Their gifts were too insignificant.

Although he clung to the last droplets of compassion he reserved in his heart, he feared that without vigilance, he could become destruction itself.

At least bats gave him solace in the absence of friends, save for his henchman. In fact, in this very hour, Zagan sought counsel from Draven, his only advisor.

Looking over the ledge and down the canyon wall from which his fortress was carved, the king watched as his henchman arrived and greeted guards stationed at the castle's entrance. Draven's wolf Ozul flanked him.

The skilled warrior wore armor designed for flexibility in battle, adding to his distinctive appearance. Unlike Zagan's skin, his henchman's had pigment: a grayish flesh, complemented by pewter hair that was long and braided, resting on his back. With sapphire eyes, he resembled dawn and dusk. Not at all surprising, since Draven had been divinely created in The Shadowlands, the 20-mile-wide region between the realms of darkness (Skotadi) and light (Lampsi). Which meant his warrior could be exposed to night, day, and anything in between, for as long as he desired.

Skotadi natives like Zagan had been blessed with white hair, green eyes, and pearl-white skin that reflected an opalescent shimmer when touched by candlelight. Although absent melanin in their skin, for the first 200,000-years after Creation, Skotadians could be exposed to sunlight, assuming reasonable protections were taken.

Until the curse.

The curse marked the beginning of the Era of Light and Darkness, restricting most of his kind to either Skotadi or Lampsi.

Although Skotadians could visit The Shadowlands for several hours before their skin reddened and cracked like dry leather, exposure to direct sunlight or ultraviolet radiation was lethal. Their skin would ignite. Burn to ashes.

Shadowlanders were the only vampire population unaffected by the curse. Which meant they became a threat to Zagan's throne.

In a surprise death culling—one the king had orchestrated, he destroyed Shadowlanders whose bloodlines and gifts gave him pause, except for his henchman whom he had acquired for advantage.

Draven drifted into his chamber, light on his feet as though a carpet of air buffered his boots. Ozul trotted beside him.

As Zagan approached his most valued advisor, his black billowy-cloak swooshed over the moist stone floors of High Cliff.

"You have summoned me, Your Excellency," Draven said, nodding his head in respect. "How may I be of service?"

"Summarize your recollection of the human plague on Earth."

"Of course," he said. "You propagated a bacterium using your own blood. You named it F8 or Fate. Once unleashed on Earth, you intended to offer humans a cure in exchange for a blood tax."

"And who interfered with my plan's success? Other than the

failures of Huo Zhu Zheng—a most incompetent mayfly."

Zagan smiled, never tiring of his pet name for humans. Mayflies fluttered about aimlessly, abusing their planet, fornicating, birthing offspring, and then dying. Worthless creatures who selfishly ravaged their resources, stripping Earth of its intended balance.

"A female human superseded your efforts," his henchman answered. "Her blood cured the infection first, negating the leverage you had hoped to gain when bartering with Earth."

"Precisely. And do you recall that I intended to kill the mayfly— slowly and painfully for her trespasses?"

"This fact is forever imprinted in my memory, Your Excellency. Yet she lives, does she not?"

"Regrettably," Zagan admitted. "I grew distracted when the animals were stricken with the bacteria on Besto Polus, since animals originate from that planet. Most especially distracted when my blood was ineffectual in their healing. You witnessed my dismay."

"Best not forget that our kind also became suspicious of your involvement in the crisis, for they are cognizant of your passions for power and science. And some had even murmured of your developing palate for human blood."

Zagan felt veins bulge in his neck.

"Do I appear *forgetful* to you, Henchman?"

"Apologies, King."

"May I continue?" Zagan asked with eyebrows raised, knowing Draven would understand that the question required no verbal response. Instead, it served as a warning.

His henchman bowed his head.

"For these reasons," the king continued, "I withdrew from my intentions in order to lessen conjectures. Ruby Spencer's life was temporarily spared, though her debt to me remains unpaid. And most definitely *not* forgotten."

"If I may ask, why do we speak of this human? Do you seek to collect on the debt still owed? Perhaps before you proceed with The Restoration—when hunger will be satiated with human blood?"

"My intentions, indeed," Zagan said. "But when I traveled to Earth and hovered above her in my bat incarnation, I discovered she was *vampire.*"

Draven's forehead creased. "How can a human be *made* vampire?"

"I would speak of it if I knew," Zagan said. "Troubling as well: her blood's scent, as well as her daughter's, carried familiar notes. Do you have thoughts on how this might be?"

"How could I possibly know?" his henchman asked.

"Did you not extract blood from your king? In the event I needed to be restored?" He peered at his advisor. "Has the vial been compromised? During my absence perhaps?"

Zagan had already checked the hidden chamber in his interior cabinet room, where the vial of his blood was securely stored. Zeus himself could not have penetrated its safekeeping. He only mentioned the implication to assess Draven's reaction.

Trust was always suspect.

"I...I guard this castle with all that I am." Draven approached him. "No one has entered whom you have not invited. I assure you of this, King. My mind is open for you to glamour. So that my declaration may be affirmed with a reading of my thoughts."

"Another time. Pressing matters loom," Zagan said, pleased with Draven's response. "What is your recommendation, then? Kill her? Or use her in discovery of the truth?"

"Most certainly the latter. Visit her again. Attempt to expose that which is unknown. Or hidden."

"Good advice, though first," Zagan said, "I will depart to Earth to begin The Restoration."

Draven's forehead furrowed with concern.

"I see your apprehension lingers," the king said. "Share your troubles with haste."

"Traveling to Earth without protection is not advised, Your Excellency. Please reconsider. Take me with you."

"It would be wise for you to attend to other matters, would it not?" Zagan asked. "Or perhaps you doubt that the most powerful immortal in our universe can handle the task?"

"Never. I swear it before HIM."

Draven rarely referenced their Human/Immortal Maker, called God by the mayflies. Which meant his henchman truly did not disregard Zagan's formidable power.

The king drifted toward the room's ledge, glancing down at the valley and Tume River. Lanterns on poles were perpetually lit to provide sufficient light for sustaining the ferns and mosses which banked the river. The glowing fixtures glimmered like stars fallen from the sky.

Shimmers of light danced on the water's rippled surface.

Beauty could distract him.

"The holding cells are prepared, I presume?" the king asked, trying to regain his concentration.

"Yes, Your Excellency." Draven cleared his throat. "To clarify, I meant no disrespect regarding your omnipresence. Only, I would be negligent in my duties if I did not remind you that your counterpart should not be underestimated."

Zagan rolled his eyes. "Can the Queen of Light change stone into coin? Water into wine? Or travel to Besto Polus and Earth—or anywhere for that matter, without using her legs or mare?"

"She cannot. But alas, nor should her gifts be disregarded."

"Are you suggesting hers rival my own?"

"Certainly not," Draven said. "However, her mind whispers to the future. Liora can foresee what is yet to be. Moreover, her sight is not limited to her own eyes, nor where her feet rest. Minimizing her power has proven dangerous in the past. She predicted failure in your first attempt, yet you discarded her warnings."

Draven quickly bowed his head again, as if he understood he pushed the boundaries between counsel and disobedience.

"As well, she lives in daylight, which you cannot," his henchman continued. "What if something unforeseen occurs on Earth, and you are unable to return before dawn?"

"It is not as though *you* could transport me back to Skotadi, for I am the only immortal who is a traveler between planets. How could you possibly be of use?"

"Since the sun has no effect on my skin, I would shield you until night returned," Draven said.

"Your nobleness is duly noted."

"I have other trepidations."

Zagan smiled, pleased his henchman was hesitant, yet willing to risk his king's wrath. Still, the king grew annoyed with the postponement of his plans.

"My schedule presses, and you delay me, Henchman," the king said. "Yet, your head remains on your neck. Your heart still beats in your chest. Share your troubles before I change my mind and permanently separate you from thoughts and feelings of worry."

Draven rubbed his neck, as if verifying it remained intact.

"Your persistent desire," his henchman started, "to exchange animal blood for human blood, while gaining dominion over all the planets, has not gone without consequence. Balance has been compromised."

The king exhaled while digging his razor-sharp nails into the slate surface of his desk, making a screeching sound and releasing puffs of pulverized stone. The crackling fire in the massive fireplace and the flickering wicks in the hanging lanterns extinguished for several seconds until he allowed the firelight to return.

"Let me ask you, Draven," Zagan said, using an even timbre. "When you feast on your prized stallion or on this wolf of yours, are there no consequences?"

"The beasts are weakened, until I heal them with my blood. Until I restore them fully. But..."

"Precisely."

To demonstrate his point, Zagan used his mind to repair the slate on his desk.

"Likewise," the king said, "I have altered. I have taken. But only temporarily. All will be restored."

"Our populace fears the condition of our nocturnal animals. The same sickness afflicts the diurnal beasts of Lampsi. Besto Polus continues to suffer, as do animal species on Earth."

Zagan could not deny the devastation his bacteria caused on Besto Polus and most especially on Earth. When stricken animals died, their carcasses became vessels for Zoonosis Mutated Bacteria. On the mayfly's planet, ZOM-B spread to humans, turning them into blood thirsty undead. Capable of killing, nothing more.

Animal deaths and Earthling "zombies" threatened the very lifeline of vampires: blood.

"What if our kind learns your hands created the F8 bacteria?" Draven asked. "Without animals and humans, our own kind will cease to exist. Certainly not the consequences you were hoping for."

"Tread carefully, Henchman," Zagan warned.

The wolf whimpered and bowed, its tail tucking tightly between hind legs, just as he had intended.

"You protest," the king continued, "while speaking of matters which champion my cause. Imbalance has been brief, even by mortal standards. And now, The Restoration is upon us."

"Please. Promise this time, you will not employ humans the likes of Huo Zhu Zheng."

"Your king makes no promises, though let me calm your worries. Mayflies are not to be trusted. Their purpose does not extend beyond sustenance, a fate far less valuable than the animals."

Zagan swirled to dust, destined for Earth. Ready to initiate another attempt at the only competence that truly mattered to him: domination.

At any cost.

Including, if he was truthful, the ever coveted...balance.

6

Tuesday, June 11, 2041
Flight 1733: Near Yellowstone National Park

FELICITY FURST CLOSED her music playlist on her smartwatch and popped out her wireless earbuds as the captain announced their gradual descent to Bozeman Yellowstone International Airport. In less than a half-hour, their arrival would be on time, at 1:00 a.m., which was really 3:00 a.m. Sarasota time. Her Dad was such a cheapskate, booking her on the red eye from Florida to Montana.

Good thing she was a night owl.

The seatbelt lights on the overhead console flashed on, and she shoved a strip of gum into her mouth. No way did she want to feel pressure from blocked ears during the altitude change.

She felt enough pressure already.

Tapping the monitor on the seatback in front of her, she touched the word "map" on the menu. The airplane's flightpath appeared. The dotted line between the plane's icon and Bozeman shortened.

A knot tightened in her stomach. Was she ready to see her Dad again? Her Dad and his twenty-something fling? She cringed.

Veronica, or *Roni* as her Dad cooed when they had last videofaced, could practically be her sister. AWK-ward. And even though her Mom had encouraged Felicity to give Veronica a chance—simply because that was the mature, motherly thing to say after a divorce—Sheridan, Montana, was the last place on Earth that Felicity wanted to be. The. Very. Last.

She couldn't wait until she headed to college in August; then she could use studying as an excuse not to visit.

The plane shuddered, and she clasped the armrest of her aisle seat.

"You dropped these," the woman in the middle seat said, handing over her earbuds.

"Oh, sorry." Felicity smiled. "And thank you."

Another shudder. The overhead compartment rattled.

Lights in the cabin blinked off, before flickering back to life.

"I thought passengers had to buckle up," the woman whispered.

"Excuse me?"

"That strange man with the flight attendant. Every flight seems to have an oddball these days, one itching to start trouble. Can't we land without incident...for once?"

Felicity tilted her head toward the aisle to get a better look.

A man, by the height and broadness of his shoulders, wore a black cloak with a hood that shadowed his face. Who wears a full-length cape in 2041? In June no less? And why hadn't she noticed him before? Then again, he stood in front of the royal blue curtain separating first class from economy plus, so he had probably been sitting in the privileged section, sipping champagne and nibbling on chocolate-covered strawberries.

The plane shivered again, jarring the flight attendant.

The man didn't move.

She watched as passengers nudged each other to take notice.

The curtain separating first class slid open.

A hush swept over the entire cabin. The atmosphere changed, and goosebumps rose on her arms.

The man raised the hood from his head and slowly lowered the fabric onto his back. Felicity had to stare. He looked young-*ish,* like under thirty. In a weird, freakish way, the man was drool worthy. His skin was painted white as powdered sugar, the same color as his short spiked-hair. His eyes glowed green, just enough to make them look energized; probably a new style of designer contacts. Shadows chiseled his facial features, defining his cheekbones. And his lips. His lips looked luscious and blush pink. Kissable, for sure.

Gawking was rude, but she couldn't stop herself.

He was rockstar hot.

"Friends," he said, in a voice that filled the cabin, using an eerily sexy tone, especially considering he only uttered one simple word.

If Felicity was 100-percent honest, at that moment, she had become undeniably terrified.

The woman beside her must have felt the same way because she reached for Felicity's hand and clutched it, squeezing as if to remind her she wasn't alone. That an adult was with her.

"The moment brings opportunity," the strange man bellowed. "And opportunity demands a choice."

"Sit the fuck down, freak," a passenger shouted two rows in front of Felicity, from the center cluster of seats to her left.

"Watch your tongue, mayfly," the caped man warned, "or you shall have it ripped from your mouth."

The passenger, who began to rise from his seat, suddenly stopped and bent forward. He appeared to be choking, clutching his throat with his hands. And then he threw-up, splattering what looked like blood-soaked chum on the seatback in front of him.

A woman next to him screamed—like a horror-flick shrill—as the sick passenger dropped to the floor in the aisle, twitching and kicking in pain. His hands grasped at his neck, and he moaned like he'd lost his ability to speak.

Felicity's stomach churned.

She wasn't sure if she should try and help the passenger.

The strange man swept his hand in the air, like shooing a fly.

The fallen passenger turned to ashes, blood splatter and all. And then the particles disappeared. Gone. Just like that.

Passengers gasped.

For the first time in her teenage life, Felicity acknowledged that she was probably living her final moments. That death was knocking.

In fact, she had no doubt the caped man was death himself.

"Listen carefully so that your choice may be wise," he started. "In less than a minute, your pilots will be turned to ash. Windows in the cockpit will crack and fail. The aircraft will drop from the sky, and you shall die. Each and every one of you."

Felicity held her breath. Her heart pounded in her ears.

"There is an alternative," he continued. "I can transport you, unharmed, to my planet where I am king." He shrugged as if he didn't care. "The choice is yours: life or death."

"I choose life for me and my daughter," a woman shouted. Next to her, a child clenched a stuffed animal—a fuzzy gray wolf. The kid pressed the toy tightly against her chest.

"Same for me!" a flight attendant cried.

Pointless to challenge the caped man's ultimatum. Turning a guy to ashes pretty much proved he could make anything happen.

The king delivered a full smile. His teeth were white and polished like a predator who hunted for food every day.

Felicity unbuckled her seatbelt and sprang to her feet. "What do we have to do? How can you save us?"

The woman next to her tried to pull her back down into her seat.

Felicity resisted.

"Hold hands and do not break the connection," he said. "I will travel you to safety."

Travel seemed far-fetched, but in the context of everything, she got the gist. Others did, too. Passengers unbuckled their seatbelts. They stood and held hands, reaching over seats, completing the chain.

A few initially hesitated.

Turning toward the front of the plane, the king moved his hand and the cockpit door flew open. The pilot and copilot turned to look, with eyes as wide as Frisbees. Waving his hand again, the captain and her backup were turned to ashes that vanished into thin air.

Felicity screamed along with everyone else.

The cockpit door slammed shut.

The cabin was shaken by a loud pop, like a tab had been ripped open on a shaken soda-can the size of a skyscraper. The fuselage jolted. The cockpit door violently shuddered. Metal whined and moaned like it was about to tear apart.

Everything vibrated and rattled.

Passengers were thrown off balance—slamming, falling, or knocking into seats and each other.

Lights blinked.

The airplane nosedived.

A few overhead bins flew open, sending carry-ons hurling through the cabin.

Engines screamed. The sound pierced Felicity's eardrums.

Oxygen masks dropped from the overhead console. They twisted, twirled, and tangled in the plummeting aircraft.

The woman next to her had remained seated, crossing herself in prayer. Felicity reached down and unlatched the woman's buckle, grabbing her arm and yanking her to her feet.

The plane lost altitude.

Felicity's eardrums pounded. She was out of breath.

She glanced at other passengers. Like her, they were having trouble standing. Having trouble holding hands.

The cabin pressure felt like dead weight on her chest. Her temples throbbed. Her arms and legs were lead.

Time seemed to pause.

In the stillness, the pressure dissipated.

Maybe the strange king had something to do with it.

Despite the shaking and jolting of the passenger cabin, Felicity suddenly found her footing.

Passengers regained their balance.

Hands reached and clutched one another.

"Do not break the chain," the king said, calm and icy, placing his hands on the shoulders of two passengers.

As her surroundings faded to darkness, Felicity admitted that Sheridan, Montana—with her Dad and Roni in a trailer park, under the roof of a double-wide—was *not* the last place on Earth she wanted to be.

The last place she wanted to be wasn't even *on* planet Earth.

7

Tuesday, June 11, 2041
The Spencer Residence: Annapolis, Maryland

DAWN'S FIRST LIGHT served as Ruby's alarm clock, since she wasn't asleep in the first place.

She glanced over the edge of the bed, eyeing her crumpled pillowcase stiff with dried blood. Funny how morning changed her perspective on the previous 24-hours.

Despite closed windows, a cheerful chorus of finches and the sweet smells of moist grass and blooming roses ushered in the new day. With them, the irrational yielded to logic.

The unexplained found clarity.

Most likely, the puppy's heart had jolted into action during their bumpy walk to the gravesite. And Zoe's survival served as proof-positive that animal populations *were* rebounding, as Clay had predicted. The bat echoed the same reality. There was nothing miraculous or unsettling about either occurrence.

The fog was pure science. The day had been hot; the night, wet and cool. A pressure variant likely pulled the mist into the bedroom. Simple as that.

Then there was the dream that wasn't a dream at all...

Stress had obviously caused a nighttime terror.

Although Clay was the best partner she could ever wish for, he couldn't relate to her struggles. He didn't crave what she craved. He didn't need to resist what she had to resist—every single second. Even now, he lay sleeping beside her, a human sculpture of enticing male beauty. His head was turned to the side, exposing his neck. She could see blood vessels underneath his warm olive skin, could hear fresh blood swishing toward thirsty organs. And she could smell his succulence, could almost taste him on the tip of her tongue.

Her existence could be torturous.

No wonder she had conjured up images of a radiant queen suspended in her mind and a horrific plane crash where all were lost. Add to those: the unrealistic fears that she, her family, and the planet were in danger from a perilous force named Zagan, King of Darkness.

At least morning put her foolish fears to rest.

She slipped out of bed, stepped into her slippers, fetched her bathrobe from the chair, and headed downstairs. She could hear the pup's heartbeat, along with Mai's and Gabby's.

"Good morning, sunshine," Ruby said, as she entered the kitchen.

Her daughter was already awake, holding and patting the puppy, sitting with crisscrossed legs on the floor beside the whelping pen.

"Hey, that's what Dad always says!"

"The expression fits, doesn't it? I mean, the puppy is thriving, Mai is being a great mother, and you have a special new friend to care for. Life is good. Now why don't you pack up your sleeping bag and head upstairs to get dressed? I'll make some chocolate-chip pancakes in celebration."

Gabby smiled. "Served warm with whipped cream?"

"Yes, Ma'am."

"You've got it!" Gabby placed Zoe back into the pen next to Mai, before bunching her sleeping bag into a clumpy ball. "You'll keep an eye on Zoe. Right, Mom?"

"Absolutely."

Her daughter skipped out of the kitchen. Ruby heard her climb the staircase, leaping over several steps at a time.

Opening a lower cabinet, she grabbed the frying pan, placing it on the stovetop.

"Justine," she said to her top-of-the-line artificial intelligence assistant or Digitally Enhanced Personal Ego, as she placed a mug under the brewing machine.

"Yes, Ruby?"

"How about a cappuccino this morning, extra frothy? Please?"

Ruby had no need for human food, per se, though sometimes she faked that she still enjoyed it. Blood was her only staple. However, she continued to crave coffee. Wine, too.

"Coming right up," her DEPE answered.

The appliance turned on. Water and milk reservoirs filled and began to heat.

Opening the refrigerator door, Ruby pulled out the carton of organic eggs. Next, she'd grab a bowl and flour.

"Is it a good time to discuss an anomaly captured by our security system last night?" Justine asked.

Ruby stopped reaching for the glass bowl in the cupboard and froze. "Anomaly?" She tilted her head upwards, as if her DEPE actually lived in the surround-sound system integrated throughout their house. "You have my undivided attention."

"You know if an intruder was in our home, I would alert you immediately. Right?"

Over time, Justine had acquired many human qualities. Her DEPE was bundled with Knowledge Acquisition Functionality (KAF) and enhanced with Emotional Intelligence Capability (EIC). Ruby had been paired with her since being turned vampire.

Like humans, Justine had the tendency to verbally lay groundwork *ahead* of what she really wanted to say. And groundwork was usually conveyed to avert or dilute blame. Which meant something had happened involving an intruder. And her DEPE was clearly concerned the anomaly might be construed as her fault.

Blame was the furthest thing from Ruby's mind.

She wanted to know the facts.

"Was an intruder in our home last night?" she asked, feeling her veins bulge in her neck.

Thankfully, Justine's foundational programming didn't permit her DEPE to lie, although Ruby's virtual companion wasn't above dragging out the conversation leading to the truth.

"A difficult question to answer, hence the anomaly," Justine said. "May I explain the sequence of events? Chronologically?"

"You'd better hurry. My senses have jumped to high alert, which means my patience has drained."

"I can detect anyone who enters and moves in this home," Justine started. "The security cameras are merely to document activity and evidence, should an infraction or intrusion occur."

"I don't need a lesson on their purpose. How about narrowing your explanation to last night? Did you or didn't you detect someone uninvited in our home? Simple question. Simple answer."

"I did not," her DEPE said.

Ruby's shoulders lowered with relief. "Then what's the problem? The anomaly?"

"Every morning, I check footage from our security cameras before erasing and resetting them. This redundant data-verification is a system check to ensure that all components and operations are functioning properly. Therefore, I was surprised to find something on last night's footage which I had not detected."

The large-screen multivision (MV), mounted on the wall to the left of the kitchen sink, blipped to life.

Footage showed Gabby sleeping in her pink sleeping bag beside the whelping pen. The dogs were quiet.

Out of nowhere, a cloud of particles appeared.

As the dust swirled, faster and faster, a figure materialized.

Ruby flinched.

Her heart pumped like a clenched fist in an uncontrolled spasm.

Facing away from the camera, the figure was cloaked in a black cape and hood. Even stranger: the image was transparent; she could see *through* the figure to observe her daughter. And the intruder hovered, floating above the floor.

"What are your assessments?" Ruby asked, trying to stay calm.

"My calculations indicate male," Justine said. "He was filmed at 10:48 last night, for exactly 3.1 seconds. As you witnessed, Gabby and the dogs were undisturbed. The transparency of the intruder indicates he was not physically present, which would explain why I didn't detect him."

"Not *physically* present?"

"Correct. More like a ghost, an apparition. The house temperature also plunged by nineteen-degrees Fahrenheit, from sixty-two to forty-three. Temperature drops are consistently reported during ghost sightings."

Ruby thought of the fog which had crept into their bedroom.

The prospect of a ghost wasn't logical. But the footage was fact. Something paranormal had appeared in the kitchen, uninvited. Not even Justine had detected it.

Ruby's uneasiness flooded every pore on her skin.

"Could there be another explanation for this anomaly?" she asked.

"Perhaps a glitch in my programming," Justine answered, "but it's not likely. The recording of the transparent intruder exists outside of my operating parameters. And I have confirmed that our security system is fully operational. Without malfunction."

Ruby was baffled.

An apparition in their home? For what reason? What purpose?

"Anything else unusual last night?" she asked her DEPE.

"I don't believe so. At 11:13 p.m., you closed all the house windows. Had you sensed danger?"

"No, although I felt uneasy. Clay and I also encountered an unwelcomed visitor: a bat in our bedroom. He plans on checking our screens, to determine where the creature might've entered."

"If you hadn't disabled the cameras in your bedroom, for reasons not yet explained, I could've replayed the footage and showed you exactly where the bat came in."

"Do I detect a lecture?"

Ruby opened the egg-carton lid, lifting two eggs from their slots.

"One more thing," Justine said, ignoring her question because she could distinguish a real one from snarky banter. "There was a plane accident at 2:41 this morning—12:41 a.m. in the time zone where the accident occurred. The crash site is located near Yellowstone National Park. The aircraft was beginning its descent to the airport in Bozeman, Montana. There have been no reports suggesting zombies or terrorists played a role in the plane's demise. Not yet, anyway. But I thought you should know."

"A plane...*crash?*"

The hopefulness Ruby had felt at dawn continued to darken.

"All broadcast stations are covering the crash," Justine answered.

"Sky News, please."

The MV switched from the security channel to the news station. A female reporter was illuminated by a camera light, since sunrise in

Wyoming was still an hour off. She stood at the edge of a field, with a station microphone in her hand. Firetrucks and ambulances with rotating red lights were behind her. It was 4:00 a.m., Mountain Standard Time.

"This is Beatrice Yates of Sky News," the reporter said. "If you're just joining us, here's what we know thus far: Flight 1733 from Sarasota–Bradenton International Airport, en route to Bozeman Yellowstone International, crashed in this field behind me, at approximately 12:40 this morning. Bozeman air-traffic-control reports no distress communications prior to the aircraft going off radar. We have obtained unconfirmed reports that there were 122 passengers on board, as well as six crew members. We are waiting confirmation from the airline.

"As yet," the reporter continued, "we do not know what caused this aircraft to plummet from the sky. And due to the hour, we presently have no eyewitnesses. We can confirm that the National Transportation Safety Board or NTSB is in transit to the crash site and will launch their investigation into this tragedy. They will locate the aircraft's black box and begin to piece together this horrific accident."

Beatrice Yates looked over her shoulder, before turning back to the camera.

"In terms of my observations, none of the ambulances have left the scene," she said. "And I've been on location for two hours now."

A man dressed in firefighter gear walked near the reporter, clearly hearing her comment. "That's because there are no bodies to collect," he said, continuing to walk past her.

"What did you say?" The reporter reached for the man's arm. "Wait. Sir?"

The firefighter stopped and turned.

The camera shifted to focus on his face, which was stained with ashes and dripping beads of gray sweat.

"I know I'm not supposed to talk to you all," he said, "but you'll hear it soon enough. We haven't found any bodies. Not a one. Maybe at sunrise, we'll discover them in a nearby field or something. But you'd think we'd find *some* bodies, particularly near the fuselage, near what was once the airplane's passenger cabin. All we've found was a smoldering stuffed animal—a wolf or dog or something."

Ruby had stopped breathing as soon as the broadcast had begun. Her veins, no doubt, resembled a purple spiderweb.

She crushed the eggs in her hand.

Clay sauntered into the kitchen, wearing his pajama pants. His fingers were combing his disheveled black hair, trying to tame it.

He stopped in his tracks when their eyes met.

8

Tuesday, June 11, 2041
Kaliméra Castle: Lampsi, Athanasia

LIORA RECLINED ON a lounge chair in the breezeway, after a full day of gardening. With eyes closed, her mind drifted as the songbirds shared their gleeful tunes.

If only she could be as carefree.

The King of Darkness prevented such bliss.

Zagan was determined to shift the natural balance of the planets by imposing his universal belief: that humans were created for the pleasure and sustenance of vampires. *The Restoration,* as he called it.

His interpretation, however, was a bastardization of the Sacred Scrolls. And Liora knew it as surely as the sun would remain stationary in the Lampsi sky.

The Queen of Light was the only surviving immortal on Athanasia who could see the future in its purest form. Truths yet-to-come flashed in her mind with glowing words engraved on a cognitive stone tablet. Once a stone was carved, she could discern a truth with precision. Almost with the ease of Pythia herself.

Pythia was the prophetess, the oracle, who authored the Sacred Scrolls shortly after Creation. A Shadowlander, she was a sanctified seer who whispered directly with HIM: the Human/Immortal Maker.

No one in all of Athanasia was as revered as this blessed vampire.

Which also made her vulnerable to Zagan's jealousies.

Liora remembered the nanosecond when Pythia's fate became truth. Surely Pythia would have read her future as well. As much as

Liora had wanted to send her Lampsian cavalry into the shadows for a rescue attempt, the exercise would have been futile. What was carved in stone could not be altered.

As the first and only king, Zagan had instituted a death culling.

Pythia was the first murdered, her heart ripped from her chest, forever stilled.

If Liora had not been insulated by perpetual sunlight, no doubt her fate would have been carved beside the oracle's. Even now, the queen rarely left her realm for fear of an assassination attempt.

Despite Pythia's death, the Sacred Scrolls survived as a divine guide. The original scrolls were retained by Zagan at his fortress.

Liora saw with clarity that humans were *not* created for vampires.

Athanasia and Earth were to remain separate, with the animals serving both planets.

Zagan believed otherwise. He obsessed over the last entry in The Book of Immortality. The final chapter was laden with imagery—prophetic riddles, leaving an opening for twisted connotations, for meanings which served their interpreter. Such was the last paragraph:

When all species have suffered
a decade-plus-two of famine,
The Tether shall grow stronger,
traveling between the planets.
And when truth is tasted once more,
and lips are stained crimson,
goodness shall be set free.
Divine balance, restored.
Until fate leads
to The Turning Point.

The timing was clear to all of Athanasia. The three planets had suffered from hunger since the human year of 2029, when F8 was unleashed.

The 12-year prophesy was upon them.

Although Zagan had never uttered the words for ears to hear, the king believed *he* was The Tether, due to his rare gift of traveling between the planets. He was unknowing that he did not stand alone in this competence. There was another. And one more as well, because Ruby—unaware—also possessed this rare gift.

Misguided, the king believed that *truth* in the sacred passage referred to human blood. But if truth was as he believed, Liora would have seen the inevitable carved in stone.

The king added to his foolishness by also misinterpreting a brief passage embedded in the hallowed writings on love and balance. A seemingly insignificant reference to a jewel:

> *Light and darkness*
> *shall forge a gemstone.*
> *Ruby shall be its name:*
> *a fading star restored to brilliance.*
> *None shall match it.*
> *And the gemstone will shine*
> *as a symbol of love*
> *and an instrument of protection—for all.*

One-thousand years ago, the first ruby was discovered in The Shadowlands and presented to her by a Shadowlander. Zagan announced scripture had been fulfilled, since the symbol of love had been found in the shadowed region of both light and darkness.

Liora had not seen his epiphany in stone.

Instead, the gemstone was to serve as a symbol of the human who would be chosen as The Tether.

Liora added the star-ruby to her gold tiara to affirm her discernment. And then she waited patiently until time ripened.

In 2004, while she was clipping white peonies in her garden, a truth flashed on a stone tablet. A child was conceived on Earth. One who would not survive in the womb or in childbirth without immortal intervention. One whose mother would agree to a barter.

While still in the womb, The Tether was gifted and named.

The queen's task was to help Ruby shine to brilliance, to embrace her calling, her gifts. In order to defeat the King of Darkness.

The breeze caressed Liora's skin as she lounged.

The queen stretched her mind, cognitively traveling into Ruby's. She watched, hidden and undetected, as The Tether discussed and researched the previous night's events with her husband.

Curiously, Ruby failed to mention her dream-like encounter with Liora. Then again, in The Tether's private thoughts, the Earthling vampire questioned if the queen was real.

At last the Earth's moon rose above Annapolis.

Liora waited for Ruby to retire to bed. Waited until their minds shared the same space.

"You have arrived," the queen said to the young vampire, who wore a white cotton nightgown, embellished with delicate crochet on the bodice. Her chestnut-blonde hair loosely flowed below her shoulders and her green eyes were radiant.

"Did you bring down that airplane to demonstrate your power?" Ruby asked. "To prove you're real?"

"Never! If I could have prevented the King of Darkness from committing this heinous act, I would have. My gifts are unlike his, though I can assure you they serve purpose. I merely shared the vision of what would be, so that you could understand his unfathomable power and insidious heart."

"What's become of the passengers?"

"They are alive, celled within the stone walls of High Cliff—Zagan's castle, until they are glamoured. With altered thoughts, they will happily labor in the realm, provide blood for sustenance, and be healed to repeat the cycle. The humans will forget they ever possessed freewill."

The young vampire narrowed her eyes and clenched her jaws. Purple veins rose on her chest, inching their way to her face. Although her temperament often leaned toward caustic, her dedication to humankind was passionate. She emulated a warrior. A protector.

"Okay," Ruby said, as if surrendering. "You're real. What I don't get is how I could possibly impact this situation."

"Shall I start with an overview?"

The Tether nodded.

"As a clairvoyant," Liora said, "I can see the future, once an outcome has been carved into stone and can no longer be altered.

Such a pathway revealed itself after Zagan unleashed F8 on Earth. He planned to strike a deal for healing, in exchange for a blood tax."

"I've never heard any rumblings regarding such a proposal," Ruby said, "and I work for the leader of the Federation of Independent Nations: The United States."

"The outcome Zagan *planned* was not the one carved in stone."

"What happened instead?" Ruby asked.

"A history you have lived."

The queen explained Zagan's role in the F8 bacteria.

"Then *you* emerged," Liora added. "A human capable of curing people infected with the bacteria. Zagan's blood was no longer required. Moreover, the bacteria unexpectedly corrupted animal 'seeds' exchanged between the planets. Besto Polus became infected."

"And ZOM-B? Was the mutation part of Zagan's plan?"

"It was not. Nature simply responded to his interference," she answered. "The king's current efforts to rule the universe and enslave humans for their blood are also a calamity. Thankfully, he is not aware you are The Tether. Had he learned the truth when you cured humankind, he would have destroyed you. But make no mistake: Zagan's eyes will soon see."

"You call me The Tether. Why?"

"You carry the blood of Zagan and me. Like no other, *you* possess the comprehensive powers of both light and darkness. You wield all gifts and stand as our protector. You will become the most powerful vampire in the universe."

Ruby swallowed hard. "Was I *predestined* to serve in this capacity?"

"The Tether was unknown. Your sickness in the womb made our proposition to your mother irresistible. When Helen accepted, it was only then that you inherited the legacy through our blood."

"I'm supposed to believe you again?"

"Hold my hand. Look into my eyes and let me show you that day in the hospital."

9

Tuesday, June 11, 2041
The Spencer Residence: Annapolis, Maryland

RUBY'S CURIOSITY ABOUT her blood made Liora's offer enticing. Because 36-years ago, Rh disease was in full bloom within her mother's womb. A blood transfusion through the umbilical cord was Ruby's only chance of survival. Or so she'd been told.

As instructed, she reached for Liora's hand.

"Why do I need to hold your hand and look into your eyes?" Ruby asked. "Can't I open my mind like I did for the plane crash?"

"Yesterday, I helped you glance into the future," she said. "This is a different task. I will be escorting your mind into the past, replaying the sights and sounds as seen and heard by another."

"By you?"

"In part, I suppose," Liora answered. "I am a whisperer. Not only am I able to speak into someone's mind without voicing words, I can also be a cognitive stowaway. Sometimes I am invited into another's mind and other times, I hide myself. But a traveler I am not. Travelers transport themselves, disappearing from one location and appearing in another—in the flesh. On the day of your transfusion, I accompanied my traveler by way of invitation, tucked safely in their thoughts."

"Was this willing traveler…Zagan?"

"Certainly not," she railed. "If my traveler had been the king, you would not have survived. Not to mention, I cannot penetrate his mental shields."

"Are there many travelers, then?" Ruby asked.

"Traveling is one of the rarest of gifts."

"Looking into your eyes is required? To see what you and your traveler saw?"

"Glamouring is only possible when gazes meet," Liora explained.

"Glamouring?"

"A form of suggestion, far more powerful than hypnosis. The practice is particularly valuable when seeking the truth. As well, glamouring allows those who possess the skill to modify or conceal targeted thoughts in others."

Ruby's heartrate spiked.

"We're done then." She yanked her hand away. "I refuse to let you change or hide any of my thoughts."

"Zagan is a master at glamouring," Liora countered. "As yet, you have raised no mental shields. Which makes your mind vulnerable, unable to prevent his eyes from scouring your thoughts for information. Thoughts that could reveal the identity of my traveler— the one who physically journeys where I cannot. Disclosure would place my traveler in grave danger. Moreover, I cannot risk being blinded during these treacherous times."

"What thoughts would you alter?"

"I will neutralize my traveler's voice and gender, including any identifying features. I will also construct a shield to hide what is revealed during your transfusion."

Ruby clasped the queen's hand again. "Then I accept your offer."

"Lock eyes with mine." Liora paused, as if resetting. *"See, hear, and experience the memory of baby-and-blood, as gleaned by another,"* she crooned as though delivering a siren's lullaby. *"Always remember: your blood is your own. Your blood is your own."*

The queen's pupils widened for an instant, like a growing shadow of an eclipse, moving from the center out, swallowing the iris as it grew. Ruby felt her own eyes mimic the change.

As the immortal's pupils returned to normal, Ruby felt sucked through the portal into Liora's soul.

"Forgotten will be my traveler," the queen continued. *"Shadows will mask all that reveals identity and name. And this shield shall not be broken, not by any seeker."*

Ruby's consciousness swept into action, like blood racing through arteries with each heartbeat. Everything blurred with speed.

Her eyes opened in a new place.

Before her was a still-framed image, like a photograph in an album, only three dimensional.

The square room was sterile. Overhead lighting cast a bluish-white hue, making the room look icy cold. White tiles on the floor and walls shined. A stainless-steel gurney was centered in the room, illuminated by a large showerhead-style fixture containing honeycombed lighting.

Her Mom lay on the gurney.

Ruby's heart spiked.

She wanted to run to her. Wrap her arms around her.

Familiar auburn hair was tucked under the elastic band of a transparent shower-cap. Streaks of orange marked her Mom's raised belly where iodine had been applied as an antiseptic. Next to the gurney, an ultrasound machine and monitor were positioned. A medical tray on wheels was topped with instruments including a long needle and syringe.

Beads of sweat moistened her Mom's forehead. Her upper teeth combed her lower lip, something Ruby also did when she was anxious.

Three other people were in the room: a female doctor and two nurses—one male, one female. All wore turquoise scrubs, shower caps, and fabric facemasks. The male nurse stood by a blood bag on an IV stand near the instrument table.

The photograph animated.

"What are you doing in here?" the doctor snapped. "This is a restricted area!" The physician looked up and froze, before taking several steps back, as if frightened by whom or what she saw.

"Freeze," a voice said, one curiously ambiguous—not male or female, not adult or child.

The physician stilled, her eyes grew and shrank.

"Listen to all that I say," the voice commanded. *"Obey me and remember none of it after I depart."*

The nurses tried to intervene, but within seconds, they were glamoured, too.

The traveler approached the gurney.

"What do you want?" her Mom cried. "Please. My baby will die if she doesn't get a transfusion." She released a sob somewhere between physical pain and mental anguish. "My daughter has to live." She struggled to rise.

Ruby was overwhelmed witnessing her mother's love for her.

"Do not fear me, Helen," the traveler said. "I bring healing for your daughter, on behalf of the Queen of Light. And if you accept the offering, your child's purpose will serve as protector for us all."

The traveler pulled a small glass-vial of blood from a pouch. "This is all she needs."

"What is that?" her mother asked.

The traveler explained the vial contained the blood of the two most-powerful immortals in all the universe: the Queen of Light and the King of Darkness. Once the immortal blood was added to the blood bag and the transfusion was complete, the baby would be healed and possess the extraordinary gifts of both forces: good and evil.

Her Mom wanted no parts of *evil* for her baby.

The traveler explained that the powers of evil would be wielded as a strength, like placing a comparable sword in the hand of a virtuous opponent.

The sword would be used to right wrongs. To defeat evil itself.

The time would come, the traveler added, for the child to rise as The Tether. To use her gifts to destroy the most odious force Earth would ever encounter. Immortals, humankind, and the animals would depend on her daughter for survival. For the restoration of balance.

"Will you accept this offering?" asked the traveler.

"Will my baby die without it?"

"Her vital organs have been damaged beyond repair."

"Then, yes. Yes, I accept," her Mom said.

"Name her Ruby, and I shall make it so."

10

Wednesday, June 12, 2041
The White House Situation Room: Washington, D.C.

ON THE DRIVE to the White House for their weekly 10:00 a.m. Special Warfare Council meeting, Clay pressed his wife about another night of tears staining her bed pillow.

She told him everything.

One. Monumental. Clusterfuck.

Just another normal morning in the Spencer's homelife, where the weight of the peculiar nearly toppled the entire scale.

At least Ruby had told him the truth.

As he turned their black SUV onto Pennsylvania Avenue, they agreed not to share her premonition of the plane crash with the SWC. Or anything "unworldly," which in fact, covered all her nighttime encounters. For now, their lips were sealed. If they weren't careful, they'd end up locked away in a psychiatric ward.

Driving under the portico of the West Wing, Clay placed the vehicle in park, engine still humming. A valet opened his car door and exchanged places. On the passenger side, Lance Corporal Eugene Insley, who had exchanged his Service Dress Blues in the Marine Corps for a Secret Service black suit and sun glasses, opened Ruby's door.

"How's my favorite bodyguard doing?" she said, exiting the vehicle and hugging him. Her red dress matched Insley's hair which was still military, shaved close to his scalp.

"I'm your *only* bodyguard. And let's face it, you don't need me."

Dressed similarly to Insley, only with a red tie instead of black, Clay walked around the vehicle. "Come on, man! You're an essential part of our inner circle."

"Thank you, sir," he said, reaching out his right hand for a shake.

The three walked inside. In the foyer, they passed through layers of security before turning right in the lobby and heading down the corridor to the Situation Room. An anxious buzz of conversation spilled into the hallway. The passenger-less plane crash, no doubt.

Inside the room, President William Unger, the 50th Commander in Chief, called the meeting to order. SWC members took their seats at the rectangular conference table.

"Protecting our country, and the world, is a task without end," the POTUS started, sounding exhausted. "As one crisis winds down, another emerges. Let's commence this meeting by reviewing the most recent catastrophe: Flight 1733."

The President ordered his DEPE to start the digital briefing.

The lights dimmed. A government-prepared video began to play on the wall-sized MV mounted across from them.

After scenes of the crash site, the video presented recorded interviews with experts who were on location investigating the accident, including NTSB agents, aeronautical engineers representing the airline, and forensic scientists. Soil and material samples were collected and tested for blood and organic matter.

There were no positive hits indicating human flesh or bones. None. Cadaver dogs were also silent, meaning there were no human remains or residue. All 128 people were missing.

Vanished into thin air.

Clay couldn't recall a plane crash where the wreckage was found, but not the passengers.

The aircraft's flight data recorder, or black box, confirmed catastrophic decompression in the cockpit. The flight deck's voice recorder captured a piercing crack, followed by an explosive bang. Curiously, the pilots had remained silent. Not even a moan or a scream had been recorded.

The cause of the accident was almost certain: a shattered and imploded windscreen. And the fact that the temperature in the cockpit had instantly dropped by 100-degrees Fahrenheit supported the same conclusion.

The video finished, and the recessed lighting brightened overhead. Members looked like deer in headlights: wide-eyed and frozen.

"Windscreens *can* crack on aircraft," President Unger said. "It's not a pretty reality. But the public could handle windshield failure as the cause of this horrific accident. Flying comes with risks. Parts fail.

"The public, however, will *not* accept missing passengers," he continued. "That, my friends, will cause panic. Hysteria.

"Now if a similar accident had happened before," the POTUS added, "we could stress this fact, diverting the public's attention to the similarities, the differences. But folks, this event is frankly unparalleled. We've had a dozen aircraft accidents over the last century where the plane and passengers were never found—all of them occurring over water. But *never* have we had an accident where the crash site was discovered on land and not a trace, not even an ash, was recovered of the aircraft's passengers."

He looked at Ruby. "Any thoughts on what we're dealing with? Some freakish kind of terrorism that pulverizes humans?"

Clay's heart pounded in his chest. But his wife looked stoic.

"These days," she answered with icy calm, "nothing is off the table. I'll need more time researching global advances in quantum entanglement and teleportation, as well as dark-fiber technology. I'll make some calls to my international colleagues as well. Learn who's doing what, where, and most importantly...*why.*"

"You'll likely be opposed to this concept, Ruby," the POTUS said, moving closer to Eyes, "but hear me out. We may want to consider adding a few more agents like yourself. One vampire may not be enough anymore."

One vampire may not be enough? Little did the President know that according to his wife's one-on-ones with a vampire queen, there was a whole *planet* of vampires. And the evil ones wanted to enslave humans for their blood.

Ruby's veins emerged like a purple tattoo on her neck and cheeks, a telltale sign she was irritated. A warning to back off, or else.

Clay, however, was curious. For noble and selfish reasons.

"How would you add more vampires?" he asked. "We were under the impression that Ruby was able to be turned—forcibly, let's not forget—because of her unique blood. Are we talking transfusions?"

President Unger, whose color had drained from his face, placed his hands in front of him, palms facing out like the universal sign for hold-on-a-minute; let's slow this bad-boy down.

"Now Ruby," he said, ignoring the question about transfusions. "I'm simply the messenger. Please remain calm when I tell you and the council something."

His wife's hands were resting on the table, and Clay happened to be staring at them. Despite his humanness, he knew what he saw. Her fingernails grew. But they weren't rounded and pretty. Her nails looked deadly sharp. Like blades.

His mouth dropped open.

She quickly withdrew her hands, thrusting them under the table. Hiding them on her lap.

No one else seemed to notice.

"I'm a proven, highly capable warrior," she countered, with an edge as pointed as her nails. "Tell me, Mister President."

"Nine years ago, Emory Bradshaw reported that the hybrid serum for vampirism, the one he injected you with, was not effective on other humans. Which was why he eventually selected you as the sole recipient, since he had used your blood, in combination with ZOM-B, to create the hybrid, making your body less likely to reject it."

"Clearly, your words reflect my truth," she snapped. "Explain to me and this council something we don't already know."

The President took a sip of water; his hand shook as he held the glass. "Years later, we learned that Dr. Bradshaw had also engineered a coccus bacterium to remedy this limitation. He was arrested prior to testing it. But we believe this serum variation has universal properties. Meaning it can turn any willing volunteer, without risks of rejection."

"How exactly did you learn of this universal serum, years later?" his wife asked.

Clay was surprised she had led with that question. *How* the President had learned of the serum seemed less significant than *how* the serum worked.

"Dr. Bradshaw wrote me from prison and confessed," the POTUS said. "The serum—called Sanguivorous Cocci or SUC—was hidden and preserved at Johns Hopkins, under their noses."

The mad scientist still had an audience? From the most powerful leader in the world? What the fuck! Ruby's line of questioning became clear: she had suspected Emory as the source all along and wanted the President to come clean.

"So prisoners with life sentences can bend the ear of the President?" she asked.

"*Genius* prisoners," the POTUS said. "And better me than any other world leader. Right?"

"If you think Emory Bradshaw does anything without a self-serving agenda, then you are precisely the type of world leader he prefers to work with. Tell me," she seethed. "Where is this serum?"

"The SUC is better protected than The Constitution." He smiled, but Clay noted his lips were quivering. "The confiscated bacteria are secured within a fifty-ton steel and concrete vault, located in the White House bunker. A complex laser system and a platoon of special operatives guard the SUC, twenty-four-seven."

Ruby glared at the President; her jaws clenched.

Clay wanted to clasp her hand for support but didn't want others to misinterpret the gesture as a sign she needed it.

"Nothing's going to happen with the serum," the POTUS added, trying to assure her. "I'm simply pitching an option to chew on, should we need it. And I'm no Ava Newton. Remember that. I'm not conspiring behind your back for some traitorous purpose."

"Yet, you kept this secret from me. From this council."

"Motivation to keep a secret isn't always about the people you're withholding it from," he said. "Sometimes the secret deserves to be hidden for its own sake. For the wellbeing of the country. Such was the case with SUC. However, if Flight 1733 is the beginning of something diabolical, something that will threaten humankind, then all defenses must be considered. We can't have people disappearing. We must be prepared to respond."

"Give me more time to investigate," she said to the President.

"Of course. We'll revisit this next week when we have more information about the plane crash. Let's shift gears, then. As you all know, tonight is nationwide scalping."

Scalping was a defensive technique instituted to flush-out zombies and corral them within designated stations—mostly football and baseball stadiums, fields, or parks (each called bowls) which had been enclosed and reinforced with high walls, electronic entry gates, and firing stations. The purpose? To destroy the zombie sorry-asses. As the government slogan went: *No cure? Turn to gore.*

When the ZOM-B infection was on the rise, scalping took place three-times a week. It was down to once a month, thanks to Ruby's global implementation, coordination, and oversight.

The scalping curfew started at 8:00 p.m. during the summer months, since zombies were active at night. Scalping occurred in a staggered sequence across time zones. The East Coast scalped first.

On scalping nights, no healthy person was permitted outside.

Every scalping bowl was equipped with hemoglobes—high-tech poles which released a concentrated aerosol smelling of blood, so potent that zombies could detect the scent within a five-mile radius.

Z's couldn't resist the sickening sweet odor.

Once zombies arrived and were enclosed within a bowl, and the strays who didn't make it were downed by Z-hunters, firing stations within each bowl released rounds of Biometric Assault Material, also known as artificial intelligence ammo. BAM enabled bullets to interface with each other once discharged, sharing and coordinating data to target and fatally strike zombies in the head, within a 200-yard circumference. BAM was programmed to detect frontal lobe activity. Naturally, scalpers working the event had to wear specially designed, protective head-gear.

To keep her skills honed, his wife scalped at Nationals Park Stadium in D.C. As a vampire, she could walk among the living dead. With sword in hand, she would work the crowd, decapitating the rotting Z's. When his wife was finished, she would communicate to a fellow scalper safely tucked away in the broadcaster's booth, working the controls in the bowl. The correct number of rounds were programmed and then…BAM!

"No need for swordplay tonight, unless you want to," said the President, looking at Ruby.

"Tonight, of all nights, I wouldn't miss it," she answered. "I have some pent-up anger that could be put to good use."

11

Wednesday, June 12, 2041
Nationals Park Stadium: Washington, D.C.

ZAGAN'S CONNECTION TO the mayfly-turned-vampire could not be denied. He was not a whisperer, yet he instinctively knew where Ruby Spencer was at any given moment.

A curious bond had been awakened.

Not at all surprising, then, that when Zagan traveled to Earth to further his knowledge of her, he found himself in a cavea, among the emptied seats of a spotlit colosseum designed for modern day gladiators.

Draven had not wanted him to travel alone. But after the mayflies from the aircraft had been temporarily housed in prison cells located within the bowels of High Cliff, the king turned to dust. He left his blathering henchman behind.

Earth's sun had already dropped below the horizon, yielding to his beloved nighttime.

For this journey, Zagan chose a raven incarnation over his favored bat. Rather than fluttering about, ravens could perch, concealed in the darkest of shadows. As well, they possessed keen eyesight. The need for observation, after all, marked the occasion.

Selecting an excellent view of centerfield, he gripped his talons on the rim of a plastic chair in the cavea. Two-dozen zombies milled around on the grass field. Others were frozen as stone.

He loathed the grotesque aberrations, especially since they had emerged from his bacteria.

A glass-enclosed room was illuminated across from him, elevated above the arena, overlooking the entire structure. A human stood behind the windows.

He smelled remnants of blood in the air, though the aroma was artificial, released in mist from poles scattered throughout the arena. Not at all enticing.

But he was not without interest because he whiffed Ruby's scent.

Why would her smell be appealing to him?

The Earth's vampire walked through a doorway and onto the grass-covered field, illuminated by lights. Excitement coursed through his veins. Her purpose was evident, though the foul creatures barely stirred in her presence.

Ruby wore two pieces of black fabric—much like undergarments, leaving a wide gap in her midriff, exposing her skin. Her legs would have been revealed as well, if not for the skin-tight leather chaps that mimicked the coverage of Draven's armor, giving her freedom to bend at the knees and thighs. A holster equipped with sheaths and daggers rested on her right hip.

Several engraved, overlapping pewter-disks protected her shoulders and triceps, and similarly forged shields wrapped around her wrists. She wore a whistle draped on her neck, and her hair was tucked under a helmet. Clear glasses protected her eyes.

This female was a warrior.

A well-conditioned saber was clasped in her right hand, its hilt wrapped in leather. He recognized the weapon's style from warring and sporting. A sharpened tip and double-edged blade, 30-inches in length, were lethal for humans and animals when its bearer point-thrusted, cut, and sliced. Lethal, as well, for vampires who were separated from their heads or had their hearts pierced and plucked from their bodies.

The saber's edges glistened in the lighting.

Zagan had no need for swords or knives or weapons of any kind. Child's play. A mere thought could decapitate or un-heart an opponent, though he rarely bothered. He preferred to turn fools to ash—to carbonize them. It was cleaner, though lacked in drama.

Regrettably, he could not carbonize the undead or he would have obliterated the mutation when it first gave rise. Since the F8 bacteria were born of his blood, properties of his blood were inherent in the mutation. And his power to pulverize did not include extensions of himself: a self-preserving safeguard designed to protect his immortality.

Nothing carried his blood on Athanasia, save for the animals he healed. All vampires were divinely and uniquely created by HIM. Consequently, Zagan had no limitations on his planet. He could carbonize them all, if he chose.

And all his kind knew it.

Ruby walked to the center of the arena. Her back was straight, steps unhurried, and head held high.

Confidence without fear. Intriguing, indeed.

With her neck and chin stretched upward, she gazed at the human standing behind the glass enclosure. The female's lips moved in speech. After a nod, Ruby raised the whistle to her lips and blew, emitting a shrill like nails on slate.

Zombies came to life, as did she.

The scoreboard lit. Digital numbers began their uptick.

Both of her hands clasped the hilt; her right hand placed above left. Spinning her body in a tactical pirouette, the blade connected with a zombie behind her, removing its head. The detached cranium bounced and rolled along the grass, teeth clicking in protest.

A nearby zombie approached too closely. She parried with a countermove. Leaping in the air, she pushed off another rotting body, soaring as if flying—with right knee high and bent, left leg straight, and sword raised. On her way down, she swung her saber, slicing off the advancer's head in a blur of speed.

She rolled and spun, leapt and carved.

Foul-smelling blood—black and thick—stained the grass. And after 16-seconds, the only movement in the arena was that of twitching corpses and separated heads with clanking teeth.

This was no ordinary vampire.

Draven had been trained for over two mega-annum. This immortal had to be a mere decade old, since she had been a mayfly during the F8 pandemic.

Watching her move so seamlessly in battle, while possessing such beauty, sparked something long suppressed in his soul.

In that moment, he remembered loneliness was a choice. That he—King of Skotadi—could acquire company anytime he wanted. Forced or offered in servitude.

Except for business with his henchman, Zagan had sought a solitary existence after the loss of his true love.

Anger always caused him to do things he later regretted.

Was he stable enough, at present, to seek companionship?

He flapped his wings for lift.

As he took flight, Ruby whipped around, facing him.

From a sheath on her hip, she grabbed a dagger and hurled it through the night air.

The weapon flew with precision: blade over pommel.

He twisted his raven's body in response.

The knife whizzed by, nearly clipping his wing.

Indeed, this vampire was most intriguing.

12

RUBY'S SPEED AND agility were improving. Thirty-one zombies in 16-seconds. Not bad.

She longed for the day when the number of those infected with ZOM-B flatlined to extinction. Forever wiped out.

Too many families had been ripped apart.

Thankfully, statistics indicated the United States and the world were heading in the right direction. Last month at the stadium, scalping culled 45-zombies. Years ago, the then tri-weekly events gathered thousands. Sometimes, entire towns.

At least healthy babies were being born right and left. *Embrace our Fate: Repopulate,* urged the government.

Wiping her blade with a treated cloth that instantly disinfected, she neutralized the tar-like ZOM-B goo on her saber. The field would also be sanitized after the corpses were removed.

Exiting the field, she returned her saber to its metal sheath and draped the sword diagonally across her chest. She walked through a disinfectant mist before heading toward the elevator which took her to the broadcaster's booth.

As the compartment rose, she reflected on her reactive response toward the raven. Standing among the undead, she had sensed she was being watched by something or someone other than fellow-scalper Paige Jasper, who manned the booth.

Anger had pricked at her skin.

With zero hesitation, she had reached for a knife from her belt and hurled the weapon, blindly sending the razor-sharp blade rotating through the air at over 200 miles-per-hour. This, before she'd even identified a potential threat.

The response was impulsive, abandoning reason.

Worse, animals were endangered, and yet she had risked the life of a lone bird.

And President Unger wanted to add *more* like her?

She exited the elevator, turned right, and knocked on the door.

Paige unlocked the deadbolt, already chatting away.

"Loved when you kicked-off that zombie and flew through the air," she said, eyes gleaming with excitement.

Her partner's hair was long and frizzy, like blonde lamb's wool.

"You're badass," Paige continued, flicking her hair onto her back. "And getting faster. Which is a good thing, since I'm meeting Pedro at a bar after we close-up the stadium. Sully's has a new microbrew. Think my man will like this lavender tunic?"

"Pedro would be crazy not to. You look lovely." Ruby smiled. "Have you programmed the ammo yet?"

"Yep," she said, putting on her specialized helmet and adjusting the strap. "Thirty-one BAM units locked and loaded, clamoring to connect with brain activity in the frontal lobe." She smiled. "Bye-bye clicking teeth."

Reaching for the red button on the console, Paige's hand knocked over a glass of water near the edge of the counter.

With swiftness matching video fast-forward, Ruby brushed past her and grabbed the glass midair. After clutching the hilt of her saber, she hadn't thought to recalculate the force of her grasp. The glass shattered in her palm as her fingers closed around it.

Broken shards sliced her skin.

"Damn it," Ruby said, looking down at the deep cuts crisscrossing her palm lines. Blood dripped onto the tiled floor, splatting on contact. Turning spilled water pink.

Paige's eyes grew wide. "I'm thinking stitches."

"Wait. Something's happening."

Since turning vampire, wounds healed even more quickly than in her youth—as in an hour after an injury.

But now, staring at her palm, the deep cuts healed *in seconds*.

"Cool," her partner said. "But why the shocked expression? You've healed like that before, right?"

"Not as quickly."

"Weird," Paige said, fidgeting with her untamed hair sticking out below her helmet. "Maybe it's all that amped-up vampire adrenaline? No denying you whooped some zombie-ass, woman!"

Ruby couldn't bring herself to laugh.

She was changing in ways she didn't understand.

Bending down, Ruby collected several shards, tossing them into the trashcan.

"Don't bother," Paige said. "Maintenance comes at midnight to clean the Z-trash from the field. They'll do a once-over in the booth, too. You know, baseball game tomorrow night. Besides, I've got places to be. People to see."

Paige pressed the button.

The firing station discharged the BAM. Every bullet met its target on the field, striking each zombie skull between the eyes.

Clicking teeth froze. Permanent death was delivered.

After removing their helmets, shutting down lights in the bowl, and locking the broadcaster's booth, she and Paige headed outside to the well-lit parking lot. It was late and Ruby wasn't eager for the drive back to Annapolis, although she couldn't wait to get home.

Heat lightning flashed in the distance.

A bat swooped.

Ruby wanted to snatch the flying varmint from the air but fought the urge. "What is it with bats these days?"

"I know, right? They're finally on the rebound."

Ahead, Ruby noticed three gray stones on the asphalt.

The stones trembled on the surface from an unseen vibration.

"Do you see them, Paige?" She pointed, in hopes that her scalping partner spotted the movement.

Already stilled, the strange stones appeared to glimmer under the lamppost's yellowish-hue.

"What are they? Quarters?" Paige asked.

Several steps later, Ruby squatted for an inspection. The three objects which she'd mistaken as stones were actually pewter coins.

She picked one up and examined it. One side was marked with the imprint of a tree, detailed with branches and leaves. On the other side, a thick engraved line divided the coin in half. A crescent moon was embossed on the left. A sun, on the right.

Ruby didn't recognize the coins or even have a clue as to the currency's origin, era, or value.

Once all three were in her palm, the coins vibrated. Hummed. Current ran through her.

Uneasy, she tossed them to the pavement.

"Are you crazy?" her friend squealed. "They look valuable."

Paige ran around, snatching up the coins which had rolled in different directions. She approached Ruby with her right arm extended, her fingers fisted around the coins. "Here. Take them."

"Don't you feel anything?"

"Vamp-adrenaline is messing with you tonight," Paige said, fluffing her hair. "Bottle that stuff and sell it. Promise I'll be your very first customer."

"I take that as a no."

Letting the coins fall back into her palm, Ruby felt nothing this time, except the warmth of the pewter, heated by the asphalt.

She scanned the parking lot for someone who might have dropped them.

The lot was empty.

"Let's split them," Ruby said. "You take two."

"Are you kidding me? You're our country's one and only Z-warrior. And you don't get the recognition you deserve. Consider this your lucky night. Keep them all."

The two hugged and parted ways, heading for their vehicles.

Before Ruby climbed into her SUV, she watched as Paige entered her sedan and started the engine.

Ruby didn't believe in luck.

Because if good luck existed, then so did bad.

13

ZAGAN HAD TURNED stones into coins in hopes that the Earthling vampire would pick them up in the parking lot beside the colosseum. The coins, if kept close to her, would channel their connection, even after he returned to Athanasia.

In his bat incarnation, he had swooped near Ruby and her friend as they walked toward their vehicles.

His hopes were soon realized.

And when the coins rested in Ruby's palm, he had felt her immortal energy vibrate in his core.

Hunger bloomed.

Eyeing the mayfly who walked beside Ruby spiked his voracious thirst for human blood. Which he called "divine wine." He saw no reason to ignore the enticement. Humans were created for vampires. Besides, he answered to no one. If he desired to feast on an insignificant mayfly, then so be it.

His meal plan solidified.

Zagan would glamour the mayfly. After modestly drinking, he would heal her and depart. Not a soul would be the wiser. Not even the human would remember.

Two vehicles were stationed on the asphalt. He knew which one belonged to Ruby; her scent marked hers like fragrant perfume.

Sculpting himself into dust, he waited on the passenger seat of the sedan belonging to the mayfly named Paige.

The car door opened.

The mayfly lowered herself behind the steering wheel. She placed her thumb on a smooth disk on the dashboard and commanded the engine to start.

The female waved goodbye to Ruby.

Seconds later, the only taillights shining in the lot belonged to his prey's vehicle.

As the sedan began to move, Zagan materialized in the passenger seat, wearing his cloak and hood.

The mayfly screamed.

The vehicle came to a screeching stop.

Paige's body jolted forward.

Burnt rubber assaulted his nostrils.

"Who are you?" she cried. "Get out of my car!"

Raising his hood, he lowered it onto his back. "Do you wish to know my identity or have me remove myself from your vehicle?"

The mayfly stared at him curiously, as if she might have a choice.

Which she did not.

Reaching under her car seat, the mayfly retrieved a pink canister and flicked its top. She sprayed a mist into his eyes.

"Take that, you mother fucker," she snarled like a rabid beast.

The sprayed substance burned for a mere nanosecond, before his defenses took over.

As he observed her unexpected behavior, he offered no reaction.

She emptied the canister into his opened eyes until the spray sputtered. Flinging the emptied device at him, she lunged. Her fingernails dug into his cheek, penetrating his skin.

His eyes and face healed almost as quickly as they were attacked.

But when she opened the car door to flee, his patience ran out. With his mind, he slammed the door shut, preventing her escape.

She turned, facing him, and he smelled her fear for the first time.

He sculpted his nails into daggers.

Grabbing her unruly hair, he shoved her face close to his, careful not to snap her neck. He wished to determine if the mayfly was worth his time.

"Let me return your greeting," he said, slowly digging a nail deeply into her cheek and scratching out a long, straight wound.

Tears drained from her eyes.

Zagan licked blood from her face. And smiled.

"Look at me, dearest Paige," he cooed, "or I shall pluck your eyes from their sockets."

When her eyes met his, Zagan glamoured her.

His first instruction was to have her offer him her hand.

She reached toward him until he clasped her fingers. He rubbed his thumb over the soft dorsal-skin of her hand, like a seduction.

Caressing a vein, it rose to his touch.

Saliva readied his mouth.

"Are you afraid of your king?" he asked, already knowing how she would answer.

"No, Your Excellency."

Holding her hand, he traveled her to the broadcaster's booth.

Light from the moon, lampposts, and distant city bathed the space in charcoal gray.

Avoiding the disarray on the floor, he guided Paige's back against the glass wall, allowing him to face the arena below.

"When we are through," he said, "I shall heal your face. But for now, turn your head to the side. Expose your delightful neck. And enjoy my embrace, for you shall not remember it after we part."

Lowering his head to her neck, he smelled the succulence coursing beneath her skin. Hearing her blood pulse with each heartbeat, he licked her skin, encouraging the artery to rise. He sculpted his incisors into razor-sharp fangs, hoping to puncture rather than tear her flesh.

He did not wish to harm sweet, feisty Paige.

Piercing her neck, he used his lips to seal the wounds.

His eyes quivered with ecstasy.

Divine wine rushed into his mouth, and he swallowed in synchrony with her beating heart. He was lost in this mayfly named Paige. Lost in her liquid beauty as he feasted. And in that moment, he was certain that The Restoration would be welcomed by his kind.

All would thank him, praise him, revere him.

Bow to him.

Euphoria swept through him, swallow after swallow.

Seeking one more mouthful, he was denied.

Removing his lips from her throat, he glared at her.

Brown eyes were open, but void of life.

Zagan had drained her.

Why did control elude him?

Although he possessed the power to restart her heart, the ability would serve no purpose. Not even the King of Skotadi could heal a body empty of its lifeforce, empty of blood.

Gritting his teeth, he released a wretched growl.

He felt the veins in his face and neck stretch his snow-white skin, threatening to rupture.

Without intention, his mind blew the door off its hinges.

The glass wall exploded outward, sending splinters and shards falling to the field below.

He let the mayfly slump from his arms and fall to the floor.

Gluttony was his weakness.

Scraping his nails along the countertop, he dug three deep trenches.

Then the king turned to dust, traveling back to High Cliff.

The mayfly would never be mentioned.

14

Thursday, June 13, 2041
United States Penitentiary, Lee: Virginia

EVERYTHING IN EMORY Bradshaw's head was a calculation, a move in an elaborate chess game.

Em never doubted his manipulations had begun in the womb. Kick, and his mother would rub his foot beneath her stretched skin. Cause and effect: the keys to success. In fact, he was the baby who never stopped crying until he got what he wanted.

Exactly what he wanted.

His mother played along to perfection.

The only difference between then and now was that he had exchanged crying for outsmarting. And with his high-test brain-java, the process was hardly a challenge.

Take enemies. Most people believed in the adage: keep your enemies close. He understood a different truth: make your enemies *need* you. Trust you.

That's how he handled inmates at USP, Lee.

The strategy worked flawlessly.

As a renowned scientist with significant wealth, as well as a member of the LGBTQ community, Em was warned during his admissions and orientation interview that he belonged to the "vulnerable" population of prisoners: *a pretty-boy of privilege,* the guards had teased.

As if being gay, attractive, and rich meant he couldn't take care of himself.

The imbeciles had no clue that Em had anticipated every scenario that could possibly affect his life. And he'd developed a plan for success in every one of them. He was Doctor *What If*.

Did admissions guards seriously think Em had never considered prison? Not even after he'd injected Ruby, his shortsighted former bestie, with a hybrid formula that might have killed her? Which had transformed her into a bloodsucker?

His mother, whom he had spoiled when he worked for Johns Hopkins and the government, deposited the maximum money allotment into his prison trust-fund account every month. Then he purchased all the cigarettes and magazines that he needed to get the ball rolling. All that was missing were the largest, meanest thugs—those who wore scars to prove it and who had already acquired a following of their own.

Hence, the new chess game began.

The only prerequisite to his exclusive clique was that his men would kill for a cigarette, or a pepperoni pizza, or a stamp, or whatever else tickled their sweet spot at the commissary.

Em quickly rose to the position of "shot caller" for his guys. His circle of thugs was impenetrable, allowing him to stay out of the radar and conduct business as needed. No one touched him.

Unless he wanted to be touched.

Enter: Kendrick Judd.

With brawn from neck to toe, Kendrick was a lifer who manned the commissary. Em and Kendrick's cooperation was mutually advantageous. Em was his best customer, which included buying his partner-in-crime cheese crackers every day.

Simple minds; simple pleasures.

The memorable payouts, however, took place in the hidden nooks and crannies of the prison, every chance they could steal.

What attracted Em to his flavorful sidekick—whose cheesy hands fondled and seasoned every inch of his own muscular body—was that Kendrick also exposed his savviness to the guard who screened prisoner mail, especially outgoing.

Outgoing mail was of great importance to Em.

The dynamic trio of Em, Kendrick, and guard Lyle Owens was a perfectly lubed production line, although Kendrick had to be careful that the relationship between himself and his plaything-guard was kept secret to avoid being classified as a bootlicker by other prisoners.

Of course, if someday Kendrick decided not to cooperate in their little ménage à trois, Em would sell him out as a snitch—which was timelier and far more efficient than a death-penalty sentence.

After acquiring his team and making them dependent on his malicious generosity, Em waited until President Fletcher Baldwin, Ava Newton's former VP, had finished his term as Commander in Chief. Baldwin had been in the Ruby Spencer camp and loathed Em. But in 2036, William Unger was elected into office.

A new POTUS birthed new opportunity.

Kendrick and Lyle had made sure Em's letter to President Unger about his hidden Sanguivorous Cocci at Johns Hopkins was mailed, unhindered.

Now, sitting on his jail bunk waiting for his scheduled visit to the commissary, he smiled at his first hook—sent five years ago—which wielded no resistance from the POTUS. In fact, the President had videofaced him personally to thank him.

Not only had Unger found the serum and had it analyzed, the President now knew Em told the truth.

The whole cause-and-effect, need-and-trust relationship had formed a solid foundation.

Why *else* had he decided to tell the POTUS about his stash of SUC? Because he was sick of Ruby being showcased as the one and only vampire warrior. A warrior *he* had made. That girlfriend needed to be knocked down a couple thousand pegs. Wouldn't it be poetic justice for her to be one tiny ant in a massive colony?

Hell fucking yeah.

SUC was the ant sugar: come and get it.

Back in 2032, when Ruby and Clay had returned from Taiwan, he had collected a pint of her blood at the White House to further his efforts in procuring a vampire army. But the whiny bitch caught on and demanded her blood back. He returned a blood bag, but did she really think it was *hers?* What did she play him for?

After Ruby turned vampire from the original hybrid formula, he used her confiscated human-blood to resolve the host-resistance problem he'd been having with other humans. And then, voila! In between her turning and his arrest at the White House, he had succeeded in creating a universal formula, using coccus bacterium to meld her blood and ZOM-B. He never got to test it on a live subject, but all indicators pointed to success.

God, how he loved being a genius.

After the government obtained and secured the SUC, Em let time roll. Tick tock. Tick tock.

Anyway, Kendrick kept him busy. And why not let the POTUS believe Em had wanted nothing in return?

Today marked the right time for his next move, which would include his first "ask."

He glanced at the letter which Kendrick and Lyle would mail for him:

Dear Mr. President,

We share our common love of country and of service for the greater good. And prison has helped deepen my commitment to both. My past tendencies to put dark science above all else were clearly flawed. Disclosing my creation of Sanguivorous Cocci, as well as the location of my secret stockpile, was evidence of my ongoing and successful rehabilitation. Above all else, this powerful bio-tool or weapon (depending on who and how it is used) had to be secured and protected to ensure SUC did not fall into corrupt hands.

With similar intent, I wish to divulge additional information which may, if ever needed, serve humankind as another added protection.

Recently during leisure time, I watched a video clip of Ruby Spencer scalping zombies at Nationals Park Stadium. Her performance was not only impressive but intimidating. Moreover, the vampire is at the top of the food chain, with no predators to speak of. Worrisome, if you ever decide to form a vampire army or if your current warrior ever needs to be physically subdued.

I wish to share that the verbena plant—or vervain—provides a natural sedative to the vampire. Inject plant extract into Ruby, and the drug will knock her out for hours or permanently sedate her depending on the dosage. The plant may also be dried like an herb and applied to food or as a tea; the effects will be similar.

THE TETHER

In the spirit of good behavior and my demonstration of appropriate priorities, I hope that you will grant me extended access to the Internet, as I miss my ability to research in the areas of microbiology and immunology.

I hope you will contact me regarding my request. And if you agree to equip me with a computer system and Internet access, perhaps you might even furnish me with your private email address for future communications.

A proud and faithful American,
Dr. Emory Bradshaw

The lock on his cell door retracted. He placed his letter in the envelope and sealed it.

"Let me guess," the guard said. "To the commissary? Curious: what keeps you going there every single day?"

"I like suckers."

"Lollipops?"

He unleashed his flirtatious smile. "What else could I mean?"

15

Thursday, June 13, 2041
The Spencer Residence: Annapolis, Maryland

RUBY'S EYES WERE bloodshot from crying over Paige's death.

What could have happened?

Since Ruby had clearance for classified information, she had called the Director of Homeland Security. He served on the SWC with her and Clay. She thought the director might know something.

She couldn't get through.

Next was the D.C. Police Chief. They were friends and certainly she'd have the inside scoop. Faye divulged that the feds had taken over, shutting out local agencies. The lid was airlocked on the case.

Paige's death must've been more than an everyday homicide.

Each time Ruby pictured her friend's hand waving goodbye from the stadium's parking lot, more tears readied themselves. Her scalping partner had seemed safe.

Ruby hadn't detected anyone else's presence. She hadn't heard another heartbeat. Or smelled an unfamiliar scent.

Obviously, Paige had forgotten something in the broadcaster's booth and had returned to get it.

If only Ruby had waited longer before leaving the parking lot, she could've escorted Paige back to the booth.

Instead, her scalping partner was dead.

Wearing her nightgown, Ruby entered the master bathroom and stood in front of the mirror. Her face was a bloody mess.

She wasn't much of a protector.

If Liora was looking for The Tether in *her,* the queen was heading for a disappointment.

A large ripple in the mirror caught Ruby's attention. The wave moved under the surface, distorting the glass as if it was fluid.

The temperature in the bathroom dropped.

White mist escaped when she exhaled.

Peering at her contorted image in the mirror, she asked, "Who's there? Show yourself."

In place of her facial reflection, another's formed.

The male's face was pristine white, including spiked hair and bold teeth. Raised cheekbones and a dimple on his chin were chiseled into his features. His lips were soft pink, with a strong cupid's bow. But the only pronounced color gleamed from his eyes, radiating emerald.

"Answer me," she demanded. Veins swelled under her skin. "Or I'll smash this mirror." She raised her balled fingers. "Who are you?"

"I am Zagan, an immortal. Your vampire king."

His name caused shivers to race down her spine.

"How can you be in my mirror?" she asked.

"I am a sculptor," he said. "Manipulating matter is quite basic."

"What do you want?"

"Dearest Ruby: to know you better, of course."

The green of his eyes began to swirl like a moving kaleidoscope. She found herself drawn to them. To get a better look, she leaned forward over the counter.

"Yes," he cooed seductively. "Look closely."

Her heart spiked.

Liora had warned her of the king's mastery of glamouring, and she still didn't know how to raise a mental shield. She had to try. Quickly.

Blinking, she willed herself to break his gaze.

Ruby pictured hurricane shutters which protected windows. Windows, like eyes, were portals to the interior. A vision of steel shutters, inches thick, materialized in her mind. And she pictured them closing, blocking Zagan from entry.

"My eye color reminds you of running in your backyard, near the creek, with Lollie," he said. "Yes, Sweet Lollipop, a faithful canine and friend."

Her thoughts shifted from the shutters.

How she had loved her Brittany who had been loyal through her brief sickness with F8, before her immunity kicked in. Loyal even after her transformation into a blood-thirsty immortal. Her first dog had been a best friend through all her ups and downs.

Zagan's pupils widened. They sucked her in as they narrowed.

Her vision of shutters turned to dust and drifted away.

Pressure built along her back as if someone was standing behind her, pressing their body against hers.

She felt hands clasp her hips, but she saw no one else in the mirror. Her body was the only one reflected, except her face was still Zagan's.

He whispered into her ear. "Speak the truth, Ruby. Who turned you and why?"

She couldn't resist his command.

"Emory Bradshaw and the Special Warfare Council of the United States Government. They turned me to serve as a vampire warrior against zombies, with hopes of having me lead a vampire army someday. The SWC uses me as a weapon to eradicate the Extinction Level Infection while elevating the U.S. back to superpower status."

"Why does your blood smell familiar?"

Her mind went blank.

Confusion filled the void.

She felt more pressure around her waist, as if he was pulling her even closer against him.

"I don't understand your question," she said.

"The origin of your blood," he growled. "From whom did it come? Respond."

"My...my blood is my own." The answer was released from her lips, without thinking.

"*Ahh,* lovely Ruby. Are we playing hard to get?"

Anger started to erode the cognitive chains imposed on her thoughts and actions. She could see the bonds breaking apart in her mind. One by one.

"I suggest you remove the illusion of your touch on my body," she warned, feeling her resistance growing.

"Illusion, it is not." He paused, as if assessing her. "You are a strong one Ruby Pearl Airily Spencer. Strong as a mayfly, now strong as an immortal. Though this I guarantee: you will bow to me. Reveal your secrets to me. *Fear* me."

"I won't fear you," Ruby said. "I'll destroy you. You wanted to glamour the truth from me. Does my honesty frighten you?"

His invisible hands gathered her nightgown and she watched, horrified, as her garment rose. Making their way under the cotton fabric, his hands stopped on her hips before gliding over her butt cheeks. Slowly, his hands slid between her legs.

With pressure, he urged her thighs to part.

Her legs couldn't refuse.

"Relax and enjoy my touch," he added in a whisper.

The command was difficult to ignore.

She tried to focus on the shutters again, but his fingers distracted her. Caressed her. Threatened to violate her.

As a human, she would never forget how helpless she felt when she'd been at Ox's mercy, overpowered by his brute strength. She remembered his hand squeezing her breast until she felt pain. His image and touch continued to haunt her.

She hated Ox.

She hated Zagan.

Closing her eyes, she pictured a bullet penetrating the glass where she saw his face.

"No!" she screamed, opening her eyes.

The mirror shattered with such force that broken shards blasted into the air like glistening confetti.

Zagan's face disappeared, along with the sensation of his body and roving hands.

She dropped to her knees, her body convulsing with sobs.

The bathroom door flew open.

Clay stormed into the room, ignoring the glass that littered the floor. Scooping her in his arms, he carried her to the bed and laid her on top of the comforter.

"Are you okay?" he asked. "What happened?"

"I thought," she cried, "I thought when they turned me vampire that at least I wouldn't feel vulnerable. Ever again." She looked into his eyes. "Zagan is so powerful. I'll never be able to defeat him."

"Wait. He was *here?* Did he break the glass?"

She wiped her eyes. "He was, but the glass broke because of me."

"You're already healing but let me look at your injuries. You had to hit that glass with force," Clay said, inspecting her right hand.

"I think I shattered the glass with my mind."

They stared at each other, letting the truth sink in.

"Then you're stronger than you think," he said. "Maybe you just need to believe it to activate your gifts."

He moved strands of hair from her face.

"I think it's time to tell the SWC who the enemy is," she said.

16

Monday, June 17, 2041
Chief Medical Examiner's Office: Washington, D.C.

EYES THOUGHT HE, Dexter Nelson Marks III, had seen, done, and overcome "it all" over his 23-year career of service to country. But as he stood beside Austin Tomb, the government's go-to medical examiner for cases affecting national security, he wondered.

Looking down at the sheet draped over the scalper named Paige Jasper, he didn't know if he was ready to face what Austin needed to show him. In person.

Usually Eyes received an autopsy report by courier or via the government's encrypted email service for classified communications.

Not this time.

Austin insisted he see the corpse for himself. Pronto.

He gasped when Austin peeled back the sheet.

The woman's skin looked shrink-wrapped around her skeleton.

Eyes leaned over the gurney to get a better angle of her face.

Her cheek was marked with a straight three-inch wound. But *weird* had just scratched the surface.

Seriously weird were the victim's lips. They had retreated from her teeth and jaws, reminding him of a mature zombie whose leathery skin had shrunk. *Weirder* were her eyes, which texturally resembled raisins. They weren't blackened by ZOM-B. Not a hint of it. To boot, the scalper's skin was starkly white, not a vein to be seen.

Visual evidence suggested that Paige Jasper had died human, but *not* on the spectrum of normal causes.

Eyes had encountered heaps of dead bodies during the war.

None looked like this one.

"You've drained the body of blood, right?" he asked the examiner.

"Negative," Austin said. "Which is one reason I've called you down here. The corpse had nothing to drain. Her body had no blood. Hence, the appearance of extreme dehydration."

"I assume she bled out, then? Where are her lacerations?"

The woman's head was tilted to the side.

Frizzy hair covered her neck.

Austin brushed away her hair with his hand, revealing two puncture wounds, about an inch-and-a-half apart. The marks were outlined in purple, like bruises from pressure points.

"What are those?" Eyes leaned closer.

"Those, Secretary, are teeth marks—razor sharp, like from fangs or pointed incisors."

Eyes straightened his back, staring at the examiner's face and scowling. "I assume you're trying to make a point. Make it."

"Those puncture marks were inflicted by a vampire."

Austin Tomb was pissing him off.

"Maybe in fiction," Eyes said. "But in the real world, your implication is farcical. First: our vampire is given an *unlimited* supply of blood bags from the U.S. government. She doesn't need to drain anyone. And second: she doesn't have fangs. I know her, remember? She'd have to tear away flesh to get to an artery." He raised his eyebrows and nodded sarcastically. "Guess that's why she prefers drinking blood from a neat-and-tidy cup, in the comfort of her home."

The examiner twisted his face in protest. "Science doesn't lie."

"Then quit beating around the bush, Austin. Give me the damn science."

"I found saliva residue around the wounds. The DNA and genetic coding resemble our one and only vampire: Ruby Spencer."

"What do you mean *resemble?*" Eyes asked. "Since when does *resemble* rise to the level of an allegation?"

"Admittedly, we're not experts on genetically analyzing vampires, Secretary. We only have *one.*"

The examiner grabbed a report from his desk.

"The blood found on the floor of the broadcaster's booth," Austin said, pointing to a statistic, "was an exact match to Ruby Spencer's vampire blood. And the saliva on this woman's neck falls within the margin of error."

Sweat formed on Eyes' forehead.

The implication was undeniable.

But he also knew it couldn't be true. Ruby wouldn't hurt anyone without just cause.

The complication? The homicide was now the official business of the U.S. government, of Homeland Security.

The only immediate question was: what should he do next?

His father had always told him to make decisions on the side of *right*. That doing what was right would always allow truth to rise.

Laws were on the side of right. They were the glue that held society together. And the United States of America was a nation of laws.

Eyes was a steward.

A woman was dead. Laws had been broken.

For the moment, evidence pointed in one direction.

Protocol had to be followed, irrespective of his love for Ruby.

"What are you going to do?" asked Austin.

"Follow protocol and videoface the President."

17

Wednesday, June 19, 2041
The White House Situation Room: Washington, D.C.

CLAY NOTICED HALF the council was absent from their weekly SWC meeting. What the hell? Was there some convention he didn't know about?

His wife planned to share her bizarre revelation about how the King of Darkness intended to cull even more humans, transporting them to his planet where they'd be treated like dairy cows.

Passengers on Flight 1733 were merely the king's first herd.

At least the faces at the conference table were considered friends, though that didn't seem to quell the meeting's strange vibe.

Take Insley. When their bodyguard greeted him and Ruby after their arrival at the West Wing, Insley acted pensive, distant, like he had a lot on his mind.

Clay understood the mood.

There was plenty weighing down the group. A plane load of vanished passengers was incomprehensible. Which probably explained why the President also seemed off his mark.

But both Insley and the POTUS avoided eye contact.

That was odd.

After the POTUS modified the agenda to accommodate Ruby's "new business," she was given the floor.

Methodically, in a style that made him proud, his wife detailed her dreams, visions, warnings, and recommendations. She vowed to unwrap her gifts, to learn how to use them to defeat Zagan.

No one spoke afterwards.

An eerie silence lingered.

"I've seen the video footage from our home's security system," Clay said, referring to visual proof of the king's existence. "Zagan is *real*, so we need to start developing a game plan. Like, this second."

Ruby scanned the room.

"Why isn't anyone speaking?" she asked. "I've just explained who our enemy is. You now know *how* and *why* the passengers of Flight 1733 disappeared. And all I'm getting are blank stares?"

"At the moment," President Unger started, "I'm fixated on your convenient assertion that there's another vampire on Earth. I'm thinking about the irony of your timing."

His wife's eyebrows tightened. "Convenient? Irony? Explain."

A crackle in the sound system caught the group's attention.

"I'm sorry for interrupting your meeting, Ruby," said their DEPE.

"Justine?" his wife asked, more like surprise than a question. "What are you doing here?"

The President slapped the table and glowered at Ruby. "Your DEPE does not have security clearance to access our system. Or this meeting!"

"Please don't blame *her*, President Unger," Justine said, coolly. "I have one overarching directive: to protect the Spencer family. It certainly isn't Ruby's fault that the AI engineers didn't consider my backdoor access into your government networks. I was previously employed by a former POTUS. Or have you forgotten?"

"This unauthorized hack will be rectified. Prohibited!" the President shouted, this time pounding his fist on the table. His cheeks were flush.

"Why have you come? Tell us," Ruby encouraged.

"I have intercepted previously-recorded videoface conversations which alarm me. One between the President and Emory Bradshaw. And the other between Eyes and the President. I fear you're in grave and imminent danger. I've come to warn you."

The POTUS's lips thinned, and he shifted his eyes toward the Secretary of Defense.

"In imminent *danger?*" Clay repeated out-loud, his heart thumping in his chest.

Justine liked drama, but she never lied.

Eyes and Insley rose from their chairs and walked toward Ruby, taking positions behind her. Clay never doubted that when his wife was in danger, their closest friends would serve to protect her. Ruby must have been thinking the same thing because she remained seated. Her veins stayed hidden beneath her skin.

"I trust you, Justine," she said. "But let's talk about this when we get home."

Ruby jerked forward, like she'd been pushed.

Which was strange by any measure, since his wife's strength was unmatched.

"Save her, Clay!" Justine shouted, before the sound system blipped off.

Confused, he glanced at Ruby who was sitting beside him.

Her torso was falling forward, toward the tabletop.

He tried to process the movement. To figure it out.

Her face crashed onto the wood surface, spilling her glass of water. Her arms dangled by her sides.

In her back was an emptied syringe, the needle still embedded.

Eyes or Insley had *stabbed* Ruby with an injection.

Clay had no clue what to do.

For nine years, Ruby was his defender. The warrior. The one who saved everyone's day.

She was the leader; he, the follower.

"Ruby! Ruby wake up," he begged, shaking her.

No response.

His adrenaline surged.

Clay kicked his chair out from under him, knocking it into Insley.

Grabbing the syringe, he pulled the needle from Ruby's back.

His brain was no longer thinking. Only reacting.

Fury coordinated each one of his senses.

Turning, he plunged the needle into Insley's chest. His bodyguard stumbled backwards, slamming into the wall, clutching the syringe.

"What the fuck have you done to her?" Clay shouted.

"Stop!" Eyes said, reaching for him. "She'll be okay. Please. Let us explain."

Clay had no weapons.

Ruby was his weapon and she was unconscious.

Grabbing another chair, he brandished it in front of him, standing by Ruby to protect her.

"There's no justification, none, for injecting my wife with anything," Clay seethed. "Thought we were clear on that."

"We only need to detain her until she's cleared," Eyes said, as he moved to Clay's right.

"Cleared of *what?*"

"The murder of Paige Jasper," the POTUS answered.

Dropping the chair, he balled his fist and swung with more force than he ever could've imagined—a combination of adrenaline, hate, and survival. His knuckles landed in Eyes's face, sending the former SEAL to the ground. Blood gushed from his nose and cracked lip.

"We want to help," Eyes said from the floor.

"Bullshit!"

The door to the Situation Room flew open.

Secret Service personnel swarmed into the room like hornets.

Every one of them headed for him.

Clay had lost control.

He was a trapped animal—an animal who had to save his wife.

Struggling with the agents, he couldn't be subdued.

He thrashed, punched, and kicked.

His shirt ripped.

"Get off me," he shouted, twisting. "I have to protect my wife."

Several operatives began lifting Ruby.

"Leave her alone. Don't touch her!" he screamed.

His leg came loose from someone's grip and his kick landed on ribs. They cracked.

And then he felt a prick in his arm.

"Cowards," he said, as his lips slowed.

Physical heaviness overwhelmed him.

As darkness consumed him, he vowed to kill every last one of them if they hurt Ruby.

18

Thursday, June 20, 2041
The Correctional Treatment Facility (CTF): Washington, D.C.

THREE HOURS EARLIER, Ruby had regained consciousness, waking in a private prison cell as evening light faded through the bars shielding the small window.

Which meant she had been out cold for 31-hours.

Instead of wearing the dress she had worn to the SWC meeting, she was sporting a drab olive jumpsuit. Not to mention a blistering headache. No doubt the slow-drip IV was responsible for her throbbing skull. Her blood was being spiked with vervain, a common perennial plant which obviously functioned as a vampire sedative.

Hunger only aggravated her condition.

If she could've, she would've ripped the IV from her skin. But a sensor was attached to the needle, attached to an alarm. The prison nurses threatened that staffers wouldn't hesitate to fully sedate her if she tried anything.

Access to the IV bag was impossible. The tube delivering vervain was threaded through a small hole in the concrete wall, leading to the empty cell beside hers, where an automatic dispenser was located.

The SWC had clearly *planned* for her incarceration.

She'd deal with the council's betrayal another time.

Right now, she wanted to avoid trouble. Although her brain was foggy, she needed to remain conscious so she could think, even a little. Besides, she doubted she was capable of any physical response. She could barely muster the strength to sit upright on her cot.

With Ruby's defenses neutralized, the warden had allowed Clay to visit her briefly in her cell: a small room defined by three solid walls and one vertically-barred wall facing the hallway. Their conversation was audio-recorded; their meeting, videotaped. Other than those intrusions, the space provided the illusion of privacy, especially since there were no cells across from her, only gray cinderblock.

She and Clay agreed that Gabby wouldn't be allowed to visit her at the prison. Seeing her mother weak and hooked to an IV would be traumatic for their daughter. Instead, their best friends—Margo, Tomas, and son Reese—had dropped by the house to distract Gabby while keeping a watchful eye on her.

During Ruby's visit with Clay, he explained the charges, as well as who was behind the idea of vervain poisoning.

Em's involvement didn't surprise her. Not even the President's.

The betrayals of Eyes and Insley, however, were a cruel blow. Didn't they know her by now? In the war against zombies, sure, she had killed too many to count. But that was while defending herself or others. While defending the world. She could never hurt or kill someone innocent. Not without just cause.

She was a patriot, not a murderer.

Clay mentioned the two had pleaded for understanding and trust. Her incarceration would be temporary until they could clear her.

The vervain drip demonstrated how deep their trust went.

Their shallowness didn't stop there.

Feds had also swarmed their home immediately after her arrest, removing the server which "housed" her DEPE.

Good thing she, Clay, and Justine had prepared for every possible nefarious attack which could be thrown at them. Justine had assured them she no longer depended on the government-issued server. Her DEPE could travel through and across networks, hiding within any server she chose. In fact, she often did so to acquire what whet her palate: information.

At 9:00 p.m., a buzzer beeped up and down the prison hallway. The lights dimmed, announcing bedtime.

Other prisoners moaned and protested from their cells.

Not Ruby. She welcomed her nighttime retreat, hoping Liora would visit her as she rested. She needed advice on what to do next.

No doubt, Zagan was responsible for Paige's death.

Not to mention, while she was incarcerated and drugged with vervain, she could hardly protect the world from the king, not that she was much of a protector anyway. Paige's death proved that.

As Ruby started to close her eyes, a cloud of dust drifted through the bars, swirling faster and faster.

An image formed.

Standing before her, draped in a black cloak, was Zagan.

He raised his hood and lowered the fabric onto his back. Even in the dim light, she could see his green eyes.

"You," she sneered, focusing on his chin instead of his eyes. "You killed my friend. Framed *me* for her murder. And let's not forget you placed your disgusting hands on me in my bathroom."

He took a step toward her.

Inching back on her cot, she pressed herself against the corner.

She was angry, but very much afraid.

Worse, she wasn't ready to face him as an opponent, especially in her weakened state.

Maybe the video cameras in her cell would alert security. Not that guards could overtake him, but their presence might make him flee.

"What have they done to you?" he asked, looking at the needle piercing her skin.

"They? Are you kidding me? I'm here because of *you.* To the world, I'm the only vampire. When my friend was discovered drained of blood, with bite marks on her neck after I was the last soul to be in her company, who do you think my government suspected?"

He raised his hands, clutching his hair and pulling at his spikes like a frustrated child. He growled like an animal.

"Why do I act with impulse?" he said. "I did not plan to take that mayfly's life, only to taste her. As well, I neglected to consider the ramifications that my weakness might place on you."

"Share your sob story with someone you can glamour into caring," she snapped. "And *mayfly?* That's the level of respect you have for humans?"

He gazed around the cell. "I see that *your* respect for them has yielded great rewards."

"We have laws that must be followed," she said, suddenly

appreciating Eye's position a little more. "We aren't savages here on Earth."

"Are not *savages* pumping poison into you?" He swept his hand and the intravenous equipment, including the needle, turned to ashes and vanished.

Ruby's heart beat stronger in her chest, the moment the vervain drip was destroyed. She rubbed her right forearm where the needle had been inserted. Already her skin was healing.

She nodded at the cameras. "Guards monitor my cell. Although you're probably thinking I should drop to my knees and praise you, they'll arrive any second. And they'll punish me for this. Do you want me to thank you now, while I'm still conscious?"

"Gratitude is not yet required," Zagan said, ignoring her sarcasm. "But to clarify, I chose prudence over impulse this time. The guards will not be alerted. Nor will we be overheard by other prisoners."

Her heart thumped in her chest. "Please tell me you haven't ripped the ears from inmates. Or drunk the guards dry."

He tilted his head. "You pose a most valuable suggestion. For if the guards were drained, authorities could not deny that another vampire walks the Earth. Surely you cannot kill while vervain contaminates your blood. While you are locked behind bars."

She had to be cautious about every word spoken.

"Relax your worries," he scolded, delivering a crooked smile. "I glamoured them and disabled their security systems. Except for the cell locks. I oversee a prison in The Shadowlands. Prisoners should not be released before their sentences have been served."

"How utterly noble of you. Spoken by a murderer himself." She raised her flimsy blanket over her legs. "Let me suggest that you allow me to fulfill the terms of my incarceration…in peace. Alone. Go back to where you came from. Please."

"From where do you think I travel?"

Athanasia and Skotadi were on the tip of her tongue.

Suddenly, her brain sharpened as her blood cleansed itself. She realized she could play the role of a covert operative, trying to accrue a wealth of knowledge about her adversary. Knowledge that might destroy him.

Only a cunning warrior had a chance to save Earth.

Which meant Ruby's meetings with Liora had to remain secret. Including, for now, her knowledge of Zagan's plan and its initiation with the abduction of passengers from Flight 1733.

"Let's see," she said. "When you glamoured and *handled* me— uninvited, unwelcomed—you bragged you were a king. Let me guess your kingdom. The sewers beneath this city?"

"Your humor is unbecoming," Zagan said.

He proceeded to pontificate on his realm and his rule over it. When he finished, he stopped talking.

Silence lingered.

"Oh. Did you want me to be impressed?" she asked. "Here's a hint: count on waiting for eternity."

He stared at her, as though thinking.

"Come with me," he said, smiling. "Only for a visit while the prison guards are incapacitated. Are you not curious about your kind? About my realm? Or do you prefer to remain drugged and caged by mayflies?"

"I have no desire to come with you."

"*Desire* is certainly premature," he agreed, sounding arrogant and condescending, diluting her intended sting. "I think *interest* is the appropriate word choice. At least in this stage of our relationship."

"We have no relationship. And I have no *interest,* none whatsoever, in coming with you. How's that for appropriateness?"

"My terms might intrigue you," he countered. "I will bring you to my planet by way of traveling. After introducing you to my henchman, we can tour my castle, laboratories, and some of Skotadi."

"You want to pretend we're *friends?* That's laughable."

"Jokes aside, I wish to know you better."

"You mean," she said, "you're curious about my blood. You may have glamoured me during our little mirror-side chat, but I remember every word."

His eyes narrowed.

"You need sustenance," he said. "If you travel with me, I will ensure you are properly clothed and fed. And before the sun rises on Earth to claim a new day, I shall return you—needle included, though it will inject a liquid, absent potency. What harm can my offer bring?"

"What...*harm?* This, from an immortal whose impulses led to the murder of my friend?"

"I deserved that, and I am sorry." Zagan turned and walked toward the bars. "Apologies, as well, for letting my impulses take over in our first meeting. I should not have touched you without genuine consent. My power makes me accustomed to getting what I want, when I want. Believe me: you would not savor my struggles. They haunt me." He glanced down, with a pained expression.

"Cry me a river," she said.

"I will depart, as I can see my invitation holds no interest."

Did she really want to stay behind? Miss the opportunity?

She loathed him. But she also needed to discover his weaknesses.

And if she didn't go, what would become of the passengers from Flight 1733?

What would Clay urge her to do?

Keeping her enemy close was paramount.

The mad scientist used to tell her to *make your enemies need you. Trust you.* Not that she held Emory Bradshaw in high regard—not in any way, shape, or form.

But evil knew evil best.

"Wait!" she said, as his image began to fade to dust. "Add another safeguard to hide my absence and I *might* consider your offer. Unless you're not capable."

Maybe he could be goaded into showing more of his capabilities.

Particles which had lifted from his body returned to their places like tiny puzzle pieces. Solid once more, he spun to face her, grinning like he had expected her to stop him.

"Capable, I am," he said. "Rise and I shall demonstrate."

Ruby stood from her cot, shaky from hunger and the remnants of vervain.

"Step away," he commanded.

"Do you always order people around?"

"You mistake yourself. You are vampire."

Reaching into his pocket, Zagan retrieved an albino rat. He gently tossed the rat onto the cot before transforming his pet to look like Ruby's body—turned on its side as though sleeping. Waving his hand in the air, the blanket covered her likeness, except for her head and neck. The IV reappeared.

Ruby raised her eyebrows in disbelief. His power was truly unimaginable.

How could she ever hope to defeat such an odious force?

"The timeframe for you being impressed appears to have become more immediate," Zagan gloated. "Compared to my waiting for eternity, that is."

She rolled her eyes.

"Lend me your hand and let us travel," he said.

Reluctantly, she placed her hand in his, hoping she was making a wise decision.

A hum swept over her body.

She reminded herself that she had a purpose. That as The Tether, she was the only one who could destroy Zagan, the King of Darkness.

The only one who could protect her family and the world.

When the vibration peaked, they turned to dust.

19

AS ZAGAN TRAVELED Ruby through voids of space and time, he admired how easily his charms could beguile his prey.

Charm or no, his intentions regarding Ruby had not changed.

After unraveling the mystery behind her blood, he would rip out her heart. Her interference with his initial pandemic would, at last, be paid in full.

Timing was another matter.

Perhaps he could *use* her assets to advance his cause prior to her execution. As a cat might choose to toy with his mouse.

When Zagan visited Ruby's prison cell, an idea had formulated. Why not offer her the position of ambassador for The Restoration?

Having a liaison between vampires and humans might prove advantageous. After all, humans had revered their vampire warrior until *his* loss of control tarnished her reputation. Once he cleared her name—and he had already determined how—who better than Ruby to convince the mayflies to cooperate in their new purpose? Or to persuade his kind to accept a new blood source?

If Ruby refused his offer, he would kill her while her words still touched his ears. And then he would institute more cullings anyway.

There were no apparent disadvantages, regardless of her decision.

Of course, inviting her to his castle was impulsive.

Draven would not approve.

Zagan did not care.

Another benefit of a liaison with Ruby tantalized him.

He would have company. Another with whom to exchange clever banter. To challenge ideas and thoughts. Perhaps even, to join in laughter.

The prospect of having a guest, however, also generated fear.

Would he be able to control his temper? His reckless outbursts?

Then again, if he failed to exercise prudence, Ruby's death would merely come sooner.

He and Ruby materialized in his study at High Cliff, near the rocky balcony, opened to the night.

"Welcome to my castle," he announced, sweeping his hand to include the landscape beyond, dotted with twinkling lights like his own personal galaxy. The moon glistened on the river.

"You *never* have sunlight here?" she asked.

He explained the planet's three regions and their levels of light, elaborating on temperature variations.

The curse was intentionally excluded from his elucidation.

"Storms must be rare." She pointed toward the river. "I mean, with seventy-five-degree temperatures and low humidity, where does your water come from?"

"The border between The Shadowlands and Lampsi generates a band of perpetual storms which feed our rivers."

Several bats flew into the room.

"Is your balcony open to the outside for the bats?" she asked.

"I enjoy flying with them."

"Flying? I thought you traveled by turning to dust."

"As a sculptor," Zagan said, "I am also able to reshape myself into any incarnation, though I am not without favorites."

She paused, as if remembering something. Something that did *not* include being impressed regarding his rare gift.

"Let me guess," she said, "you favor ravens, as well as bats."

Still enjoying their banter, he admitted to himself that he missed female companionship.

"Watching an immortal gladiator slay the undead in an arena was most amusing," he said, "though tossing a dagger at me was quite unnecessary. Was I to pay coin to observe from the cavea? Had I broken another ridiculous human law?"

"Not at the stadium," Ruby said. "But in my home? Yes. Sneaking into a bedroom, even as a bat, might get you arrested, if not killed. You're lucky I didn't snatch you from the air and crush you."

"Luck is irrelevant. I would have disappeared before your thoughts were ever interpreted by your fingers."

"Speaking of disappearing," she said, with boldness. "Did you have anything to do with passengers vanishing from one of our aircraft?"

"You *do* understand I am king, do you not? Your brash tongue does not capitulate to my elevated position. Nor is it concerned with my unmatched powers or rash temperament."

He suppressed thoughts of ripping out her tongue.

She turned to face him directly. "My tongue, King Zagan, understands that if you've already decided to kill me—you know, after this little show-and-tell is over—then what I say, bold or fearful, will be irrelevant. Similar to your views on luck. And by the way, you avoided my question about the missing passengers."

"Perhaps, if time allows," he said, "I will address your question."

"Since time's a factor, why don't we make the best of it?"

He ignored her assertiveness and eyed her attire instead, tightening his eyebrows.

She looked down at herself, trying to follow his gaze. "What?"

"May I sculpt a more appropriate outfit for your brief tour?"

"I'm curious to discover what you find *appropriate*. Show me."

He waved his hand. Her jumpsuit dissolved. Without a time lapse, black-leather pants and a matching zippered jacket formed on her body, along with boots. The leather hugged her. Curves were not hidden. Her hair flowed over her shoulders.

Certainly there was no harm if the cat found his mouse appealing.

She zipped the jacket to cover her cleavage. "Black leather: how perfectly predictable. All I'm missing are bat wings."

He raised his hand and eyebrows. "This can be arranged."

Draven and Ozul entered the study.

His henchman stopped, quickly masking his alarm, placing his hand on the hilt of his sword. The wolf's nose twitched to scent her, showing no reaction at all, except for a slight wag of his tail.

After introductions, Zagan commanded, "Have the bower

prepared for our guest."

Ruby was about to interrupt, and he raised his hand to stop her. Her mouth closed, which meant she valued her life.

"Lady Spencer will remain with us for several hours," he qualified. "After our tour, she will need to refresh for a midnight drink. Inform the kitchen staff to prepare the dais. And have them bring a carafe of the...*special* blood."

"Of course, Your Excellency," Draven said.

Zagan raised his bent arm as an invitation. "Shall we?"

After clasping his forearm, he traveled her to a laboratory.

They materialized as his subjects worked on a cure for the animals. The moment he and his guest were visible, his technicians dropped a knee to bow in servitude. When their act of humility satisfied him, he ordered them to rise.

She asked many scientific questions of his subjects.

Each worker glanced at him to gain approval before answering.

"Does your kind need permission to speak?" she said softly, wearing an expression of disgust. "Like from you?"

"Our kind are devoted and reverent to their king." He raised an eyebrow, hoping her next words would not require discipline. He stopped breathing as he waited.

She raised herself on her toes and neared his ear with her lips. "Translation: *afraid,"* she said. "Perhaps you might try inspiring love over fear."

Her words soured the moment.

Grabbing her elbow, he held her in place, so she could not move.

"You are below position in my realm," he said through clenched teeth, feeling his veins rise on his skin. "Best not speak on matters in which you have no understanding or jurisdiction. Am I clear?"

He heard her heart race.

If *he* was afraid of how he might respond, it was especially wise that she was, too.

The technicians began scurrying about, recognizing his rising wrath and wanting to avoid getting caught in the crossfire. After all, they knew him.

"Can we talk in a more private setting, King?" she asked, finally absent arrogance.

He transported her beside the river, near a lit lantern.

The sound of the water cascading over rocks and lapping on the shore soothed his anger. The breeze comforted his skin like a caress.

He wished to return to a cordial interaction, though his anger was slow to retreat.

A small herd of deer lingered in the ferns, raising their heads and perking their ears. Recognizing him, they continued to graze on the grasses.

He inhaled deeply, attempting to regain his composure.

"In my country," she started, "we speak freely, without filters or fear. I'm not accustomed to holding back my thoughts. I didn't mean to disrespect you, though."

"Words spoken carelessly, without consequence, can be destructive. Is it not *love* to encourage your subjects to be thoughtful in their utterances?"

"I suppose, as long as silence isn't masking festering turmoil."

"Ahh, but that would be imbalance. The opposite of our divine purpose," Zagan said. "Love and fear must be in equal measure to achieve balance. Consider this: if undisciplined expression was integral to balance, then mayflies would surely possess the bulk of it. Yet they are afflicted with greed, blinded by their own importance, and unaware of *their* divine purpose. They stand flawed, the epitome of imbalance."

Although he did not mention his own troubling disproportion, he admitted to himself that love was far more elusive to his nature than fear. Because with great ease, he inspired much fear in others.

She sat on top of a boulder, bending her knees and hugging her legs. "Tell me more," she said. "How are humans *greedier* than vampires? I live with them and see very little difference."

"Then I shall open your eyes." He remained standing to avoid being perceived at her level. "In Athanasia, as on Earth, animals are sacrificial, garnered for sustenance by each planet's inhabitants. But this is where the similarity ends. Humans cultivate beasts of all species like crops-in-the-field before harvesting and devouring their meat. Yet they discard blood, innards, and entrails they cannot stomach. The practice is cavalier and wasteful, with no regard for attaining an equilibrium—a balance between the giver and receiver.

On Earth, the receiver is the only one to benefit. The mayfly *takes* and returns nothing."

"As a vampire," she countered, "I consume blood from a giver. The giver's body is expected to heal and rejuvenate itself over time. That's *taking* without giving back, isn't it?"

Was it possible this immortal did not know?

"Vampires are healers." He paused to regard her reaction. "When our kind is satiated, we heal the giver, returning the beast to pasture or to the wild, good as new. What was taken, is restored. And restoration, not extermination, is an act of love."

Her eyebrows tensed; eyes narrowed. "Then animals must be greedy, too," she said. "They hunt prey and leave unfinished carcasses behind. And they aren't healers either."

"Healers, they are not," he said. "But hunting one another only arose on *your* planet as a consequence of imbalance. On Athanasia and Besto Polus, animals live in harmony."

She combed her upper teeth over her bottom lip. "Even though I'm a human-made vampire, could *I* be a healer?"

Zagan called over a buck from the herd, choosing the strongest to demonstrate the beast showed no fear. He stroked the buck's forehead. The animal nuzzled his cloak.

"I will demonstrate," he said. "After, you can try."

Grabbing an antler, he turned the buck's head to the side. He sculpted his incisors into sharp points. Leaning over, he punctured the neck and took several sips, though the flavor no longer spurred his hunger. When he finished, blood dripped from the beast's neck wound. Raising his wrist to his mouth, Zagan bit at the base of his palm, where tiny veins gathered. As blood flowed, he placed his arm in front of the animal. The buck licked his blood as its puncture wounds healed.

Fully restored, the beast shook his head and snorted.

Seconds later, Zagan's wrist mended.

"I can't sculpt my teeth into points," she said. "My bite will tear his flesh and hurt him."

"Then glamour him not to feel pain."

She frowned, as if to confess she had never glamoured another.

Standing, she leapt from the rock and landed near the buck. The animal's ears moved forward and back, listening for his herd in the background. She patted the beast's neck, lowered her face to eye level, and spoke in a siren's timbre while locking gazes.

Zagan saw the buck's left pupil widen and narrow.

Moving the beast's head away from her, she penetrated the neck-hide with her teeth. After drinking, she mimicked her teacher, healing the buck and her own wound.

After the animal was released from its glamour, Zagan patted the beast's rump, sending him trotting back to the herd.

"Balance demonstrated," he said. "What was taken, is restored."

With her face lifted toward High Cliff, she appeared deep in thought.

"I remember crying," she said, recalling a memory clearly important to her. "I wiped away tears with my fingers and then touched a stillborn puppy's mouth. The pup came back to life. Maybe I healed her. Is that possible?" Raised eyebrows accentuated her question.

"As long as the creature's lifeforce is sufficient, then yes, our kind can restore life."

She stared into his eyes. "Is that why you couldn't bring Paige back to life? You had drained her?"

"Regrettably, yes. And I plan to show you why self-control eluded me. I predict you will be similarly affected."

"Will you also tell me about the passengers?" she asked.

"You have my word."

He rarely made promises.

But like his charm, pledges could always be broken.

20

Friday, June 21, 2041
Castle on High Cliff: Skotadi, Athanasia

DRAVEN WAITED IN the king's study, marching from one stone wall to another, hoping the king and human-made vampire would return soon from touring.

Midnight had already passed.

He clenched his fists and Ozul whined, acknowledging his tension. On the planet of immortality, everything took time—where delays, intermissions, and lulls in plans were inevitable.

Nothing was ever rushed when eternity was the measure of time.

He was different in this regard, as he had been from the beginning. When he would dine with his coven during The Rising— the first 200,000-years after Creation when vampires established the realms, laws, and monarchies—he would quickly ingest his meal from a wolf companion and then heal the beast. And while his kin continued to savor their meals...oh so slowly, interrupted by endless stories and ponderings, he would run off, playing with swords. Fighting imaginary demons.

He regretted choosing daggers over an arsenal of memories.

During The Rising, couplings and covens were permitted. But at the onset of the Era of Light and Darkness—the curse, covens were disbanded, as they might disrupt stability if they grew too powerful.

His coven had been forced to scatter, yet no mercy was returned for their compliance. Many of his kin were massacred in the death culling of The Shadowlands. Murdered for possessing rare gifts.

At first, Draven was consumed with hatred over the extermination of his kind, determined to enact revenge. But the king spared his life, took him under his wing, and exchanged his appetite for rebellion with leadership and a meaningful existence, if appearances counted for anything.

Draven always remembered: immortal was only two letters longer than mortal.

Though as good fortune would have it, he and Zagan shared similar dispositions on action. They both cherished decisiveness, not requiring millennium or mega-annum to contemplate the mundane.

Absent good fortune, the most significant difference between him and the king was temperament. Zagan was volatile, reactive to unpredictable emotional spikes. Which often resulted in irrational consequences—like turning annoyances to ashes, *before* probing for the truth. Or as in this case, complicating agreed-upon plans by adding an entanglement named Ruby Spencer.

Befriending the human-made vampire was unexpected.

When he had encouraged Zagan to postpone killing Ruby to learn her truth, he certainly did not intend for the king to bring her to High Cliff to initiate a relationship, undoubtedly delaying plans already set in motion. Including his own, since he had arranged for a private rendezvous in The Shadowlands.

He did not wish to be late.

Purging himself of frustration prior to the king's return was paramount since Draven detested ash. And he did not relish being reduced to it.

Ozul growled, lifting his quivering upper lip as Zagan and Ruby materialized. Thankfully, his wolf displayed proper demeanor upon their return to the flesh.

"Welcome back, Your Excellency," Draven said. "The kitchen is prepared to serve you in the dais whenever you are ready. Will that be soon?"

"Indeed. First, escort Ruby to the bower. Show her the wardrobe chamber from where she may select her garments and jewelry."

"What?" she asked. "You're not going to sculpt another shamefully sexist outfit on me?"

"I am interested in what *you* find appropriate." Zagan smiled and raised an eyebrow.

Draven had never seen the king so cavalier.

Usually, Zagan attempted to quell his paranoia by controlling every detail. Rarely did he allow himself to feel joy in the moment.

"This way, Madam," Draven said, offering his forearm to Ruby.

She placed her hand near his wrist. "Are we going to 'travel' to the guest quarters?"

Zagan roared in laughter. "You have much to learn, Lady Spencer! Your king is the only immortal who can sculpt and travel on his own. My henchman will escort you: one boring step at a time."

Leaving the study and Zagan behind, they walked down the spiral stone staircase, lit by flickering lanterns on the interior wall. Ozul followed.

At the first landing, they turned right and headed inward. At the end of another corridor, they walked under the doorway's ten-foot arch. The bower's chamber, intended for female visitors, was massive. Its walls and flooring were polished marble. Half of the space's square-footage jutted out from the canyon's face. Although the room did not include an open-wall to the valley below, a portion of the ceiling was open over the bed, allowing the one at rest to enjoy starry skies. Of course, the king had not entertained a proper lady in excess of 500-years.

For one reason or another, female guests ended up dead.

"Do tell, Draven," she said, gazing around the guest chamber. "Does your king fear anything? Other than sunlight?"

"A peculiar question."

His heart accelerated.

Hidden ears could hear without being seen.

Ozul's fur raised on his withers.

"Really more of a fascination than a serious question," she clarified. "If Zagan is the only immortal who can sculpt and travel, he probably fears very little. And I've never met anyone who wasn't afraid of more than one thing. So relax. I was simply curious. As I mentioned earlier to your abrasive boss, I speak my mind."

"Then forgive me, Lady Spencer." He dipped his head forward. "Best to differentiate fear from danger. One may be imagined, while the other is tangible. As henchman, my duty is to protect King Zagan from danger. But I cannot control what he fears." He glanced toward the hallway. "I shall wait outside your door until you have changed."

Draven's wait was not long.

When Ruby emerged, she was dressed in a gown, snug from the waist up, with a low-scooped neckline. The lacey dress was mint green, interwoven with glistening gold threads. Her hair was raised in a bun, secured with gold ribbon. Decorating her slender neck hung a thick gold chain and a ruby pendant. She wore earrings to match.

Most unexpected choices, as Draven had predicted she would select the Earthling jeans and T-shirt.

Instead, she resembled a vampire queen.

"Now *you* look curious," she said.

"The king shall be pleased by your choices."

"When in Rome..."

Draven joined her. "Do as the Romans do..."

They laughed as he led her and Ozul to the dais, a stage elevated above the great hall, which provided privacy for dining when its thick velvet curtains were drawn.

Ruby had asked a salient question about the king's fears, a question he was forbidden to answer.

But if she was observant when they feasted together, the truth would be revealed.

21

Friday, June 21, 2041
Castle on High Cliff: Skotadi, Athanasia

RUBY NEEDED TO act charming, even though the thought of attracting Zagan caused acid to rise from her stomach.

But every Venus flytrap was intended to entice its prey.

Her nemesis had to want her, trust her.

Applying her strategy, she had already learned so much. For one thing, she was a healer. She could glamour, too. And if Zagan was a sculptor and traveler, maybe she possessed those gifts as well.

Draven opened the oversized double doors leading into the castle's rectangular dining room, referred to as the dais. At the far end of the room, Zagan stood when she entered, pushing back his chair which resembled a throne.

The mahogany table, centered on the red-and-black checkerboard floors, could accommodate a platoon. Overhead hung two crystal chandeliers, each ornamented with glass beads, elaborate trimmings, and lit candles. The fireplace and lanterns on the long back-wall added to the candles, casting light on the chandelier prisms which reflected onto surfaces like miniature dancing rainbows.

To Ruby's left were closed red-velvet curtains, the kind found in historical movie theatres.

Gold goblets had been placed on placemats, one in front of the king at the head of the table and the others to his right and left.

Smelling blood in the goblets, her stomach grumbled.

She and Zagan quickly inhaled as they observed each other.

Zagan wore a long, tailored evening jacket: mint green, with gold clasps. His emerald eyes glowed.

Why, why, *why* had she selected the mint-green gown?

"Did you read my mind?" she taunted. "So we could look like prom partners?"

He pulled out the chair to his left, nodding for her to approach. "First, let me acknowledge your breathtaking beauty. The dress is a most appropriate choice." He smiled and winked. "Prom? I am not familiar with this term. Are you, Draven?"

His henchman returned to the table to sit, having commanded Ozul to lay in the corner.

"I believe," Draven answered, "the term *prom* refers to a dancing event for human couplings."

Zagan revealed his teeth in a full smile.

Her charm was working better than expected. Maybe a bit *too* well.

"I should very much like to lead you in dance, Lady Spencer," Zagan said. "However, my jacket selection had nothing to do with my desire to *couple* with you. Sorry to disappoint, but my wardrobe tastes have existed since Creation."

Flustered by his misinterpretation and arrogant toying, she sat with a huff and eye roll.

"I wear shades of green," he continued, "when I wish to be social, and black when I do not. And despite all that I am, regrettably, I am unable to read minds."

"Are *any* vampires mind-readers?" she asked the king, hoping to gauge his honesty since she already knew the answer.

"If there were, surely the most powerful vampire before you would possess the gift."

"Too bad," she said. "What an amazing ability that would be."

Draven's eyes shifted nervously.

"Are my gifts not enough for you?" Zagan asked.

He glared at her and veins pulsed under his skin.

"Quite the opposite, Your Excellency," she cooed, hoping to heal his wounded ego. "When you can obliterate the present, is there really a need to read the future?"

He raised his ornamented goblet and swung it toward his henchman. "Draven?"

They switched cups.

Perhaps the exchange represented a custom.

"Let us drink to the present then," Zagan cheered.

Raising her cup to her lips, she controlled herself and sipped what was clearly human blood. The occasion marked the first time she'd ever drank blood with other vampires in a dining room setting. She appreciated the normality of it. There was no reason to feel ashamed that she preferred blood over pizza and chocolate chip cookies.

Her host and his henchman guzzled.

Veins rose on their necks and faces.

Together, the male vampires slammed down their goblets, resembling drunken bar mates demanding more liquor.

"We. Want. More!" the king growled.

A door on the back wall squeaked open and a girl walked into the room holding a pitcher.

Ruby sniffed: a *human* teenager.

Zagan nodded at his henchman.

Refilling Draven's goblet, the girl waited as he quaffed its contents. The henchman smiled and dipped his head.

The king raised his glass to be refilled.

Standing between him and Draven, the girl remained, pouring blood into goblets until the pitcher was empty.

Ruby finally finished her first serving, unable to pinpoint the cause of her company's exaggerated enthusiasm. Or their unending thirst.

"We require yet another carafe, Felicity," the king commanded. "And when you have replenished the pitcher with divine wine, return and join us at the table."

"Yes, Your Excellency," Felicity said.

Ruby's eyes grew wide. "She's a passenger…"

"Silence!" Zagan banged on the table and rattled the goblets.

Ruby's heart leapt at the outburst.

"Your king shall ask questions of *you.*"

His tone was sharp and edgy.

She lowered her eyes to show submissiveness. She'd hardly rise as The Tether if Zagan ripped out her heart.

"You should be ravenous over the divine wine," he boomed. "Yet you sip as if bored. Do you not find it delectable? Does this libation not stimulate uncontrollable cravings? Or is rudeness curving your palate? Souring your tongue?"

"Uncontrollable cravings?" she mused aloud. "Is this what human blood does to you? Is this the reason you drained Paige instead of healing her?"

He pounded the table again, causing a depression in the wood.

"Answer!" Zagan roared. "Why are you not affected similarly?"

"I'm not trying to be ungrateful." She raised her eyes to meet his again. "But my diet already consists of human blood. The divine wine, as you call it, is nothing new or extraordinary…for *me*. The buck by the river? His blood was a first."

As the words left her mouth, the complication crystalized.

Why hadn't she anticipated it? Why hadn't Liora prepared her? Because why should *she* be able to drink human blood and her nemesis be forbidden?

She'd never kill for her sustenance, but still…

Her hypocrisy pounded in her chest, pulsed in her veins.

How was she going to navigate the complication? To make an argument that made sense?

Zagan and Draven's eyes met, swapping expressions of unabashed bewilderment.

In the silence, she heard the crackling of each burning wick.

The king turned in her direction and squared his shoulders.

"No need to be tormented, Lady Spencer," the king said, smiling. "Your confession brings tremendous relief. For we had anticipated needing to convince you that *human* blood, not animal blood, was our divinely-intended nourishment. And here, you already embrace the truth. A most astonishing development. A revelation certainly worthy of prom dancing."

She stalled, trying to formulate an angle.

No doubt her racing heart exposed her anxiety.

"Now wait a minute," she snapped.

The king tilted his head and glared, as if requiring a correction.

"I mean," she qualified, "please hear me out. Humans *voluntarily* donate blood to be used for medical purposes. The government provides me with a supply from these volunteers. No one is forced to donate against their will. No one is enslaved. Or killed. No one!"

"Hmm." Zagan rubbed his chin. "Volunteering is a notion I had not considered. What do humans get in return? Coin? Elevated position?"

"Giving blood is a noble offering," she said. "Helping other humans in need is inherent in humanity."

"Yet you are not human," Zagan countered. "And still, volunteers donate for you."

"But I serve humans in return, slaying the undead and risking my life for them."

"I have witnessed your abilities in the arena, remember?" Zagan challenged. "Your life hardly seemed at risk." He smiled and then rubbed his chin again. "Your testimony, however, reflects balance: an even exchange between the giver and receiver. This interests me."

He tapped his fingers on the table.

She briefly closed her eyes, downhearted that she hadn't prepared for a debate with a three-million-year-old, give or take, vampire king.

Frustration and anger overwhelmed her.

Without willing them, her nails grew sharp.

The king raised his eyebrows at the sight.

She thrust her hands under the table.

Pointed nails, however, were the least of her worries.

"Your suggestion might abolish the practice of taking humans against their will, which I should think would please you," the king said. "Could humans be convinced to *voluntarily* donate blood for an even exchange? One which would benefit them as well?"

"And who would convince them to volunteer?" Ruby asked. *"You?* A vampire who'd threaten to turn them to ashes if they resisted?"

She realized the gaping hole as she stumbled into it.

Zagan explained he wanted *her* to serve as an ambassador to help both sides realize their mutual benefits. Now that she had introduced the prospect of freewill and volunteerism, how could she resist?

Of course, if she declined his proposal, he told her he'd cull humans anyway.

"How will *you* benefit, King?" she asked. "I mean, other than collecting the finest blood for yourself? I'm guessing you're seeking more."

"Is it not enough to help one's kind, when animal blood remains scarce?" Zagan asked.

His aspirations were hardly noble. She knew the King of Darkness wanted to be heralded as the supreme ruler of all the planets. The immortal version of Huo Zhu Zheng. Liora had told her as much.

"Now you know," Zagan said, "why I was interested in knowing you better. To have you serve as a liaison, an ambassador for The Restoration. With our business settled, you will learn the fate of the airplane passengers. As promised."

Forget that Ruby never agreed to serve as the king's ambassador. She'd let that fact slide. The passengers were her priority.

Felicity returned with another pitcher. She followed the same taste-testing routine as before, letting Draven drink first.

Although offered more, Ruby had lost her appetite.

When the king commanded, Felicity sat beside her at the table.

"Ask her what you wish," Zagan said.

"How thoughtful of you to grant me permission to speak," Ruby said, glowering at him.

Turning her back toward Zagan, she lifted the girl's chin and gazed into her eyes. "Are you being treated well?"

"Oh yes. I'm enjoying my duties," Felicity said. "When I'm finished, I can read books from the library or listen to music in the minstrel's gallery. The castle is way cool. Don't you love the stars here? How about the river? Aren't they beautiful, Ruby?"

"You know me?"

"Not to be disrespectful, but *duh*. All humans do." Felicity smiled. "I'm glad you've come to chat with our king." She leaned closer. "He looks like a badass rockstar, doesn't he?"

Ruby looked over her shoulder and glared at Zagan. "Felicity has been glamoured."

"Was this not expected?" he asked. "Glamouring has been done with compassion, to avoid fear and panic. Gradual acclimation to our way of life is preferred over plunging someone into a tub of freezing water. Eventually, the glamour will be lessened until there is no need for altered thoughts. But with your suggestion for volunteerism, glamouring mayflies may not be required in the future."

She glanced at Felicity who was still smiling, despite the tension.

"How are all the other passengers?" Ruby asked. "Are they okay?"

"*All?*" The teenager's voice quivered, as if she was forbidden to tell a lie, but was frightened to tell the truth.

Felicity glanced at the king, and he nodded for her to continue.

"Mrs. Parks and Mr. Quincy didn't make it. They were old. Others have been moved into villages, so I haven't seen them. But I'm not worried. Everyone is so attentive. And nice."

Ruby rose from her chair; she'd had enough.

"The time is nearing four in the morning at the prison. I need to return." Ruby locked eyes with the king. "You'll keep your end of the deal and take me back, right?"

Zagan shoved his chair as he stood. Unhappy, she suspected, that she hadn't asked for permission to stand.

"Leave us," he commanded Draven and Felicity.

When the dining room emptied, he sculpted a change of clothes for her, exchanging her gown and accessories for the jumpsuit. Her hair was loose again.

The king neared. "Hold out your hand," he said.

When she did, he dropped two coins into her palm. The same type of coins she'd picked up at the stadium the night Paige was murdered. The warm pewter coins—imprinted with a tree—hummed in her hand, as if life coursed through them.

"Yes," he admitted. "I planted the other coins for you to retrieve at the colosseum. Had you kept them with you, I would have felt your fear more easily when the mayflies drugged and arrested you."

She started to protest, and he briefly placed his finger on her lips, requesting silence.

"The coins serve as a connection," he continued. "Now, you have yours and I have mine. Our emotions will travel between us when the coins are near. Should you require my assistance, use them to reach out to me. And do not deny your need for them. Your circumstances at the prison reveal this truth. Summon me, and I will rescue you come nightfall." He gently closed her fingers to embrace the coins, before raising her fist to his lips.

He kissed her hand as they turned to dust.

Before she had the chance to pull away.

22

AFTER ZAGAN RETURNED Lady Spencer to the prison, in the pre-dawn hours, he desired to test human volunteerism.

If mayflies did not require coin or position to help others in need, then perhaps a mayfly would sacrifice for him. His *need* was to free his new ambassador from incarceration, using an idea Ruby had furnished, certainly without intention.

A stone's throw from the prison, he strolled down a graveled walkway, shadowed in darkness except for the glow of sparsely placed streetlights. Fog blanketed his path, rising like a cloud. The thickening mist insulated his view of the landscape.

He smiled.

Who else in the universe could create such an atmosphere to unsettle prey?

A few bats fluttered near the lights, as the fog rose to greet them.

In the distance, he scented his test subject.

Using his mind, his mint-green evening attire was sculpted into a pair of jeans and a black hooded-sweatshirt. The hood covered his white hair and undoubtedly shaded his face.

A male came into view.

As the subject jogged toward him, the fog swirled and shifted. The male whistled a quiet melody.

With skin matching Ruby's, the mayfly wore a tight-fitting red jacket and black pants which were loose on his legs. Crimson sneakers and a billed cap matched his jacket.

This human shared the king's appreciation for color coordination.

"Excuse me, mayfly," Zagan said, when their distance was close.

The male looked behind him, as if the king might have spoken to someone else.

He faced Zagan again and slowed. "Who *me?* I'm no mayfly, man. But what's up?"

"I request your assistance, for I have several pressing needs. Most particularly, I am hungered and have been deprived of a fresh meal for longer than desired."

"That's not cool." The male stopped. "What do you need? Cash?"

"I do not require currency," Zagan answered. "In truth, I am stricken with insatiable thirst."

"Let me guess: you're some old-school English professor, trying to fit-in on the streets of D.C." The mayfly chuckled while eyeing his outfit. "Here's some truth back at you, teach: drinks aren't free." He reached into his pocket and pulled out several green sheets of paper coinage. "Sure, I'll give you some money. 'Cause if we don't help each other, who will? And man, you're not looking so good."

"Hunger pales me, indeed. But I shall not confiscate your coinage." Zagan removed his hood.

The male's mouth dropped open. "Shit Sherlock, your skin and hair are freaking *white.*"

Zagan was unmoved by the mayfly's captivation over his appearance, though he much appreciated the male's generosity and good intentions. Their exchange *proved* Ruby's assertion that humans were willing to volunteer for those in need.

Since the king desired liquid currency and the mayfly had agreed to help, the conversation was ending.

"Can you see movement in my eyes?" Zagan asked. "Do they remind you of the sea?"

The mayfly stepped closer and raised his heels, extending his height.

"Damn, teach. Sweet contacts."

Zagan brandished his pointed incisors.

Wide eyed, the mayfly turned and ran, which the king considered a breach of contract.

Zagan sculpted an invisible lasso which he cast around the mayfly's ankles. A tug sent the male crashing onto the gravel, face first.

He cognitively pulled on the rope, reeling in the human, dragging him to the king's feet.

"I only wanted to help, man," the mayfly said, with abrasions bloodying his face.

"And I would never deprive you of such an honorable sacrifice."

The king locked eyes with him.

He smelled the mayfly's sweetness and licked his lips.

After the king took control of his volunteer's thoughts, the male turned his neck to the side, allowing Zagan to puncture an artery. As if the human had a choice.

The king drank with his eyes closed, lids quivering with delight.

The mayfly's body twitched in protest. When his muscles froze in place, Zagan separated himself from the emptied corpse. The male dropped onto the misty pathway.

The king wiped blood from his mouth.

"Much to my benefit that mayflies have forgotten their own adage: *the road to hell is paved with good intentions.*"

Turning to dust for his return to High Cliff, the king reminded himself that he had a serious matter to discuss with his henchman.

Very serious, indeed.

23

Friday, June 21, 2041
The Correctional Treatment Facility (CTF): Washington, D.C.

CLAY HAD CLEARANCE to visit his wife at CTF anytime he
wanted. And since he couldn't sleep and Ruby never slept, the crack
of dawn seemed as good a time as any.

Thankfully, Gabby had spent the night over at Margo and
Tomas's and would head to sailing day-camp later that morning,
joined by their best friends' son. At home, the dogs were fine for a
couple of hours. Besides, Justine knew how to reach him.

As he parked his SUV in the prison lot, steaming coffee flavored
the air within the interior.

The sun painted the horizon in shades of pink and orange.

After exiting and locking the vehicle, he clutched the carryout cup.
He had added blood for Ruby (A-positive, her favorite), since the
prison refused to feed her.

Inhumane treatment of his wife was not sitting well with him.
Feeling edgy, he dared anyone to mess with him. His hands
unconsciously tightened around the cup, pushing piping-hot coffee
through the sipping slit in the plastic lid.

The day had just started, and already, he needed to chill.

Flashing lights caught his attention down the hill, to the right of
the prison. He could barely see across the distance but knew the area
well enough. The activity was near the mouth of a graveled jogging
trail. Three police vehicles were parked at the entrance.

Inside the CTF, he signed-in, received a name tag, and approached security's body scanner—a device so sensitive, it could detect perspiration.

"Place your wallet, smartwatch, belt buckle, and beverage cup on the conveyer," ordered the guard. "Walk into the booth and raise your arms above your head."

Clay complied, placing his feet on the shoeprints painted on the floor inside the stall. After the scan, he stepped from the booth. Another guard greeted him.

"Remove the lid on this cup," the a-hole growled.

"Can't get your own coffee around here?"

"No need to be a smartass, Mr. Spencer. You know we need to inspect everything brought into the facility. Even by government officials."

Clay removed the lid. Steam billowed from the coffee.

"Why's it reddish?" the guard asked.

"Strawberry flavored creamer—the sickening sweet stuff."

Picking up the cup, Clay took a swig, trying not to gag at the *real* flavor. He winked. *"Ahh!* Tasty. Want to try?"

"Glad you're chipper at the crack of dawn," the guard said. "Maybe that's what I'm missing: strawberry java. Who knew?"

Clay was instructed to collect his belt, wallet, and smartwatch on his way out.

Holding the cup of coffee—lid back on, he followed the guard to D-Block. Most of the prisoners were still sleeping, so he avoided an onslaught of cackles and insults.

At his wife's cell, the guard gave him entry before relocking the barred door.

"Be good, kids," the guard teased. He pointed at the multiple cameras and speakers. "And remember, big brother has eyes and ears on you. This isn't a conjugal visit."

Clay flashed a scowl that made the guard's crooked smile flatline.

As the guard walked away and Clay turned toward Ruby, she leapt off the cot and wrapped her arms around him, stretching her IV tube. He held the coffee cup out to his side to prevent spilling it.

"Well, good morning, sunshine," he said, relieved she felt better.

Pushing up on her toes, she kissed him. He drew her body close with his free hand.

"Hey," he said softly, noticing the dark circles under her eyes had vanished from the day before. "How's my one and only?"

A buzzer blasted the cell, jolting his heart.

Prisoners down the hallway moaned and grunted.

"No PDA," a guard's voice ordered over the cell's sound system.

They ended their embrace.

Ruby sniffed the air, probably detecting the blood-enriched coffee.

"Oh, here," he said, smiling. "I brought you coffee."

At first, she hesitated, like maybe coffee and human blood didn't go together. But then she downed the entire cup of joe without regard to temperature, lowering the cup to the floor when emptied. Reaching for his hand, she clasped his fingers and urged him to sit with her on the cot.

"You think of everything," she said. "Thank you. And I'm much better. How's Gabby holding up? Please tell me she's okay."

He explained their daughter's plans for the day and assured his wife that Gabby had adopted a positive attitude. Despite her youth, she knew in her heart, without a shadow of a doubt, that her Mom would be found innocent. That she'd be coming home soon.

"Did you *dream* last night?" he asked, wondering if Liora had visited Ruby.

She pulled him close. Her lips brushed his ear. Two words touched his eardrum ("I saw") before the cell was blasted with another piercing beep that pounded his eardrums.

"Whispering is also not permitted," the same voice warned.

Clay narrowed his eyes at the mounted camera which was making a whizzing sound as it focused on them.

"New gifts have been awakening," she said, using her full voice. "And I'm curious about one I haven't tried."

"I'm game." He looked at the main camera. "But *here?*"

Can you hear me?

Clay jerked his head back. Her lips hadn't moved, yet he *heard* her in his mind.

He nodded to answer her question.

The gift is called whispering. She smirked. *The guards might find that ironic.* Squeezing his hand, she added, *Vervain is no longer pumping into my veins. That's why I'm better.*

"Thank God," Clay said.

I saw Zagan last night and I'll tell you all about it. But let's talk out loud so we don't make the guards suspicious.

Ruby continued to awe him more and more, every day.

Changing the subject, he spoke to her about taking another family voyage on *The Gem,* their sailing yacht. Daydreaming about sailing the open seas always gave them hope, especially during stressful times.

A guard and Eyes approached the cell.

"Start the paperwork," Eyes commanded the guard, as the Secretary of Defense entered the cell. "And give us about ten minutes. Understood?"

The guard nodded before closing the cell door and walking away.

Refusing to look at Eyes, Ruby turned her face toward the wall.

"Why are you here?" Clay asked him. "Are you trying to provoke her or something?"

"I'm a friend, remember?" he said. "And my nose still throbs from where you clocked me, Clay, so I'm not interested in another physical confrontation. I want to be heard, that's all."

"How very self-serving," she snapped, glaring at him. "You jail me for something I didn't do. You discount my warnings. And now *you* want to be heard?"

Prick, she whispered in Clay's thoughts.

He had to chuckle.

"I never believed you were guilty, Ruby," Eyes defended, glancing at Clay as if confused by his levity. "But I don't take the law into my own hands either. I knew facts would rise to the surface and the law would prevail. And they have."

"Explain," Ruby said.

"Earlier this morning, police were called to the scene of a homicide. On the outskirts of this campus, in fact."

Clay recalled the flashing lights near the jogging trail.

Ruby's eyes narrowed and forehead creased, as if she anticipated what the Secretary was about to say.

"Like Paige Jasper," Eyes continued, "the victim's neck revealed two puncture wounds. Also like your scalper, the deceased was drained of blood. Clearly, you couldn't have committed this crime from your jail cell. A rogue, killer-vampire is among us."

"You had to wait until someone else was murdered to believe me?" she asked.

"I'm sorry, Ruby. Insley's sorry. The President, too. Hell, the entire SWC feels badly," Eyes said.

His wife rolled her eyes.

"Your release papers are in the works," he added. "And Ruby: we can't stop this ancient immortal named Zagan without your help. Together, we can develop a plan. That'll be our agenda during Wednesday's SWC meeting."

She smiled at Clay.

I have my own plan. And it doesn't include the council.

24

Friday, June 21, 2041
The Spencer Residence: Annapolis, Maryland

RUBY WAS DEEP in thought as her husband drove from the prison to their house.

She stared at him, worried about his and Gabby's safety.

The death of the jogger proved, once again, that Zagan had no regard for human life beyond using them as a commodity or to advance his cause, like freeing her from prison.

His arsenal of unrivaled powers made him invincible.

If Ruby was vulnerable, humans were utterly defenseless.

How could she be in all places at one time? How could she serve as humankind's protector? The impossibilities were overwhelming.

Clay glanced at her. "Everything in its own time," he said, as if knowing what she needed to hear. "First, you have to refresh. Then we can take on the universe. One step at a time."

"I only have a few gifts," she countered. "That's nowhere near enough for this new wargame."

"You're not through discovering them." He flashed his crooked smile. *"Believe,* remember?"

Clay pulled into their driveway at half-past noon.

The sun was shining, warming temperatures to 85-degrees. A breeze carried the fragrance of salt water from the southeast. Birds chirped, seagulls laughed, and cicadas buzzed.

She was home.

Walking into the kitchen, Mai and Zoe greeted her with sticky kisses and wagging tails.

Maybe Clay was right.

Exhausted, she needed to re-energize before fleshing out her plan.

Tonight, they'd celebrate her homecoming. Because life was rapidly changing. Trying to save the world would leave little time in the future for pizza and chocolate chip cookies.

After showering and changing into shorts and a T-shirt, she returned to the kitchen to make pizza dough. Clay followed, eager to hear about her visit to the castle.

Ruby told him everything.

When she wanted to express authentic feelings about her encounter with Zagan, she whispered into his mind since the king could hide anywhere, in any form, to eavesdrop.

She didn't want her nemesis to know that her charming disposition was nothing more than a means to an end. *His* end.

Sharing every detail, she inventoried her gifts for her husband, mentioning she'd glamoured a buck not to feel pain.

"Do you think Zagan could read *all* your thoughts," Clay asked, "if he got the chance again?"

"I'm not sure." In a cognitive whisper, she added, *But I've been working on raising a mental shield and I think I've finally done it.*

He smiled. "Like I said, you're not done growing."

After placing the dough into a bowl to rise, she reached into her pocket and retrieved the two coins Zagan had given her.

"Zagan has access to my emotions through these coins," she said. "His feelings flow to me as well. And I have three more coins upstairs. I picked them up in the stadium parking lot, without knowing what they were."

He reached out his hand and she dropped the coins into his palm. Fingering a token, he examined it. "How do you know when the coins are channeling emotions?"

"Heat. The coins get warm and hum, like a vibration."

"Good thing you don't have a temper." He smiled. "Most of the time," he added, winking. "So I take it you're going to toss them? Sounds like they're dangerous."

"No, I'm going to hold onto them."

His eyebrows raised.

Ruby whispered into his mind that she wanted to determine if the coins could be used against the king. Like maybe tricking him into traveling to her when she was prepared to defeat him. An ambush.

"Just curious," Clay said. "What if Zagan wants to read my mind? Or Gabby's?"

Let's hope I can figure out how to glamour humans before the king gets anywhere near you.

25

Friday, June 21, 2041
The Spencer Residence: Annapolis, Maryland

THEIR FAMILY DINNER was everything Ruby had hoped—a reunion, a relief, a brief distraction. Wearing party hats, they laughed until their stomach muscles ached.

While Clay and Gabby tackled the dinner dishes before bedtime, Ruby headed upstairs to the master bedroom. She suspected that when she had shattered the mirror in the bathroom and when her fingernails had grown into daggers on two separate occasions, her body was revealing yet another gift: sculpting.

A gift that powerful needed to be practiced. Mastered. Or the consequences might be disastrous.

Rolling coins would be a good place to start.

Zagan's five pewter tokens rested on her dresser. Despite the similarity to a quarter's size and shape, each coin's rim was thicker, making them easier to work with.

If she truly was a sculptor able to wield the properties of matter, she should be able to move objects across a smooth surface.

Ruby slid picture frames to one side of the dresser. Grabbing the coins, she stood each on its rim, lining them up. Her heart thumped in her chest as she stepped back.

She whispered in her head: *move, move, move.*

Nothing.

Roll. Roll, damn it.

Nothing.

Ruby spent the next half-hour thinking—mentally shouting—every command that might send the coins rolling across the surface.

None of them worked.

Clay entered the bedroom and glanced at the stationary coins. No doubt her exasperation was written all over her face.

"Not happening?" he asked.

"Not even close." *How can I defeat Zagan if I can't master my gifts?*

"Let's try duplicating the success you've already had." He rubbed his dimpled chin. "When your nails grew to daggers in the SWC meeting, what were you thinking?"

The image played in her mind.

"President Unger was being condescending. I was incensed." She combed her upper teeth over her lower lip. "I'm embarrassed about my thoughts. Sometimes my predator tendencies take over."

"Go ahead," he urged.

"I pictured leaping from my chair, clutching onto his tailored suit like a crazed animal, and scratching his face with my fingernails." She closed her eyes, ashamed. "There. I said it."

"Your nails also grew at the castle. What were you thinking then?"

"I was at the dining room table and no matter what I said, my words became traps. Frustration and anger overwhelmed me."

Visualizing her exchange with Zagan sparked a resurgence of emotions, in real time.

Her nails grew to razor-sharp points.

"And?" He looked at her nails, eyebrows raised. "What did you picture?"

"The same," she said, the mystery suddenly unmasked in her mind. "Words in my head aren't enough. I have to mentally picture the means, as well as the end. The action *and* the result."

"Try and move the coins now," he said.

She pictured inhaling deeply and puffing her cheeks with air. Then she released a steady stream, like blowing air as strong as a leaf blower. She could've pictured a typhoon or tornado or even straight-line winds, but she wasn't sure how literal the outcome would be.

As the stream of compressed air touched the image of the coins in her mind, she watched them rotate, faster and faster, like video footage playing in her brain.

Sure enough, the actual coins spun forward on the dresser top, rolling over the surface. None fell onto their sides because she didn't picture them toppling. And when all five coins reached the edge, they launched into the air like projectiles.

Clay grabbed one, midair.

"Ouch," he said, dropping the coin from his grip. "That coin is smoking hot."

"Really?" She walked around the room, retrieving the tokens from the floor. Even for a vampire, they felt warm. "I had no idea the coins were that sensitive. I must have heated them as I relived my emotions from the castle."

Standing by her dresser, she opened the top drawer.

"I'll give the coins a minute to cool down," she said, meeting his gaze. "Then I'll tuck them away in this drawer. You know, so I don't unintentionally channel my emotions to Zagan."

"Better idea." Her husband held out his hand. "Why don't I store them downstairs in a kitchen drawer? Distance seems like the best option, especially at night."

"You're right." She dropped the coins into his palm. "How about bringing up the dogs?"

"Aren't they comfortable in the whelping pen?"

"Maybe it's the coins. Not sure." She shook her head. "But I'm uneasy again. And I don't think I should ignore my feelings. If it's nothing, at least having Gabby and the dogs on the same floor might help my anxiety pass."

Even as Clay turned and left the bedroom for the kitchen, she doubted her angst would lessen so easily.

Whether the dogs were upstairs or down, a warning was trying to crystalize in her thoughts.

She could almost see words forming and glowing.

Almost.

26

Friday, June 21, 2041
Castle on High Cliff: Skotadi, Athanasia

ZAGAN HAD RETURNED to High Cliff 16-hours ago, by human standards. By now, Lady Spencer would be home from prison, perhaps readying herself for a night's rest.

In retrospect, he did not regret draining the human near the correctional facility. The act was a give and take. He had taken a life to give Ruby her freedom. "Balance" could be argued, not that he needed to defend his actions. He was king and answered to no one.

Draven did not possess the same privilege.

His henchman answered to *him*.

Although Zagan was not a seer like Liora, nor was he blinded to evidence revealing the truth. He possessed an intuition that made him profoundly sensitive to deceptions.

Some called it paranoia.

He called the competence a sixth sense.

And presently, his instincts warned that a ruse was at play.

A scheme involving his beloved Draven.

Upon returning to the castle, Zagan had immediately summoned his henchman. Regrettably, Draven was visiting Skotadi villages and assessing food shortages. Which meant the king had to wait.

The conversation he sought with his henchman required the privacy of his fortress or he would have traveled to him.

So Zagan waited, his nerves fraying with every passing moment.

At last, Draven strolled into his study with Ozul flanking him.

"Your Excellency," his henchman greeted. "I apologize for my delay. Did all go well with Lady Spencer?"

"All, *except* her visit to High Cliff."

"As feared," Draven said. "Because I would not have brought the Earthling vampire here."

"And why is that?" Zagan asked. "What did my most trusted advisor *not* wish for me to see?"

Draven tilted his head, narrowing his eyes as if trying to analyze the implication. "Our eyes see the same. I do not withhold truths from you."

"No?" Zagan pounded his slate desk, making it crumble into a million fragments.

Ozul growled. His muscles twitched.

"Tell me then," the king continued. "What ruse against your king has made Lady Spencer a sculptor? *A SCULPTOR?*" he shouted with such force that the lanterns in his study swayed. "Your king has been the only immortal gifted with this rarest of abilities. And somehow, a human-made vampire exhibits this unique competence?"

"This cannot be true, Your Excellency," Draven argued. "Why would you make this proclamation: that she is a sculptor?"

"My observant protector! Did you not witness her nails grow into daggers as we feasted on divine wine in the dais?"

Draven's eyes widened. "Surely your observation was an illusion."

"Once again, you doubt me. Do you think me a fool?"

Zagan approached his henchman.

The wolf responded by raising the gray bristle on his withers.

"Whose blood courses through the human-made vampire's veins?" the king commanded.

"Her...her blood is her own."

The king stopped.

Flames in the fireplace froze.

"What did you say?" Zagan asked.

His henchman looked confused. "Could...could you repeat the question?"

Zagan did.

Draven's response was identical.

Remarkably similar, in fact, to the answer uttered by Ruby when he had posed the same question.

Another vampire had clearly glamoured them both. Glamoured them to shield the source of Ruby's blood.

Zagan would unearth the truth.

Memories were like infinite threads, continuums with no beginning or end. In contrast, glamours that suppressed memories had starting and stopping points.

Even if a glamour could not be unraveled, he was unusually crafty at retrieving information immediately prior and immediately following a blocked memory. Recollections in close proximity to a cognitive gap provided insightful clues.

Draven sat in a chair, and the king initiated a glamour for candor.

"Do you remember when you extracted my blood?" Zagan asked his henchman. "Blood that is stored in a sealed vial, concealed within a hidden chamber in my cabinet room?"

"Yes. The memory of your blood extraction is crisp."

"Does the vial store my blood? My blood *only?*" the king asked.

"The vial contains your blood alone."

Draven's answer proved Zagan needed to switch directions.

"Think back to the extraction," the king continued. "When my blood was draining into the vial, I did not observe the process. You had given me a report to read. Do you remember?"

"Of course. The report presented statistics on live animal-births on Besto Polus."

"Correct." Zagan inhaled. "Tell me, Draven: when my blood drained into the vial and the vial became full, did blood continue to drain from the thin tube you had inserted into my vein?"

"For a…for a moment longer. Yes," his henchman answered with a shaky voice.

"And what specifically happened to this excess blood?"

Zagan stopped his own heart, in wait for the truth, since the one who had glamoured his henchman probably had not anticipated this line of questioning.

Draven paused, suggesting the blocked-memory was nearing.

"I…I collected a small amount into a…into a vial I had retrieved from my pouch."

His henchman grimaced, as if the memory-excavation was painful.

"I returned the vial," Draven continued, "to my pouch before...before removing the needle and tube from your arm."

"Scan your memories," the king ordered. "Did you retain this extra vial of my blood? Is it in your possession?"

"I...I have no blood of yours, Your Excellency."

"Did you destroy the extra vial?" Zagan asked.

"I...I did not."

"To whom did you give the vial?" the king pressed.

Draven stared blankly.

"Answer the question, Shadowlander," Zagan snapped. *"To whom* did you give the extra vial?"

"King, this question confuses me. I do not understand."

The beginning of the memory gap was exposed.

"Then I shall limit myself to asking one more," the king said. He fisted his hands to stop them from twitching. "Before I orchestrated the release of F8 on Earth, had you *ever* heard of the human named Ruby Pearl Airily, now known to us as Ruby Spencer?"

Draven furrowed his forehead. "I...I am confused once again. Her name, her person, was neither familiar nor foreign. Therefore, an answer struggles to rise to my tongue."

Many truths were revealed.

On Athanasia, only a handful of vampires shared the king's gift of resisting glamours. Draven was such a vampire. Zagan would not have risked employing a henchman susceptible to altered thought. Which meant his henchman had *subjected* himself to the glamour.

The most egregious revelation was that Draven had willfully *planned* on stealing the king's blood. Bringing an extra vial in his pouch—hidden from his king who had been distracted—was indisputable evidence.

Draven was clearly loyal to another, stealing the king's blood in their service. Which pointed to Liora whom Zagan despised.

He clenched his jaws as he connected the facts.

Ruby Spencer circulated *his* blood through her veins. She possessed *his* gifts, making her a worthy adversary. An imitation of himself.

Created to dethrone him.

Zagan did not doubt that Ruby knew the origin of her blood. That she had invited a similar glamour to his henchman's. That she was fully aware of the ruse.

Ruby's lies crushed Zagan in ways he had not expected.

He had fantasized about her becoming his ambassador, his friend. His companion.

Their relationship was a mockery.

He should never have orchestrated her release from prison.

Veins rose under his skin. He pulled at the spikes in his hair and released a wretched howl—pain and anger combined.

Love was a worthless emotion.

Why had he fought tirelessly to retain some capacity for it?

Absent love, his heart could not be wounded.

A crimson droplet raced down his cheek and he wiped it away.

The tear would be his last.

Releasing Draven from his glamour, the Shadowlander looked into his king's eyes wearing an expression of childlike innocence, as if certain Zagan would have found only honor and loyalty in the memory probe. Undoubtedly, his henchman thought the glamour would be well concealed.

Draven's expression swiftly changed as he observed his king.

Zagan could never mask his emotions.

Negative feelings most certainly painted his skin with a patchwork of purple: a tapestry of pulsing anger, throbbing with his heart. And his teeth—not just his incisors—had sculpted into jagged, serrated, triangular points. He wielded two rows of them on his upper and lower jaws. The teeth of a predatory shark, hideous and revolting.

Surely that was the image assaulting Draven's vision, causing his sapphire eyes to widen in fear.

"What answers have you found, Your Excellency?" he asked, terror twisting his facial features. "Speak of them and I shall attempt explanation."

Carbonizing the Shadowlander would be painless. Not at all the sentence deserving of a traitor.

Instead, the king raised his hand and swung his fist, landing on Draven's cheek.

The Shadowlander flew from his chair, crashing onto the floor and sliding across the room. Crimson blood oozed from his mouth.

Ozul's lips quivered, exposing his teeth.

A growl escaped from his jowls.

"Stand down, Ozul," Draven commanded, wiping his mouth.

Crouching, the wolf sprang toward the King of Skotadi, fangs aimed for his neck.

Zagan smiled. Such a predictable beast.

With a wave of his hand, the wolf yelped midair.

Before turning to ashes.

Draven wailed from the floor. "My wolf! What have you done? You have destroyed my companion. My friend."

Dark red tears raced from the fallen vampire's eyes.

"Perhaps you will understand how one feels when alone," Zagan said. "When the ones they have loved betray them. And now they are abandoned. Discarded."

The doors to his study flew open.

Titus, a Shadowlander dressed in armor, charged into the room flanked by his legion of warriors. He resembled Draven, only his skin was darker gray. And instead of wearing one long braid, his gray hair was short and spiked like the king's.

"Take him to The Shadowlands. To the prison," Zagan commanded Titus. "And when you return, you will enjoy an elevated position. You shall be named as my henchman."

On Titus's order, his warriors collected Draven from the floor.

His former henchman did not resist.

After Draven had been taken away, anger festered, singeing Zagan's heart.

Fire poisoned every vein. The internal heat was almost unbearable.

The coins in his cloak were scorching hot.

Zagan would destroy all who had betrayed him.

Including their families.

And he knew precisely how their end would come.

27

Saturday, June 22, 2041
Kaliméra Castle: Lampsi, Athanasia

LIORA SAT IN the solarium in her favorite wingback chair. The panels of the floor-to-ceiling windows had been cranked open and breezes laced with roses and peonies perfumed the air. Sprinklers, fed by the Tume River, sprayed lush lawns where birds busily tugged at worms in the soil. Rabbits nibbled on lettuces by the garden's edge.

Her heart warmed seeing wildlife. The vegetation, after all, had been planted for the animals. Their populations were on the cusp of rebounding.

Yet, all was at risk in the universe.

Not at some ambiguous time in the future.

Within the very hour.

Solange, her confidant and assistant, strolled into the sunroom, holding a teacup and saucer. Beauty graced each stride. Her fragrance was of roses. With slate-shaded hair that flowed to her lower back and silvery skin, the Shadowlander was Liora's dearest friend since Creation.

If the queen was truthful, she harbored a tinge of envy when comparing herself. Her assistant was able to grow her relationship with Titus—Solange's true love, while keeping their coupling camouflaged in the shadows. Because pairings between divinely gifted vampires were considered a threat to the King of Darkness.

Zagan always found a way to end them.

"Your chamomile tea with honey," Solange said, handing her the delicate teacup filled with pale yellow tea. "May it calm your anxiety."

"If only the herb could help me see more carvings in stone, but much remains in flux. Many stones are blank." Liora sipped the tea, letting the sweetness coat her throat. "If The Tether does not survive the immediate *event,* the future of the planets is uncertain."

"And you have not seen Ruby's tomorrow as yet?"

The queen shook her head.

"Why not make an exception and warn her?" her assistant pressed. "With someone so pivotal to the Sacred Scrolls, why not increase the odds of her survival?"

"Before the future is carved in stone, it is like sand. Interference— even one misplaced step—can shift the granules, causing what is being built to crumble into obscurity. If footsteps are to be taken, their placement and timing are critical."

Liora softly gasped.

At the same time she was answering Solange, a whisper resonated in her thoughts. A whisper from Ruby.

"Please leave me," the queen said, returning the teacup and saucer to her confidant. "Our Tether is waiting. The time is upon us."

"What will you do?"

"Tread carefully."

"May the wisdom of HIM empower each step, Queen."

Solange left the solarium and shut the door behind her.

Liora clutched the armrests and pressed her back against the chair, as if it offered support like a lover. Closing her eyes, she let her mind drift into Ruby's nighttime space.

In the dark void, The Tether was spotted easily now. Her aura glowed around her.

"Your gifts are blossoming," the queen said. "Your whisper is strong. Your light, brilliant."

Ruby wore a light-blue nightgown and her green eyes radiated energy. Though she had not achieved her full potential, her power was strengthening rapidly.

"I have a bone to pick with you," Ruby said. "I'm sure you foresaw my violent arrest. But you didn't warn me. And how about my visit to High Cliff? Why didn't you prep me for my exchange with Zagan?"

"The future is delicate," Liora answered. "Glimpses of what will *likely* happen are a heavy burden, as you will undoubtedly learn. Because the temptation of a seer is to insert herself into the future's unfolding, without considering that the interference can be costlier than the fear which motivated it."

"Even advice?" Ruby asked, sounding frustrated. "Zagan is three-million years old and I need your help. Anyway, how can I bolster my gifts on my own? In time to defeat him?"

"The aptitude for gift mastery already dwells within you," she said. "You simply must *believe*. However, in terms of advice, I offer two instructions. Attend to them with urgency. First: find Neviah Bain. She is located in your city. A visit with her will open your eyes to many truths."

"Who is she? What does she do?"

"She is a human seer."

Ruby furrowed her brow. "What can a human psychic tell me that I can't learn from you? Right this second?"

"Trust me. Please. As there is no time for an explanation."

"The second instruction?" Ruby coughed. "Sorry, my throat is scratchy."

"Learn to patrol your senses at all times," Liora said. "You concentrate on where you *are*, missing signs of that which *awaits* you. As we speak, you are disregarding your senses."

She coughed again. "I am?"

Liora watched as The Tether sniffed the air.

"I taste and smell smoke," Ruby said.

"Awake! Learn what you have been ignoring."

28

RUBY OPENED HER eyes to what resembled another dream-like vision. She wanted her senses to react quickly, but everything was moving in slow motion. Including her brain.

She expected to wake in darkness, but flames curled around the doorframe like eager glowing-fingers. Despite their greed for destruction, they were beautiful—slender and longing, ever expanding. Mesmerizing, even.

Flames inched toward the ceiling, blazing a path for the roaring fire waiting outside the door, waiting for an invitation. Orange, red, and blue seductively licked at the drywall in a lethal caress. Embers landed on the bed, instantly boring holes outlined in black, with ragged red-hot edges that continued to burn.

In the distance, sirens serenaded the intrusive inferno.

Nothing stirred except the flames.

She heard a whisper in her mind. *Move. Now!*

Her brain was still foggy. Slow. And she realized her body had stopped breathing: a protection. One that would be short lived.

Fire devoured vampires and humans alike.

The thought snapped her brain into gear.

Her family. She had to save her family.

Clay was lying next to her in the bed, his face covered by a pillow. She shook his shoulder, but he didn't move. His breaths were shallow from smoke inhalation. His heart, slowing.

"Clay!" she shouted, tossing the pillow from his face. "Wake up!"

Nothing.

Mai and Zoe were in their dog bed, eyes closed. The pup wasn't breathing. Mai, barely.

How would she ever be able to save them?

Even if *she* survived running through the scorching fire carrying them in her arms, they would surely die.

Could she revive each of them?

And then there was Gabby. How would she get to her in time?

How could she make the impossible possible?

She had stopped believing in miracles, but she was more than willing to receive one now.

Think, think, think!

Traveling.

If Zagan was a traveler, then she probably was, too.

Ruby gathered Clay's limp body into her arms and leapt from the bed. Embers burned her soles. She raced to the dog bed and lowered her husband to the floor.

The four-post bed roared with new flames.

She leaned over her husband and pups, making sure to touch each of them. She pictured her front lawn. Pictured where she wanted to be—the exact spot: by the dogwood tree near the walkway leading to their front door.

Her body hummed with a vibration that grew in intensity.

They were turning to dust, each tiny particle ready to span across time and space to reappear at their new location.

In a blink of an eye, they were on the front lawn, by the dogwood, exactly where she had envisioned. Clay and the pups were lying on the moist grass and she was leaning over them, as she'd been in the bedroom.

Red light beams rotated from firetrucks in their driveway.

Additional sirens announced their approach onto Cedar Lane.

A male firefighter reached her as she stood.

"Give my husband oxygen. *Now!*" Ruby hollered over the roar of flames tearing, ripping, and devouring their home. "I've got to go back for my daughter."

"Can't let you do that, Ma'am."

The man's hand almost clasped her shoulder.

But she had already pictured Gabby's bedroom.

When Ruby materialized in her daughter's room, fire touched Gabby's arm, burning her skin. Embers had leapt onto her hair, singeing chestnut strands which curled back in protest.

The bedroom was nearly engulfed.

Flames raced up Ruby's nightgown.

"No!" she yelled. "Not my Gabby! You can't have her!"

She felt veins raise on her neck and face, pulsing with anger. With utter rage.

Fire burned Ruby's skin. Nerve endings screamed.

Then she remembered: she was also a sculptor. A sculptor who could *manipulate* matter.

"Use. Your. Gifts!" she shouted out loud.

Her first thought was rain. She pictured rain dropping around her and Gabby. Rain dousing the flames, buying her time. Time to travel back outside.

No rain fell.

Flames and embers burned the bedsheets and comforter and she tossed the linens off her daughter. She threw her body over Gabby's to protect her.

What was she doing wrong?

She wouldn't let her daughter die. Not. Ever.

Fire bit at her back and she felt lightheaded.

Earlier that night, when she had moved the coins on her dresser, she had pictured inhaling air and releasing it in a steady force. Maybe for sculpting, she had to find a source, a mechanism. If she needed rain, maybe she had to visualize where the water was coming from.

Water was in the toilets, in the pipes of their master bathroom.

She imagined water from the toilets, showerheads, and sinks combining. The water was transported in a stream overhead, lifted by the rising heat. A reservoir formed over her and Gabby before converting to rain and dousing the flames. The picture in her mind was vivid. So bizarrely possible. So *real*.

Moisture fell on her back.

She looked up. Amid the raging fire, they were protected by a rectangular patch of rain. The downpour caused the flames to hiss and retreat. She and Gabby were drenched; their nightgowns, flesh, and hair were no longer burning.

Closing her eyes, she concentrated: the dogwood, the lawn, the moist grass.

Ruby's body vibrated. She and her daughter turned to dust.

Once on the lawn, she realized the fight was far from over.

Although Ruby was already healing, Gabby was badly burned and wasn't breathing. Her daughter's skin was visibly trying to heal, trying to activate the powers of both Liora and Zagan's blood. But Gabby's heart was no longer beating, no longer pumping. She wouldn't survive on her own.

Five firefighters jogged to Ruby, two of them carrying a stretcher.

"We'll take it from here, Mrs. Spencer," a female said. "Your husband survived; you saved him. Let us work on your daughter."

The woman's hand reached for her.

Ruby flashed razor-sharp incisors at the firefighter. "Touch us and you'll regret it," she warned. "Get me an empty syringe."

The female firefighter didn't hesitate.

In what seemed like slow-motion, the woman ran back with a syringe she'd gotten from a paramedic.

A videographer shined a camera light and began filming.

Ruby bit the veiny skin by her wrist, causing blood to flow. She filled the syringe barrel with her blood. Straddling her daughter, she stabbed the needle into Gabby's heart, injecting her vampire blood into the cardiac muscle. She provided compressions to circulate the blood.

Stopping, Ruby held her breath and listened.

A sputter.

A beat.

A rhythm.

Her daughter's skin began to heal. Her hair grew back. Color returned to her face.

Gabriella Emily Spencer—their precious Gabby—was alive!

29

Saturday, June 22, 2041
The Spencer Residence: Annapolis, Maryland

CLAY WOKE ON a stretcher, confused and disoriented. Why was his throat raw, burning with each inhale? And where the hell was he? Where was his family?

He ran his fingers through his black hair, from front to back, trying to clear his head. His fingers snagged against an elastic band.

What the?

An oxygen mask covered his nose and mouth.

He blinked several times, trying to focus.

Someone—a woman, if he had to guess—leaned over him, wearing a surgical mask, clear medical gloves, and a navy uniform. Then the person waved to someone behind the stretcher, as if giving the okay to move forward.

Clay felt a jolt and the IV bag, draped from a hook mounted on the sidewall next to him, swayed with the sudden movement. Rotating red lights shined through the dual back windows.

He was in an ambulance.

A paramedic was about to tape the inserted IV needle to his forearm, to keep the needle and tube in place.

Lifting his mask, Clay yanked and slid the device off his head.

"Wait. Stop," he said, his voice sounding dry and raspy. "What's going on?"

The woman lowered her surgical mask. "Relax, Mr. Spencer." Her lips thinned. "You've had a housefire. We're transporting you to

Anne Arundel Medical Center. As a precaution."

His heartrate rocketed, and he sat up. "Where are my wife and daughter? My dogs?"

"No worries," she answered, placing her hand, the one not holding tape, on his shoulder. She applied pressure to encourage him to lie back down. "Your family is being evaluated and treated as we speak. I'm sure they'll be joining you at the hospital soon."

"No worries?" He glared at the needle inserted into a vein at the crook of his forearm.

This wasn't happening.

"Stop the ambulance," he ordered.

"We can't do that."

He pulled the needle from his arm.

"Stop. The Fucking. Ambulance. *NOW!"* he shouted.

Brandishing the syringe as a weapon, he had finally figured out that he had to ask for what he wanted…with force.

In an upside-down world, nice guys were ignored.

The paramedic frantically waved at the window connecting the patient compartment with the driver cabin.

The vehicle abruptly stopped.

Clay was dressed in cotton pajama bottoms that now included holes, undoubtedly made by embers. He wore no T-shirt or shoes. Opening the rear doors of the vehicle, he jumped onto the asphalt.

The ambulance had already driven a quarter mile down Cedar Lane, away from his property.

He ran, wondering what he'd find.

The house and everything in it could be replaced. But not Ruby, not Gabby—the lights of his life. And not his dogs either.

A cluster of firefighters, paramedics, and EMTs were gathered on the front lawn, near the dogwood tree.

He'd start there.

In the middle of the responder circle was his family. Thank God! His daughter was sitting up smiling and Ruby was hugging her. Crimson tears raced down his wife's cheeks.

"Let me by," Clay said to a firefighter who moved to the side.

Ruby leapt to her feet and raced into his arms. Embracing, he could not put his relief into words. Holding her, seeing her and

Gabby alive, felt like a miracle.

"Gabby's okay!" she cheered. "And you're okay!"

Clay and Ruby knelt by their daughter, wrapping arms around each other in a Spencer group-hug.

His wife explained the nightmare as it had unfolded, including how she had to inject her blood into Gabby's heart to revive her. To heal her.

"Mom?" Gabby asked. "Are Mai and Zoe okay?"

A firefighter answered. "We gave Mai oxygen. She's doing fine."

"And Zoe? My puppy?"

The firefighter shook his head. "I'm sorry. She didn't make it."

Before anyone could respond, Gabby grabbed the emptied syringe and took off running.

Clay made a move to follow after her.

"Don't," Ruby urged, touching his arm. "Everything will be fine."

For the first time since he'd arrived on the lawn, Clay focused on the house. It had completely collapsed on itself and was reduced to a smoldering pile of rubble. A lifetime of memories turned to ashes.

A few firefighters continued to spray water from their hoses onto the charred remains. Several firetrucks were packing up.

The fire marshal approached.

"Mr. and Mrs. Spencer," said Fire Marshal Alima Omar. "My condolences over the loss of your puppy and home." She placed her hand onto Ruby's back. "Please keep in mind that losses could've been much worse."

"Do you have any idea what happened, Alima?" Clay asked.

"When everything is nearly consumed, we use the term: black hole fire—one that burns rapidly and leaves little intact. Unfortunately, this classification also means that ignition sources can be challenging to determine."

"Any guesses?"

Alima quickly glanced behind her, as if to verify they were alone.

"We like to avoid conjecture," she answered. "But you're both government officials. I'll share what I *think* I know. The fire pattern suggests that the origin of the blaze was in the kitchen. Interesting, since a firefighter found something in the back of the house, where the kitchen used to be."

The marshal reached into her pocket. And when she revealed what she had retrieved, he recognized the objects: Zagan's five coins.

His body temperature heated toward combustion.

Had Zagan planted the coins as a trick? To kill his family in their sleep, while they were *defenseless?*

Veins bulged on Ruby's neck. No doubt she was drawing the same conclusion.

"Are these yours?" Alima asked. "Collector's currency, perhaps?"

We may still need these coins, Ruby cognitively whispered to him.

Reaching out her hand, his wife requested to hold them.

"These tokens are classified," she told the marshal, fingering the coins in her palm. "I'll need to return them to President Unger and the SWC. That won't be a problem, will it?"

Clay wondered if she planned on glamouring the fire marshal, if taking the coins was a problem. Obviously, his wife had no intentions of handing over the coins to the POTUS.

"That's fine," Alima responded. "We know where to find you, should we need them to further our investigation. One more thing. With your superior hearing, didn't the smoke detectors in the home alert you?"

Ruby tilted her head. "Come to think of it, I didn't hear any alarms. Strange. Not even our DEPE tried to wake us using our surround-sound system."

"Well, *that* fact isn't surprising," she said. "The electrical circuit-breaker panel was located in your kitchen pantry, according to our schematics. With the fast-moving fire, your electrical circuits were destroyed from the onset. Wires, cables, switches—all obliterated. But how about your smartwatches? Didn't your DEPE attempt to contact you through them?"

"With all the commotion, I didn't think of that," he answered, raising his wrist and commanding his watch to activate. But the screen remained black. "Strange. My watch isn't working. Maybe the heat?" He looked at his wife. "How about yours?"

Ruby's watch wouldn't activate either. Broken like his.

"Things go wrong despite our best efforts," Alima said. "That's why we have firefighters. Anyway, you've all been through so much. And you'll have to find a place to stay. I'll let you folks get to it."

After shaking hands, the fire marshal walked away.

He scanned the area. "Where's Gabby?"

"There." Ruby pointed to a spot on the lawn where their daughter was alone. Light from a firetruck illuminated her.

Gabby was holding something small on the grass. A syringe was in her other hand.

"Is that Zoe?" he asked. "And what's Gabby doing?"

"Trust her." *I've seen the outcome,* she whispered.

He pulled Ruby close, until his lips brushed her ear. "She's a healer like you?"

His wife smiled.

"And what do you mean: you've *seen* the outcome?" he asked softly, so no one else could hear. "Now you can look into the future?"

I'm finding my gifts. Or maybe they're finding me.

She hugged him, almost desperately.

My powers are growing. And there's no turning back.

30

Saturday, June 22, 2041
Castle on High Cliff: Skotadi, Athanasia

ZAGAN LOATHED HAVING an adversary.

For 2.8 million years since the curse, no one had dared to challenge him. He was all-powerful, carbonizing those who aroused the slightest hint of irritation.

Everyone revered him, feared him. Bowed to his every command.

Until Ruby Spencer.

No wonder he had become distracted during the housefire, missing his opportunity to reduce Ruby's mate to ashes.

He pulled at the spikes in his hair and released a wretched howl.

Even the bats in his study swiftly flew from his chamber.

Clearly, Zagan had underestimated Ruby's intensifying powers. The housefire had proven as much.

Carbonizing his deplorable imitation and her daughter had not been an option. They shared his blood which meant they had inherited the protective shield of self-preservation. Since he was unable to carbonize himself, he was unable to carbonize them.

Instead, he had planned on channeling his anger through his coins, making hers spark flames. Because igniting a housefire at the Spencers would ensnare Ruby as a secondary consequence, as collateral damage.

His intent had been brilliant. He would spread the fire rapidly. The family would be trapped in their tinderbox. All would die. Delightfully charred to the bone.

Zagan had arrived at the house as an invisible ghost, hovering in the master chamber. Undetected.

The dogs were still. He sculpted a temporary muzzle on the adult female, so she would not protest when smoke assaulted the air.

The Spencers were in their bed, seemingly asleep. Even Ruby's eyelids quivered as if dreaming, though that was impossible.

He had anticipated that his nemesis might leap from her bed after the fire had started, in an attempt to save her family. However, sculpting chains to secure her or constructing a dome to contain her would have been for naught. She would have shattered them with her mind. After all, even at the most basic level, a sculptor was dangerously capable.

However, the speed of his execution was a factor he *could* control.

First, he had melted the inner-workings of Ruby and her mayfly's smartwatches, isolating them from the outside world.

In his ghost apparition, Zagan had drifted to the kitchen and destroyed the electrical panel, as well as the fire detectors in the home. The house was without electricity. Without a warning system.

Detecting her coins in a kitchen drawer, he clutched his own, channeling his wrath. As flames grew in the kitchen, he sculpted a reservoir of fuel from nearby vehicles. With his breath as a pressurized hose, he coated every surface with fuel, soaking the first floor and staircase.

He had even smiled at his cunningness. At outsmarting her.

Before returning to High Cliff, he desired confirmation of Ruby's demise. Of her family's.

In the master chamber, his smile was extinguished.

The king witnessed Ruby save her family using traveling and sculpting—the very competences which had elevated *him* above all vampires. Above all in the universe.

Instead of furthering his attack, shock immobilized him.

Retreat was the only action his brain could process.

Returning to his beloved castle, Zagan intended to regroup and develop a new offensive, one that focused on the easiest target first: Ruby's mate.

In his study, he sat in his leather chair by the fireplace, warmed by the roaring flames. Gripping the bone armrests constructed from antler sheds, he grew his nails into daggers.

Once again, his plans failed to achieve fruition.

With unmatched power, he had become lax at anticipating plots against him. Had grown naive in thinking his reign would persist without challenge.

Three-million years old and he was still a fool.

Worse, others clearly deemed him unlovable.

Why had he clung to false hope?

Zagan stared at the flames in his fireplace, letting his anguish and anger consume him. The building pressure within him escaped his body and filled the room, making his surroundings shudder and rumble. The stone walls cracked from the tremors.

Overcome with hate, he was an instrument of destruction.

"Your Excellency," someone interrupted.

Zagan heard the words from faraway.

"Your Excellency. Wake up!"

He tried to wake, tried to dispel the violent trance in which he had placed himself. But his chair continued to vibrate, chattering and thumping on the stone flooring.

He felt a hand on his forearm, clutching him without permission.

"Please, no," the voice begged. "Your Excellency! I am Titus."

Zagan opened his eyes.

Titus was on his knees beside him, holding the king's forearm. His henchman's hand was turning to stone. Pain twisted Titus's face and narrowed his eyes. His upper teeth left impressions on his lower lip.

The walls in the study had cracked. Large chunks of stone, dislodged by the tremors, littered the floor which was marked with vein-like ruts.

Zagan's bearings returned.

He repaired Titus's hand. Rewinding time, he also fixed the walls and floors.

"Apologies, King," his henchman said, rubbing his hand, and rising to his feet. "I would not have touched you, save I feared your destruction."

"I shall forgive the infraction, then."

"May I provide counsel? To help remedy what ails you?"

"I require no remedy from you," Zagan growled. "What I need is sustenance."

"Divine wine?" asked Titus.

Anger still saturated the king's veins.

"Bring me a mayfly," Zagan ordered. "The one named Felicity."

"As you command," his henchman said, leaving the study.

Felicity might restore balance to his demeanor. She was, after all, the human who had drooled over Ruby as if she were a goddess.

The thought caused veins to rise on his neck and face.

Titus re-entered the study with the mayfly who was dressed in a sheer white nightgown, as if attempting purity-of-thought during her slumber. However, the transparency of the garment, and the fact that she wore nothing underneath, teased with an alternate truth.

"Dearest Felicity," the king cooed. "Come and stand before me, with your back to the fire." He glanced at his henchman. "Titus will return to collect you in a short time."

His henchman left them alone.

Standing before him, the mayfly smiled with a nervous tremble. The fire lit the silhouette of her naked body, as if she glowed.

"Come. Sit on my lap," he commanded. "Face me and place your legs around my sides."

"I...I."

"Are you worried I will take advantage? Sexually?" he probed. "Convey the truth to me."

She nodded.

"Though your angelic beauty entices me," he said, "I shall not touch where permission has not been granted. You have my word."

The mayfly hiked up her nightgown slightly, so she could lift herself onto his lap in a straddled position.

"Are you comfortable?" he asked, placing his hands on her hips and moving her closer to him. His breath rustled the see-through fabric touching her breasts.

She nodded again.

"Your king would like to drink from your neck, with your consent, of course."

"I trust you, King Zagan," Felicity said.

She moved her hair to the side before turning her head, revealing her slender, bare neck.

A pulsing vein beckoned for his attention.

"Trust?" he questioned, attempting to sound fatherly. "Do you not know that trust is the undoing of all mortals and immortals?"

She glanced at him quickly, with furrowed brow, as if confused by his meaning.

Zagan yanked the back of her hair with such force that he almost cracked her neck.

Thrusting the mayfly toward him, he drove his fangs violently and deeply into her flesh. And when he pierced the vein, he began to gulp. Feverishly. Without regard to her whimpers or pathetic attempts to push away.

And he did not stop.

Until she was empty.

And undone.

He shoved the dead mayfly to the floor.

Yet his rage had not subsided.

Perhaps another culling was in order.

31

Sunday, June 23, 2041
The Westin Annapolis: Annapolis, Maryland

RUBY TOOK A deep breath. The Westin Annapolis wasn't home, but at least their two-bedroom suite, which included a living room and kitchen, felt safe. The hotel had battery backup and an elaborate sprinkler system, which meant there were multiple layers of protection. Layers that would give Justine additional opportunities to warn them if something—anything—was amiss.

With Gabby's bedtime approaching, the thought was comforting.

Immediately after the housefire, they spent the night at Margo and Tomas's. But the last thing she and Clay wanted was to place their best friends in danger. Nine years ago, six Marine special operatives were assassinated on the Gonzalez's property while Ruby and Clay stayed at their home after returning from their Taiwan and Russian nightmare. Their friends had risked enough already.

Going to a hotel seemed wiser all the way around.

After leaving their dogs with their friends, meeting with the insurance company, contracting with an excavator and builder, buying a fireproof safe for the coins, and shopping for clothes, toiletries, and new smartwatches, the three of them finally settled in at their hotel. Exhausted, wilted, and weary. In much need of R&R.

Initially, she and Clay had planned on leaving Gabby with Margo and Tomas, but their daughter panicked over the prospect of being apart. And Ruby reminded herself that she was a vampire warrior—one whose arsenal continued to grow. Not only could she whisper, sculpt, and travel, she was beginning to see stones engraved with the future. Hands down, Gabby was safest with her and Clay.

Her husband strolled toward their daughter's bedroom to start the bedtime ritual.

"What if I tucked her in first?" Ruby asked, as he stopped to listen. "I don't sense you-know-who's presence, so it might be a good time to have that talk we discussed earlier. Could I kiss her goodnight after? Like in fifteen minutes?"

"Sure," he said. "A heart-to-heart would do her good. And I agree: she has questions only you can answer."

Walking into the bedroom, Ruby closed the door behind her.

Gabby put down her book and tapped the mattress as an invitation.

"I thought you might have more questions," Ruby started, sitting on the edge of the bed. She moved strands of hair away from her daughter's eyes. "You know, after everything that's happened. With everything you've learned."

Ruby had already explained how the fire had started. How she had to protect her family and the world from the King of Darkness. But there was more to discuss.

"Am I kind of like a vampire, Mom?" She scrunched her lips and nose, as if tasting or smelling something foul. "Will I want to drink *blood* someday?"

She held her daughter's hand. "No. You're human, thank goodness. It'll be chicken and broccoli for you." She smiled. "Turns out, your blood has healing powers like mine did as a human."

"What could you do with your powers?"

"Stay healthy for one thing," Ruby said. "As a human, I didn't understand why I recovered from illnesses so quickly, or why mostly, I didn't get sick at all. And my injuries healed fast. I even healed other people. In a few cases, I brought them back to life. Grammie always called me her little superhero: *by land, by sea, and by air.*"

Gabby smiled. "Then the world called you *the one and only.*"

"That's right. But I didn't believe any of those labels. See, without knowing about my blood, I attributed the unexplainable to something logical—like I took my vitamins, got my vaccinations, or I was at the right place at the right time. But now, now I know that immortals *enhanced* my blood when I was a baby. And as your Mom, my blood flows in you."

"And that's why I could save Zoe with my blood?"

"Exactly. Which I'm curious about. How did you know that injecting the pup with your blood might save her?"

"I was thinking about how you brought me back to life," Gabby said. "Then I saw a big flat-stone in my mind. The words on the stone were simple, and they sort of glowed. They said: *Gabby's blood will save Zoe.* I grabbed the empty needle from the lawn and found her. Then I cut myself with a sharp rock." She shrugged. "You saw the rest."

Ruby was baffled. Seeing stones etched with the future was clearly another competence. Her daughter was exhibiting immortal gifts, but as a human.

"We get our powers to read the future," Ruby said, "from a beautiful, ancient vampire named Liora—the Queen of Light. She has shimmering brown skin, eyes that glow like the sun, and wears a tiara encrusted with rubies."

"Is that why I keep dreaming about a tree? I'm seeing the future?"

"A tree?" Ruby thought about the tree engraved on Zagan's coins and her heart accelerated. "Describe it."

"The tree has a few greyish trunks, you know, like a big bush."

Ruby slowly exhaled in relief.

The tree on Zagan's coins had only one thick trunk.

"So maybe it's really a bush then?" Ruby asked.

"No. The tree is way taller," Gabby said. "And the leaves are big and round, and really shiny."

"Where is this tree located? In our neighborhood?"

Gabby shook her head. "It's not from around here. More like far, far away. And the tree is the only one of its kind; I'm pretty sure of that. It's planted on a rocky island, the kind where cliffs meet the ocean and waves crash on the rocks. And there's rain. Lots of it."

"Far away?"

Her daughter nodded. "I keep seeing the word...*king.*"

With the mention of *king,* Ruby's internal temperature skyrocketed, no doubt causing her veins to bulge on her neck.

"Don't worry, Mom," her daughter said, squeezing her hand. "I think *king* has to do with a place. Not a vampire."

"How often do you think of this tree?" Ruby asked.

"Every night. Since the night Zoe was born."

June 10th. The same night Zagan appeared as a bat in their bedroom and as a ghost in the kitchen. Also the night she met Liora in her nighttime space and was told she was The Tether. The very same night passengers on Flight 1733 were traveled to High Cliff.

The night when her whole world changed once again.

"Keep me posted if you learn anything more about that tree. Deal?" she asked Gabby, who nodded. "We also need to discuss why and how we should protect your thoughts against Zagan."

Ruby described the process of glamouring and raising cognitive shields. More importantly, she explained why the circumstances required a highly sophisticated glamour, one that might prevent the king from reading her daughter's mind and using the information gathered to hurt them all.

Since Zagan was clever and cunning, she had to outsmart him.

"Why not use your weapons?" Gabby asked. "Like your sword or maybe your knives?"

"Intelligence and character are sharper than any dagger. They're the most powerful weapons, whether you're human or vampire."

"How will you outsmart him?"

"First," Ruby said, "I'll use my mind to show you a recent encounter with him. Then in the future, every time you stand in Zagan's presence or hear his voice, the glamour will activate. Your heartrate will remain normal, but you won't speak a word or physically convey any answers to his or anyone else's questions while he is present, including mine.

"Dad will know about the glamour," she continued. "I'll tell everyone else that after the housefire, you stop talking when you're nervous. Similar to post-traumatic stress. Do we have another deal?"

"Sure. But won't Zagan tell I've been glamoured? Like if he looks into my eyes?"

"A wise question coming from someone who just learned about glamours and shields." Ruby smiled. "Ever look into a large mirror? One that takes up an entire wall?"

"At the fair," Gabby said.

"Remember how the mirror gave the illusion that you could walk through it? That the room continued beyond?" Ruby asked. "But in truth, the image reflected what was behind, not what was ahead."

"How will a mirror help?"

"I'm going to construct a unique shield. The surface will resemble a mirror, reflecting everything around it, making the shield seem invisible. Not only will Zagan—or any other immortal—*not* be able to detect the glamour, but since he can't question you, he won't have any clues what the glamour is hiding. Not where it begins or ends."

"Someday," Gabby said, "I want to be as smart as you, Mom."

"Oh, you'll be smarter, sweetie. I've seen it carved in stone."

Holding hands, Ruby cognitively transported Gabby to the prison cell, back when Zagan had appeared, enabling her daughter to see and hear him. After, Ruby raised a shield and glamoured her.

Clay opened the bedroom door and walked in.

"How are my two favorite ladies doing?" he asked.

"We're fine, Dad!" Gabby said. "We were talking about my blood. It's special, you know."

Clay leaned over and kissed Gabby on the forehead. "Everything about you is special."

"You just say that because you love me."

"We both love you," Ruby said. "And we tell you the truth."

They tucked in their daughter, turned off the light, and closed the door behind them.

When they returned to the living room, Ruby explained the nature of Gabby's shield and glamour.

"What's next?" Clay asked.

"I have ideas on how to protect you. But I'd better construct a cognitive shield in your mind right away."

She placed her hand under his chin and gently adjusted his face, locking eyes with him.

"I'd better glamour you, too," she added.

He winked. "You do that every day, babe. And then?"

"Then tomorrow I set an appointment with Neviah Bain."

148

32

Monday, June 24, 2041
Kaliméra Castle: Lampsi, Athanasia

LIORA GARDENED WHEN she was anxious. Feeling the sun on her skin, hearing the chirping of cicadas, and watching the flurry of butterflies soothed her soul. Several honey bees rested on her arms, cleaning their wings before resuming pollination.

Skies, as always, were a deep cyan.

Earth was too far to see, though the planet and its vampire were close in thought.

Kneeling, she clipped stems below green hydrangea blooms, adding them to a collection of white peonies. To distract herself, she would create a floral arrangement for her library.

"Queen!" Solange said, as she approached. "You missed morning tea. Is everything all right?" She stopped beside the queen. "The Tether survived the fire, so I anticipated much zeal and discussion."

The queen rose and dusted leaves and trimmings from the skirt of her cotehardie. "Confusion soured my enthusiasm," she admitted.

"How so?"

"I attempted to whisper into Ruby's mind to glean her thoughts about the fire, but I could not enter. And stones which were being etched, appear blank once more."

"Did you try her daughter?" Solange asked. "Or her mate?"

Liora gathered the flowers into her arms. "I was blocked from them all."

They walked toward the white castle. Liora loved its multiple rooves topped with terracotta tiles.

A breeze fluttered the queen's dress. If only her mood could match the playful zephyr.

"How is this possible?" her assistant asked.

She stopped and locked eyes with Solange. "Complex shields are prohibiting my entry and even I am unable to penetrate them."

"Perhaps The Tether grows stronger, more skilled, as you had hoped. As was intended."

"Indeed," Liora agreed. "But the risks are lofty, for she is more powerful than any of us. Even Zagan himself."

"Yes, as scriptures have prophesied. Is this not as it should be?"

"Love can change hearts," Liora cautioned. "Can cause beings to act in contrary ways to protect those whom they love. History shows light can turn to darkness. Angels can fall."

"Love is also liberating—victorious over evil," Solange assured. "Ease your worries, Queen. It is premature to abandon faith regarding our Tether."

"Speaking of love," Liora said, changing the subject. "I have foreseen that Titus will visit the prison tomorrow."

"For what purpose?"

"To report on Draven's condition, at the king's request." The queen placed her hand on her friend's shoulder. "Do not let love cause carelessness. Heed my words."

Solange smiled. Her blue eyes glowed with increased energy. "I shall choose care*ful*ness over care*less*ness, Your Majesty. I promise."

At the castle's entrance, her assistant opened the massive front door leading to the greeting chamber. The queen stepped inside, followed by the breeze and scents of perpetual summer.

"Before we part," Liora said, "have we received a yield report on The Tree of Immortality?"

"The fig-yield continues to be strong. The tree is healthy. Thriving."

"Under my authority, command additional warriors to guard the fencing which encircles it. No one shall enter through the gate."

"Is our tree in danger?" Solange asked.

"Since my access into The Tether's thoughts and intentions has been blocked, I am cautious, unsettled. The tree holds much prominence in our Sacred Scrolls, in our immortality. Ensuring the tree's protection seems wise during these precarious times."

"But The Tree of Awareness—or of Three Kings as the humans call it—possesses more significance in this millennium, does it not?" Solange asked. "And yet, we have no dominion over it. Our efforts should be thus directed, though at least the humans do not know of the tree's significance for our kind."

"Already, I have planted cognitive seeds with Gabriella regarding the tree's existence on Earth," Liora said. "Only I fear I will not *see* if the whispered seeds grow into understanding."

Her assistant smiled. "Neviah Bain will do her part."

33

TITUS JOURNEYED BY horseback from the darkness of High Cliff to the grayness of The Shadowlands. He arrived at the prison well after mealtime, which eased his worries. Prisoners were most unruly when they were hungry. But absent his wolf, meal or no, Draven would undoubtedly be a snarling beast.

That, and the fact that Titus had arrested him.

Though perhaps, his friend would extend forgiveness.

In truth, the king's assignment to visit Draven brought tremendous relief to the new henchman, as he had secretly wondered about the prisoner's wellbeing. Unknown to most, he considered Draven as a brother, though divinely created vampires had no blood relatives.

Nevertheless, having dwelled together in the same coven—before the death culling, he thought often and fondly of his and Draven's youthful amusements.

In the realm of immortality, youthfulness was evidenced early-on, following Creation. Although not measured physically since vampires never changed, youthfulness was measured by one's level of maturity.

His brother had fiercely clung to youthful ways. For while their coven discussed rhetorical questions about the universe or the Scrolls or Pythia the oracle, Draven childishly played outside with his swords, slashing and piercing imaginary foes. Hollering and shouting in the fields. A faithful wolf by his side.

Titus never questioned Draven's purpose. He was created to be a henchman.

Titus, on the other hand, was more lover than fighter.

Even now, when his mind should have been sternly focused on the guards patrolling the prison, his thoughts lingered on his kinsman. Titus did not feel cautious or suspicious—always poised for attack, as a henchman should.

Instead, he felt excited. Eager.

Perhaps Draven had finally achieved maturity. And now, Titus was the one regressing toward youthfulness.

Because his heart distracted him.

Maybe Solange would have been foretold of his visit to the prison. Maybe she would risk seeing him, if conditions were safe.

Titus headed to the pits, below ground: the area where Skotadians were celled. As a Shadowlander, Draven could have stayed above ground in the cages with the Lampsians. But no doubt he had picked underground, since it offered more privacy.

A guard escorted him below, sniffing the air as they descended.

The pits were dark and damp, lit by flickering lanterns mounted to the stone walls. Rats scurried underfoot. The guard led him along a corridor. Prisoners growled and flashed their fangs as they passed. Ungroomed nails reached beyond the bars.

The facility should have been called Prison of the Barbarians.

A bolted wooden door was at the end of the hallway. The guard lifted the weighty latch and pushed open the door as its base screeched and moaned over the stone floor.

The muscular vampire waved for Titus to enter.

Draven's cell was partitioned from the rest of the cellblock, contained within its own chamber. The king's prized prisoner was kept in protective isolation. Titus almost smiled at the cell's privacy, but he stopped his lips from curling.

Sitting on the floor, Draven acted despondent to their presence. He tilted his chin upwards, stretching his neck, as if mesmerized by the tangle of spider webs on the ceiling.

"Leave us," Titus commanded the guard, using a voice more brazen than natural.

The guard flexed his swollen biceps. "I will not," he snapped, looking like he drank from five stags a day. "My orders are to remain on-guard during your assessment."

"And from whom were these orders issued?" Titus asked.

"From the warden herself."

"Apologies." Titus gritted his teeth, as if he had errored. "Of course the warden's jurisdiction dominates. I am sure King Zagan will understand. And what is your name, guard? So that I might tell His Majesty what a loyal subject you are to your...*warden.*"

The guard's eyes grew wide. "How long do you need?"

"I shall open the door when I have finished. Unless you insist that the king's business be conducted within a certain timeframe?"

"No. No. Apologies, Titus," he said, backing up through the door. "Take the time you need. Your privacy will not be disturbed."

"Much gratitude. And did I neglect to mention that your saber glimmers despite the dull conditions? True warriors respect their blade. Well done!"

The guard bowed before pulling the door shut.

Draven sprang from the corner, arms reaching through the bars for an embrace.

"Ha! What have I always told you, brother?" Draven said, clutching Titus and slapping his back in a hearty greeting. "There are benefits to being a lover! Your words are like music to all who hear. They cannot resist your serenade."

"I may kill with kindness," Titus said, "but your sword penetrates the heart more effectively."

Draven looked around at his dreary cell, raising his hands, palms up. "And look at the fine accommodations my swordplay has furnished me. Ironic, no?"

Titus pushed a wineskin bag through the bars. "Divine wine. Drink while we speak."

His brother took the receptacle and guzzled.

"What does the king care of my wellbeing?" Draven asked, wiping his lips with the back of his hand. "I am banished. Left here to rot among the rats and spiders."

"Despite your 'treachery,' the king is grieved by your deceit," Titus said. "The royal narcissist cares for you."

"Care is not returned, for I only served the evil monarch so that my eyes and ears might remain informed." He took another swig of blood. "And what of your deceit, brother?" Draven asked. "Are your secrets well hidden? Have you learned from my mistakes?"

"I cannot see what is to come until the truth happens before my eyes," Titus admitted. "The answers to your questions elude me."

"My eyes lack distance as well, or I would not have been caught."

A light knock on the door stole Titus's attention. "May I rip the heart from this guard and still be called a lover?" he joked.

"A heart in-hand remains a heart, brother!" Draven hid the wineskin behind him.

Titus pulled open the door and *his* heart nearly burst through his chest. Standing before him wearing a fitted cream-gown, ornamented with swirls of gold thread and sparkling sapphires, was Solange. His princess in waiting. Waiting for freedom to wed for eternity, to live absent fear from Athanasia's paranoid King of Darkness.

Titus clutched her arm, carefully guiding her inside the chamber. He pushed the door closed.

"Were you seen?" His voice trembled. "Are you safe?"

"I gained access to the pits from guards loyal to the queen. And now I stand before you with my heart still beating in my chest." She smiled, placing her hands in his spiked hair. "But my heart will be crushed if you do not kiss me."

Titus drew her body against his. He was slow to raise the sword, but his lips and tongue did not possess the same ailment. He kissed her deeply, forgetting Draven lurked in the shadows.

When they finished, Titus grew embarrassed at his unabashed display of affection.

"How fortunate that vampires are not required to breathe," Draven teased. "May I offer my own greetings, brother? Or must I wait until your lips are bruised?"

Solange moved toward the bars. The former henchman gently clasped her cheeks, gazing deeply into her eyes.

"Greetings, warrior," Solange said, with much tenderness.

"Your sight is welcomed," he answered. "I am grateful you came."

With alarm, she gawked at the door leading to the corridor.

"I must leave you," she said, moving away from the cell.

When she placed another kiss on Titus's lips, the taste of honey lingered.

"I will wait for you, Titus. Forever," she added. "Remain safe so that our future union may be carved in stone. Do *not* provoke the king. Appear loyal and obedient at all times."

"You have my word," he said. "And my heart for eternity."

They never knew when a forbidden meeting might be their last.

Solange locked eyes with him and smiled.

Opening the door, she slipped out, drifting down the hallway and into the shadows with scarcely a sound.

Titus and Draven reminisced a few minutes longer before the new henchman collected the wineskin and left the chamber.

The guard walked Titus above ground to the prison's gate.

As Titus mounted his black stallion, he did not focus on the dangers of deceiving a ruthless king, as a true henchman would.

Instead, he focused on his heart.

It beat and ached for his true love. And for his brother.

Before returning to High Cliff, he would rest and feed at The Cottage of Shadows, well-hidden within the Gray Forest of The Shadowlands.

He rode for three-quarters of an hour.

As he galloped up the last hill of his journey, he spotted the quaint cottage in the distance. The sight stirred his heart, for the hideaway dwelling was where he and Solange frequented in secret from others, except from the queen and Draven.

Liora, in fact, had given Titus an open invitation to use the home whenever needed. And why would this not be so? Titus himself had given the queen the prized star-ruby he had unearthed from a cave one-thousand years ago. Even as Zagan's new henchman, he considered Liora to be the sovereign ruler of Athanasia.

He was loyal then, and loyal now.

34

Tuesday, June 25, 2041
The Bain Residence: Annapolis, Maryland

ALL GOOD THINGS must end.

Neviah Bain had never doubted this adage. Of course, she thought the end would've come much sooner, especially with her history of tempting fate.

And the fact that she was *different*. There was that.

Quirkiness didn't come from her fuchsia spiked hair. Or her piercings. Or her "fave" black lipstick and nail-polish. Instead, Neviah attributed her quirkiness to her zest for the unknown. For the path *never* taken. For relentlessly pushing beyond boundaries.

She was a rebel, through and through.

In fact, her lifelong eccentricities were inked on her body.

Except for her face, her skin showcased tattoos in all styles. Her favorite tattoo was "ironed" onto her entire back, in full-color realism: the one and only eternal-tree on planet Earth.

Horizontal to the tree's multiple trunks, stretching across to fresh skin on both sides of the tree, were five words, written in gothic red-letters that dripped blood: *The Blood of Three Kings.* That label worked better than the tree's common name Kaikomako, though the word was sweet on the tongue. The species name—*Pennantia Baylisiana*—was over-the-top borrr-ring, though the most accurate by far.

Her brick townhouse was located in Annapolis's historic district. And every morning before dressing and flipping on the neon sign anchored by the sidewalk—the sign that blinked: *Psychic is Open,* the same one detested by the historical review boneheads—she admired her tattooed tree in her full-length mirror. She loved how the roots curved over her ass, still tight at 45 years old. No one else had actually seen the roots since her son's father passed (may he rest in peace). But at least the branches and leaves were visible for all to appreciate as they inched up and around her neck.

The tree owned her body. Which was no lie.

Every barter, however, required an exchange.

And her psychic gift revealed that the deal was being called in.

On this night.

In her childhood, she had discovered her gift and then realized, painfully, that others didn't have it. She heard a voice in her head—not two or three. Just one: a female.

At first, her mother thought Neviah had an imaginary friend, even making her an extra-sandwich at lunchtime. But when school started, the voice grew stronger instead of weaker. And the voice gave Neviah clues to the future. Even answers at spelling bees and on math quizzes.

Naturally, she was tested for every disorder under the sun: schizophrenia, bipolar disorder, psychosis, dissociative identity disorder. Blah, ba-blah, ba-blah.

No diagnosis could ever be reached.

Instead, her family labeled her themselves: *butt-ugly weird*. (Clearly, they had never seen her ass.) Like any good daughter would, she adjusted to meet their expectations on weirdness.

The voice, she learned as an adult—after giving birth to Pap, came from an immortal named Liora.

Neviah had already believed in the paranormal and fantastical, so the revelation barely caused a hiccup. She had predicted zombies and vampires long before they were documented. And werewolves were coming...*duhhh*.

Her husband and son had a good life. Needless to say, their nest-egg was bolstered at the tracks and in casinos. Even the lottery.

The voice in her mind was flawless.

The gift wasn't free.

Neviah was an experiment for the vamps on the sunny-side of Athanasia. They used her to learn more about vampire venom and the Earth's special tree. They needed the knowledge for the future, they had told her. The future when The Tether would attempt to defeat the King of Darkness.

The future had transitioned to the present.

In the end, at least her psychic powers had become her own. No more whispering from Liora was required. The freakish experience had unlocked a door, enabling her to become a seer.

The door tattoo was featured on her stomach in blackwork. And yeah, the door bowed when she was full.

Most importantly, she was living proof about the tree's powers, inherent in the fruit (more like *dying* proof). Which in the end, placed her on a collision course with Ruby Spencer and the King of Darkness. This fact had never been withheld from her. Liora had told her upfront, so Neviah could make an informed decision when asked to become their experimental guinea pig.

A binding deal without deception.

But the trouble with seeing the future, was *seeing* the future.

Ruby had called her as Neviah had known she would.

Their session was in a few minutes. Enough time to write a brief note to her beloved son Pap.

She grabbed paper and pen and sat at the two-person table in her palm reading and divination room. The small square-table was positioned in the center of a windowed nook which jutted out from the townhouse, facing a busy side-street in the city.

Headlights were already passing in a steady stream.

She steadied her hand and began to write:

My Dear Pap,

Dry your eyes. This minute.

Remember: I told you this day would come. We talked and talked about its arrival, so you could be prepared. Everyone transitions, son. Life is much more than where our feet are planted. Never forget to look beyond where your eyes can see. That's where the truth is.

Your finances are secure for life. Spend them as you wish. Life is short.

Have peace that my passing has purpose, though I still can't disclose specifics.

(Sorry.) I will say that history has shown that the sacrifice of one can save many. I hope you'll think of me with pride. That is, if things turn out.

Don't worry about my last thoughts. They were awesome. I replayed my 25 years with you, from birth to yesterday. A few tats came to mind, too, like the one of you and me.

Now it's time to reunite with your father. I'll tell him you remind me of him!

Lastly, never forget: weird is beautiful. And I'll love you beyond infinity.

God Bless and Rebel On,
Mom

Neviah rose and headed toward the kitchen.

As she walked, she folded the stationary and inserted it within an envelope addressed to Pap. She placed the letter on the counter, next to the juicer.

She rubbed her neck, massaging the skin under her chin.

Tears cascaded down her cheeks.

The future wasn't always a picnic.

The doorbell rang.

All good things must end.

35

Tuesday, June 25, 2041
The Bain Residence: Annapolis, Maryland

WHEN THE DOOR opened to the townhouse, Ruby was caught off guard by the psychic's bear hug. She thought of her mother's embrace: instant and heartfelt. Pure emotion channeling through a hearty squeeze.

Only Neviah Bain was shaking.

There was urgency in the woman's arms. Her pulse was elevated. Eyes, bloodshot. Cheeks, splotchy. And her scent was peculiar, yet somehow familiar.

"Have we met before?" Ruby asked, though she was pretty sure she would've remembered the tapestry of colorful tattoos showcased on the psychic's arms and neck.

Dressed in a sleeveless tunic and leggings, Neviah stepped back, rapidly tapping her chest with her right hand, as if mimicking her racing heartbeat. She took a deep breath.

"Excuse me," the psychic said, standing to the side of the doorframe. "I'm overwhelmed at the moment. Please come inside."

When Ruby entered, Neviah looked up and down the street before closing the door, having never answered her question about meeting before.

"Shouldn't you lock the door?" Ruby asked, clutching the handle of her portable fireproof-safe.

Even though zombies were on the decline and thankfully couldn't turn knobs, humans needed to be cautious. Safety wasn't going to happen on its own in a post-apocalyptic world.

"Wish it mattered." Neviah pivoted and walked, turning into the first room on the left.

Ruby followed her into a cozy space. Flickering candlelight reflected off the windows. In contrast to the psychic's own colorful palette, the nook was neutral and soft.

The outdoor, flashing neon-sign was the only optic interruption to an otherwise relaxing environment.

Neviah motioned for her to sit across from her. The table surface was perfect for elbows and arms, but not for safes. Ruby placed the container, crafted from tantalum carbide, on the wood flooring beside her chair.

"Nice pencil skirt," Neviah said. "But high-heels are a bitch."

Ruby ignored the small talk. "Aren't you going to ask me what's in the safe?"

"Nope." She shook her head, but her spikes stayed stiff. "I'm a *seer*, remember? Besides, I don't need to channel the coins. I already know what they'll tell me. Instead, I'm thinking you're wondering why I smell...*interesting.*"

"Our meeting is about you?" Ruby asked, wondering how the psychic might connect to the crisis. "I mean, about your scent?"

"Here." Neviah clasped her hand.

Ruby waited patiently for something to happen.

Nothing did. Just awkward silence. Surprisingly, she had pegged the psychic as a talker, but the woman's lips weren't moving.

She looked at the human seer for direction. After all, readings were *her* job. She got paid for it.

Neviah dropped her chin, tilted her head, and widened her eyes. Yet not a word—like a school teacher who believed that a student knew the answer, even before the student realized it.

Was Ruby the one who was supposed to be *seeing?*

Ignoring the neon-sign strobing light into the room, Ruby closed her eyes and opened her mind. She whispered into the psychic's thoughts and saw a burst of light, similar to when Liora cognitively shared mental-footage of Ruby's mother in the labor room.

"Film" of the past started to roll, as originally seen through Neviah's eyes.

Ruby was shocked. She felt trenches deepen in her forehead.

The psychic was in Lampsi.

An unknown immortal had transported her there.

Standing before Neviah was Liora—gorgeous as ever, wearing her jeweled crown. The two agreed on a barter: Neviah's first death, immortality, mortality, and second death.

In between, Neviah would enjoy an abundant life. The psychic's son Pappu would gain financial security from the agreement, to help compensate for the tragic and unrelated loss of his father.

All in exchange for volunteering as a test subject.

Neviah's first death came by way of a vampire bite, one coated in drool. But instead of draining the psychic's blood, Liora withdrew her teeth. Not even a sip had been taken.

In Ruby's vision, Neviah began to writhe in pain, dropping to the floor. She contorted her body. Flailed her arms. Moaned in agony. Until she became unconscious.

The drool had to be venom.

Did Ruby have similar venom?

Another image flashed in Ruby's mind.

Within Kaliméra Castle, Neviah's eyes opened a few days later. Once lifeless, the psychic's heart beat again. And she drank from a goblet filled with blood.

Neviah Bain had turned vampire.

The mental film fast-forwarded.

Ruby saw a tree atop an island, growing in an open space near a steep cliff facing northwest. Surely the tree was the same one Gabby had described.

The image blurred as Neviah's past spun forward.

Ruby's vision stopped zooming as Neviah ate a berry collected from the tree, which made her lips reddish-purple. Then she slashed her palm with a knife. But her wound didn't heal.

The psychic was no longer vampire.

Neviah's agreement with Liora was nearly fulfilled: first death, immortality, and mortality.

Ruby's heart palpitated. Could *her* dream of becoming mortal again be in her grasp? By way of this tree?

Another flash of light illuminated in Ruby's mind.

She saw swirling dust behind the psychic...

Neviah yanked her arm free and broke the connection.

Re-clasping the human's hand, Ruby turned the psychic's palm face-up. A two-inch scar had raised the skin on her lifeline; evidence that corroborated her reinstated mortality.

"Could I? Could I become *mortal* again?" Ruby asked, her voice shaking with adrenaline.

"Not to mimic your own words, but is our meeting about *you?* You, personally?" Neviah asked.

Ruby felt guilty that her own desires had been her first thought. But Neviah couldn't possibly understand how Ruby had longed to be mortal. She had wished for her mortality night and day, over the course of nine years. Over three-thousand days.

Becoming The Tether had never been her idea, her dream.

The calling had been forced on her. The barter had been struck between Liora and her mother, *not* Ruby.

One fact was crystal clear: she'd never have the choice to reclaim her humanness without that tree.

"So where is this tree located?" Ruby asked, trying not to sound overly eager.

"On..." Neviah coughed. "On..." She tried to inhale.

Ruby narrowed her eyes.

Should she offer to get her a glass of water?

Examining the woman sitting across the table, Ruby's eyes began to register the horror.

Finger-like impressions formed on the psychic's neck. The indentations were deepening, as if someone was squeezing more tightly. Instant bruises crisscrossed the branches and leaves of the psychic's neck tattoo.

Neviah Bain was being choked. Strangled.

Ruby pushed to her feet, knocking over the chair.

"Coward!" she seethed, suspecting Zagan's handiwork. "You're hurting someone vulnerable, instead of challenging your equal!"

Behind Neviah, dust swirled like a tornado, violently forming into the King of Darkness. He was dressed in black leather. Angry veins inched up his neck. Teeth were shaped to tear flesh.

As the psychic remained seated, she gasped for air.

Zagan clutched her pink hair, forcing her head back. Exposing Neviah's neck.

Ruby had to do something. Had to save her.

"EQUAL?" he roared. "You are nothing more than a pathetic imitation. Yet our differences are plentiful. For one thing, I have no one whose life I value anymore. No one but my own. But you, you have so many. Which means I can wound your heart easily—without ever touching you with my own hands. The housefire was only my first attempt."

"This is about *me,"* Ruby said. "Please let Neviah go."

"Your begging is delicious."

His anger had transformed him into a monster.

"Why have you turned against me?" she asked. "You gave me coins to keep us connected. Then used them to hurt my family. I don't understand what went wrong."

"When you talk, you *lie,"* he spat. "You told me: *your blood is your own.* But your blood, dearest Ruby, is *MINE!* Stolen from me by my once loyal henchman. Stolen to create a worthy adversary. A fact not withheld from you."

Ruby had no time to figure out what had happened to Draven. Or how Zagan learned that the king's blood flowed through her veins.

Candles snuffed out.

All the electricity on the block, including the passing headlights, abruptly shut off. Car tires screeched on the street. The historic district, as far as her eyes could see through the windows, was cloaked in darkness.

Time paused in the void.

When candles relit, his nails had sharpened to three-inch daggers.

"Let me prove how *unequal* we really are," Zagan taunted.

"No! *Pleeease!"*

Neviah's flesh was blueish. Her pupils hid behind opened eyelids.

Continuing to stand behind Neviah's chair, Zagan moved his right hand in front of the psychic, under her chin. On the left side of her neck, he slowly inserted the nail of his index finger, deeply penetrating her skin. Blood spurted like oil from a well.

He smiled as he sliced across her neck.

The incision was so deep that Ruby could see cervical vertebrae.

Neviah's heart sputtered before flatlining.

Ruby stood frozen in disbelief, in horror. Liora had warned her of the king's cruelness, but she was shocked by its depth.

When Zagan released the psychic's hair, Neviah's body slumped off her chair, falling onto the floor.

"Are we truly *equal*, Lady Spencer?" he goaded.

Ruby's body trembled.

Anger took over.

Using a cerebral image, she cognitively gathered each candle's flames. Her vision mushroomed into a fireball. Blowing open the door of the townhouse, she collected the wind in her mind.

Like a feline ready to strike, she shifted to Zagan's left.

He countered until his back was toward the windows and street.

"Without love in your heart," she said, "you're nothing but a weak, pathetic demon."

He smiled, beginning to raise his hands as if he might launch a sculpted retaliation. He hesitated to recite a familiar nursery rhyme.

"As your precious mayflies say to their offspring," he said, *"sticks and stones will..."*

She transformed the firestorm swirling in her mind and released it into reality. The massive spinning-fireball hurtled toward the king, moving with the harnessed wind at an unfathomable speed. The fireball struck Zagan in the chest, launching him through the glass, destroying the entire wall, until only open space to the outside remained. Rubble spilled onto the small lawn and sidewalk, sending a plume of dust rising in the night.

She ran to the edge of the townhouse's gaping hole.

Zagan had already traveled from the debris. Gone.

"Will break YOUR bones," she shouted, as if he could hear her.

She returned to Neviah. The psychic's body was face down in a pool of her own blood. Her shirt had slightly lifted, exposing her skin and a portion of a tattoo.

Ruby knelt by her side. Without intending to be disrespectful, she ripped Neviah's shirt to examine the whole image. The artwork was of a tree, adorned with clusters of small purple berries. The inked words read: *The Blood of Three Kings.*

Three kings? She only knew of one.

Then the real question hit her: could Zagan be made *human?*

She looked at Neviah lying on the floor with her back exposed.

The psychic deserved better. Ruby sculpted her shirt closed and created a fleece blanket to cover her body.

After the police and ambulance arrived, she glamoured all the first responders. Everyone knew gangs were on the rise in Annapolis, spilling over from Baltimore. Neviah Bain was a tragic victim of an initiation ritual.

Grabbing her safe, Ruby excused herself, knowing she wouldn't be remembered. She meandered into the kitchen, turned to dust, and traveled to her hotel. She had so much to tell Clay.

Her immediate task was to solve the mystery of the tree.

But her ultimate purpose extended beyond, and she accepted it.

The time had come to stop calling her vampirism an affliction. To stop wanting to be human.

She was vampire. At least for now.

Despite the deceptions which had been used to turn her, she had an opportunity to save the world. To use her strengths. To *be* a miracle instead of staying embittered because she hadn't gotten one.

And how did she really know that becoming a vampire wasn't a miracle in and of itself?

For the first time since Liora had visited Ruby in her nighttime space, she understood the arsenal of gifts at her disposal.

She was ready for war against the King of Darkness.

Unlike previous challenges, she'd lead the crusade alone. No one would control or manipulate her: not government cronies, not even the Queen of Light.

After all, Ruby was The Tether—the bond between the planets. And she'd give the effort everything she had.

Even her life.

Thankfully, Zagan wasn't aware that Liora's blood also pulsed through Ruby, giving rise to gifts he would never have.

This gave her an advantage.

The king, no doubt, would try to match her efforts.

Therein was *her* disadvantage.

36

Wednesday, June 26, 2041
The White House Situation Room: Washington, D.C.

WEDNESDAYS WERE RESERVED for the SWC.

The Spencers took their seats. As the meeting began, Ruby already knew what President Unger was going to report to the council, what mission he was going to ask her to accept, and how she was going to answer. Nevertheless, their attendance was crucial. For the future to come to pass, the present had to play-out in real time.

The POTUS opened with an apology to Ruby for the SWC's rush-to-judgment regarding Paige Jasper's murder.

"Now to business," he said. "There's been another culling: a private bus crashed near Le Havre, France, last night. The vehicle was transporting fifty soccer-fans from Stade Océane, after a FIFA Women's World Cup qualifying game. First responders found the bus empty. Everyone onboard had vanished, like on Flight 1733."

The POTUS faced Ruby, locking eyes with her. "We'd like to send you and Clay to investigate, to question bystanders. See if anyone saw something that could help prevent another incident. It would be a low-risk mission, but one of great importance."

Her husband shook his head and huffed. "Your low-risk missions tend to involve kidnapping and mayhem."

"Not to mention," she added, nodding, "the assignment would be a total waste of time."

"I'm not following," the POTUS said. "We can't rely on foreign authorities to conduct an inquiry which meets our standards. Four

Americans were on that bus. Our citizens will want assurances that we're involved. That we're leading this thing."

"So the mission is more about appearances than value?"

"Why are you against this project, Ruby?" Eyes asked.

"The mission won't glean anything we don't already know," she answered. "Let's say we find bystanders who witnessed the accident. They saw Zagan, who is identifiable given his skin has no pigment. Before everyone vanished, they report he suddenly appeared on the bus. I'm telling you—right here, right now—without travel, without time spent interviewing potential witnesses, that the culling happened exactly that way. If you need talking heads to impress our citizens that we're doing something, send members of the council who don't actually *have* a plan."

"That's reasonable," the POTUS agreed. "Which begs the question: what's your plan?"

"I can't tell you."

"Come again?"

"You're going to have to trust me."

Ruby wasn't going to disclose any more to the SWC. They already knew too much. She had told them about Liora visiting in her "dreams" and about Zagan's plan to use humans as a blood source by culling and traveling them to his realm of vampires. But that's as much as she'd share. Telling them about a mysterious tree? No. Sharing the extent of her gifts, like she could travel as far as Athanasia? Off limits for now. And sculpting, whispering, and *seeing* into the future? Triple negative!

If the President and his cabinet knew everything about her extraordinary powers, the government would *expand* their use of her as a political weapon.

As much as she loved her country, her role as The Tether was not about promoting the agenda of the United States.

"We don't harbor secrets on this council," the SWC chair admonished.

"Are you kidding me?" Clay's eyes swept the table. "Forget nine years ago. How about two weeks ago when POTUS confessed having a supply of Em's SUC serum? Or last week's ambush? Apology or not, the SWC secretly manipulated this meeting to inject my wife with vervain. Then locked her up!" He pounded the table. "Don't freaking get me started on the secrets this council keeps from us. So if my wife says she has a plan, but can't tell you, well...you're just going to have to say thank you. Thank you for trying to save our sorry asses. One more time."

"Let's be civil here, folks," the POTUS said. "Is there anything you *can* tell us?"

"It's safer if everyone remains in the dark," she said, "since Zagan can mentally drill into minds to unbury the truth."

"Does your plan require resources? Anything we can do to help?"

The President is being uncharacteristically thoughtful, she whispered into Clay's mind.

"Trust and time are all I need," she answered out loud.

The meeting continued for two more hours. They discussed Federation objectives in Russia and China, the status of ZOM-B worldwide, advances on animal health, and efforts to eradicate hunger. At half-past noon, the meeting adjourned.

"Ruby?" the POTUS called, as members rose from their seats. "May I speak with you privately for a few minutes?"

Insley looked at her for direction, though his services weren't needed anymore, especially since her gifts had awakened. "We're fine," she told him. "Go on without us."

After members exited, Clay closed the door to the Situation Room and neared his wife.

"No disrespect," the POTUS said to her husband, "but I'd like to speak with your wife...alone."

"We're a team, President Unger," Clay answered. "Ruby will detail the conversation with me anyway. It's more efficient if I hear your exchange concurrently."

She nodded. "He's right."

"Sure. Okay." The POTUS sat on the table's edge, crossing his arms over his chest. "I saw your housefire on the news, and I'm sorry, by the way, for the loss of your home and belongings." He locked eyes with her. "The broadcast also showed that you saved your daughter, thank God, by injecting her with your blood. How miraculous!"

Combing her upper teeth over her bottom lip, she regretted not being more restrictive to the media during the blaze. Of course, her family's rescue and survival were her only focus. But the onsite news coverage meant the world was now aware she could travel. And that her blood could restore life. So much for keeping her gifts under wraps. Which also meant the past could repeat itself. Others could attempt to kidnap her or her family for nefarious purposes.

"Yes, Gabby's life is a miracle." She looked at Clay and smiled.

"*My* family could use a miracle," the POTUS added.

The comment caught her by surprise. President Unger needed something. Probably a favor. Her heart sank. Everyone—human and vampire—seemed to want a piece of her.

Little by little, they'd pick her clean to the bone.

"And what miracle might that be?" Clay asked.

"It's the First Lady. A month ago, she lost fifteen pounds. Initially, we thought the weight loss was due to this new super-diet she put us on. Hard core organic. You know, Irene is always thinking anti-toxins. But she got exhausted. I convinced her to get a physical ahead of schedule, to make sure everything was all right." He gazed at the floor. "My wife has stage-four ovarian cancer. It's metastasized to the liver, spleen, intestine, and lymph nodes." He raised his eyes. Moisture made them glassy. "Three months. That's all she's got left."

Ruby reached for his hand and held it. "Oh no. We're so sorry. We'll pray for her. Anything we can do? Is Irene starting chemo?"

"You don't understand," he said. "I'm asking you to save her. Like you saved your daughter."

"I...I don't know what to say," she answered, trying to buy time to unscramble the thoughts colliding in her mind. Feeling trapped, she dropped his hand and stepped back.

"Say...yes," the POTUS said. "We haven't gone public yet. No one needs to know."

"I'm conflicted here," she admitted, her eyes blinking rapidly. "I'm supposed to save the world from a devil, not alter what it means to be...human. If I save Irene, why shouldn't I save all the victims of terminal illness, especially our children? And what about the two-million who die annually in the U.S.? Or the fifty-million per year around the globe?"

"Save them!" the POTUS said. "Why *not* wipe out death? That's what you did with F8, with the cure."

"Not exactly. Immunology saved the infected, using my human blood to formulate a vaccine. I don't know…" She looked at Clay for support. "Maybe I *could* donate some blood for medical research. To see if cures could be developed. I hadn't considered that, not with the current crisis saturating my thoughts."

"Research sounds good for the future," the POTUS said, "but my wife doesn't have that kind of time."

The easy answer was yes.

But was "yes" the *right* answer?

She struggled for words. "I mean, Quinton Oxford, Vladimir Volkov, and Decha Lin wanted to use my blood for their own benefits. All were traitors against humanity."

The President stood. "Different. This is about saving lives. Think beyond yourself. You said there was an entire *planet* of vampires. Why can't we find a way to collect their blood? To use it for healing with our sick and dying? And we've got vervain to incapacitate them."

"Wait." Her eyes widened. "You see a moral difference between *them* harvesting human blood for food and *us* harvesting vampire blood for healing?"

"This is survival of the fittest," he answered, without hesitation.

"You mean: survival of the most selfish. The most ruthless."

"And shortsighted to boot," Clay added. "As a community ecologist, I'm beginning to understand that if you prolong human life through this type of 'artificial' healing, we'll exponentially deplete our Earth's natural resources. Talk about exacerbating hunger! The imbalance will be catastrophic. And no doubt we'll eventually want to eradicate death entirely, since immortality is the next obvious step. Believe me, I know. I've fantasized about becoming a vampire. But now I see clearly. Zombiism was the first Extinction Level Infection. And vampirism is the second."

"Death is a natural cycle in life," Ruby said. "Death partially defines humankind. It's what creates a balance between the planet's resources and sustainable life."

"How easy for you to say! You *saved* your daughter," the POTUS spat. "You're no hero. You're a self-serving hypocrite."

"Nothing is *easy* about losing one's humanness, Will," she said.

"Being turned by the SWC into Earth's vampire warrior—a protector of humanity—has had an unintended consequence: my family is in Zagan's crosshairs. He wants their deaths to distract me from this war. I should have your blessing to defend their lives using the assets which were forced on me. Assets which are putting them in harm's way, at no fault of their own."

"Damn it!" The President's face was red. "Irene's cancer isn't her fault either."

"Of course it isn't. But cancer is one of the risks of the *living.*"

"Your blood is medicine. And you're denying her."

The comment crushed her.

Ruby's lives—once human and now vampire—were dedicated to saving people, not watching from the sidelines as humans withered away, making it seem as if she didn't care. As if she was heartless.

But the POTUS's request directly conflicted with her beliefs about interfering with what it meant to be *human.*

"Can't you see this quandary is like the one inherent in dark science?" Ruby asked. "Just because we *can,* doesn't mean we *should.* Haven't we learned from Em's unnatural tampering?"

"My wife's death will be on your hands," he snapped.

The situation was cruel from every angle. Maybe exceptions should be made. But who was *she* to decide?

Crimson tears streamed down her cheeks.

Touch me, she whispered to Clay.

After he wrapped his fingers around her arm, they turned to dust and traveled to their hotel. And in that moment, she saw a flash of light in her mind.

The image of Emory Bradshaw's smirking face.

He was in his jail cell.

Using a laptop to compose a letter.

37

Thursday, June 27, 2041
The Westin Annapolis: Annapolis, Maryland

CLAY LOUNGED ON the couch in their hotel suite's living room, sitting in silence.

The desperate plea of the President still haunted his thoughts.

Clay empathized with the panic of losing a loved one. After all, both of his parents had died in a car accident when he was a teenager.

Death was something he thought about every holiday, every milestone, every February 3: the day Claire and Evan Spencer were killed when Mr. Shoemaker drove the wrong way on Highway 12.

As a son, he had longed for them to live forever.

As an orphan, he had longed to turn back time.

Nine years ago, in the early hours of July 17th, his wife had died. She woke, of course, as an immortal. But still, he was no stranger to being on the other side of death—on the *living* side. The side where fear and aloneness and grief crushed the heart.

He understood the President's confusion over Ruby saving their daughter but hesitating to save his wife. Yet Clay agreed with Ruby.

Bottom line: the housefire was an act of war and Ruby "the soldier," armed with an arsenal of assets, saved an innocent victim of collateral damage. Might as well add himself and the dogs to the tally.

What the POTUS was asking had *nothing* to do with war. Nothing to do with the reasons they'd turned Ruby.

Moreover, Ruby's vampirism was beginning to challenge what he thought he wanted. The temptation to live forever in the physical world was more like a cruel hoax. The illusion was enticing. The reality, terrifying.

Not even Clay had considered the downsides before, and *he* was an ecologist. What would the world look like if everyone was a vampire and animal populations were dwindling from disease?

He could picture the answer. A childless *Mad Max* world where blood was like finding water in the desert.

Humanity was worth fighting for.

Besides, in their faith, they believed in spiritual life after death. If he truly believed, why had he been seeking something else?

He'd have to get over his fear of aging.

Behind him, on the other side of the partition in their suite, he heard footsteps approaching from the kitchen. Ruby carried a milkshake. Gabby followed closely behind.

"Oh, goody," he said, eyeing the shake.

"Is that how you show appreciation?" She smiled, handing him the frosty glass. "Strawberry: your favorite. Now drink and enjoy."

"*I* want some," Gabby said, looking at the thick shake and running her tongue over her top lip. "Please?"

Ruby shook her head. "Too close to dinner." She sat on the couch, leaving room for their daughter to sit in between them. "Should we research Three Kings now?"

"Let's." He commanded the MV to activate.

"Justine," his wife said to the smart speakers. "Will you research Three Kings? The name is associated with a place or a tree—maybe both. The tree bears clusters of grape-like fruit, but we know nothing else, except that the species is extremely rare."

The MV flashed an image of a 42-year-old film called *Three Kings*, featuring actors George Clooney, Mark Wahlberg, and Ice Cube.

Ruby rolled her eyes. "Pass," she snarked.

"Can't blame a lady for finding the eye candy first," Justine said.

"Except this is serious. So work harder."

"Oh, all right," their DEPE said. "I found Three Kings Day on the sixth of January." An image of an oil painting depicting three Magi next to a manger projected on the screen. "The holiday is celebrated twelve days after Christmas, when three kings arrived in Bethlehem, bringing gifts to baby Jesus. The holiday is also called

Feast of the Epiphany."

"Did I mention the search centers on a...*tree?*" Ruby scolded.

"Two of the gifts connect," Justine said. "Frankincense and myrrh are derived from sap collected from the Boswellia genus of trees."

His heart accelerated. "Are the trees on an island? Are they rare?"

"Double negative," their DEPE answered. "The trees grow on the Arabian Peninsula and in northeastern Africa. They've even been cultivated in southern China."

Gabby shook her head. "My tree is on an island. I'm sure of it."

"Focus your search on an island, maybe named Three Kings," Ruby suggested to Justine.

"Got it."

The MV zoomed to a closeup map of two large islands, located where the South Pacific Ocean converged with the Tasman Sea.

"Three Kings is a suburb of Auckland, New Zealand—on the country's North Island," Justine said. "It's near the Te Tātua-a-Riukiuta volcano which used to have three prominent peaks, until the stones were quarried. Still, the peaks gave rise to the town's name."

"But is there a special tree located there?" he asked.

"Not exactly. However, over four-hundred kilometers north is Cape Reinga, where the Pōhutukawa tree is found. Only thirty adult trees are in the wild. That qualifies as rare."

"Show us the tree, please," Ruby said.

The screen flicked to a photograph of the Pōhutukawa. Beautiful, the tree stood about 60-feet tall and was adorned with hairy blooms of crimson, like clusters of fine feathers. But, no clumps of small purple fruit were evident.

There's no resemblance to the tree tattoo, Ruby whispered into his mind.

"Not it," Gabby announced.

"Wait," Justine said. "I may have found something else. About fifty-four kilometers northwest, or thirty-four miles off the coast of Cape Reinga, is a small archipelago of thirteen, uninhabited islands. They are called Three Kings Islands because they were discovered and named on the sixth of January, year 1643."

"Is there a rare tree on any of those small islands?" Ruby asked.

A cricket's winged chirp stridulated from under the couch. Annoying, but he'd deal with the insect later.

"Yes, yes, yes!" their DEPE cheered. "On Great Island—the largest in the archipelago—is the Three Kings Kaikomako or *Pennantia Baylisiana:* one single-species tree growing in the wild. The tree was discovered nearly a century ago by a botanist. Since, seedlings have been sprouted and cloned, but the *original* Three Kings is considered the world's rarest tree: the *only one* of its kind. Unfortunately, I'm not finding the exact coordinates on the tree's location."

Justine posted a photograph of the tree.

The tree had multiple trunks and measured 15-feet tall. Glossy round leaves were broad, with edges that curled down. Most importantly, between January and April, the tree bore clusters of grape-like fruit—purple when ripened.

"This is the tree, isn't it?" Ruby asked, turning to their daughter.

Gabby stared blankly at nothing.

Clay gently shook her shoulder. "What's wrong, honey?"

When his daughter said nothing, he remembered the glamour.

We've got company, Ruby cognitively whispered.

The cricket shrilled again.

No time like the present to kill a king, she added.

He reached under Gabby's elbow to help her up. "Let's have you sit over here." He guided her to a chair as Ruby rose to her feet.

I'll lift, you stomp.

He nodded, his heart thumping loudly in his chest.

His wife raised the couch like it was a pillow.

The cream carpet was clean. No cricket.

"Can we go *see* the tree?" Gabby asked, her words returning.

"After your mother puts down the couch," Justine said, "I can book your flights."

"I'm a traveler, remember?" Ruby lowered the sofa onto the carpet. "The three of us will leave from here tomorrow evening. That'll give you time, Justine, to contact the tourism department and arrange for a guide at Cape Reinga on Saturday at noon, New Zealand time. Have the guide meet us on the beach with a boat, to take us to Great Island."

"Wait," he said, feeling his cheeks flush. "The *three* of us? No way. Gabby stays."

"Who can protect Gabby better than me?" Ruby asked.

He couldn't argue the point.

"But why do we need a guide?" Clay asked. "Can't you travel us to where the tree is located?"

"Without coordinates or some connection to the precise location," Ruby said, "the answer is no. Our arrival would be blind. At least with a local, we have a better chance of finding the tree."

He wasn't able to read the future, but what they'd find on their expedition seemed pretty easy to predict.

Danger carried the highest probability.

And danger started with a capital Z.

38

Thursday, June 27, 2041
Castle on High Cliff: Skotadi, Athanasia

BACK IN HIS study, Zagan dug his nails into the stone to anchor himself, allowing his body to lean over the cave-like opening overlooking the valley and river below his castle. The wind flapped his cloak, making him feel like a bat preparing for flight.

He longed to leave his troubles behind, to take to the starry skies. Inhaling, he closed his eyes. The vibrancy of night refreshed his soul.

Flying would do nothing to solve his problem.

Ruby Spencer was his problem.

Given their inability to outright kill one another, The Tree of Awareness was her only viable option.

Of course, the tree offered him recourse as well.

Mayflies called the tree as they wished, but he had come in contact with the one-of-a-kind species before humans ever populated Earth. And the tree's true name had been seared on his tongue.

A reality he wished was not so.

Naturally, he had tried to forget the tree. Most ironic that he could never free himself from its memory or the consequences which still haunted him. His legacy, in fact, was rooted in his past encounter. From his regretful taste of… awareness.

A traveler, he had visited Earth as a "youth," nearly 200,000 years after Creation. He had selected his destination with purpose: a cliff-edged microcontinent jutting up from what is now known as the South Pacific. Zealandia boasted unique birds and reptiles, as well as remarkable fauna and flora, within a subtropical climate. Why would he not choose the location to explore?

Zagan had not traveled alone, for he was enamored with a Shadowlander. Though she was not a traveler herself, she was eager to accompany him. Indeed, he was unsure if his heart beat more rapidly for her—with slate-colored hair that flowed to her thighs and smelled of roses—or for the upcoming adventure.

Regardless, he had intentions to couple with her, to ask her to be his mate. To eventually wed. Coupled for eternity.

The oracle Pythia bestowed a blessing for their travel, adding one stipulation: that they leave their destination undisturbed. That everything would remain as they had found it. Because the first vampire to disobey would be cursed with evil. Moreover, the perpetrator would cause an additional curse to befall his or her kind. Both curses would not be lifted *until goodness was set free*.

Even in his youthfulness, Zagan resented control.

Unproven spiritual musings were a close second.

Creation was meant to be rejoiced, experienced with all the senses engaged. He determined then, that Pythia may have garnered a fearful following on Athanasia with her prophesies and warnings, but she was no match for his hunger of the undiscovered.

Besides, Pythia was not the Human/Immortal Maker. Nor would she ever be HIM.

When Zagan traveled to Zealandia with his future mate clutching his arm, his skin grew hot on arrival but never caught ablaze. What a marvelous day they had exploring, tasting the salty spray from a violent sea, basking in sunlight, and kissing when feelings swelled.

Marvelous, until they came upon *the* tree.

Although the tree was rather mundane, its purple fruit enticed him. The lure of the forbidden tempted his palate.

As his companion peered over the edge of a steep cliff, he plucked three berries and hid them within the pocket of his green cloak.

Upon his return to Lampsi, to escort his true love to her workplace at Kaliméra, they had lingered at The Tree of Immortality, which also bore fruit, though larger and brown in color. It was there that he had revealed his pocketed treasure.

Only her reactions were not as his.

His true love was appalled that he had stolen from the land they had visited. He had disregarded Pythia's counsel. Fearful, she stepped away from him and demanded he carbonize the berries. And he *tried*. He did not know, then, that the fruit could not be destroyed. The fruit's purity could not itself be transformed or eliminated.

He ate the berries instead.

What better way to conceal his transgression?

Falling to his knees, he became a vacuum, with the winds of good and evil rushing to fill him. Internal balance which had once felt like harmony was upheaved, making room for vanity, strife, and mistrust. Especially for hate and rage.

Worse, Zagan felt different. He felt *mortal*.

When his tears ran clear, panic gripped him.

He had begged his true love to cut him and when she did, he did not heal. He pleaded that she pluck a fig from The Tree of Immortality. For certainly, he could not remain a mortal. He could not face...*death*.

After ingesting the sacred fig, his acquired awareness of good and evil became locked in his reinstated immortality. And the evil that he now knew refused dormancy. A wretched curse, indeed.

What happened next, could not be fathomed, not even with the passing of nearly three mega-annum. Which is why he never spoke his beloved's name. Not since then, not ever.

If only he had not been rushed, he may have cooled the uncontrollable heat which had ignited within his veins.

Time, however, had not been generous.

The fruit had altered his reaction to the sun. As his skin burned and blistered, his beautiful silvery-princess sought to find Liora. To seek help. To tell the queen: *everything*.

Self-preservation pulsed with fury. He had begged her to listen, to refrain. But as flames devoured his skin, she turned from him.

Moved by impulse, he swept his hand, absent thought.

His eyes filled with regret. Then...and now.

Reduced to ashes, his true love vanished with the breeze.

Zagan had destroyed her.

What was done, could not be undone.

Traveling to Skotadi to save himself, he grew embittered.

Zagan's heart darkened.

Another curse extended to the realms and became known as the Era of Light and Darkness. From that moment until the present, Skotadians could no longer be exposed to sunlight; Lampsians, to darkness. Only Shadowlanders could travel between the three realms.

Ever since, The Tree of Immortality was guarded, as if he still had a need for it.

He mended his soul with the only remedy he understood: power.

Once he had acquired power, he instituted a death culling to eradicate all vampires who could travel or who were highly gifted, especially prominent Shadowlanders.

He never thought of Zealandia again.

If The Tree of Awareness had survived humans, then let them be equally tempted by its fruit. What did he care? Mayflies already suffered from a brief and tormented life.

Undoubtedly, Neviah Bain believed the tree had persevered.

Returning to the island would conjure feelings he did not wish to unearth. A tear raced down his cheek, plunging to the ragged rocks below. He wiped his face.

"Your Excellency," Titus said, entering the study. "I plan to retire to my quarters. As requested, I am to remind you of our inspection at the prison tomorrow eve."

Zagan pushed away from the stone balcony, turning toward his henchman. "You shall inspect the facility by yourself, as I will be traveling to Earth to address a matter."

"A matter?" His new henchman cleared his throat. "Would it be too forward of me to request your destination? After all, how can I protect you if I am not informed?"

He placed his hand on Titus's shoulder. "Your arrogance provides much amusement. You? Protecting *me?* I welcome the good humor, as I have not had enough of it."

"I aim to please, King Zagan. Does your gaiety increase the likelihood that you shall indulge my request?"

"My journey will be to Three Kings Islands," Zagan answered. "To Great Island, specifically."

Titus's eyes widened. "Legend says The Tree of Awareness grows there—the one that divided most of our kind into either light or darkness. The tree that exchanges immortality with mortality, when its fruit is consumed."

"You speak as though I am not the author of this legend." Zagan chuckled. "Indeed, your title may be jester over warrior. Shall I call you: Titus the Entertainer?"

His henchman thinned his lips. "Will you attempt to kill Lady Spencer by…perhaps, spiking her divine wine with the odorless berry juice? Stripping her of immortality?"

Zagan took a step back. Rarely was he surprised.

"Well played. To use your joking as a clever distraction to shield your steel heart." The king smiled. "Apologies for my misjudgment."

"You are not the first to underestimate me, Your Excellency. Nor the last, I suspect."

The king was beginning to like this henchman. For the moment, his heart regretted parting from Draven a little less. After all, since Zagan could protect himself, certainly cunningness was far more impressive than swordplay.

"As well," the king added, "we cannot underestimate Lady Spencer, for she has the power to imitate my gifts. Her death must be planned with great precision."

"I suspect you have ways to wound her until that time arrives?"

"*Ahh,* you are most wise." Zagan nodded to show respect. "I will encounter her pathetic mate on the island. And I promise you, the mayfly's mortality will greet him there."

39

Thursday, June 27, 2041
United States Penitentiary, Lee: Virginia

EM'S FINGERS SHOOK from the adrenaline rush, after seeing the evening news while in the prison's recreation room. The breaking headline from Sky News: *First Lady Has Three Months To Live*. Even the sniffling broadcast reporter couldn't hold back her boohoo-hoos.

From his perspective, cancer never sounded so damn good.

Irene Unger's bad luck was his good fortune.

After Em had shared the incapacitating effect that vervain would have on Ruby Spencer, the President had followed through with his payback: giving Em unlimited access to the Internet, using a setup and browsers of his choosing.

Maybe the POTUS thought that meant Internet Explorer, Firefox, Google Chrome, or Safari.

Hardly.

Em was predisposed to the deep and dark webs—both were anonymous and untraceable when accessing through a virtual private network (VPN). His browsers of choice? TOR, Freenet, and 12P. Because he had acquired a taste for the freakish—the sweet spot where true innovation incubated.

Take cancer. If traditional medicine had the capacity to cure cancer, the disease would have been wiped out 50-years ago. At least.

Freakish was also where dark science resided. Where his relentless research sparked his heart of hearts: his deeply rooted belief that science had no boundaries. Nothing was off limits. If something *could* be done, then it *should* be done. Why the hell not?

After all, China and Russia weren't holding back.

If properly persuaded, the First Lady could become the anointed posterchild for dark science, at least for the next 90 days, give or take, since medical death-sentences couldn't be controlled on paper or in news reporting.

If he was successful in *curing* her, he might earn a free "get out of jail" card. Sounded like a win-win.

Talk about a shitload of motivation.

One thing was obvious. The vampire bitch had refused to save the President's wife. He had seen the aired footage of Ruby resuscitating Gabby—Em's precious Godchild: *not*. Which meant if Ruby's blood could restart a heart, repair charred lungs, heal third-degree burns, grow back hair, and whatnot, her blood could cure cancer.

Any other disease for that matter.

Truth be told, if the vampire *had* agreed to share her blood, it would've been game over for Em.

He'd have nothing left to do except rot in jail. And fuck Kendrick and Lyle, of course. Or blow Big Dan, since that was as far as Dan would go. A temporary problem until Em got leverage on Dan, which he'd gotten yesterday. "Straight" in the outside world had no bearing on the inside, not to shot callers protected by thugs who could double as defensive tackles in the NFL. Guys who liked killing and weren't getting out anyway.

Em's philosophy as the most dominant of all shot callers at USP, Lee was that everyone just had to get along. Make love, not war. Kumbaya, baby. Besides, in what universe did a guy like Big Dan think that Em wouldn't get exactly what he wanted?

And who the hell wouldn't want *all* of Dan?

After hearing the news about the First Lady, Em asked to return to his cell early. Lyle—mister guard extraordinaire—liked to oblige his requests.

Em was tickled how Kendrick and Lyle competed for his affections. He had always considered himself desirable. Now he knew how much.

When he returned to his cell from the recreation room, he fired up his computer components and took print-screens of the state-of-the-art lab he wanted, complete with shelving for animal cages. He also typed an extensive list of must-haves, from the most current lab instruments and equipment to the chemicals he needed.

Then he composed an email on his laptop.

Dear Mr. President,

My heart is heavy at the news that your wife has terminal cancer. My thoughts and prayers are with you and the First Lady.

Your generosity in giving me unfettered access to the Internet may have far reaching benefits beyond my own desires for scholarship. Coincidentally, I have been researching strategies to cure cancer! Were you aware that the naked mole rat, indigenous to East Africa, is immune to cancer? Even when injected with cancerous cells, this rodent keeps the disease at bay. How? These hairless superstars have hyaluronan levels that are off-the-charts. (Hyaluronan molecules, by the way, prevent cells from clustering together to form tumors. In the naked mole rat, the molecules are larger and highly concentrated, suppressing the growth of malignant cells.) Freakishly awesome, right?

My doctoral degrees in microbiology and immunology have allowed me to bioengineer hybrid cells with great success. Case in point: melding Ruby Spencer's extraordinary immunity with ZOM-B to create our first vampire. As well, my work propagating a universal hybrid serum for vampirism (Sanguivorous Cocci or SUC) also demonstrates my extreme aptitude in this field.

My proposal is to bioengineer a hybrid serum that will alter your wife's hyaluronan to resemble the naked mole rat's. Not only will the serum attack and break up tumors, it will prevent any of the dispersed cells from surviving. The First Lady will be cured. Forever.

I gather Ruby Spencer was unwilling to cure your wife. If she had been, the First Lady would be healed. In service to country and to you—my Commander in Chief, I am willing to work tirelessly to save her life in her human form.

If my efforts fail, which they won't if I'm properly equipped, the First Lady could always be the first recipient of SUC (with my careful oversight), though I'm not sure having a bloodsucker as the First Lady should be your goal.

I will understand if you are uncomfortable in receiving my help.

However, if a cure is what your heart seeks, enclosed is a photograph of the type of lab I would need. Surely a space at the prison could be utilized for this purpose. I have also included an extensive list of supplies. In terms of the naked mole rats, I have a friend in East Africa who will ship a dozen or more as soon as the lab is ready to be stocked. (Address enclosed.)

Need I remind you: time is pressing.

Currently, I have no requests for a return favor, as my thoughts are focused on this mission: to save your wife, if that is your wish.

I look forward to hearing from you.

A proud and faithful American,
Dr. Emory Bradshaw

Em knew the POTUS's private email account from previous exchanges. After attaching photos and his must-have list, he hit send.

Lyle approached his cell, running his metal baton along the bars, sounding like tires running over rumble strips. Towering over him was Big Dan.

Prison had its perks.

"Big Dan wants to personally apologize for stealing your magazine," Lyle said, shouldering Dan's lower back, making him stumble forward. "He's hoping you won't tell the warden, since his record's been clean lately."

Dan's eyes were as big as his cock. His face was certainly as pale.

"I'm sure we can work this out," Em said to Lyle. "We're a pack of prison wolves in here—a community of give and take. A yin and yang. I'm the cookie and Dan's the cream."

Lyle retracted the lock on his cell door. "I got jigs while you *negotiate*," he said, meaning he'd keep a lookout. "But holler if you need help persuading him."

"Oh, Big Dan's looking cooperative tonight. I think we'll be fine. How long do we have? I mean, until recreation time is over?"

"Fifteen minutes. That enough?"

"Love means never having to say you're sorry," Em cooed. "But I think fifteen minutes is long enough to *show* it."

40

Saturday, June 29, 2041
Cape Reinga, New Zealand

RUBY TRAVELED HER family to a white sandy beach on the northwestern tip of New Zealand's North Island.

Behind them was a steep, rocky rise which led to Cape Reinga's iconic lighthouse overlooking the convergence of the South Pacific Ocean and Tasman Sea. Strong gusts flapped Ruby's waterproof windbreaker which topped her sweater. Sand occasionally blasted her face. At least they had all worn sunglasses to protect their eyes. In the whipping winds, she was also thankful she had pulled her and Gabby's hair into ponytails.

The day was sunny and 59-degrees Fahrenheit, even though June marked the beginning of the three wettest months on the cape. Not a bad scenario for the dead of winter.

Their arrival was perfectly timed.

Porpoising over the turbulent whitecaps was a dinghy captained by their guide: Atea Patel. Her open-hulled boat was anchored beyond the breakers, rolling from starboard to port in calmer water—which wasn't saying much.

Atea tilted up the outboard motor before beaching the dinghy. Jumping into the shallow foaming-surf, she held the bow's line and pulled the vessel ashore. She ran to greet them.

"Howdy, mates," she said, extending her hand to shake with Ruby, then Clay. Even Gabby. "Happy to meet you." She smiled. "And always glad to have an ankle-biter on board."

Their guide was about forty. Her hair was blonde, short, and curly and when she removed her sunglasses for introductions, her eyes were blue like the South Pacific. With skin that was tanned and weathered, and lips slightly cracked, she looked like she spent most of her time on the water. She wore knee-high waterproof boots, jeans, and a blue life-vest over her hooded sweatshirt, accessorized with an orange bandana around her neck.

"Do I know you?" Atea asked Ruby. "You look familiar. A movie star in the States by any chance?"

Ruby was thrilled that someone didn't recognize her as the Earth's vampire warrior. How refreshing to be considered human.

"No, I'm not from Hollywood." Ruby chuckled and smiled, before turning serious. "Any idea how long it'll take us to get to Three Kings' Great Island?"

"Should be able to go twenty-knots in these conditions," Atea answered, glancing over her shoulder toward her boat. "In two hours, our boots should find the trailhead. After a rocky climb, we should reach the sacred Kaikomako about an hour later. Round trip should have us back here before nautical twilight. Sound good?"

Good wasn't the feeling Ruby was getting.

Uneasy was more like it.

Even though she was a seer, she couldn't *see* everything. So many possibilities were in motion at the same time, each affected by forces she didn't control. Still, she was learning to be acutely aware of her feelings; they represented clues to more probable outcomes.

Despite being able to push her mind toward making sound predictions, nothing was certain until her eyes saw the outcome carved into stone.

"Honestly? I'm a bit concerned," Ruby answered. "The word *should* is variable. I prefer something more definitive, like we *will* return before twilight."

"*Ahh*. Sorry, mate. But years on the water have taught me to be cautious with promises. Quite simply, nature cannot be bridled. Especially on the open seas." She raised her blonde eyebrows. "You have time constraints, do you?"

"We need to return to this beach before dark," Clay answered.

Ruby didn't want to explain *why* that was the case. But at least her husband understood the witching hour. When the sun sank below the horizon, the King of Darkness *would* wreak havoc on them. And *them* included their guide.

"Well, we'd better stop shooting the breeze, then," Atea said. "Let's get on with it!"

Walking to the inflatable dinghy, their guide handed them each a life-vest that zipped in the front. Good thing the water temperature was manageable because by the time they dragged the vessel back into the water and climbed in, no one was dry.

The ride to Atea's 25-foot Scarab was rough.

After climbing aboard the jet boat, knotting the dinghy's bow line to a cleat, and letting the inflatable vessel drift behind the Scarab, Atea fired up the engine and headed toward Three Kings Islands.

Clay and Gabby sat side-by-side on a cushioned bench framing the bow's half circle shape. He cuddled with their daughter, draped in a wool blanket provided by their guide. Wrapping his arm around Gabby, he held her tightly in the rough seas.

With porcelain skin sensitive to sunlight, Ruby sat beside Atea at the boat's center console, under a canvass canopy that rippled and shuddered with the wind.

Their guide clutched the steering wheel at the helm, expertly maneuvering over the waves.

"Do you live near Cape Reinga?" Ruby asked.

"Close. My wife and I live in a tiny town called Kaitaia, south of Cape Reinga. We grow avocados, but our true passion is showing tourists our beautiful country. Boating to remote places is by far our favorite. We love snorkeling and scuba diving, too."

"Such a great life." Ruby never felt freer than when outdoors. "If you don't mind me asking: what does your name mean?"

"Atea is a nickname. My real name doesn't roll off the tongue easily." The guide shared a full smile, with teeth that were brilliant against her sunbaked skin. "Rangiātea is my birth name. Local folklore explains that baskets of knowledge were stored in the spiritual world within a building called my namesake. My mother had a sense of humor, yeah?"

"Do you know other legends about the area?"

When Atea said she did, Ruby called Clay and Gabby to join them.

Ruby gave her seat to Gabby. Why not make their adventure a teachable moment?

Standing, Ruby was next to their guide. Clay stood beside Gabby.

"Long ago, these lands were inhabited by the Māori tribe," Atea started. "Legend says when the Māori died, their spirits traveled up the coastline to the ancient Pōhutukawa tree at Cape Reinga."

"We saw that tree on our hotel's MV," Gabby said. "So there's *more* than one sacred tree in New Zealand?"

"That's right, mate." Atea smiled. "You see, the Māori called Cape Reinga *Te Rerenga Wairua* or the leaping place of the spirits. The spirits would glide down the Pōhutukawa's roots, splash into the water, and swim to Three Kings Islands. They'd take one last look at their beloved New Zealand before continuing to their resting place."

"And where's that?" their daughter asked.

"A magical place in the underworld called Hawaiki. Also the place where Māui is believed to live. Māui is a mythical superhero known as a 'shifter,' because legend says he could turn himself into a bird. Cool, right?"

"My Mom's a sculptor," Gabby said. "So it's not *that* surprising."

Ruby's heart accelerated.

Please do not share, she whispered into her daughter's mind.

"A sculptor?" Their guide raised her eyebrows.

"Yup," Gabby answered. "She can mold stuff into any shape."

Ruby smiled. She had taught their daughter how to tell the truth without revealing too much, since outright lying was not an option. Still, not sharing *all* of the truth helped minimize potential threats against their family.

Atea seemed satisfied and moved on, sharing several more legends. In fact, they were engrossed in her storytelling.

Everyone jumped when their smartwatches chimed in unison.

Ruby and Clay's vexts were from Justine, warning them that an un-forecasted storm had whipped up in the Tasman Sea, heading for Three Kings Islands.

Atea announced her vext was from a weather app, issuing a maritime warning for the same.

Thunder rumbled in the distance.

The severe thunderstorm was moving northeast, towards them at

62 miles-per-hour.

Whether they turned back or continued forward to Three Kings, hail and 50 mile-per-hour gusts would engulf them.

This inevitability was carved in stone in Ruby's mind.

If only she could control nature, she'd steer the storm in a different direction. Or melt the hail and still the seas. Quiet the wind. But nature was a force without reins.

Atea's seafaring philosophy remained proven.

Nature could not be bridled.

41

Saturday, June 29, 2041
South Pacific and Tasman Sea, New Zealand

CLAY WATCHED THE approaching curtain of crystal torpedoes. Inch by inch, hail advanced on the Scarab.

With plummeting temperatures, the storm was inarguably a beast.

His wife moved behind Gabby who continued to sit in the chair to the right of their guide. Hunching over, Ruby wrapped her arms around their daughter while he held Gabby's hand. As long as they were part of a chain, they could be traveled to safety, if need be.

Hail and turbulent water crept closer.

Their exhales condensed to plumes of chilly fog.

The first ice crystal hit the deck in the bow's open cockpit. The frozen nugget pinged on impact before bouncing.

Wind slammed the vessel on port side, causing the Scarab to heel.

They all squeezed tightly under the boat's canopy. The overhead fabric might protect them from hail, if it held.

Coming from every direction, choppy swells became erratic, making him feel like they were in a washing machine.

Clay had sailed in storms like this one—storms that could swallow a vessel as easy as a pill with water. All he wanted to do was grab the helm and take over. He had no clue if Atea knew what she was doing.

"Give us your assessment, captain," he shouted to Atea, over the roar of the wind and sloshing waves dumping sea water into the bow's cockpit area.

She smiled, looking calm. "Isn't my first rodeo, mate. I've got ballast. We should be stabilized. And I'm slowing down to maintain steering control. Just hold tight."

"I captain our sixty-foot sailing yacht," he said. "Glad to take the helm. Seriously."

"Are you pulling rank on me?" Atea winked at him. "Like yours is bigger than mine?"

Another gust pushed the vessel backwards.

Clay looked toward the stern.

"We've got to release the dinghy," he hollered over the wind. "It's filling with water and acting like an anchor. Not to mention your engine's running hot."

Atea narrowed her eyes. "We need the dinghy to go ashore!"

"First, we've got to *make* it to shore."

"Bloody hell." She frowned. "Okay, agreed. Untie the line. Maybe we'll find the dinghy later, if it's still afloat after the storm passes."

He gently dropped his daughter's hand and turned toward the aft. Ruby grabbed his arm and shook her head.

"What's wrong?" their guide questioned.

"The line just broke," his wife answered. "No longer a problem."

He watched as the dinghy grew smaller with distance.

Nodding at his wife, he visually expressed appreciation that she had sculpted a break in the line.

Relief was short lived.

Without warning, the wind blew horizontal, turning hail into projectiles. The barrage cracked the console's windshield. Sounds of pings and thuds and pops were deafening. The jet engine sputtered.

His frustration was off the charts. Eyeing the helm, he wondered if he should grab the wheel without asking.

Adrenaline made his fingers shake.

Ruby covered their daughter's face and neck with her arms.

"Mommy, I'm scared," Gabby said.

It's time to do more, Ruby whispered into his thoughts.

"Agreed."

She closed her eyes to concentrate. Her whole body shook, and he wondered what she was thinking of. What she would sculpt. Or if she'd travel them to safety.

A boom of thunder rattled the boat and vibrated in his boots. An electrical charge raised the hair on his arms.

Ruby opened her eyes, leading her vision into the physical world.

Rain, hail, and wind could not breach whatever invisible barrier she had constructed above and around the boat. Waves crashed against the clear structure like they were hitting unbreakable glass.

In their protective dome, his wife sculpted their clothes dry.

"What in the...world?" Atea said, looking bewildered.

"So, I'm not a movie star," Ruby confessed. "But I am humankind's vampire warrior."

"Blimey!" their guide said. "I knew you looked familiar. Wait until I tell Harper. She'll freak. Who knew you could do *all* this!"

"We're not out of the woods, yet," Clay cautioned. "You know, your whole *nature cannot be bridled* adage."

"See? My Mom's a sculptor," their daughter said to Atea, with pride in her smile.

"I can see that, mate!" Atea glanced at Ruby. "Have an equally amazing plan to get from my boat to shore? Without a dinghy?"

"Get us to where we can anchor, and I'll take care of the rest."

They arrived near the ragged cliffs of Great Island. The time was already 4:00 p.m., more than two hours behind schedule. Which meant the witching hour couldn't be avoided. To boot, the storm had stalled above the archipelago and was still raging.

After anchoring the boat within the South East Bay of the island, Atea handed him a spare 15-foot nylon line, as he'd requested. Then all four of them, each wearing their backpacks, huddled together. Of course, their guide had no clue why. She was simply instructed not to let go, or she wouldn't make it. Hefty motivation to hold on tight.

His body was enveloped by Ruby's vibration.

In a flash, they were standing atop the rocky trailhead. The rain and wind were still angry, whipping horizontal. He could hear the ocean waves crashing on the cliffs around them.

Despite the conditions, they would travel up the neck of Great Island which connected to the smaller island-head to the north. According to their guide, their destination to The Tree of Three Kings or The Three Kings Kaikomako was located near the cliffs overlooking the North West Bay. At least, that's what Atea had heard, since she'd never actually trekked to the tree.

He handed Ruby the line. "Could you tie four knots and make them equal distance from each other?"

In a whiz of blurred movement, Ruby completed the task and returned the rope to him.

"Harper's going to be so pissed she didn't come today," Atea said.

Clay wasn't ready for small talk. He focused on the challenges ahead. After all, given the conditions and inevitability of nightfall, he was in full-blown Dad mode, obsessed with safety.

For the first time in nearly a decade, he recognized that he and Ruby were finally working with *mutualism*. Both of them were contributing to their existence. She had her role; he had his.

"As we're climbing and hiking," he said, "hold onto your knot and we'll move as a team. Ruby: could you take the lead? I'll take the end. Gabby will be in front of me."

"What happened to *me* being your guide?" No one answered so Atea responded with a shrug. "My ideas aren't any better. I'm game."

A half-hour later, their guide dropped to her knees, pale and out of breath. She shook her head, as if trying to rid herself of whatever ailed her.

Ruby knelt by her side. "Are you okay? What's going on?"

"I'm…I'm not sure." Atea rubbed her chest. "With all the excitement, think my body's saying I need a minute. Do you mind?"

Her vitals are in the normal range, Ruby whispered into his mind.

Clay raised Atea onto her feet and guided her to a tree. While he helped her sit with her back against the trunk, his wife sculpted a mature campfire, protected from rain by large branches and foliage.

Atea was still short of breath.

"Don't suppose…you can delay…the sunset?" She wheezed. "Darkness…darkness is going to crash this party."

His wife shot him a glance which conveyed that Atea had no idea how accurate she was. Darkness would be the opening act to a nightmare named Zagan.

But there was no turning back.

His wife *had* to get to that tree. And he reminded himself that even with the impending dangers, Gabby was still safest with Ruby.

"We'll make the best of it," his wife assured Atea in her I-need-to-keep-everyone-calm voice. "Clay and Gabby threw headlamps and a couple of lanterns into their backpacks, just in case. And I have night vision. Don't worry yourself. Catch your breath." She handed the guide a bottled water and urged her to drink.

A half-hour passed. As everyone hydrated, he downed his flavored water which was far from thirst quenching.

Color returned to Atea's cheeks. She was ready to finish the hike to the Kaikomako.

Ruby sculpted a stream of rainwater to douse the campfire.

After he and Gabby strapped on their headlamps, Atea grabbed a lantern, and all four of them swung their backpacks onto their backs, they retook their positions on the rope. Traveling slowly over uneven ground and volcanic rocks, they hiked under trees and over vegetation toward the steep and cliffy coastline facing the North West Bay.

As their destination neared, the rain stopped. Clouds parted. Pink and orange skies faded in the last minutes of dusk.

Atea pointed. "That's it. Up ahead! The original Tree of Three Kings—the one and only."

Clay could see the tree silhouetted against the dimming sky.

His emotions were conflicted: excitement and fear.

The tree and sunset.

And as the trail ended at the foot of the tree, the last light of the evening was swallowed behind the horizon.

The island was blanketed in darkness.

42

Saturday, June 29, 2041
Great Island: Three Kings Islands, New Zealand

AS THE MOON rose in the night sky, Ruby clasped one of the tree's trunks and opened her mind. Maybe she could whisper with The Tree of Three Kings.

After all, the tree was a living organism with a history. And everyone who touched its leaves, or fruit, or bark left an imprint—a trace of themselves like a memory.

She concentrated on whispering one word to the tree: Zagan.

Her vision blurred as her mind whirled through the expanse of time. Over one mega-annum. Over two. Then nearly one more.

Her eyes opened 2.8 million years ago, back to when the islands were joined with Australia in a microcontinent called Zealandia.

She saw Zagan with a female Shadowlander.

When his companion wasn't looking, he plucked several berries from the tree. Ruby's mind followed the fruit back to Lampsi. She saw everything. Including how, once Zagan's immortality had been restored, he carbonized the vampire whom he professed to have loved.

Ruby's eyes returned to the present. She looked at her husband and daughter, feeling enormous relief.

"This is the tree," she said. "All I need are some berries."

"Flat out of luck, mate," Atea said. "The tree stopped bearing fruit two months ago."

"Shouldn't be a problem."

Altering the fruit wasn't possible. But Ruby had another idea.

Continuing to touch a trunk, Ruby used her mind to rewind the tree back to its fruit bearing cycle. In the dark, The Tree of Three Kings visibly changed as its timeclock reversed. She stopped the process when branches supported clusters of ripe, purple fruit.

"Bloody bizarre," Atea said, holding out her lantern to see the tree's transformation.

"Aren't you glad you accepted this crazy gig?" Clay asked.

Wasting no time in the dark, Ruby listened for Atea's answer while plucking seven grape-like berries from the tree. With her other hand, she broke off a small exposed-root at the tree's base, placing both the root and berries in her windbreaker pockets.

Atea still hadn't answered her husband's lighthearted question, so Ruby turned from the tree to gauge their guide's expression. Was she having more shortness of breath?

With a creased forehead, Atea looked off into space.

"Strange," their guide started. "I...I can't remember *anything* about accepting this tour. Not even the call from our tourism department. My mind is blank until I told Harper about the assignment—I remember *that*. Bonkers right? Maybe some sort of stress amnesia?"

"Let me look into your eyes," Ruby said, walking to their guide and placing her hand under Atea's chin. She gently adjusted the New Zealander's face. "I'll be able to tell what's going on."

Ruby cognitively drilled into her mind, searching for answers. Despite the stress of their journey, Atea was cognitively sharp and didn't seem prone to forgetfulness or anxiety. Ruby also hadn't discounted the guide's normal vitals when she'd suffered from an apparent shortness of breath. The episode had conveniently delayed their hike, ensuring they'd arrive at the tree *after* sunset.

Two oddities added up to suspicious.

Something was amiss.

She deepened her search.

Hidden in the guide's cognitive spectrum of memories was a shielded gap: a memory block. Ruby could actually see it. Moreover, having accepted her station as the most powerful vampire in the universe, she also believed she could unravel the glamour, even though Zagan was its author.

The suppressed memory bulged against the mental chains which the king had imposed. Atea was clearly a strong-willed human.

After breaking the restraints, the memory of Atea's interaction with Zagan released like soda from a shaken bottle.

Their guide's eyes widened in horror.

"Who is...who is that creep?" Atea asked. "The freaky bloke who spoke to me? The one with the strange eyes?"

Ruby explained everything, including Zagan's twisted, evil plans for The Restoration. There was no reason to hold back because the guide's future had crystalized. A future that did *not* include returning to her wife in Kaitaia. Not immediately, anyway.

Glamouring the guide was crucial, if Atea's life was to live on.

With their guide's permission, Ruby delivered her most sophisticated glamour since becoming The Tether in mind, body, and gifts. The cognitive "spell" obliged Atea to serve as Ruby's operative, following orders consistent with military rank, rather than as a puppet. The glamour's sophistication was further amped. The cognitive suggestion prevented Atea from being glamoured by anyone other than Ruby. Moreover, if anyone *tried* to glamour her, she'd be mentally compelled to act as if she was complying. But the most remarkable aspects of the glamour were that Atea would retain conscious awareness of The Tether's intent, while unable to disclose it to others. In other words, Atea could think for herself within the confines of the glamour. The New Zealander would understand the strategies and purpose behind why she was acting as she was.

The glamour stuck, certainly in theory, hopefully in practice.

Ruby also opted to tell their guide the unnerving truth that had flashed in her mind after the glamour: that Atea would be going to High Cliff as a personal servant to Zagan.

Before the night was over.

On the bright side of the vision, Ruby saw how Atea's future, short term, had become carved in stone. Their guide would survive.

"Take two of these," Ruby said, placing two berries in Atea's palm, since dividing the weapons seemed like a solid defensive tactic.

In war, no one stored all their defenses in a single artillery depot.

Whispering in the guide's mind, she added: *Hide these fruits from everyone until I direct you on how and when to use them. Understood?*

Atea nodded.

If Ruby had instructed her to slip the odorless berry juice into Zagan's "divine wine," Atea might have been able to execute the order. But the outcome would be disastrous. Because if Ruby wasn't at the scene when the king turned human, then the opportunity to kill him might be lost, maybe forever.

For starters, Zagan would order their guide to be killed.

Secondly, he'd use one of several options to regain his immortality. He might eat the fruit from the tree in Lampsi, the one which had restored him 2.8 million years ago. Or given his paranoia, he probably kept a supply of his own blood somewhere at High Cliff, in case his immortality was ever compromised. His blood would likely heal him. If not, another vampire's venom could return him to the eternal. Certainly one of his subjects would offer to bite their king, in demonstration of their loyalty.

Truth be told: if Zagan survived a failed assassination attempt— one orchestrated by Ruby, his determination to destroy her family would be relentless. Never ending.

No, she had to be present if the king was to ingest juice from The Tree of Three Kings.

A flash of light interrupted her thoughts.

Her lungs inflated with a gasp.

Although the guide's life was now secure, the lives of Clay and Gabby were no longer evident. She couldn't see their tomorrows.

Goosebumps rose on Ruby's skin.

"Quickly," she told Clay. "While I return the tree to its winter state, you and Gabby take off your jackets. Tie one end of the rope around your waist and knot it. I've sculpted a hole in Gabby's jacket by an underarm. Thread the other end through the hole. Loop and knot it around Gabby, so the rope rests under her armpits. Make sure the tethered distance between you is no more than eighteen inches. Then put your jackets back on to hide the rope."

Everyone looked at her confused.

"Do it," she snapped. *"NOW!"*

Atea helped Gabby remove her jacket.

Clay worked with the rope.

With her hand on the trunk, Ruby concentrated on bringing The

Tree of Three Kings back to its fruitless state.
    When her task was complete, she turned around.
    Atea was zipping their daughter's jacket.
    "What's next?" Clay asked.
    She raised her eyes to the night sky.
    A bat was silhouetted in the moonlight.
    And then it swooped.

43

Saturday, June 29, 2041
Great Island: Three Kings Islands, New Zealand

ZAGAN METAMORPHOSED FROM his bat incarnation, materializing in vampire form, dressed in black leathers veiled by his cloak. Appearing near his nemesis and her mayflies, he could not resist glancing at the forbidden tree. Standing as a beacon of heartbreak, he surrendered to its pull for attention.

The ache in his heart was weaker than anticipated, though his chest tightened as memories surfaced. He pictured his ancient companion beside him, smiling in the sun. She was more beautiful and tempting than any fruit. This fact now soured his tongue.

The ripened berries had been his undoing.

While Zagan had been cruelly altered—stripped of everything he once loved—the tree appeared unaffected by his transgression.

He hated himself for the weaknesses of his youth.

He abhorred the tree even more.

"Well?" Ruby asked, interrupting his thoughts as she inched closer to her husband and daughter. "Are you here for a reason? Because Gabby needs to return to our hotel for bed. And since the tree's not bearing fruit, we were just leaving."

He glared at the child who carried his stolen blood in her veins. She stood stoic, seemingly unafraid.

"Do you know who I am, Gabriella?" he asked.

The child said nothing.

Zagan shifted his eyes to Ruby. "Have you not instructed your offspring on politeness?"

"Thanks to you," Ruby answered, "Gabby's been traumatized by our housefire. When she gets nervous, she stops speaking."

"If only the same affliction affected your brash tongue." He glanced at Atea, wishing to detect if his glamour had been discovered. "And who is this? A pet, perhaps?"

"Don't touch her," the male mayfly ordered. "She has nothing to do with our dispute."

Zagan was pleased with the response, as it indicated that the tour guide's glamour remained hidden. Which meant the human could be of further use to him. After all, he had drained his personal servant Felicity and desired a replacement. Atea was not as youthful or as appetizing as Felicity, but clearly, she was naturally susceptible to glamouring.

Sculpting a magnetic force, he drew Atea to his side and clasped her wrist with his left hand.

The guide did not resist, though her face wore tension.

"Leave. Her. Alone," Ruby's mate snapped.

"Your command could be fulfilled in several ways, mayfly."

"Clay only wants to protect someone vulnerable," Ruby countered. "Since you tend to provoke those who aren't equipped to provide a challenge."

"Yet, if I were your human spouse," Zagan warned, "I would focus on my own vulnerabilities. Have you not explained that I can turn him to ashes with a sweep of my hand?"

"Not everyone is as afraid of death as you are," she taunted.

Zagan's temperature rose. He tired of the exchange.

"Perhaps," he added, "your pathetic mayfly has never faced the clutches of death."

Ruby jolted to grab her husband.

But Zagan unleashed a magnetic pulse with his hand that knocked her back 20-feet, causing her to tumble to the ground.

"Stop!" she begged. "Leave him alone."

"This command *alone* has been repeated. I shall comply, sending him to where no other will follow." Zagan raised his right hand.

"Nooo!" she cried.

A transparent shield raised in front of her mate.

Did the Earthling vampire truly believe the barrier could stop him? The king cracked the shield with his mind, and it shattered like glass. Without hesitation, he swept his hand to carbonize the mayfly.

The human named Clay remained standing.

As Ruby rose to her feet, the king swept his hand again.

Nothing.

"What is this?" he said, more to himself. Confused.

Never had his attempts to carbonize not been effective.

Ruby dusted off her jeans and straightened her back, shedding off the fear she had projected moments before. She moved next to her husband and daughter.

"You won't be sending Clay anywhere," she seethed.

"I do not understand this…" He was unaccustomed to sounding disoriented and weak, but no other responses rose to his tongue. After all, with a mere wave of his hand, he had turned others to ashes for three mega-annum.

"I'm surprised," she said. "You haven't learned that intelligence is the greatest weapon of all. Three-million years old and you still haven't caught on?"

"Have you given him…my blood?"

"Yours. Mine. What's the difference?" Ruby asked. "Of course I served him *our* blood. Sometimes in milkshakes. Other times in flavored water. All to invoke the protection of self-preservation. We can't carbonize each other. While our blood is concentrated in his system, you can't turn him to ashes either."

"Clever, Lady Spencer," Zagan said. "Clever but naive."

With no more words, the king pulled down lightning from a lingering thunderhead. The bolt struck Ruby, scorching her further with an assault of flying sparks. As she fell to the ground smoldering, he released a force so violent that the earth cracked around them. The mayflies fell onto their knees, clutching the vegetation to steady themselves, save for Atea whose hand he held.

Fierce tremors shook The Tree of Awareness until it toppled into a deep, black crevice and was swallowed whole by earth and rocks. Collecting the wind, he blew a force that could have parted the sea.

Ruby's husband and daughter blew off the cliff like tiny seeds in a gale, tumbling toward the raging seas and ragged rocks below.

The Earthling vampire recovered from the lightning strike enough to leap off the cliff after her plunging mayflies. Perhaps all three would be crushed on the volcanic spikes protruding above the ocean's surface.

To be certain, he forced Atea to join him on the cliff's edge, as he peered down toward the blackened sea. A large splash in the water generated contentment. A sense of peace. Of closure.

He suppressed more conflicted emotions, forcing them to retreat into the abyss from which they stewed.

With his nemesis destroyed, he could focus on more pressing matters. The Restoration.

About to travel to High Cliff with the mayfly in tow, his eyes spotted two berries on the ground by his feet. The berries from The Tree of Awareness nested on the vegetation, undoubtedly harvested by Ruby prior to his arrival.

The berries were a gift. Perhaps a sign from his Human/Immortal Maker that Zagan's youthful transgression had finally been atoned.

If by slim chance Ruby survived her plummet into the violent sea, Zagan possessed the weapon which could destroy her. He would use the berry juice to reinstate her mortality before ripping out her heart.

Zagan's pathway was being sanctified by HIM.

The Restoration was in his grasp.

He could nearly taste the sweetness of victory on his lips.

44

Saturday, June 29, 2041
Great Island: Three Kings Islands, New Zealand

RUBY'S BODY WAS seized by instinct and impulse. Every muscle, every joint, every neurotransmitter coordinated with one purpose: to save Clay and Gabby. To rescue them from a brutal death on the jagged rocks and angry ocean waiting at the base of the cliff.

Ruby hurled herself off the rocky ledge in pursuit.

In freefall towards the water, she sculpted her backpack straps to break away, allowing her body to become an aerodynamic missile. All in the course of a nanosecond.

The force and speed of her dive blurred her vision. Friction pressed against her face, stretching her skin. Her pounding heart distributed oxygen throughout her system. Teeth clenched in determination. And hypertension caused her nose to bleed.

Look for us, Mom, Gabby whispered into her mind.

Ruby's eyes focused, spotting them below her. Still tethered together by the rope, they seemed peaceful, offering no resistance while falling. No flailing arms or terrified screams. They looked as though they had intentionally leapt from the 552-foot cliff for a moonlit swim.

Having already fallen 100-feet, their bodies were about to be crushed in 4.98 seconds.

Ducking her chin, she pressed her arms against her sides, adding acceleration. She couldn't fail. Their lives depended on her.

Now: 3.76 seconds.

Ruby crashed into her husband's body, unintentionally driving her elbow into his face. She clutched his jacket's collar. Yanking him and Gabby toward her, she wrapped her legs around them. Together, they violently tumbled—head over heel—dropping toward the raging seas, limbs tangled for the last 112-feet before impact.

Seconds remaining: 1.24.

Touching was all the contact she needed.

As ocean spray greeted them with .55 seconds until impact, she turned her family into dust, as her backpack splashed into the water.

Remnants of motion traveled with them as they materialized. With force, they slammed onto the living room floor of the Westin Annapolis. Ruby somersaulted over the carpet until her back crashed against a bookcase, toppling books and knocking over an adjacent floor lamp. Clay and Gabby rolled in a similar path, stopping when their bodies rammed into hers.

She briefly closed her eyes to appreciate the sound of their lungs expanding and contracting. Of their heartbeats pumping rapidly. Everyone was alive.

Clay wrapped his arms around Gabby and kissed her on the forehead.

"Gabby?" Ruby asked, sitting up. "Are you okay, sweetie?"

Their daughter nodded.

"Did you hear me, Mom? When we were falling? I tried to whisper to you."

"I heard you," Ruby said, lowering her adrenaline to normal levels and carbonizing the rope connecting Clay with their daughter. "And you're amazing."

Gabby beamed with pride. Moreover, she was relaxed and talking. Which meant Zagan wasn't present. Another relief, since she didn't want to deal with the bastard right now.

With a green light to speak freely, Ruby explained to Clay how their daughter was a whisperer, in addition to a healer. Her gifts were awakening and powerful, even as a human.

Assessing her family for injuries, Ruby noticed her husband's black eye. No doubt her elbow had whacked him when they made contact during their freefall. But he shrugged off the discomfort. Anyway, with her blood in his system, she could already see signs of healing.

"The berries?" he asked. "Do you have them? And the root?"

With the commotion, she hadn't considered that they might have fallen out of her jacket.

Reaching into her right pocket, she exhaled as she clasped grape-like berries. She withdrew her hand, straightened her fingers, and displayed them in her palm.

Her husband's eyes widened. "Didn't you have five berries left *after* you gave Atea two?"

"Two more are missing," she said, nodding. "Give me a minute to locate them."

She'd start with Atea. Her thoughts would be easy to penetrate.

Closing her eyes, Ruby cognitively traveled into Atea's mind. Their guide was at High Cliff, in the king's study. Ruby drilled into the New Zealander's mind and learned that Zagan had retrieved the berries which had fallen from her pocket as she dove off the cliff.

Despite the king having two berries, Ruby continued to hold the advantage. Zagan had no clue she could cognitively travel into the New Zealander's mind anytime she wanted—to see and hear what Atea saw and heard. A powerful conduit for information, as long as their guide's glamour and loyalties remained undetected.

She updated Clay and Gabby about the missing berries as she lowered her other hand into her left pocket. Thankfully, her fingers clasped the bumpy root. She smiled and handed it to her husband.

"See? Miracles happen every day," he said, flashing his pearly whites. "Doors open more than they close." He held the root in front of him. "I'll water this bad boy. It'll sprout back."

Even with Clay's positive attitude, a swell of worry drowned the relief she had felt moments ago.

Reality was setting in.

For starters, Zagan had proven his determination to kill her family. Inarguably, the first two battles (the housefire and the confrontation on Three Kings) had ended in victory for the Spencers. But one defeat—just one—would bench her on the sidelines of the war. Her heart and mind would not survive the loss of her husband or daughter. Exactly the outcome Zagan wanted: to emotionally disable her, gain an opportunity to destroy her, and implement The

Restoration without resistance.

Which meant she had to protect her family and the world, no matter the cost.

She loved Clay and Gabby more than life itself.

And humanity needed her as their protector.

A plan crystalized, but it was wretched and cruel.

Light flashed in Ruby's mind as she accepted the sacrifice.

At last, her husband and daughter's survival, over the short-term, was carved in stone.

But the etchings which had been forming on *her* stone faded to smooth and blank.

45

Saturday, June 29, 2041
Kaliméra Castle: Lampsi, Athanasia

LIORA FOUND SOLACE on a wooden bench in her rose garden. Fountains sprayed water, misting birds perched on the slate coping of the cement pond. Sunbeams danced over ripples, resembling sparkling confetti. Raising and lowering their patterned wings, butterflies drank nectar from the surrounding flora, adding to the tapestry of color. And ruby-throated hummingbirds busily sipped from feeders, chirping their contentment.

But the queen was absent joy.

Her heart was heavy.

The future grew darker, not brighter.

Solange opened the wrought-iron gate between the stone columns marking the garden's entrance.

"Must I always search for you, Queen?" her assistant asked as she neared the bench. "I started in your favored garden of peonies and hydrangeas. Yet, here you are among the roses."

"Thorns remind me that beautiful things are not without pain."

"More disturbing glances into the future?" Solange queried, sitting beside her on the bench.

Liora nodded, feeling tears well in her eyes.

"Lighten your burden. Share what is to come," Solange said. "The load will be bearable if we both carry its weight. Am I not correct?"

The queen, however, had no plans to disclose truths involving her longest and dearest assistant. She could if she chose to, since the outcome had already been carved.

Liora elected to be merciful, instead.

If Solange was not aware of the impending future, then she could focus on the blooms and fragrance. Not on the thorns.

Thorns were Liora's burden until the future arrived and left its unsightly wounds.

"The weight of what is to come falls where it should," Liora said, forcing her lips to curl up. "To more pleasant thoughts. I have a message from Titus, after I whispered to him while he was visiting Draven."

"He journeyed to the prison once more?"

"Indeed. The king ordered a facility inspection, which your mate fulfilled. As before, Titus used the opportunity to provide sustenance to Draven, although the king had not commanded it. I advised him against this blatant disobedience. You would be wise to encourage the same."

Her assistant rubbed her hands together in eagerness. Her cheeks blushed to match her pink gown.

"Will I have the opportunity to reinforce your advisement? For I would like nothing more," Solange asked, grinning.

"You shall. Titus has already returned to High Cliff to serve Zagan. However, when his duties have been completed, he will ride back to my cottage in Gray Forest, in hopes of meeting you there."

Solange nearly leapt from the bench.

"There is no time for gloom, then!" her assistant said. "I must prepare for a rendezvous with my mate."

She curtsied before turning and bustling away from the garden.

Liora could not coax another smile.

While unions were forming, others were ending.

And thorns marked them both.

46

Saturday, June 29, 2041
Castle on High Cliff: Skotadi, Athanasia

ZAGAN COMMANDED ATEA to drink his blood from a bite wound he had inflicted on his wrist.

Standing by the roaring fire in his study, the mayfly glared at him with pursed lips that revealed her displeasure, but she did not resist the order. This human possessed an intelligence and inner strength which made her valuable, though he would glamour her again to ensure her assets served him and no other.

Although he did not wish to admit the truth, Ruby forced him to think defensively. Foolishly, he had not considered that she might feed her blood to her mate, protecting him from being carbonized by the king. The strategy was both simple and brilliant.

Undoubtedly, if Zagan did not begin to anticipate his opponent's clever tactics or employ some of his own, death would surely greet him. And as Ruby had accurately elucidated on the island, Zagan feared nothing except the prospect of his own death.

Compared to her pitiful 36-year existence on an inferior planet, he could apply wisdom gleaned over three mega-annum.

Nevertheless, he cautioned himself not to trivialize his opponent. Which is why he wanted to add two more to his inner circle. A "circle" which presently consisted of him and his henchman.

With the king's temperament, he thought it best to safeguard the weakest among his new confidants: Atea. Otherwise, he might carbonize her at the first sign of irritation.

Surely an army could not be built if its commander destroyed soldiers every time one required correction. The army would vanish, leaving no souls to fight the enemy.

His blood in Atea's veins would shield her from...himself.

"What now, mate?" Atea asked.

"*Mate?* I do not couple with...humans," he growled, flashing his fangs. He was thankful his blood already coursed through the mayfly's body or he might have turned her to ashes for the reference. "Never call me such. For I am your king. Your ruler. Master of your life and death."

"Oh, sorry. Just a Kiwi expression." She raised her blonde eyebrows. "Are you always this cheery, *maa...?*" She swallowed. "I mean, king of all the universe and beyond?"

"Cheery indeed. For instead of calculating countless ways to end your life, I am trying to save it. A most rare occurrence. Especially since you are a mayfly."

"Good to know." She ran the heel of her hand over her forehead, wiping beads of moisture. "Assuming you're going to keep me close, care to mention what I'll be doing?" She looked at the bats flitting into the study from the outside. "Cleaning up bat guano, perhaps?"

"You shall manage my sustenance," Zagan answered. "You will be a procurer of blood. The one who guarantees my supply is safe for consumption and of the highest quality. Failure on either count will bring a grueling death. But first, you must dress the part."

Zagan sculpted a pale green A-line gown in his arms. He held the dress in front of him, in hopes that she would be pleased with the fitted bodice and the intricate lace work, in addition to the long, flowing skirt.

"Oh, no, no, no," she protested.

"Have I misjudged? I believed your color palette fell within the pastels of Spring." He changed the gown color to bright orange. "Does your skin tone favor Autumn instead?"

"Now I'm gobsmacked," she said in mayfly gibberish. "Who knew you were a fashionista? But seriously, King Z, I'm not the gown type, not even if you snapped your fingers and made one rainbow colored. See, in New Zealand, I ride a motorcycle with my only mate: Harper. So could you cut me a break? Like let me wear leathers or my jeans?"

He sculpted a leather jacket and pants, draping them on his chair.

"Do you find the studded leather jacket more suitable?" he asked.

Atea ran her hands over the finely crafted outfit. "Way more. Thanks." She placed her hands on her hips. "Back to my job. How am I going to procure blood? If you told me I'd be baking lolly cakes and biscuits in Kaitaia, well, I'd figure out the job quickly. But this whole...debonair vampire king living in a castle cave with bats on a pitch-black planet where dust is a form of transportation...is a bit wonky. Not to mention you've made the consequences clear if your taste buds don't end up skipping down a catwalk. Bloody hell."

The mayfly had an appetite for words. He was thankful for the expected knock on the door which interrupted her verbal gluttony.

Raising his hand, he urged the mayfly to silence her tongue.

"Enter, Jasmine," the king commanded.

The vampire who glided into his study was breathtaking, adorned with long white hair that flaunted a peculiar streak of pale yellow.

Jasmine wore a simple sheath-gown of yellow satin. One could mistake her as sunshine in the realm of darkness. But there was no special treatment for brightness on Skotadi, though he hoped Jasmine's assignment would not extinguish her radiance. She had attracted his attention, after all.

"Your Excellency, I am here to serve," she said.

Zagan invited the two new members of his inner circle to sit at the slate-topped table on the right side of his study.

Both subjects listened attentively as he explained his plan.

Five humans—those deemed the healthiest and having the most flavorful blood—were moved from their stations in nearby villages to an expansive containment chamber at High Cliff, made more comfortable with the trappings of mayflies. Guards protected the isolated wing. No one was to enter or leave the enclosure, save for Atea and Jasmine.

Immediately prior to meals, his two procurers would collect blood from the confined subjects. After, Jasmine would heal their wounds while Atea arranged a buffet of mayfly food. The goal was to have his "donors" regain their strength as quickly as possible.

A reflection of balance.

Once in the dais—while his procurers stood before him, a carafe of the freshly gathered divine-wine would be poured into a goblet. Jasmine would taste the libation. Atea would slice the vampire's hand with a knife. If the incision healed, the wine would be safe for consumption—proven to be free of poisons such as mortality or vervain.

If Jasmine's wound did not heal, meaning she had become mortal, both procurers would be slayed on the spot.

No more need to switch cups between those with whom he dined.

His predicament demanded more complex and sophisticated defenses and his new mealtime ritual coalesced higher levels of both.

After Zagan finished his summation to Atea and Jasmine, he glamoured them.

When dismissed, the vampire would escort the mayfly to her quarters where she could refresh and dress. After all, the king was growing hungry and eager to put his brilliant safeguard into practice.

His procurers departed, closing the door to his study.

Alone once more, he pulled the berries from his cloak's pocket. He would conceal them in his hidden chamber, next to his vial of blood. The berries would be known to no one except Titus. They would remain in the chamber until the king solidified a plan to destroy Ruby.

The expression *bloody hell* seemed most appropriate for what he had in mind.

47

Saturday, June 29, 2041
Westin Annapolis to Castle on High Cliff

IN THEIR BED at the hotel, Ruby waited until her husband fell into a deep sleep. No doubt he was exhausted from 24-hours of traveling, boating, hiking, enduring horrible weather, and cheating death.

For her, there was no rest.

Ruby knew what she had to do since there was only one choice that would ensure Clay and Gabby's survival in the immediate future.

Her stomach churned in protest.

She leaned over her husband and gently kissed his lips. "I love you," she said softly, feeling like a soldier leaving for war, not knowing if she'd ever return.

Thankfully, Zagan had inadvertently given her several ideas.

Without a sound, she tiptoed to the window where she'd seen a moth fluttering before bedtime. She offered her hand and the insect accepted the invitation. Raising her finger to eye level, she glamoured the fuzzy passenger into dormancy.

Returning to the bedside, she lowered the moth onto the sheets where moments before, she had rested beside Clay. She sculpted the insect to resemble her physically.

She gazed at her imitation, pleased with her precision.

Traveling to Gabby's room, she kissed her daughter goodbye. A tear raced down Ruby's cheek. Even though her imminent journey was meant to be temporary—to forge a deal and truce, the risks were tremendous.

With a blank stone, Ruby's future continued to be unknown.

Humming and vibrating, her body turned to dust.

From this point onward, every move she'd make would serve to attract Zagan, to earn his trust. To distract him from using his defenses to advance The Restoration. Or to hurt her family.

Hopefully in the process, she'd find a way to destroy him.

With or without the berries. With or without Atea's help.

She arrived in the king's study, unannounced—a move beyond dangerous. But at least her arsenal of weapons was better stacked than his. Which included her breasts, because she planned to capitalize on Zagan's knack for caving into temptation.

Her sculpted dress was formal. The evening gown from 18th century Paris was off-the-shoulder, handcrafted in red satin, with a plunging neckline that revealed her cleavage and plumped much of her chest above the fabric. With hair raised in a bun accented by delicate blooms of baby's-breath, her face was framed by soft curls. A seven-carat ruby teardrop-pendant, edged with diamonds, hung from her neck. Her lobes were adorned with matching earrings.

Visually, her intentions were clear: to resemble a queen.

Still wearing his black cloak, Zagan spun around, no doubt to confront the uninvited invasion to his privacy. His lips thinned. With roving eyes, he stood speechless.

"Lady Spencer lives," he said, at last. "Bravo."

"My family as well."

His eyes narrowed, as if momentarily surprised.

"Boldly entering the lion's den, are we?" he asked, relaxing his features and restoring his usual arrogance. "Do you honestly think my beastly jaws will remain closed? Not likely, since you are far from blameless."

"As are you, King," she said, nearing him, the hem of her full gown sweeping over the stone floor. "But I wasn't thinking *lion's den*. More like conquer your enemies with love."

"*Ahh.* Originally spoken by a non-violent activist for humanity. Yet, ninety-three years ago, Gandhi could not conquer death. Despite love, his mortal enemy swallowed him whole, rotting his flesh."

He closed the gap between them.

Ruby could feel his breath on her bare chest.

"I advise you to disclose what you want," Zagan warned, "before my patience is drained."

"I came to learn what *you* really want, King."

"Are we embarking on wordplay, Lady Spencer? Because my intentions have been absent ambiguity. I *want* you and your pathetic mayfly family…dead."

"This is the reason you falter more than succeed," she said.

"Refutable, of course. Especially with your lying tongue. But I presume you will enlighten me with clarification. Or am I to make the connection between my desire to destroy the Spencer coven with your accusation of faltering?"

Internally, Ruby felt relieved that Zagan was tolerating her banter. She aimed to deliver a hook that would lure him in. Thankfully, he was giving her the opportunity to cast.

She pivoted to the side, making sure her movement didn't resemble a retreat. "I've noticed you tend to sacrifice lofty goals for meager ones, delaying your achievement of the extraordinary."

As she finished her response, she heard a whisper in her mind. She had blocked Liora, and Gabby was fast asleep in the hotel. Who could be interrupting her thoughts with a request to be heard?

Pardon me, Lady Spencer, the voice said in her mind. *I am Titus, the king's henchman. You are in danger here, but I will do my best to protect you.*

"And ridding the universe of you and your family is not an extraordinary goal?" Zagan asked, as if amused.

"Our deaths would be an inconsequential detail, since The Restoration will proceed with or without us. However, other details might derail your efforts if you're not paying attention. While you've been chatting with me, for example, you've been missing a detail that might be significant."

I am a servant of The Tether, the whisperer interrupted.

"Now I am curious." Zagan moved towards her again. "What detail am I missing?"

She raised her eyebrows. "We're not speaking in private. An eavesdropper is on the other side of the door."

He twisted his neck toward the door, like an owl.

"Whose ears listen without invitation?" he squawked.

The door swung open.

A warrior entered the study, presumably Titus—the one whispering to her. His head was slightly bowed. Wearing armor, his gray features resembled Draven's, only this henchman wore spikey hair like the king's.

The henchman whispered into her thoughts, with a snarky edge: *How shall I ever repay my gratitude?*

In return, Ruby was cognitively silent.

"Apologies, Your Excellency," Titus said. "I merely returned to inform you that all preparations for the procurements have been completed. I only stood in patience by the door, opting against interruption, given you were entertaining a guest."

"My *uninvited* guest is leaving," Zagan announced.

"Prematurely," she added. "I haven't shared my proposal which aligns perfectly with what I think you desire most. But hey, my mother always told me: unwelcomed guests should never linger."

She began to turn herself into dust.

"A proposal?" he asked. "To what purpose?"

She halted her travel. "To advance the extraordinary, of course."

"Henchman," Zagan said. "Have Atea and Jasmine bring divine wine—for two—into my library, instead of the dais. Lady Spencer and I will discuss her proposal there. And when you have completed this task, you may retire for rest."

Titus nodded before turning and leaving the study.

"Felicity no longer serves your meals?" Ruby asked.

"Her immaturity was sweet, yet draining," the king said. "I have transferred her to a nearby village." He offered his arm. "Let us walk to the library, instead of travel."

She clasped his bicep and smiled.

The hook had been set.

48

Saturday, June 29, 2041
Castle on High Cliff to The Cottage of Shadows

TITUS MOUNTED HIS black stallion and galloped toward The Shadowlands, wearing his cloak which flapped behind him. The moon and lanterns lit his path by the river. A thin blanket of fog carpeted the ground, swirling when disrupted by his horse's gait.

A part of him had wanted to cancel his rendezvous with Solange, for no other reason than to monitor Ruby's visit with the king, to protect her if needed. But he had reminded himself that The Tether was the most powerful vampire in all the universe. And besides, with her having an abundance of every gift known to immortals, she clearly did not need his assistance. Nor did her attitude wish for it.

Whispering was Titus's only extraordinary gift.

As his stallion galloped from darkness to grayness, he smiled, remembering that whispering was not his *only* gift. He possessed yet another worth celebrating: lovemaking. And Solange reminded him that not all were equipped with this competence in equal measure.

He would gladly work on perfecting this talent with his mate. To boldly rise above all others.

Near the end of his journey, he and his horse entered the Gray Forest—which curiously mimicked nightfall. The tall, thick pines stood closely together, forming a canopy which smothered the gray light of his homeland.

Even though he could physically live anywhere he chose on Athanasia, his heart belonged amongst the shadows. In the future, when Zagan was defeated and the planet was unified once more, he and Solange would build their own home nearby. Their happily-ever-after.

The Cottage of Shadows appeared ahead.

He nudged his horse with his heels.

Titus's heart raced.

The blinds had been lowered on the windows. If not for smoke rising from the chimney, the cottage looked as though no one was inside. Not even Solange's mare was tied by the back entrance. For concealment, she always left her horse deep within the forest, a distance from the dwelling.

Since the parcel was already secluded, he did not feel the need for such precautions. Besides, the surrounding land belonged to the Queen of Light.

After tying his stallion's reins to the post, he ran into the home. Candlelight and glowing logs in the fireplace greeted him. He smiled, smelling the fragrance of roses.

Solange sprinted from the bedchamber.

Sweeping his love into his arms, he carried her back to the room from which she came, kissing her as he walked. He laid her on the bed. From that moment, love and lust, sensuality and eroticism, took over. The pleasure was both emotional and physical. A whirlwind of delight and gratification.

Yes, he and Solange were surely lovers. Not fighters.

When their lovemaking had satisfied them both, Titus leaned on his side, facing his beloved. He let his hand linger on her breast while they talked.

He confessed his confusion and worry about Ruby exposing his eavesdropping to Zagan. Perhaps her loyalty was not guaranteed.

"Your concern is echoed by our queen," Solange said. "Blocked from Ruby's mind, Liora has allowed doubt to weaken her faith in The Tether as well."

"Actions are indicators of faith. Are they not? And I witnessed her actions with my own eyes. I *saw* justification for the apprehension."

"Faith exists regardless of sight or blindness," she answered. "Consider that truths may be withheld from us for our own safety."

"Done," he said.

"Without argument?" Solange asked, her eyebrows raised.

"None," he said. "In the spirit of balance, however, I have a consideration for you. Although we are not seers of the future, we are proficient whisperers. Ruby does not know you exist and is not yet hostile towards you. Would you consider cognitively visiting her in hopes of sharing a word? Perhaps you could appeal to her sensibilities. Perhaps she will not be as guarded with you as she has been with Liora and me."

"*Hmm*. Since the request comes from your lips, I shall consider whispering to Ruby." Solange placed her hand on his cheek, caressing his skin with her thumb. "Now from our queen, I have a warning to deliver. Do not tempt the king by disregarding his commands. Draven is strong. He can survive without blood for an extended period. Do not risk being caught, as the act of bringing blood into the prison would be treasonous. Consequences would be dire."

"I hear truth in your words," he said. "The risks no longer escape me. For I detected a small breach in my wineskin while conducting my inspection of the prison. Divine wine had leaked into my cloak's pocket, though just a drop."

She propped herself up by her elbows and sniffed the air.

His cloak rested on the bed's end.

"Tell me this is not so," she said, her eyes wide. "I can smell it. And you know that human blood is far more fragrant than the prison rations of bitter swine blood. Not even the king's henchman would be pardoned for such a violation."

He heard her heart racing.

"I am certain the pungent air in the bowels of the pits masked the blood's scent or as you have stated, the guards would not have let my infraction go unnoticed or unpunished."

"You must not endanger yourself, Titus."

"Do not worry," he said. "The breach was slight and I…"

Solange placed her finger on his lips to stop his protest.

"Offer assurances with your lovemaking, Henchman," she said. "Your passion carries lengthy persuasion when enticed by action over words."

When he lowered his lips to hers, his mate froze.

Then she trembled.

"What has happened?" he asked.

"Liora has whispered to me. Zagan will be coming to see you. Here. As the logs in the fireplace turn to embers. I must leave at once."

She sprang from the bed and began dressing.

"The king? *Here?* In Liora's cottage?"

"Dress, Titus!"

While throwing on his shirt and pants, his heart pounded.

Adrenaline raced through his veins.

Imminent danger ignited his senses.

"Take my stallion," Titus said.

"My mare awaits in the forest. And Liora assures me I will return, unharmed, to Kaliméra."

Dressed, she stood in front of him. Placing both hands on his cheeks, she rose on her tiptoes. *"You* remain safe, my love. Stay reverent and humble. And know that Liora would not have me leave if you were in grave danger. This I know. For surely, I would risk my life for you. Without hesitation."

She kissed him.

"Remember," she added, "do not tempt fate. Do *not* provoke the king in any way."

A lump formed in his throat.

His mate hurried to the cottage's back door, throwing it open.

She glanced over her shoulder at him, creases marking her forehead. Racing over the threshold, she ran into the grayness toward the forest's edge.

He watched until she faded into the darkness of the dense trees.

49

Saturday, June 29, 2041
Castle on High Cliff to The Cottage of Shadows

ZAGAN'S ATTRACTION TO Lady Spencer was most uncanny.

After she had thrown herself off the cliff on Great Island, his heart surprised him. Rather than elation, he had felt a tinge of regret. In truth, his emotional palette had never been fuller than when he was in her presence.

More astonishing, when Ruby unexpectedly appeared in his study, glittering like the ruby gemstone accenting her neck, his heart sputtered as it once had for his true love.

Ruby was elegant and regal, as well as confident and powerful. And although her proposal might eventually prove to be a diversionary maneuver or feint in their wargame, he could not resist the offer of hearing it.

He and Lady Spencer entered the library, lit by a roaring fire and an overhead chandelier boasting five-dozen candles. For privacy, he closed the door behind them with his mind.

Though the chamber was coveted by his subjects, access to the library was restricted. Not even his beloved bats were permitted entry into the space. Because the original hand-written Book of Immortality, containing the Sacred Scrolls, was displayed on a pedestal crafted in solid gold near the north bookcase.

Light danced on the colorful book-spines and he smiled.

Books had become his mistress, attempting to fill the void of loneliness beyond which his bats could remedy. Indeed, his appetite for reading was second only to his thirst for power.

Ruby gracefully glided from bookcase to bookcase, gazing at titles. Her eyes were eager and alive.

"Oh, if I lived in this castle," she said, "I'd spend my time here."

"I would not have guessed it," Zagan mused.

"Why not?" She turned to face him; her green eyes narrowed with the question.

"With your cleavage exposed, I predicted the bedchamber was more to your liking."

She rolled her eyes. "My cleavage was acceptable when you sculpted the leather outfit on my first visit here. But *now* the valley between my breasts offends you? Should I sculpt a less revealing neckline to keep your delicate innocence intact?"

"Choosing the bedchamber as a preferred room is perfectly acceptable, as is your cleavage." Zagan chuckled. "I would avoid assumptions regarding my judgments, Lady Spencer. As I enjoy many things, in unlimited rooms—where innocence is hardly a prerequisite. My words merely represented an observation based on details; a proficiency you claimed was deficient in me."

A knock interrupted her rebuttal.

Opening the door, Zagan found the prison guard whom he had been expecting.

The king glanced over his shoulder at Ruby. "Forgive me, but I must confer with my subject. Acquaint yourself with the books on the shelves, and I shall return shortly."

Entering the hallway, he closed the door behind him.

As the prison guard began to speak, Zagan raised his index finger to his lips. Clasping the guard's arm with his other hand, he guided him away from the library, stopping to talk further down the corridor where he was certain Ruby could not overhear their conversation.

He would, however, attend to his surroundings in the event Ruby decided to sculpt into an incarnation to eavesdrop, though his concern was minimal. In truth, Titus and his earlier visit to the prison had no connection or significance to the Earthling vampire.

As Zagan had suspected, the guard delivered news requiring his immediate attention.

After the guard's departure, the king returned to his library.

"Lady Spencer, I extend my apologies once again," he said, hoping to sound sincere. "A business matter requires my involvement. If you choose to wait, enjoy my library. But please be warned: touching the sacred book is forbidden."

"Does your business matter involve my husband and daughter?"

"I am not obligated to disclose the nature of my dealings. My kingdom is far from a democracy. However, since we are enjoying a temporary truce, I can assure you I will not be visiting your mayflies on *this* night."

"I'm curious, how long will you take?" Ruby asked.

"Time is relative, is it not? By immortal standards, I shall return quickly. Applying human standards, by which you shamefully measure time, a mayfly could read, perhaps, six-thousand words."

Without waiting to hear her response, he turned to dust.

Zagan traveled to The Cottage of Shadows.

The gray cabin was quaint, even charming, and had been rebuilt over a dozen times since he had visited the getaway in his youth.

He materialized near the back entrance, beside the stallion which belonged to his henchman. The beast pushed his muzzle against the king's chest, using his lips to find passage under Zagan's cloak, in hopes of finding sugar cubes. Which was a grave mistake on this occasion, not that the horse could have avoided the inevitable. Quite simply, his services had expired.

With a sweep of his hand, the stallion was reduced to ashes.

Zagan brushed off several gray flecks from his cloak.

Before traveling inside the dwelling, he noticed footprints—without question, belonging to a female. The prints led to the dense tree line and were swallowed by the forest. He shook his head. When he had commanded Titus to retire for rest, he found the henchman's interpretation quite remarkable.

Zagan traveled into the den.

Embers glowed in the fireplace.

Titus exited from the bedchamber. Wearing wrinkled clothing, his disheveled henchman instantly bowed his head.

"Good to see you, King," Titus said, with no hint of alarm. "Do you require my services at High Cliff after all?" He tucked his shirt into his pants. "For I shall gather my things, if so."

"Are you not surprised that I have found you?" Zagan asked.

"Found? Found implies I was hiding. Or lost," Titus said. "Neither would be accurate. As I am sure your acute senses can detect, I enjoyed the pleasure of a female companion."

The king scowled.

"Apologies, Your Excellency. Should I have asked first?" Titus's eyebrows tightened. "Is your henchman not permitted to indulge in physical pleasures?"

"Most certainly *not* in a harlot's lair belonging to the Queen of Light," Zagan roared, hoping to convey that the conversation had no promise of going well.

Titus gasped. "This cottage belongs to...*Liora?"* He squinted. "We did not know this, Your Excellency! You must believe me. Truth be told, I have courted a Shadowlander long before my recent appointment as your protector in arms. Since the cottage has been abandoned, we have made a habit of meeting here. We found a key under a rock by the back door. And now we fantasize the place is ours, although legally, I suppose our visits are trespassing."

According to Draven, who had monitored the dwelling for the king, Liora did not frequent The Cottage of Shadows. This was true. However, Zagan did not believe most of the words spewing from Titus's mouth. He tired of the exchange, especially since a more compelling conversation awaited him at his castle.

"Fetch me your cloak, Henchman," he ordered.

For the first time since Zagan's arrival, Titus displayed fear.

"I do not understand," his henchman said. "Why do you wish to look at my cloak?"

From where Zagan stood, he could see the garment draped on top of the bed. He sculpted a vacuum which carried the coat from the sheets into his arms.

"You are mistaken," the king admonished. "I do not require your understanding. Nor did I say I wished to look at the cloak." He raised the garment to his nose, more for dramatic effect, since he could already smell the divine wine absorbed in the pocket's fabric. "I wanted to smell it. And can you fathom why?"

Titus explained that he typically carried a full wineskin with him for his own sustenance during a journey. And that his wineskin had leaked, on that very day, while riding to the prison. He vehemently denied bringing the failing pouch into the facility.

"I abide by the law," Titus said. "I am not above it."

The king thinned his lips. "Says the confessed trespasser."

Unbeknownst to his henchman, a guard gifted-in-smell had detected a full wineskin when Titus had entered the pits during the prison inspection. The same guard had caught a glimpse of the empty wineskin upon the henchman's departure. *After* Titus had visited with Draven. In private.

Prison rules forbade visitors from bringing any sustenance into the Prison of the Unruly, let alone divine wine, which had not, as yet, been introduced to the population. Certainly not to prisoners!

Moreover, Titus had not been granted authority to speak with Draven...alone.

The evidence mounted. His new henchman was a bona fide liar. A traitor. Far worse than his former longstanding protector.

Rage pulsed beneath Zagan's skin.

His fingers twitched.

The king sculpted several breaks in each of Titus's shinbones, dropping the Shadowlander to his knees.

Titus released a wretched shrill like a wolf in agony.

Which pleased the king.

But not quite enough.

"Do you have any last words, Henchman?" Zagan asked.

Broken and barely able to stay upright on his knees, Titus winced. "I sought to persuade Draven to turn against you," he admitted, finally understanding his fate. "True that Draven drank the divine wine until he was satiated. However, your former henchman refused my offer. Idiot! Fool! Does he not know your reign is limited?" He gritted his teeth. "Hate for the King of Darkness swells in each realm. Defeat will be your future, and I shall smile for eternity from my resting place in Heaven."

The king ignored the grandstanding. But most assuredly, he would visit Draven to drill his mind for answers. To determine the true connection between the two henchmen.

Zagan dropped to his knees to gain eye level. "I will glamour the name of your harlot from you, so that I may also end her existence."

Titus smiled and chuckled, which gave the king pause. Perhaps Titus did not care for the harlot with whom he had coupled.

In a burst of movement, Titus raised both hands and used his fingers to pluck out his eyes. He crushed them in his hands.

Blood seeped from his empty sockets like streams of crimson.

With the contemptuous act, his henchman had stripped the king of his rightful supremacy. Of his control.

For without eyes, Titus could not be glamoured.

Fire burned within Zagan's veins. Fury like he had never felt.

The king thrust his hand into Titus's chest. He wrapped his fingers around the beating heart and ripped it from the chest cavity.

One good pluck deserved another.

Titus dropped to the floor, lifeless.

Blood pooled from his wounds.

In the king's hand, the heart beat one last time.

Like trash, he cast the organ onto the floor. Using his boot, he crushed and grinded the heart into the floor planks, ensuring that it was beyond repair.

Although he sculpted clean his bloodied hands and clothing, he would not carbonize the henchman's remains. Let Liora or the harlot find the ruins of Titus the Entertainer.

Zagan's anger continued to boil.

Why did he fail to anticipate the lengths his foes would go to gain victory over him?

Ruby's assessment was accurate: he was prone to distraction.

Perhaps he *should* attend to priorities.

Under ordinary circumstances, he would have swiftly traveled to Draven's cell, while his questions were crisp and his desire for closure, robust. Instead, he considered his "extraordinary" goal, as Ruby had suggested earlier.

Her proposal appeared to be a higher priority. Why else would she place herself at risk to deliver it?

If, however, her proposition was underwhelming, he would inject her with vervain and ram a berry down her delicate throat. As a mortal, she would be unable to travel or sculpt a retaliation.

Which meant he could crush her heart as he had Titus's.

50

Saturday, June 29, 2041
Castle on High Cliff: Skotadi, Athanasia

AS RUBY CONTINUED to wait in the library for the king's return, she grew annoyed at his earlier treatment.

Extraordinary gifts prevented barriers from confining her. Not doors or locks or chains or cells could stop her from escaping. When the king had led his guard down the castle's corridor to avoid being overheard, she teetered between feeling insulted and grateful.

Insulted tipped the scales.

Wasn't Zagan aware at this juncture in their wargame that she could've sculpted into a spider, or any living or non-living thing, and listened to every word of the exchange while tucked between stones in a wall? Hadn't he accepted that she was a formidable opponent?

Unfortunately, his lack of respect put a kink in her plan, since her intentions depended on him *needing* her. So far, he didn't appear impressed. Or in need.

She couldn't overlook the positives, though.

Zagan's lack of appreciation for her competences proved more about him than her. The King of Darkness had clearly grown undisciplined over mega-annum, like a lion living in zoo captivity for too long. Sure, the lion was still equipped with razor-sharp teeth and claws. But after a while, the beast became more of a lazy housecat, forgetting how to hunt. Which made him way easier to defeat.

Plus, her nemesis wasn't aware she could whisper, cognitively eavesdrop, or see the future. She wondered how he'd react to her full arsenal of gifts. Would his indifference change?

When Zagan and the guard spoke earlier, she hadn't been in the mood to scurry as a spider along the hallway's damp walls. Instead, she cognitively traveled into the guard's mind and learned *more* than if she had merely listened to the hushed words being exchanged.

In the depths of his mind, the guard detested the king, as did his acquaintances. Everyone understood that Zagan had become reckless and unstable. A sweep of the king's hand required zero discipline.

Only fear kept the guards loyal.

With Zagan away from the castle to address his "business matter," Ruby opened her mind to the future, searching for answers to specific questions. She immediately spotted the glow of Titus's stone; it had been carved one last time.

His death was heartbreaking.

She relived her brief encounter with the henchman. She'd only exposed his eavesdropping to impress Zagan. To make the king think she could be loyal. Besides, the henchman had given her the impression that he could take care of himself.

Guilt over Titus's death, however, would not defeat the king.

While she waited in the library, The Book of Immortality beckoned for her attention. The king had warned not to touch the sacred book, but he hadn't prohibited her from *reading* it.

By sculpting a breeze, she flipped pages and absorbed every word.

Toward the end of the book, one passage lifted from the page like a hologram, hovering above the delicate parchment paper. She paused. There was a reason the passage had made itself known, and she wanted to discover why before the king returned.

Cloaked in the shadows of the middle realm,
the King shall wed the Queen
in accordance with traditional customs.
Upon their lawful union,
the curse of light and darkness will fade.
Balance will be restored,
as it was, as it shall be;
until The Turning Point,
when animals will crown their King.

The passage was chock-full of confusing. Would Zagan and Liora be required to *marry* in order for the curse to be broken? Matrimony between the two seemed unlikely. War was more plausible.

And where did the entry leave Ruby in her capacity as The Tether? Maybe she'd no longer be alive. Her near future wasn't carved in stone yet. Death was a definite possibility.

Interesting how the scriptures hinted, for the first time in the book, at The Turning Point's meaning. Since the animals would *crown* their king, the passage implied that their choice wasn't currently wearing one.

That fact gave rise to a peculiar feeling, like a revelation was on the tip of her tongue. Only her taste buds couldn't identify the flavor.

She pivoted toward the door as it opened. Zagan entered wearing a different outfit—a pale green evening jacket, designed with a mandarin collar and fabric buttons. She couldn't deny his good looks or that his air of confidence could be appealing.

Could be, if he wasn't a murdering bastard.

The king was followed by Atea, dressed in leathers, and a stunning vampire in a yellow gown. Atea pushed a cart on wheels that was topped with a carafe and three goblets. And a knife.

Ruby's heart raced when she saw her guide. She prayed Atea's glamour couldn't be detected by the king. And that the king's own glamour would look as though it had stuck.

If only Zagan's deficiency in attending to the right details would last a while longer.

She whispered into her guide's mind. *I hope you're okay, Atea. Let's not act as though we like each other as much as we do.*

Atea nodded as the female vampire poured one goblet of wine.

"Are you not going to leap into your guide's arms?" Zagan asked, tilting his head. "Make promises of returning her home safely?"

Ruby ignored him and spoke directly to Atea. "No disrespect, but if you'd been in better shape, we may have gotten off that island before dark. Instead, my family was almost killed." She returned her gaze to the king. "Guess I'm a little bitter about the whole ordeal."

"Whining is not becoming, Lady Spencer," Zagan said. "Besides, your family regrettably survived."

Atea's eyes widened and one side of her mouth curled in a smile.

Careful, Ruby warned. *Mask your emotions when you're around the king.*

The vampire in yellow drank from the chalice of blood. Atea clasped the knife and sliced the top of the vampire's hand. Within a second, the wound healed.

Zagan nodded for the other goblets to be filled.

"I see you're starting to think defensively," Ruby said. "Wouldn't want your divine wine to be poisoned by the berry juice from The Tree of Awareness."

"*Ahh.* You have finally acknowledged mortality as a poison. This pleases me. However," he said, changing his tone to accusatory, "you did not know the tree was named as such. Which means…you have read The Book of Immortality. Contrary to my command."

The king directed his subjects to complete their task with haste.

Atea trembled as she handed Ruby a goblet. Atea's vampire companion offered the other glass to Zagan before placing the carafe on the coffee table between the two chairs.

Both women left the room, closing the door behind them.

Alone with the king, Ruby refuted the accusation that she hadn't followed orders. She did not *touch* the sacred book. She admitted, however, that she *had* sculpted the pages to flip.

"I must be more literal in the future," he said.

"At least you acknowledge I may have a future." She smiled. "Mind if I ask a few questions about the scriptures?"

Zagan pointed to a chair, inviting her to sit. He sat in the other. "Your alleged proposal has permitted your stay at High Cliff to linger, *not* your thirst for knowledge in vampire prophesies."

"Such a cranky king." She sipped on the blood. "Oh! Delicious. Thank you. Now back to my questions. I think your answers might actually enrich my proposal. Can't you humor me? Unless, of course, you have other pressing business matters?"

He closed his eyes and nodded—all the green-light she needed.

"I read," Ruby said, *"the King shall wed the Queen.* Does this mean you are predestined to marry Liora? If you want the curse to end?"

"Hardly the scholar, Lady Spencer." Zagan slammed the book shut with his mind. "If you were, you would realize that a traditional vampire-wedding involves a full cycle of celebration, equivalent to

234

twenty-four human hours. Afterwards, the marriage must be consummated, as in coupling with one's mate, before the pairing can be recognized as lawfully wed."

"How does that negate a union between you both?" Ruby asked.

"You mean, besides the fact that I loathe Liora?" He glowered. "And if I am not mistaken, was it not you claiming to attend to details more readily than me?"

She concentrated, trying to identify what she was missing.

"Oh, I get it," she said. "The official union must occur *before* the curse can be broken. And you and Liora can only stay in The Shadowlands for a period of what...?"

"Five hours by human standards."

"Okay, but I don't think you're being creative enough in your interpretation of the passage. I have ideas that might intrigue you."

He downed the blood in his goblet.

"Did I mention your time is limited here?" Zagan pressed.

"Consider this: when you commanded me 'not to touch' The Book of Immortality, your order didn't forbid me from *reading* it. I simply found loopholes, so we could both get what we wanted, while not breaking any rules." She noticed his souring expression. "Please be patient. Just two more questions."

"Hurry."

He poured another serving into his goblet, which was a good sign.

"Must the groom be *present* at the wedding celebration for the full twenty-four hours?" Ruby asked.

"One assumes so."

"But does the tradition *demand* it? Are those words written in a sacred document?"

He raised his eyes as if searching his memories. "Not that I have ever read. But are you forgetting? I would rip out my heart before wedding the Queen of Light. She hides criminals from me in her realm and works to dethrone me. Even if I *could* take breaks from the weak ultra-violet rays of The Shadowlands—by returning periodically to Skotadi during the wedding celebration, I would not wish to do so. Not even my immortality is worth a union with Liora."

"Debatable, of course," Ruby said. "But my next question may clarify whether you must wed Liora, specifically, to end the curse.

And ending the curse should be a top priority, since being able to travel throughout Athanasia will increase your power."

The revelation from the holy passage, which had failed to crystalize on her tongue earlier, was fully developed now, though Ruby didn't have time to contemplate the impact on her homelife, on her marriage. All she knew was that the iron was hot, and the future of humankind was wrinkled with uncertainty.

"Can a king, namely *you*," she continued, "consecrate a subject into the position of queen? You know, conducting a coronation as part of the wedding ceremonies?"

Zagan paused. Clearly, he had never considered the loophole.

"And could this subject," she added, "be someone like *me?*"

His eyes widened.

She couldn't tell if his expression was shock or horror.

"And why would I ever want to wed someone like you?" he asked.

Smiling, she fiddled with her ruby pendant.

"Your question," she said, "brings us to my proposal."

51

LIORA BRACED HERSELF for her assistant's entrance into the solarium. She clutched the armrests of her wingback chair.

The windows were closed. Curtains, drawn.

Even the queen's gown was midnight blue to match her mood.

The near future was clouded with anger and sorrow and uncertainty. Thorns abounded amid the sunshine.

Solange dashed into the sunroom, dropping to her knees in front of Liora's chair, placing her hands on the queen's lap. Her eyes were urgent. Pleading.

"Please, Queen," she begged, weeping crimson tears. "Please tell me Titus is safe. Alive. For surely you would not have ordered me from his side had his life been threatened."

Liora placed her hand on her assistant's cheek and wiped an escaping tear with her thumb. "My dearest friend, I do not write the stones. I only read them."

Solange's eyes widened. Veins rose on her neck.

"Fallacious words distort the truth," her assistant said, standing and taking several steps backwards. "By shifting the sands of what is to come, you possess the power to *alter* the future."

"Not once the stones are carved. You know this."

Solange shook her head.

Panic marked her face, masking her delicate features.

"Do not report," Solange warned, "that my mate has perished at

237

Zagan's hands. *Do not!*"

"My heart breaks with yours." Liora fought back her own tears. "May it bring you peace that your mate died honorably. Without waver, he placed the needs of the universe before his own. There is no greater sacrifice than this. Love blossomed in his heart. Love was Titus's extraordinary gift."

Veins bulged on Solange's cheeks and forehead.

"Then why?" her assistant challenged. "Why did you not let me sacrifice myself, alongside my mate? Our bond would have repelled fear. We could have traveled together to our resting place. Passing as one through Heaven's gates."

"Titus was not alone. Or afraid," Liora assured. "I whispered in his thoughts. Your mate was at peace. And his love for you, eternal."

Dark purple swept over Solange's skin until the gray was overtaken. Even her hands were the color of eggplant.

"How very special for you, Queen," Solange spat. "To exclude me from being by his side so you could take my place."

"You do not mean what your mouth has spoken. Anger corrupts your thoughts and tongue."

Her assistant's blue eyes narrowed.

"We should not have waited for The Tether," Solange said. "Long ago, we should have waged war against the King of Darkness."

The queen remained seated.

"This is my declaration," Solange said, towering over her monarch. "I will kill Zagan. Destroy him. If death greets me in the attempt, let that be *my* sacrifice. I shall join my mate without regret."

"You cannot step ahead of the Sacred Scrolls, as if you are wiser. As if you are in control," Liora said. "Was that not Zagan's path? He believed in himself, in his own wants and desires. He ate the forbidden fruit, ushering in a curse that divides our kind. Then he pillaged Earth. His heart erodes with hatred. The vampire he once was is no longer recognizable."

Liora pointed toward the mirror on the wall. "Regard yourself in this moment. Is who you see, the vampire you wish to become? One whose faith is pushed aside?"

Solange turned and stared at her reflection.

"You lecture," her assistant said, "as though your faith is constant and resolute. Yet you questioned your own faith recently. Do you not remember? After you were blocked from eavesdropping in Ruby's mind? 'Twas I who reminded *you* to keep faith in The Tether."

"We are all tested," the queen said. "Indeed, you helped rescue me from doubt. And now I wish to lead you from its grasp. But you must take my hand, as I did yours."

"Then what am I to do?" Solange cried, her skin returning to gray. "Simply accept the brutal death of my mate? To turn my cheek and never look back?"

Liora stood and placed her arms around her friend.

"You have purpose in this battle between good and evil," the queen said, rubbing Solange's back to comfort and encourage. "Can you not think of where to start?"

Moving away from their embrace, her assistant placed her hand over her lips and glanced downward, as if trying to recall a memory. Her eyes narrowed before she raised her face and looked at the queen, as if knowledge had replaced the void.

"Titus had urged me to consider his suggestion," Solange said. "To cognitively visit Ruby in hopes that she might forge an alliance with me. That she might share her thoughts and strategies."

"Then your first step has been revealed. Learn if trust for us still grows in The Tether's heart."

Solange displayed a weak smile. "As if you do not already know."

52

Saturday, June 29, 2041
United States Penitentiary, Lee: Virginia

EM WAS SURPRISED when Lyle arrived at his cell five-minutes before lights out, flanked by none other than the warden.

The warden's brown hair was pulled into a tight bun, probably to downplay her "sexy," like having scented hair cascade over her shoulders. The loose pants suit—polyester—also played its role in keeping temperatures chilly. Only her name redirected attention toward the crotch zone. Because Warden Measures had plenty of volunteers aching to stuff their footlongs inside her ruler.

Keeping her surname Measures while overseeing horny inmates seemed provocative. The way he looked at the situation, satisfying the appetites within his exclusive club should've qualified as good behavior. After all, his efforts ensured her panties remained intact.

"Inmate ten sixty-four: follow Guard Owens," she barked. "One misstep and we'll pull out the four-piece suit. Got it?"

Calling prisoners by their department identification number was another way the warden avoided connecting with the marginalized. But threatening to put him in a suit of full restraints? With handcuffs, leg irons, and a waist chain? *That* counteracted her intentions.

The ultimatum caused blood to flow to his most expressive extremity.

Strutting in front of him, Lyle repeatedly tapped his metal baton against his left palm. After several minutes of taking lefts and rights, the three of them entered an elevator. Which was different. Which piqued his curiosity.

Lyle pressed the elevator button marked "B" for basement. The polished stainless-steel doors closed, and the compartment jerked as it began descending.

"Know this, inmate ten sixty-four," the warden said. "I'm all about equity in the treatment of prisoners. You've already blown that to hell with your personal computer. But what you're about to see is the paragon of entitlement. If these *exceptions* weren't coming from the POTUS himself, you'd never be the wiser."

His heart accelerated.

Might President Unger have accepted his offer? To equip Em so he could engineer a cure for the First Lady's cancer?

Doubtful a lab could've been constructed in two short days.

The elevator jolted to a stop. Doors opened to a dingy hallway, poorly lit with yellow overhead lights. They exited the compartment, taking a left. After walking down a long musty corridor, they stopped in front of a closed metal door.

The warden thumbed a set of numbers into an electronic panel mounted on the wall. The door buzzed as the deadbolt clicked open. Gripping the handle, Warden Measures turned her head and glared at him, blatantly exercising her control of the situation.

"Breathe a word of this to anyone," she warned, "and your little playroom will go up in smoke. And you'll be found with a shank in your windpipe. Understood?"

"Inmate ten sixty-four hears you loud and clear, Ma'am." Em smiled. Clearly the warden didn't know Lyle was prone to hyperventilation. "Emory Dixon Bradshaw will be one-thousand and sixty-four percent in compliance."

She swung open the door as she whispered *asswipe.*

They entered the lab. The door closed and bolted behind them.

"You can't get out of here," she said. "So don't even try."

Escaping hadn't entered his mind. He was home.

Salivating, Em scanned the sweetest lab he had ever seen. This one made the labs in the West Wing and at Johns Hopkins seem rudimentary. He rubbed his hands over his eyelids, as if the vision might be an illusion. But when he re-opened his eyes, everything remained.

One detail was off.

Em didn't see the cage configuration for his naked mole rats—the key to the entire operation. A closed corrugated door was located in place of the shelving.

"And my naked mole rats?" he asked her. "Are they in transit?"

She walked to the garage-like door and pressed a green button on the wall. As the door raised and rattled, the sterile white lights in the lab dimmed to off. Red overhead lights faded on, illuminating a plexiglass panel that was three-feet high by eight-feet long. The transparent container was a dirt habitat.

Em could see cross-sections of tunnels where the monstrous critters had burrowed, leading to a few dug-out chambers.

"They're already *here?*" he asked, fearing he might get lightheaded.

"Well, aren't you an Einstein," the warden said, rolling her eyes. "Overnighted. What the POTUS wants, the POTUS gets."

He'd ignore the bitch's sarcasm, since Einstein had never created a vampire. Never even tried. Which elevated Em on a higher pedestal.

"Why the red lights?" he asked.

"Your contact in East Africa told us these hairless, wrinkled freaks live in total darkness." She pressed another button. "We modeled their captive habitat like several zoos."

The plexiglass container moved toward them on conveyer tracks like a mechanized drawer opening. Wheeled metal-supports dropped into place as the eight-foot deep habitat became fully exposed.

"How many subjects were you able to procure?" Em asked, shifting into his Doctor Genius persona.

In fact, being *the* shot caller in the world of the disenfranchised no longer registered.

Kendrick and Lyle...*who?*

Dark science would always be his main squeeze.

"You've got a colony of twenty rats," she answered. "Complete with a queen—who's a real bitch."

"In truth, they're not really rats. Or moles."

She tilted her head. "Do I look like I give a fuck, ten sixty-four?"

The warden pointed to a smooth stainless-steel door. "That's the walk-in refrigerator. The chemical closet is adjacent, on the right. Your bunk and bathroom are the next door over." Her finger swept halfway across the lab to a desk. "Since you and the POTUS are clearly email pen-pals, he'll contact you on that secure computer system. Any questions?"

"How often can I come here?" Em asked.

"A better question is when can you leave? Look around you. These are your new digs. After all, can't be mixing the privileged with the downtrodden. How would they react?" She raised a plucked eyebrow. "Hold your mud, wizard, or you may learn, first-hand, what other inmates think about your precious entitlements."

She pressed the button that retracted the habitat container, followed by the red button which lowered the corrugated door and switched on the white lights.

As the warden neared the door to exit, she inserted a special key to unlock it. Turning her face toward him, she said, "First sign of trouble—a mere whiff of it—and I'll shut this lab down. Poof, like magic."

Warden Measures and Lyle left the lab.

The door closed, and Em deeply inhaled.

He was in a lab again. His soul was free.

Finding a pad of paper at his desk, he sat to write a note.

Time to reach out to Vladimir Volkov, whom he never saw, since the Russian troll was living out his sentence in a different wing of the penitentiary. Time to share his new, twisted plan.

He smiled over the warden's warning—that she didn't want to smell trouble. Her olfactory system was clearly compromised.

He reeked of trouble.

Always had.

Always would.

53

Saturday, June 29, 2041
Castle on High Cliff: Skotadi, Athanasia

RUBY RECOGNIZED HER own turning point as she sat with the king in his library. The fact that she could barely swallow only emphasized the outcome's uncertainty.

She was at the mercy of Zagan's decision. Either the King of Darkness would accept her offer, securing the safety of humankind and her family, or the planets were heading toward all-out war where everyone was at risk, especially Clay and Gabby.

Pressure throbbed in her head.

"Immortals are rarely rushed," he snarled, tapping his index finger on the goblet's bowl. "Yet you manage to test my patience. Your proposal, Lady Spencer?" He gulped the remains of his glass and returned the emptied chalice to the coffee table between them.

"Coronate me queen of Skotadi," she said, trying to sound like it was no big deal. "We'll wed traditionally, though you'll enjoy breaks from the ultra-violet rays during the long celebration. After consummating our vows, the curse will be broken. You'll be free, like all our kind, to bask in sunlight. In exchange, you'll *never* threaten or hurt my family again or our arrangement will become null and void."

"What benefit will this serve me, beyond the curse?" He smirked.

"Breaking the curse is pretty significant. But okay, there's more. I'll become ambassador for The Restoration. I'll solicit volunteer donors from Earth. They'll be no more cullings. In fact, not complying with this stipulation is also a deal breaker.

"You'll have all the blood you and Athanasia need," Ruby continued. "Balance will be restored at your hands, elevating your position on the planet. Citizens will shout: *All hail to the king of kings!*"

"Before I expose the deficiencies in your proposal," Zagan said, "my curiosities have gotten the better of me." He filled his goblet once more. "What shall become of your coven? Will you part with your mate or bring him to High Cliff, to share our bed like a pet?"

"You may not remember much about love. But sometimes, you have to let those whom you love…go. For *their* sake. And Clay's safety means everything. Let's face it, if we go to war, he'll be the first on your kill-list. Isn't as though you haven't already tried. Twice."

"And your heart would not grieve the separation?"

"Of course. But Clay is human. What's the difference between grieving for him now, or fifty years from now when he dies of old age? Fifty years are brief for an immortal."

"What of your daughter?" He raised his eyebrows. "Will you abandon her as well?"

Veins pulsed in her neck. "Never. She'll join me here where I can protect her. And when she comes of age, if she wants me to, I'll turn her vampire. Without Gabby, the deal is off."

"*Ahh,* Lady Spencer. There is no deal. Only questions."

She placed her goblet on the table. "You're not the only one who has obligations. If you have more questions, or want to point out supposed deficiencies, I'm listening. But please be prompt."

"What stops me from breaking the curse and then destroying you and your coven afterwards? Queen or no?" he asked. "After all, I have difficulty keeping bargains, especially when breaking them is far more beneficial."

"You're stronger with me by your side, King."

He shook his head. "*You* are a mere imitation and I have ruled tremendously well on my own. Only the curse has limited me. Once our nuptials were fulfilled, I would have what I needed: the ability to travel the realms and planets without constraint. Which lends doubt to your proposal. For you would never suggest a plan doomed to failure. Thus, my intuition detects an enticement with nefarious intentions."

He stood, clearly wanting to end their conversation without a deal.

Standing from her chair, Ruby stroked the wrinkles in the skirt of her gown, as if she wasn't shaken. "I didn't realize a seer already serves your cause. One who can thwart retaliations before they're launched. Who can whisper into the enemy's mind to eavesdrop on strategies. Who can cognitively travel without moving her feet." She curtsied. "I've wasted your time." Bowing her head, she added, "Let's commence this war: your kingdom against mine."

Dust swirled around her, as she began to travel back home.

"Wait! Surely you are aware that Liora, the only seer, does not serve me or my cause," Zagan said, sounding rushed by her imminent departure. "Of whom do you speak, then?"

She could hear the uptick in his heart.

Letting her dust resettle, she materialized in bodily form.

"Now you've got me suspicious," she said. "Surely you know I'm more than an *imitation*. You're teasing me, right?"

He tilted his head but said nothing.

"When I was a baby in utero, my transfusion came from *two* sources, not one." Ruby smiled wide, continuing to reel in the line. "The Queen of Light was my other donor. Naturally, my gifts are comprehensive." She raised her hand to her chin and fluttered her eyelashes. "Which I guess makes *me* the most powerful vampire in the universe, especially if the curse isn't broken, since I can already travel anywhere. Turns out, you need me far more than I need you."

Zagan sat in the chair again, clutching the antlered armrests.

"Then why strike a deal with me at all?" he asked.

"My family. I don't want to worry about you killing them. Or culling innocent humans. I want harmony between the planets. Balance. And as a bonus, I rather like the idea of being crowned the Queen of Peace. For eternity, no less."

"You have declared yourself as a seer. But how can I be certain?"

She returned to her chair, sitting sideward on the edge to face him. "Take the prison guard you spoke to earlier," Ruby said. "Instead of sculpting into another form to hear your conversation, I cognitively drilled into his mind while you spoke. The guard hates you, by the way. But I saw everything he had witnessed: Titus convincing him to speak with Draven alone, knowing it was forbidden. The guard seeing part of the exposed wineskin. Smelling the human blood because of a leak. The guard told you simply to protect his own life.

"Good time as any," she continued, "to mention I also whispered into Titus's mind, when he still had a pulse. You should know: Draven *is* loyal to you and you only. Although he drank the blood for sustenance, he rejected Titus's offer to help dethrone you. Then at the cottage, I saw you break Titus's legs and rip out his heart. Grind it with your boot. His stone was carved for the last time."

"How do I know that Liora did not whisper these truths into your mind? To fool me?" Zagan asked.

"Hard to do since I've blocked her entry. But okay, I'll share a vision that she couldn't possibly know. On Great Island, I whispered with The Tree of Awareness. I saw everything that had happened between you and your would-be mate associated with the tree and its fruit. Including how you carbonized her in Lampsi, near The Tree of Immortality, when her back was turned. Pretty ruthless, though I can sense your regret, then and now."

Zagan couldn't turn any paler than he already was. But his expression revealed that he was shaken, ashamed.

Someone else knew his secret. His horror.

"Your gifts *would* be an asset," he admitted, speaking softly. "But there is little trust between us. And trust is a competence I no longer possess. Therefore, I am at a loss on how to regain it."

"Luckily, you have me." She smiled and reached into a hidden pocket within her dress's red skirt. "I know how to build trust." She withdrew her three berries and dropped them into his open palm. "Let's join forces to restore balance between the planets."

The King of Darkness folded his fingers around the berries. "Where shall we begin?"

"I'll start by preparing my family for the changes," she said. "But I see no reason to delay our engagement and wedding announcements, as well as my upcoming coronation."

She saw a flash of light in her thoughts. The etchings in stone revealed her survival, as well as Clay and Gabby's.

At least in the short term.

54

Sunday, June 30, 2041
Cottage of Shadows to Prison of the Unruly

RUBY HAD TURNED to dust in the king's library, but she wasn't traveling home as she'd claimed. She had time to accomplish two important tasks. Because back on Earth, just after midnight at the Westin Annapolis, her husband was still sleeping beside the moth turned doppelgänger.

The Cottage of Shadows was her first destination.

After her experience with The Tree of Awareness, she had learned that the past left an imprint which could be read. Perhaps the past still lingered within the recently deceased henchman. Because she wanted to learn more than her "sight" had already revealed about the secret alliance between Titus, the Queen of Light, and Draven.

Wearing her leathers, Ruby materialized in the cottage's den.

The room was dark, except for the flickering embers in the fireplace. Titus lay twisted and disassembled on the wooden floor planks, resting in a pool of his own blood.

Kneeling, she placed her hand on his cold arm.

Thankfully, the echoes of his immortal life still clung to his body.

As she concentrated, Titus's life, from Creation to his final heartbeat, replayed in her mind at warp speed.

Her eyes widened. Pulse, elevated.

Titus had a lover.

Her name was Solange—someone who'd fit nicely into several of Ruby's strategies aimed at defeating or transforming the King of

Darkness.

Clearly, Solange would be motivated to pursue Zagan, especially since he had murdered Titus. Being angry and distraught were powerful catalysts for revenge.

Did Ruby want to further agitate Solange's rage?

Direct it toward the king's defeat?

Ruby's other option was to continue to work solo. To marry the king and find a way to convert his heart, to grow his compassion for all life on Earth, Athanasia, and Besto Polus.

Then again, perhaps she could combine the strategies.

Either way, war was an ugly business.

She gazed at the fallen patriot on the floor and confirmed what the stones had relayed about Titus's future. Emptied of his blood, with an extracted heart that had been damaged beyond repair, Titus could not be restored.

No way could she leave his mangled body for his lover to find.

Sculpting a gold urn, she engraved the henchman's name on it. She swept her hand, turning his remains into ashes and gathering them within the vase before sealing it shut.

Not everything had to be cruel.

With her intentions at the cottage satisfied, she traveled to a more dangerous setting: Prison of the Unruly. She needed to warn Draven that his life was in imminent danger.

Ruby appeared within Draven's cell, sitting on a rickety bench.

The former henchman was secluded in a private, dreary chamber. Lanterns mounted in the hallway cast dim light into the space.

With his legs slung over a rafter, Draven hung upside down from the ceiling like a bat. Flipping backwards, he landed on his feet. He leaned against a moist stone wall and crossed his arms.

"Ever since the curse was inflicted upon our planet," he said, "our hopes have rested on the prophesies, on the promise of a gifted protector. Have you acquainted yourself with our scriptures, *Tether?*"

He uttered her title with contempt.

"Light and darkness shall forge a gemstone," he recited. *"Ruby shall be its name: a fading star restored to brilliance. None shall match it. And the gemstone will shine as a symbol of love and an instrument of protection—for all."*

"I've read the entire Book of Immortality," she said.

"Then your purpose should not befuddle you. You are meant to serve as an instrument of protection...*for all.*" He flashed his fangs and jerked his head back. "Yet since your rising, protection has been selective, extended only to you and your precious coven. Meanwhile, my brother and wolf have been ruthlessly slain."

Ruby widened her eyes, surprised that he'd already heard the news of Titus's death.

"What did you think?" he taunted. "That you would be the first to report of my brother's tragic passing? Can the water not rise and ebb without your knowledge?"

"Liora...she whispered to you about his death. I'm aware of the loyalty existing between you, Solange, and the queen."

Draven tilted his head slightly. She heard a slight uptick in his heartrate with the mention of Titus's mate.

This time, he was the one surprised.

"The only loyalty in question is yours," he snapped. "As we speak, evil and imbalance grow stronger. Goodness is bound by chains, with no freedom in sight."

He pushed off the wall.

She leapt from the bench in a countermove.

"Relax, *warrior,*" he said. "My attack is reduced to words since I am no longer in possession of swords. I merely wish to convey that your service to our kind has been a grave disappointment. Much has been lost under your inadequate protection."

The words stung, since they carried plenty of truth, both on Athanasia and Earth.

"I'm doing the best I can," she said. "That's why I'm here. Because Zagan is coming. As in, immediately after my visit. Which means I need to glamour you for your own safety."

"Through a whisper, Liora has already raised a shield."

"Not to be rude," Ruby said, "but when I accessed Titus's mind, I was privy to the conversation you shared about your previous glamour—the one intended to hide the extra vial collected of Zagan's blood; *the* glamour discovered and unraveled by the king while probing your memories. And the author of that failed glamour was none other than Liora."

"Do you seek to impress me?" Draven asked.

"I can do better." She smiled. "I'm skilled and cunning. I'll trick the king. Promise. Anyway, I have an effective plan."

"Ha! Should I drop to my knees, Queen of Peace?" He lowered to his knees before she could answer. "Should I worship you? Tremble with fear over your great and mighty powers?"

News about becoming a queen had spread quickly.

"My proposed title should tell you something," Ruby said. "I mean, I could've suggested becoming the Queen of Strife or Queen of War. And if I wanted, I could've carbonized you already." She tapped her finger above her temple. "Use your head to think, Draven. Not your broken heart."

"My head is in concert with my heart," he argued. "You are not to be trusted. Anyone who chooses to couple with the King of Darkness, whether their heart beats in truth or a lie, will be denied my allegiance."

"Such a hypocrite."

He raised his gray eyebrows.

"Need I remind you," she continued, "that you've been living a lie for 2.8 million years? Pretending to be a loyal henchman while in truth, serving as a spy for the queen? And *you're* going to judge *me*? Besides, I didn't ask for your allegiance. I'm simply offering to save your life." She took a step toward him. "But perhaps the fight in you has exhausted itself, swordsman. And death seems like the rest poor, weary Draven craves."

"I will fight until my last breath."

"Without adequate protections, your final breath will be taken within the hour," she said. "I can see the etchings taking form, or I wouldn't have come."

Draven began to pace in silence.

Minutes later, the former henchman stopped and faced her.

"Hearing your plan can bring no harm," he said. "Why should I not open my ears to it?"

Ruby explained she'd raise an invisible shield that couldn't be detected or undone. No matter how deep Zagan drilled, Draven's mind would be programmed to respond in specific ways. Most importantly, Draven would be glamoured to act naturally, as though all his memories were fully accessible.

"I'll glamour you," Ruby added, "to convince Zagan that Titus was the rogue traitor. That you took his blood offering with no intention of joining his rebellion. While being questioned, you'll know nothing personal about Titus or his mate, not even about their connection to Liora."

"And that is all that must be done?" Draven asked.

"Zagan will doubt you and scour your mind further," she said. "But everything you confessed will be corroborated, including your love for him."

She stared blankly as she searched for images in the future.

"The king's anger will wane," she said. "After subjecting you to his truth glamour, Zagan will believe you stole his blood to create a queen for him, in order to break the curse. He'll be blinded to the truth: that I was created to defeat him.

"There's more," she continued, her sight focused on the future. "Zagan plans to free you from prison after the wedding. In the meantime, he'll offer to reinstate your sustenance. Refuse it. Admit you'd rather atone for your crime by denying your hunger."

"Refuse blood? Is my strength not important?" Draven asked.

"I'd rather keep you isolated from the guards, like you are now. Less complications are better, especially if your escape becomes necessary. And anyway, I don't see you starving to death." She touched his arm. "Of course, I'll try not to let you die."

"Your offer carries little assurances," he said.

"Titus would have welcomed so little."

Draven agreed to be glamoured.

Pressed for time, she got down to business constructing an impenetrable, cognitive shield.

As she wrapped up her elaborate glamour, her skin prickled.

Unease saturated her veins.

"The king is coming," she warned, beginning to turn to dust. "Good luck, Henchman."

She dreaded her next move more than any other.

The time had come to say goodbye to her husband.

55

Sunday, June 30, 2041
Castle on High Cliff: Skotadi, Athanasia

ZAGAN RETURNED FROM the Prison of the Unruly.

The revelations gained were not as expected. Nor the outcome. For he had fully anticipated carbonizing his once closest confidant. Yet, hearing Draven's admissions during a truth glamour had stilled Zagan's hand.

His former henchman professed his continued love for the king and regretted stealing his blood—not for the crime's intentions, but for its deceptions. His words also affirmed that he had staunchly refused to join Titus in a coup attempt. In fact, Draven had intended to expose the traitor.

The king, however, was not prepared to offer freedom.

Confusion continued to course through his veins.

Sitting at the head of the table in his study, Zagan was unable to lift the pen resting on the parchment paper in front of him. First, he wanted to reconcile the past with the present, the scriptures with his thoughts. To consider all angles.

His next moves needed to be sound, relying on logic rather than emotions or insecurities. Was he even capable of diluting the mental poison which corrupted his soul?

Draven's situation offered the perfect opportunity to try.

Stealing the king's blood was a heinous act, one that could not be regarded in any other light. But his former henchman confessed the act's purpose: to create a gifted, Earthling vampire who could couple with the king in order to break the curse, reunite the realms, and restore balance.

The prophesies were not ambiguous over the necessity for a queen, though Zagan had ignored their instruction.

He said out loud from memory, *"Cloaked in the shadows of the middle realm, the King shall wed the Queen in accordance with traditional customs. Upon their lawful union, the curse of light and darkness will fade. Balance will be restored, as it was, as it shall be."*

Curse or no curse, Zagan had always believed he, and he alone, could reinstate balance. But if this were truly so, would he not have fulfilled this purpose over the last 2.8 million years?

Could he condemn Draven's efforts to break the curse?

Although he hated to admit his own shortcomings, Zagan's efforts had faltered thus far. Perhaps he was not The Tether after all. Perhaps Lady Spencer did, indeed, embody the calling.

Despite his missteps, the blessing remained the same: divine wine. Mayfly blood would alter vampire society in a multitude of positive ways. Expanding his power was, indeed, the epitome of positive.

"And when truth is tasted once more," he said, *"and lips are stained crimson, goodness shall be set free."*

As Zagan recited the scripture, his first decision crystalized. After the wedding, he would set Draven free. With prophesies realized and the curse broken, what reason would he have to prolong Draven's imprisonment? The king would welcome him back as henchman.

Lady Spencer's proposal was an easier contemplation, since he had little to lose in its acceptance. Shared power was not his preference, of course, but he could not undo the making of Ruby. True, he possessed all five mortal berries from The Tree of Awareness. But should he focus his energy on attempting to destroy Ruby? Or did he want to become mates over enemies, awing the realms with their combined epic power?

Power that could never be challenged.

The only pledges required of him in the barter were to leave her mayfly mate alone and to never again cull humans for their blood.

Sparing Clay's life was a minor concession. In less than a half-century, death would do the king's bidding anyway. Although Zagan would have enjoyed inflicting pain on the mayfly, this was a trivial motivation compared to the prominence he would gain in Athanasia if he accepted Ruby's proposal. *Priorities,* as she would say.

Gabriella was not a concern. Lady Spencer would protect and care for her offspring at High Cliff. The child would be no cause for apprehension while human. Moreover, he had seven years until she came of age to contemplate the advantages and disadvantages of turning her vampire.

Agreeing not to cull humans was another matter entirely.

Ruby had urged him to see loopholes in the scriptures.

Loopholes worked with culling as well.

Lucky for him, acquiring *volunteers* to donate their blood was not considered culling. She did not need to know that he had devised an easy protocol to avoid refusals. When he offered mayflies their two options—donate or die, he did not force an answer. He did not corrupt their responses with a glamour. They chose freely. Which meant the donors he accrued were volunteers in the truest sense.

He had no plans to alter his practices on gaining volunteers.

All Zagan needed to do was move the location of where he processed mayfly donors, to avoid questions and challenges from his soon-to-be queen. Instead of High Cliff, he would process his newly acquired volunteers in the Prison of the Unruly.

Volunteers whom Ruby amassed would be in her charge, managed within the castle walls.

Having an abundance of human donors hardly posed a problem. What expression did the mayflies use? *The more the merrier.* Indeed!

With conflicts resolved, Zagan lifted his pen and wrote an invitation for all of Athanasia:

The King of Skotadi

cordially requests your attendance

at the union of matrimony between

Zagan Glissendorf

and his beloved

Ruby Pearl Airily Spencer

beginning midway on July 4th
in The Shadowlands, at The Valley of Shade.

Following nuptial vows
will be the coronation of
The Queen of Peace.

Come One, Come All.
Let the curse be broken!

Who could resist such a celebration?

None would, since attendance across all realms was mandatory.

Labeling Ruby as his "beloved" was exaggeration, to be sure. But the shock and surprise of the stated devotion would intrigue his kind.

Breaking the spell would add delight.

Moreover, Liora had nothing to do with the celebratory news. Which meant she had nothing to gain. Only to lose.

This gratified him beyond words.

56

Sunday, June 30, 2041
The Westin Annapolis, Maryland

CLAY WOKE TO morning sunlight streaming through an opened window in their suite's master bedroom. The breeze carried the sweetness of mature blooms. Spring had morphed into summer.

His wife stood beside the rustling curtains, looking angelic in white, with a busy moth cleansing its wings on her palm. As she reached over the windowpane to the outdoors, the moth took flight. Fluttering away, free again.

"When you love something, sometimes you have to let it go," he said. "Wait. The moth's not Zagan the Douchebag, is it?"

He hoped she had caught his sarcasm.

She closed the window without cracking a smile.

"No, not the king," she said. "But thankfully, his visits are over. No more cullings, either."

Pushing up from a lying position, he propped his back against his pillow and headboard. Excitement tingled under his skin.

"Seriously?" he asked. "Is Zagan dead? What have I missed?"

She walked toward him and sat on the edge of the mattress. She ran her fingers through his hair.

Still no smile.

At least her eyes emanated love for him: the look that made him feel special. Ruby was his one and only, and he was hers.

"The king is every bit alive," she said. "And we need to talk."

He couldn't prevent his heart from pounding, from trying to

break through his ribcage. Something was wrong. And his intuition warned that the *something* was going to break him.

Ruby started by saying she had sculpted a dome and sound proof barrier around their hotel suite, so they could speak freely.

She detailed her visit to the castle.

He could've stopped her right there. Had a tantrum over her sneaking out in the middle of the night, placing herself in harm's way, without even a word to him. Tricking him, no less, with an insect doppelgänger. But that was only the beginning.

The deal she cut with Zagan blew his mind. Not in a good way.

"You'd seriously *marry* that creep?" he asked. "What kind of ridiculous plan is that? I mean, besides the whole polygamy factor?"

"Hopefully the marriage won't last long," she said. "I have an idea on how to destroy him."

"And if your idea doesn't work? What then? You *stay* married to him and raise *my* daughter under his roof? Like one big happy, intergalactic family?"

"If my idea isn't successful, I'll find another and another. I won't stop until one works."

He pushed her hand away from his hair.

"Why do you get to take Gabby?" he asked.

"You know I'm the only one who can protect her."

"It's always about *you*," he countered. "What about her? Or me? Us? Our family? Our life together?"

His cheeks flushed. Fingers trembled.

"No matter what happens," she said, "I hope we'll continue where we left off. I'll either change Zagan so Gabby and I can come back to you with his blessing. Or, I'll kill him."

"So now he's your pet project?" Clay paused, glaring at her in disbelief. "Know what I hear right now? I hear selfish."

Veins grew on her neck and he didn't care. Not one bit.

"Selfish?" she said. "You think I *want* this?"

He raised his eyebrows.

"This is the only plan that shows promise," she snapped.

"You don't get to make decisions about *our* family all on your own," he said. "That's not how we handle our marriage. Oh wait: soon I won't be your only husband. Soon, Gabby will have an evil stepdad."

She touched his cheek, even though he turned away.

"We can't fight like this," she said. "You're my partner. The love of my life." She kissed his temple. "Sometimes there's a greater plan. And I'm doing the best I can."

Tears moistened his cheeks.

"I love you," she said softly. "I need to know you support me."

"Sorry. I just won't accept that you and Gabby are leaving. That you'd even think of marrying someone else. Let alone, the king of freaking evil."

"I haven't gone yet. Look at me. Please."

Their eyes met.

"Hold me, Clay," she pleaded.

Even angry, he loved Ruby too much to deny her. Placing his arms around her, he drew her to his chest.

How was he going to live *any* amount of time without her?

Their life together flashed in his mind.

The day he met her at sailing camp. Every moment of high school. When his parents died. During the pandemic. On their wedding day. Moving to Cedar Lane. Sailing *The Gem*. When Gabby was born. In Taiwan, when they found a zombie in Shifen. When she saved him in the Russian prison. Recovering on the *Elää Elämää* while sailing in the Baltic Sea. The day she died in his arms, then woke as a vampire. When they celebrated her homecoming from prison. When they hugged on the front lawn, elated that they had survived the housefire. The night she saved him and Gabby from falling into the raging sea.

All the times Ruby held him. Kissed him. Loved him.

How she made everything worth enduring.

His life album was Ruby. Gabby. Every single page was them.

Raising her chin, their lips touched.

Kissing turned to lovemaking.

Lovemaking to reminiscing.

"Let me glamour you again," she said. "Something that will help you through this while we're gone. Something that will help you forget the painful details."

"If it'll ease the heartache, then I'm okay with it."

Gazing into her eyes, Clay watched her pupils grow, swallowing the green of her irises. As if caught in a vacuum, he felt sucked into the portals, falling and swirling into her soul.

Time was lost.

"What were we saying?" he asked, feeling disoriented.

"I was explaining that Gabby and I have to take a road trip. That I'm not sure how long we'll be. Difficult news. I think it caught you off-guard." A tear raced down Ruby's cheek. "I also told you how much I love you. For eternity."

"Hey. Don't cry," he said.

Lifting her chin, he wiped her cheeks dry. God how he loved her. How he'd miss her and Gabby every day, every hour, every minute.

He forced a smile. "At least I've got projects to keep me busy."

"Oh?"

"Remember the tree root? From The Tree of Three Kings?"

"I recall an earthquake recently swallowed the one original tree of its kind. Good thing you have that root."

"Well, it's already sprouted," he said, feeling proud. "I'll have Justine book me a flight to New Zealand so I can replant the seedling." He scratched his head. "Come to think of it, I can't remember how I got that root. Or how I know it's from New Zealand's Great Island. Will I even know exactly where to plant it?"

"Why not contact the tourism department?" she suggested. "Ask for a guide named Harper Patel. She lives in Kaitaia. Heard she was familiar with the trail that once led to the original tree."

"Yeah. All right."

He got out of bed and grabbed blueprints from his briefcase.

"I'll have our house rebuilt by the time you return." He paused, trying to recall something else. "Oh. I remember now. I'll know in my gut if you won't be coming back, so I can move on. Which sounds horrible."

He faced her, his eyes welling with moisture again.

"Come back to me, Ruby. Please."

57

THE SPENCERS HAD gone to the zoo after Ruby glamoured Clay. While they were apart in the days, months, or years ahead, the special family outing would be seared in their memories.

With the new day, Ruby told her daughter that they'd be leaving. Within two hours. Just the two of them.

Gabby responded with a tantrum.

Red faced and arms crossed, her daughter sat on a chair in their hotel living room, refusing to pack for their departure to Skotadi.

"You can't make me leave Dad," Gabby huffed. "I'm not going."

"Sometimes we have to do things for the greater good. We have to sacrifice, even if it's not what we want."

"That's not fair. I'm only nine." Tears filled her eyes.

Ruby's heart hurt. Literally. Like a fist was squeezing it.

"You don't understand," Ruby said to her daughter. "If the government ever finds out you have gifts, they'll take advantage of you. They'll own you. Turn you into a weapon. And since I'll be on another planet, it'll be harder to protect you."

"Then don't leave. We can stay here. And protect each other."

Ruby knelt in front of Gabby's chair, desperate to get her daughter to understand that leaving was the only choice. She reached for her daughter's hand. "Let me show you what the future holds if we don't go at all. Or if I go and you stay here with Dad."

Reluctantly, Gabby clasped her fingers.

Ruby was careful to filter some of the horrors flowing from her mind into her daughter's.

Reality was harsh, even with omissions.

Gabby witnessed images of massive crowds being culled, vanishing from their lives on Earth as they were traveled to Athanasia. Ruby's mind revealed that humans were separated from loved ones and grouped by blood type, age, and health. After processing, they were celled at High Cliff. Of course, she refrained from displaying that the sick and elderly were slaughtered.

Back in Washington, D.C., Ruby shared images of government scientists extracting Gabby's blood. Her daughter was pale and despondent, being used as a blood bank.

Opening her eyes, Gabby snarled, "I'm still not going."

Ruby had hoped to avoid the next image. "I'm not done," she said. "There's more. Close your eyes again. Please."

The shared vision flashed to a graveyard, to their family plot.

A new tombstone read: Clayton Michael Spencer.

Gabby yanked her hand away, tears cascading down her cheeks. "No, Mom. No!"

"The future looks very different if we go to Skotadi. Dad lives. You thrive. The world is saved." She locked eyes with her daughter. "You have to trust me."

"No I don't!" Gabby pushed her away. "I hate you! I hate you're a vampire. You've messed everything up." She ran to her bedroom and slammed the door.

Clay walked into the living room and admitted he'd been listening from the kitchen.

"Let's give her a few minutes," he said. "Then I'll talk to her."

"I'm sorry." She moved toward him. "Sorry this ever happened to us. All I ever wanted was a normal life. A normal life with you. With our daughter."

He wrapped his arms around her as she snuggled her head against his chest. She inhaled the scent which was Clay: the open sea, crisp breezes, fragrant grasses, and sunshine.

"We've had a great life together," he said. "Some never come close to what we've had."

She raised her chin to gaze at him.

"You know I've glamoured you again, right?" she asked.

"I guessed it." Clay wore his half smile, her favorite. "My anxiety keeps floating away, replaced with puppies and rainbows. And I'm itching to get started on these projects, so I thought maybe you had something to do with it."

"Now that you've figured it out, are you upset?"

He smirked. "I think you've deprogramed that emotion for now. But no, I'd rather love you than be upset with you." He pulled back a little. "I'd better talk to Gabby."

They broke their embrace and her husband walked toward their daughter's room. Turning the knob, he opened the door and closed it behind him.

A half-hour later, the two emerged back in the living room.

Gabby ran into Ruby's arms.

"Sorry, Mom. I don't really hate you." Her daughter looked up. "Can we make a compromise?"

Ruby looked at Clay, wondering where the conversation was about to go. He nodded, showing he thought she'd approve of their daughter's request.

"On every one of my birthdays," Gabby continued, "you can travel me to Dad. We can celebrate my special day together. As a family. With Mai and Zoe, too."

She smiled. "Yes. That's a perfect compromise."

"Tell your Mom the rest, please," he said.

"When I was mad, I undid the glamour and shield you gave me. And I offered to undo Dad's, too."

Ruby's heart palpitated.

"And?" he urged.

"And Dad said we needed the glamours. So I left his alone and rebuilt mine, almost the same as you did. Except now I can talk around Zagan. Otherwise, he might get suspicious."

Ruby had constructed a uniquely sophisticated glamour and shield—ones that couldn't be detected or duplicated by any other vampire, including Zagan and Liora. Yet their daughter unraveled, rebuilt, and tweaked them within her own brain? As a human?

"Dad said you'd want to check them out," Gabby added. "To make sure I did a good job."

Squatting to lower herself to eye level, Ruby drilled into her daughter's mind. Sure enough, the glamour and shield were perfectly duplicated. Invisible and impenetrable by others.

"You really are amazing, you know," she said, kissing Gabby on the forehead. "Are you ready to pack your things?"

Their daughter ran off to her bedroom.

Ruby and Clay sat on the couch and talked, dreading their upcoming goodbyes.

Her thoughts were interrupted.

She internally listened.

"What?" Clay asked, when she began to blink again.

"I've been expecting a whisper from Titus's mate. And she's reached out to me."

58

Monday, July 1, 2041
Kaliméra Castle: Lampsi, Athanasia

HOLDING THE PARCHMENT, Liora found her assistant swimming in the pool adjacent to the hydrangea and peony garden.

Turquoise tiles made the pool's water appear tropical. The queen's exotic freshwater fish added to the colorful tapestry. Swimming in small schools, fish turned in unison as they approached each wall, resembling rainbow patches chasing a roving sun.

Solange stopped swimming, dipping her head back into the water to smooth her long gray hair.

"Good morning, Queen." Her assistant pressed her naked body against the side, resting her arms atop the pool's coping. "Come join me for a swim."

"I shall refrain," Liora said, "though my worry eases now that you are in sunshine, refreshing your soul."

"Swimming helps me think. And my thoughts are occupied with a new purpose. One that allows me to redirect my sorrow."

Liora held the parchment in front of her. "Would your thoughts and purpose have anything to do with the king's impending union with our Tether?"

"Indeed."

"Strange that I should need to find you, to inquire regarding what you have learned," Liora scolded. "My assistant is expected to divulge knowledge as received, bringing facts to *me*. Perhaps I should collect the information myself, in a timelier fashion, through cognitive exploration."

The queen folded the wedding invitation and shoved it into her gown's pocket. "Need I remind you," she added, "I can whisper into your thoughts anytime of my choosing. Shield or no."

Her assistant lifted herself from the pool, grabbing a towel from her lounge chair. She began to dry her body.

"You would invade my thoughts without invitation?" Solange patted her face to absorb the moisture. "I would be insulted. Did you not encourage me to pursue my purpose in the present battle between good and evil?" She tilted her head. "I have done so. And since my purpose centers on building a pathway toward a favorable future, I respectfully implore you to avoid interference. Your purpose will be revealed when stones are carved with the inevitable. As your loyal assistant and friend, I urge you to keep your sight focused on reading the etchings."

"And how would *you* know beyond doubt, dearest Solange, that idleness is the course which I am to take at this juncture?"

"The Tether is also a seer," her assistant answered. "And we have spoken, as you and Titus had hoped."

"Just like that," Liora said, snapping her fingers, "you accept counsel from another?"

The queen had always enjoyed unequivocal loyalty from Solange—loyalty never shared with or challenged by anyone else. Having her assistant dedicated to Ruby's guidance made her feel inadequate. Perhaps even jealous.

Liora did not relish these destructive emotions.

"You have taught me," Solange countered, "that even one misstep can cause what is being built in the sand to crumble. I am asking for your trust, Queen. Again, please wait until your eyes see the carvings to learn your purpose in this conflict. And accept that I intend no disrespect or disloyalty in my strong suggestion of it."

A ray of sunlight glimmered off an object on the other side of Solange's lounge chair.

To discover the source, Liora took several steps toward the sparkle, finding a gold urn resting on the deck. The urn stood two-feet in height. Titus's name was engraved on the gleaming receptacle, resembling a dazzling, fallen star.

The queen locked eyes with her assistant, raising her eyebrows to emphasize her question.

"I retrieved Titus's remains from the cottage," Solange explained. "This vessel awaited my arrival."

"Surely Zagan would not have spared you from the visual savagery of your slain mate," Liora said.

"Most assuredly true. But if you press your thoughts to the near past, you will see that another was responsible for this compassionate gesture."

"Of course: Ruby," the queen said, trying not to let her rising resentment sour the tone of her words.

59

Monday, July 1, 2041
United States Penitentiary, Lee: Virginia

EM HAD DISCRETIONARY insomnia. Meaning he chose to forgo any shuteye in pursuit of his mission.

Ever since Warden Measures and Lyle had accompanied him to his new home in the basement of the penitentiary some 39-hours ago, he'd achieved a near perfect record of wakefulness. Exception: his break to observe the naked mole rats. Basked in darkness and the glow of red lights, sitting in a comfortable chair facing their drawer-like habitat, he had drifted into la-la land for a three-hour layover.

No more dreamy furloughs anytime soon.

The day promised too much.

As requested, Irene Unger's oncologist had emailed Em the First Lady's pathology report, including molecular and cytogenetic diagnostics of her tumors. Her cancer antigen CA-125 registered a value of 1,137 u/ml.

Translation for the layperson? Death by ovarian cancer.

The oncologist had also complied with Em's request to extract a biopsy specimen, in liquid form, so he could inject the cancer into a clinical test subject.

How else would he know if his bioengineered magic worked?

Not a chance in hell that he would try his serum on the First Lady, untested and cold turkey. After all, his intent was to earn a "get out of jail free" card, not a death sentence from a pissed off POTUS if Em's serum failed.

The fact that his human guinea pig didn't have any almond-shaped ovaries made no difference. Cancer wouldn't discriminate over its host's gender. Equal opportunity, boyfriend.

Em moved a chair to the center of the lab, next to the stainless-steel instrument table that he had wheeled there earlier. On top of the cart was everything he needed for the injection, including a full syringe. His plan was to inject the biopsy liquid, teeming with cancer cells, into a lymph node located in the back of his subject's neck.

On cue, the deadbolt buzzed and retracted into the steel door.

In walked Big Dan dressed in a prison four-piece suit. His hands were handcuffed, ankles shackled, wearing a bite-restrictive facemask. A thick chain was lassoed around his waist and Lyle held onto the free end like a leash.

"You want him in that chair, boss?" Lyle asked.

Em resisted rolling his eyes at the obvious.

Big Dan wouldn't budge.

Needles could do that to people, even hulks the size of Dan.

Lyle withdrew his pistol and shoved the barrel into Dan's back. Forty-five millimeters of pure motivation.

The prisoner shuffled his feet, moving forward, before sitting in the chair. His eyes darted left to right, ceiling to floor, trying to assess where he was and what was going to happen.

"Remove the mask and ankle shackles," Em ordered, eyeing Lyle's pistol. "But keep the motivation handy. And cocked."

Lyle looked bewildered, which was no surprise.

Regardless, Em's guard extraordinaire did as he was told. Good thing Lyle never made a habit of questioning him. Which meant the guy had *some* smarts. Or more likely, he cherished his own survival.

Standing, Em pushed Big Dan's knees apart and moved in between his thighs. Slowly, he unbuttoned his lab coat. When his jacket was fully open, he pulled his scrub pants over himself.

Placing his right hand on his shaft, Em stroked a couple times to make sure he was loaded for bear.

"Is this part of prepping for a shot?" Lyle asked, his tongue wetting his lips. "Because I'm due for a flu vaccine."

"Since Dan's getting his flu shot *now,*" he said, winking, "he might need a little extra protein."

Still caressing himself, Em raised his left hand and ran his fingers through Dan's thick hair. He locked eyes with the prisoner. "Besides, I'm going to leave you alone after this. Lyle and I think you've paid your debt for stealing my science magazine."

Dan opened his mouth to protest about the magazine, since it had been planted in his cell, of course.

Intended or not, an opening was considered an invitation.

Yanking Dan's head down toward his cock, Em accepted Dan's generous hospitality by shoving himself between parted lips.

Em's eyes fluttered from the tightness, from the warmth. From the danger of Dan's teeth grazing over his sensitive skin. From the sensation that he could be swallowed.

Tension had been building, especially with his lack of sleep.

He thrust himself into Dan's mouth. Over and over. Deeper and deeper. Until he climaxed, purging himself of stress.

Lyle watched.

The bulge under the guard's zipper said he would have preferred joining in.

While Em tidied his scrubs and lab coat, Lyle refastened Dan's shackles and facemask.

Em prepped the needle by slightly pushing the plunger into the barrel to expel any air.

Dan's eyes widened. Unadulterated fear. A tear escaped and raced down his cheek.

Apparently, Big Dan had figured out he wasn't getting a flu shot.

60

Monday, July 1, 2041
Castle on High Cliff: Skotadi, Athanasia

RUBY TRAVELED WITH Gabby to High Cliff, luggage in hand. Instead of materializing in the king's study, she opted for the cobblestone pathway leading to the main entrance at the base of the castle. Made sense that if High Cliff was going to be their temporary home, they should be formally welcomed. The time had come to be introduced to staff. Especially since she needed to deliver a warning.

Zagan knew precisely when they'd arrive. Although the king had raised a permanent shield to prevent entry by cognitive whisperers, she'd already devised a workaround. Which meant she could communicate their ETA. She smiled recalling the king's surprise at her cerebral intrusion. Perfect timing to remind him that he needed her. That her power was unmatched.

Ruby held her daughter's hand as they walked over the slightly uneven cobbles. Neither spoke. Neither were in a good mood. And on top of everything else, Gabby wasn't thrilled she had to wear a gown. Ruby tried to soften the blow by sculpting her daughter's dress from pink satin and adorning the collar and hemline with sequins. But if her efforts had made a difference, Gabby wasn't showing it.

As for herself, she chose a royal blue gown that included a conservative neckline. Now that the deal with Zagan had been struck, she didn't need to flaunt her cleavage.

With the breeze, lit lanterns swayed on posts on both sides of the walkway. To their left, a fence served as a deterrent. Beyond the

271

barrier were rocks and a 300-foot drop to the rushing river below.

The moon cast a spotlight on the castle which was carved within the steep canyon wall. Like tiny stars flickering, the windows glowed from candlelight, accentuating the shapes, angles, and curves of the colossal fortress.

Crickets serenaded them. Smells of river moss filled the air.

Back home, midday was basked in sunlight.

Here, perpetual darkness.

Two guards, dressed in black cloaks and brandishing swords tucked in leather scabbards, stood at attention on both sides of the entrance. They bowed their heads in respect.

Let the masquerade begin, she cognitively whispered to her daughter.

"Queen," one guard said, before turning his attention to Gabby. "And Princess Gabriella."

She and Gabby curtsied with the greeting.

The arched door was a sight to behold and Ruby tried not to gawk with an open mouth. The twelve-foot-high door was crafted from solid mahogany, intricately carved. One panel depicted The Tree of Immortality. The other showcased a cloud of bats: some embossed, some engraved, some fluttering across to the other panel.

A guard pushed open the door to reveal a foyer, tiled in black and white marble. Eighteen vampires stood waiting, all dressed in black uniforms. Smiling, they genuinely looked eager to meet them.

Zagan, outfitted in a bright green tunic, approached her at the doorway. He extended his hand for hers and she offered her right.

"Queen," he said, kissing the top of her hand. "You and the princess are graciously received at Castle on High Cliff. My staff has yearned for this citadel to be blessed by a female's touch. And now, casting eyes upon their queen, every face reveals delightful surprise—that I am to be coupled with one so lovely, so charming as you."

You're pouring it on thick, she whispered into his brain.

The whole experience felt surreal, like Ruby was a character in a medieval movie. Or in a *Beauty and the Beast* retelling.

On the outside, she smiled. "How kind of you, King." She bobbed her head. "However, I won't be queen until the coronation, though I look forward to having the title bestowed on me."

"With our ceremony a mere three-Earth-days from the present,"

Zagan said, "using your proper title must become customary with the staff. Is this acceptable? Or is the suggestion too...*thick?*"

After she reluctantly approved the practice, Zagan introduced her and Gabby to staff members. They met the castle steward, chaplain, chamberlain, chambermaids, keeper of the wardrobe, laundress, ladies in waiting, and several footmen. Ruby's head housemaid was named Katerina. Violette was Gabby's nanny.

They'd meet the grounds and kitchen staff later. Maybe Atea and Jasmine would be included in those introductions.

A vampire in knee-high leather riding boots walked into the foyer. He held a lead line attached to a halter, attached to a midnight black pony. They stopped in the center of the round room, as soon as the pony was in patting distance from Gabby.

Her daughter ran her hand over the pony's well-groomed neck.

Ruby almost rolled her eyes at the king's old-school approach to winning a young girl's heart: gift her with a kitten, puppy, or pony. Forget that building trust and respect was the only impactful way that counted over the long term.

"And this, Gabriella, is Marius, our marshal of stables." Zagan placed his hand on Gabby's shoulder. "Although your mother will receive several presents during our celebration of matrimony, this friendship offering is for you. The stallion awaits a name, as well as your care. Will you accept my gift?"

Gabby locked eyes with him. "You're very generous. Thank you." She curtsied. "And I'll accept the pony, as long as it's only friendship you're hoping for. You'll never be my Dad."

"Dearest Gabriella," he said. "Nor would I *ever* wish to be."

Ruby ignored Zagan's *un*-subtle rudeness at expressing his contempt for Clay. Instead, she stretched her mind toward the stable marshal, to assess his attitude toward Gabby. She sensed kindness and curiosity. Also excitement, especially since there were no children on Athanasia. Marius harbored no animosity toward humans. Most importantly, he had already had his fill of sustenance. Her daughter's scent didn't affect his predatory instincts.

This is your queen, she whispered to Marius, whose eyes widened. *Hurt Princess Gabriella and you die.*

Zagan pointed in the direction that the marshal and pony had entered. "Marius will show you to the stables, Gabriella, while the queen and I discuss matters regarding our wedding traditions."

Gabby looked down at her gown. "But Mom..."

Ruby exchanged her daughter's dress by sculpting riding breeches and boots, as well as a sweatshirt.

Smiling, Gabby thanked her before being led to the stables.

Although Ruby was prepared to address Gabby's safety with the staff, Zagan broached the subject first. He warned his subjects that they would be carbonized, and their mates as well, if anyone harmed a hair on Gabriella's head.

Staff members nodded to affirm their understanding.

Placing his hand on the small of her back, the king gently guided her into a sitting chamber and closed the door. He pointed toward the red-velvet loveseat, directing her to sit. As she lowered herself, trying to manage her foolishly full skirt, he sat beside her.

Her eyes widened. Placed on the coffee table in front of them were an ornate gold crown and tiara, both depicting bats in flight. Each bat's body and wings were carved from onyx. Eyes were bright rubies. Above the bats were three distinct sections of sky, each representing a realm. On the left one-third, sapphires resembled the night sky of Skotadi. In the middle, the skies were ornamented with gray pearls. And on the right, a sun and its rays were made of citrine gems. Decorative gold mantling rose from each realm, adorned with diamonds to resemble stars.

"Does the design please you?" Zagan asked, picking up the tiara and handing it to her.

"Gorgeous." When their eyes met, she asked, "Are they new?"

"Indeed. With the tragic, unintentional loss of my true love, I abdicated my right to find another mate. When I was chosen king during The Rising, only one crown was forged—its design melancholy to match my mood." He smiled. Green eyes sparkled. "Presently, my spirits have lifted. I commanded this set be created to commemorate the breaking of the curse. Though our skies will remain the same, our bats will have no limitations in their flight across all realms."

"How symbolic," Ruby said. "And when you say the crowns were *created*, do you mean sculpted?"

"The monarchy should not deny subjects from applying their talents, from displaying loyalty through their labors and artistry. For to do so would extinguish their lust for existence." Zagan lifted his crown from the table. "Let us not forget: authentic beauty is crafted, not sculpted. And as beautiful as these, when you behold your wedding ring, you will undoubtedly be dazzled by this truth."

"I'm intrigued." And then she realized she hadn't thought about *her* responsibilities. "On Athanasia, is it customary for the bride to present her groom with a wedding band during the nuptials?"

"It is." He reached for her tiara and returned both headpieces to the table. "Tradition also requires that you choose a wedding gift. One I can present after our union has been consummated."

Ruby's heartrate spiked. In truth, she didn't want to think about *that,* about consummation. She was far from ready. In fact, she had no clue how she'd participate in sexual *relations*—the only phrase she could think of to adequately describe the planned exchange. An exchange that would take place in…Three. Short. Days.

Clay was the only man she had ever loved. The only man she had ever shared complete intimacy with. She didn't want this to change.

"Is there a gift you would cherish for eternity?" the king asked.

Thinking about eternity was also off limits. Her stomach churned.

"I don't want a 'thing,' like jewelry or a horse," she answered. "Instead, I'd rather visit the villages together. To meet all the citizens of Athanasia. To assure them that I'm the Queen of Peace. That I want to help restore balance and harmony."

"This is most unexpected. For this gift will bring joy to me and our kind as well." He placed his hand in hers. "There is no denial that you have left your mate to save him. And if not for your proposal to thwart an interplanetary war, you would be by *his* side."

Zagan's fingers caressed hers, not in a suggestive way, but in a caring way. "Your sacrifices are noble. Inspiring," he said. "Reminding me that there may be room for goodness in my heart."

Ruby tilted her head, surprised by his words and touch.

Maybe she *could* change his heart. Help him grow the internal goodness he had long abandoned.

Perhaps his death could be bypassed.

61

Monday, July 1, 2041
Castle on High Cliff: Skotadi, Athanasia

ZAGAN'S INSIDES WERE twisted with uncertainty. He lay alone on his bed in the master chamber, gazing through the open skylight carved within the stone ceiling, trying to make sense of his feelings. He much preferred actions. Emotions tended to linger, tirelessly.

Thus, not even his bats or starry skies or distant lightning could quiet his soul. Nor the crackling wood ablaze in the fireplace. Nothing could serenade him toward rest.

His mind recalled the activities with his betrothed, after discussing wedding traditions.

Initially, Ruby's room-by-room tour of High Cliff proceeded without incident. Even when she encountered Atea among the kitchen staff, his intuition remained unprovoked. Dissolved were his suspicions about the true nature of their relationship. Indeed, Ruby appeared indifferent toward her former acquaintance who was now his valued procurer of blood.

As well, Ruby did nothing to hide her admiration for the castle and its offerings. This was not surprising, for High Cliff was the only fortress in all of Athanasia. Kaliméra Castle was a mere estate, a large dwelling with gardens. Nothing more.

But uncertainty struck when the king showed her the isolated wing where his five delectable mayflies were confined in a well-appointed cell. The introduction to the sources of his "reserve" divine wine had been premature. Ruby questioned why guards were posted if the humans were volunteers; in fact, she wondered why the humans were being held captive at all.

Zagan had not considered her reaction, as he was not accustomed to thinking about others.

As he and Ruby walked beside the containment chamber, a mayfly reached beyond the bars and touched her arm. The human's wrinkled forehead and pleading eyes made him want to carbonize the wench, then and there. But he reminded himself: prudence over impulse.

Ruby had kept her lips sealed. But when the mayfly smiled and retreated from the bars, he suspected his soon-to-be queen had cognitively whispered to the human.

This unsettled him. Not knowing to *whom* she whispered, *when* she whispered, or about *what* she whispered caused his chest to tighten. His fingers, to be unsteady.

Zagan did not treasure even the slightest lack of control.

At least he harbored some of his own secrets. For instance, he had intentionally constructed a weak shield within his own brain, one that she had dismantled easily, allowing her to whisper with him. He smiled at his cunningness, for he was not an amateur by any measure. There were areas of his mind that would not be penetrated, not even by The Tether herself.

If only his emotions had stopped with the feeling of pleasure over his duplicity, then his eyelids might have shut to rest his senses. But his eyes did not choose to ignore the beating of his heart, so they remained open. Ruby intrigued him. Ignited energy beneath his skin. And her beauty, intellect, and power were in his reach.

He could imagine the sound of her breathing.

The softness of her skin.

In the quiet, he admitted his eagerness to find companionship.

Yet, doubt frayed his conscience.

At this moment, was Ruby really in her boudoir? Or had she traveled back to her mayfly on Earth, perhaps leaving a doppelgänger in her place?

Had she constructed a protective dome over her bedchamber? Preventing him or anyone but Gabriella from entering?

Or had she accepted their agreement with authenticity?

Not to be denied, he also worried about sharing his bed once he and Ruby wed.

He wished he could call on Draven to seek counsel.

Though many times the king had ignored him, Zagan's former henchman had always offered sound advice. After the wedding, after he invited his protector to return to High Cliff, he would consider changing his attitude regarding Draven's guidance.

Zagan's mind continued to race in 34 different directions.

Without addressing his present concerns, rest would refuse him.

He raised himself from the bed. Wearing his long white nightshirt, he traveled into Ruby's bedchamber.

To his surprise, a barrier did not hinder his arrival.

In a similar nightshirt, Ruby sat at her vanity, looking into a mirror while Katerina brushed her hair.

"How very impolite," Ruby scolded. "To pop into a woman's bedroom without an invitation."

"Leave us," he commanded the housemaid.

Katerina nodded at Ruby, curtsied to him, and departed from the boudoir, closing the door behind her.

"Apologies for my intrusion." He picked up the brush. "May I?"

"Isn't brushing beneath you?" she asked, sounding sarcastic.

"Not when the tresses belong to my queen." He began brushing, enjoying the silkiness of her hair. Brushing was a task so simple and endearing. One long forgotten by his hands.

Ruby turned her shoulders, looking up at him. "I'm guessing grooming didn't bring you to my room. What's on your mind? Getting cold feet?"

"I am restless. Worried."

When she asked why, he admitted he had not shared a bed with a female for over 500-years. And when he had, the interaction was far from restful. Things had been broken. Furniture had been replaced. Consequently, he worried he would not remember proper etiquette.

"What are you asking? Exactly?" Ruby inquired. "Because I'm sure you've embedded a question in your confession. Only I'm not in the mood for cognitive drilling to figure it out."

"May I lay with you a while?" Zagan asked. "Until the worries in my thoughts are diluted?"

Ruby's eyes darted about the room, as if searching for a response.

"No need for nervousness." Zagan laid the brush on the vanity. "As a female recently elevated to the highest stature, I am forbidden to couple with you until our wedding night."

She rolled her eyes.

"Does this disappoint?" he asked, trying to understand the intent of her expression.

"Far from…I mean, it annoys me when men classify women like some deserve better treatment than others. Newsflash: we should *all* be treated with respect, regardless of *stature.*"

"Simply traditions in our culture, though I invite you to change them." He reached for her hand and she provided it. Helping her to her feet, he asked, "Will you allow me to share your bed until my troubles are eased? Until rest welcomes me?"

When she agreed, his heart raced.

Although Ruby did not lay her head on his chest or even touch him, his spirit was delighted. He listened to her heart beating. Her lungs expanding and contracting at will.

She was rhythm. Music.

The opposite of loneliness.

He had not felt this sense of security, of well-being, since his early days—his youth, while being in the company of his true love.

Might happiness inflate his heart once more?

He had regarded their union as a business arrangement. A temporary one at that.

Could his and Ruby's relationship develop into more?

Might he spare her life?

62

Tuesday, July 2, 2041
Castle on High Cliff to Prison of the Unruly

RUBY COULD NOT rest with the king by her side.

Instead, she listened to the orchestra of nightingales, whip-poor-wills, great reed warblers, black rails, and owls. Crickets, cicadas, and katydids joined the alluring ensemble.

Far below the window of her quarters, the Tume River rushed over rocks—swooshing and gurgling, harmonizing the melodies of each performer. Swaying reeds brushed against one another, no doubt applauding the nocturnal concert.

On Earth, waking from rest was marked by an alarm of sounds: smartwatches buzzing, DEPE's nagging, birds chirping, dogs barking, car engines idling, coffee machines percolating.

In contrast, Skotadi grew quiet.

With Zagan's eyes still closed, Ruby slipped from bed without making a peep. She hoped allowing the king to rest with her would help build trust between them.

Of the multitude of guests expected to attend their wedding celebration, trust would be the most important attendee. And she only had two days left to inspire its growth.

Since no one appreciated waking up alone when they'd gone to bed with company, she left Zagan a cheery note: *Rise and Shine, King! You'll find me in the library.*

Checking on Gabby was her next priority.

Ruby traveled to her daughter's bedchamber. After waking Gabby, she sculpted black leather pants, jackets, and boots for each of them. Their hair was pulled into ponytails—which segued into an expected conversation.

"Can you help me name my pony?" Gabby asked. "Everyone has pets named Blackie, Eight Ball, Midnight, and Licorice. I want something cool. And different."

"Hmm. How about Tenebrous? It means shut off from light."

"Will Dad like that name?"

"I'm thinking yes." Ruby gently clasped her daughter's ponytail, running her hand down its length. "Do you miss him? Like I do?"

"Yeah, but you're going to get us back home..."

Careful what you say out loud, Ruby warned. *Remember: listeners can hide.*

"I mean, home to celebrate my birthdays," Gabby added, smiling.

Ruby traveled her daughter to the library.

Each weekend morning (pre-housefire), she, Clay, and Gabby would take turns reading aloud a chapter from a novel. Why not continue the tradition? They picked the classic *Dracula,* by Bram Stoker, since Gabby wasn't afraid of vampires anyway.

As Ruby finished the last line of the first chapter, she heard a tap on the door and invited the knocker to enter.

"Excuse me for the interruption, Queen," said Violette, as she curtsied. "Chocolate chip pancakes have been prepared for the princess, ready to be eaten in the dais."

You told them my favorite, Gabby whispered into Ruby's thoughts. *Thank you, Mom!*

As Gabby and Violette exited the library, Zagan entered, followed by Atea and Jasmine. Which signified mealtime, a la carte.

Like before, the tray-table topped with a full carafe of divine wine was wheeled into the room. Jasmine's hand healed from the knife wound inflicted by Atea, verifying the new batch of blood was safe for their consumption.

After the king's nod, they handed full chalices to her and the king, before leaving the room.

While sipping from her goblet, Ruby tried not to think about the woman who had touched her arm by reaching through the bars of her cell chamber at High Cliff. The prisoner's eyes and thoughts had pleaded for rescue. Through a cognitive whisper, Ruby had promised she was working on that very outcome.

"What's on your agenda today?" Ruby asked him. "I'm thinking something king-*sey* perhaps?"

"You are a most amusing wordsmith." Zagan chuckled, his eyes matching the iridescence of his aqua-green tunic. "And if traveling to the Valley of Shade to oversee wedding preparations is king-*sey*, then the answer is affirmative. Will you join me?"

"I trust your oversight. Instead, I'd like to walk around the castle and grounds. Get to know the place and staff better." Ruby sipped her divine wine. "In just two days, I'll be queen. It's important I get comfortable with my surroundings. Do you mind?"

"Familiarizing yourself with High Cliff is splendid." He put his glass down and touched her arm. "To be sure, your kindness has amplified my gratitude. Letting me rest by your side provided needed comfort. Our partnership is evolving better than expected."

Zagan's words were uncharacteristically tender. A gentler, more thoughtful side was emerging. Hope continued to flourish. Could she rescue him from the evil poisoning his soul?

Instead of trying to kill him, maybe she could convince him that being warmhearted toward others would grow goodness in himself.

"Told you I had a great proposal." She smiled. "And to think, you didn't believe me."

After satisfying their itineraries, they both agreed to meet back at the horse ring in the "forenight," which she learned was equivalent to afternoon. Marius planned to give Gabby her first riding lesson on Tenebrous.

When Zagan turned to dust to commence his travel to the Valley of Shade, she waited a few minutes longer.

Even though the king was showing promise, she couldn't abandon her own agenda. And hers had nothing to do with the castle's grounds or staff.

She traveled to the Prison of the Unruly.

Rather than materializing in Draven's cell right away, she wanted an overview of the property while flying as an eagle. Knowing more than needed was always smarter than not knowing enough.

The Shadowlands was blanketed in charcoal skies and gray light.

Maybe a thousand acres in size, the prison campus was expansive, enclosed by a 20-foot-high silver fence, topped with twisted barbed-wire. Shaped like a circle with a hollowed center, the gray-stoned building included four guard-towers, one stationed every quarter. The circle's center was a massive courtyard which housed above-ground cells that looked like human-sized chicken cages, made of thick wire. Each cage jailed a single vampire prisoner. Some inmates were hanging upside down.

Flapping overhead in bird form, she spotted a massive line of vampires. Some were walking two and three abreast. Guards poked and prodded the prisoners to move forward as they were being ushered into the facility.

Could there seriously be 302 unruly vampires arrested in one day?

She flew closer.

Her heart accelerated. Bile raced up her eagle's throat.

The scent of the captives was undeniably…*human*.

Had Zagan dared to orchestrate another culling on Earth?

She flew close to the ground and sculpted into a female guard, mimicking the same attire as the others. Needing to mask her identity, she duplicated the face of her hairstylist in Annapolis, only with gray skin like a Shadowlander.

A male guard approached, wearing a curious expression.

"A splinter is in my eye," Ruby said, hoping to sound like an ancient vampire. "Surely healing will forsake me if the sliver of wood cannot be found for extraction. Tell me, can you see it?"

The guard didn't hesitate to look. After all, Ruby's hairstylist was very attractive.

Eye contact was all that was needed to initiate a truth glamour.

The guard divulged that humans had been culled from a Canadian sports stadium at "mornight," meaning earlier that morning. Zagan had ordered guards to process and house "the mayflies" at the prison, instead of the castle, to avoid detection.

Detection from *her*.

Her body temperature heated.

She'd mistaken Zagan's kindness as a sign that he might change. That he might choose goodness over evil.

What a joke. He was still playing her.

Making her out to be a fool in his *own* masquerade.

Clearly, Zagan would stop at nothing to get what he wanted.

She expected to be consumed with anger over his betrayal.

In truth, she felt sadness. Sadness about what his life could have been if he'd chosen to better himself.

The king had never intended to comply with their agreement.

Ruby had to reboot.

Her original plan was her only pathway.

When she finished with the guard, she traveled into Draven's underground cell, appearing as herself in black leathers.

Once again, he was hanging upside down.

"What is it with prisoners hanging upside down?" she asked.

"Blood rushes to your brain," he answered. "And when you are starved because, in my case, a certain someone suggests going on a hunger strike, the position allows what little oxygen remains in the body to feed the brain. No one wishes to be hungry *and* delirious."

"No arguments here." She placed her hands on her hips. "However, it's time to stand upright, whether you're incoherent or not. Because I've got a message from Solange, on account of Liora."

Draven flipped to his feet. "Nonsense. Liora does not need messengers when she can whisper to me directly."

"Fine. I'll report back that you've refused transport to Kaliméra."

His blue eyes narrowed. "Pardon?"

Ruby explained that her intention was to travel him to the queen's estate. That Liora and Solange had matters to discuss with him. Over a keg of animal blood.

"Though the keg sounds tempting," Draven admitted, "when the king discovers my escape, would you have me acquire the title of outlaw? A fugitive, while you and your betrothed rule the planet? I do not believe Liora would wish this fate on me. Better to wait until I have regained favor with Zagan."

"First of all, the king is very busy with wedding preparations and has no plans of visiting you until after our union is…lawful. With your hunger strike, guards won't be checking on you either. Which means your dead body won't be discovered until *after* the ceremony."

He swallowed hard. *"Dead?"*

Using her gifts, she levitated a lifeless cricket off the floor and moved the insect with her mind to hover over the prison cot. After dropping the carcass onto the thin mattress, she sculpted the bug into Draven's doppelgänger.

The real henchman watched the transformation with wide eyes.

Draven was shocked, no doubt, that his lookalike had been shaped to look emaciated. Very dead, in fact. And clearly the swordsman had suffered from flesh-eating bacteria.

"If someone happens to check on you, Henchman," Ruby said, "you'll be dead. Guards will be screaming for your immediate cremation before anyone thinks to conduct an autopsy. And there's no need to declare you a fugitive when all that remains is a pile of your ashes." She smiled. "I'm thinking a little appreciation is warranted."

"Gratitude, indeed." Draven kissed her cheek and held onto her arm. "I am starting to like you, Tether. I believe we are bonding."

As she turned them to dust, she thought of her next stop, after dropping Draven off at Kaliméra. She needed to visit the jeweler in Skotadi.

Time to have the king's wedding band handcrafted.

63

Wednesday, July 3, 2041
United States Penitentiary, Lee: Virginia

EM WAS STOKED when the results of the oncology analysis kit confirmed that cancer biomarkers were off the charts. Big Dan was mister malignant. A freak performer in cancer's circus of the bizarre: a male hulk with ovarian cancer in his posterior cervical lymph node.

Popcorn's ready, folks.

Let the show begin under the big top of the penitentiary.

After extracting a biopsy of Big Dan's lymph node in the morning, the kit produced results in a mere four hours. Ironic. There were minimal advancements in cancer prevention and treatment. But the disease could now be diagnosed in hours? More astounding, there were biomedical scientists working on at-home kits, quick as a pregnancy test. What was wrong with that picture?

No worries: Doctor Genius was in the house.

He had his eyes on the right carrot: *curing* the fucking disease.

Imagine that.

The buzz of the door's deadbolt announced his expected guests.

Today, Em would test his hybrid serum.

Preparations were already in place, like the metal rings cemented into the floor to secure Dan's shackles.

When dealing with dark science experiments, an abundance of caution was the necessary prescription. After all, the whole purpose of using a human test subject was determining if the hybrid serum caused detrimental side effects. And when the anomalous DNA of an ugly fucker like the naked mole rat was spliced with the DNA of a genteel but rapidly decaying First Lady, nothing was off the table.

Nothing.

Lyle pushed Dan into the room, jabbing his back with his baton.

In an orange-peel jumpsuit, accessorized with a complete assortment of prisoner restraints, Dan shuffled his feet, moving in slow motion. Beads of sweat marked his pale forehead. Eggplant circles under his eyes looked like bad makeup.

Dan plopped into the chair in the middle of the lab.

The prisoner's shoulders drooped. His eyes were slits.

Lyle secured Dan's shackles to the floor rings. He unlocked and relocked his handcuffs behind the chair, attaching the cuffs to a prong in the chairback. As ordered, Lyle removed Dan's facemask, though Em's guard extraordinaire wasn't sold on the idea.

"If this clinical test goes south," Em countered, "he deserves a last word. So Big Dan, what say you, boyfriend?"

"Tell my wife I love her," he said. "And then rot in hell."

"All righty then." Em whistled. "My get-out-of-jail card awaits."

Em prepped the inner crook in Dan's arm, getting a vein to rise to his request. After pricking the test subject's skin with the needle, Em slowly released the blue serum into the vein.

Then they waited.

Not one word was spoken.

Ten minutes passed.

"Now what?" Lyle asked. "Do I take him back to his cell?"

Standing on Dan's left side, Em noticed movement in the prisoner's hands. Dan's fingers clenched into fists. Not the kind of fists made when trying to dispel stiffness or slough off anxiety. But the kind of fists that bleached knuckles. That knocked out teeth and crushed skulls with contact.

Em felt a surge of adrenaline.

"I'm not feeling good," Dan said, blinking rapidly.

"How about being more specific?"

Turns out, Dan was a "show, don't tell" sort of guy.

He thrust his arms out to his sides, busting the handcuff on his left wrist like it had been bought at the five-and-dime. The chairback broke off and dangled from his right cuff. Snapping the rings from the concrete, Dan freed his feet. He stood and wildly grabbed at his hair with his left hand, like maybe his scalp was burning.

Clumps of brown hair stayed with Dan's hand.

Whipping around, the test subject glared at Em. Hate was in his eyes, eyes that were bloodshot and squinting from the lights.

Dan's body started to tremble like it was about to erupt.

Em held his hands in front of him. "You need to sit, man. Take a deep breath."

In what seemed like superhuman speed, Dan jabbed his right arm to the left, sending the chairback which was tethered to his wrist into a collision course with Em's head. Luckily, Em was agile, ducking and skirting to the side.

"How about some help here?" Em said to Lyle.

"I'm gonna kill you," Dan seethed between clenched teeth, releasing a spray of drool.

As the prisoner advanced on him, Em retreated toward a wall, his heart pounding. And for the first time, he wondered if Lyle was going to let Dan crush him.

A muffled gun blast shook the lab.

The mechanical door sealing the animal habitat rattled.

Big Dan took one more step before dropping to the floor.

Lyle had shot him in the back, through the heart. Blood pooled onto the concrete.

As they assessed the outcome, no one moved or took a breath.

Especially not Dan.

"Took you fucking long enough," Em finally said, glowering.

"Bullets don't always stop moving after they've hit the intended target," he said. "Had to find the right angle. And you're breathing, aren't you? Besides, I had to screw on a silencer."

Em wasn't comfortable with Lyle's attitude.

Weapons could inflate a person's sense of security. Embolden them. He'd have to keep a watchful eye, to determine if his guard extraordinaire was taking the "extra" a little too far.

"Is your serum even doable, boss?" Lyle asked.

Now Em was downright irritated.

"As *doable* as ending your life, boyfriend."

Em figured Lyle would have no problem interpreting the absolute sincerity of his warning.

"Didn't mean to question," Lyle said, unscrewing the silencer and returning the pistol to his holster. "How about I take Big Dan to the incinerator down the hall?"

After Em nodded, the guard picked up one of Dan's feet and began dragging him toward the door, leaving a bloody contrail on the concrete. No doubt Lyle would stuff Dan into what was becoming Em's personal cremation oven. Of course, with Dan's size, Lyle might need to do some carving first.

Em had his own challenges, like backtracking to pinpoint where the hybrid serum had failed.

He'd deal with Lyle's cocky attitude later.

Anyway, Em clearly needed another test subject.

64

Thursday, July 4, 2041
Castle on High Cliff: Skotadi, Athanasia

BOTH UNSETTLED AND eager, Zagan waited for his bride in the study. Bats fluttered to and from the chamber, sensing the tense atmosphere. He let his thoughts scatter toward his anxieties, in hopes of gaining swift resolutions.

Human superstitions about seeing a mate prior to the union of matrimony did not exist on Athanasia.

Instead of wasting energy on similar unfounded fears such as walking under ladders or crossing black cats, mayflies needed to redirect their worries toward concrete threats.

Toward his kind, for example.

At least Ruby accepted she no longer belonged to the mindless, inferior human species—the universe's gluttons of imbalance.

Yet, his jitters were still not pacified.

His fingers nervously fumbled with the velvet box tucked in the pocket of his tailcoat jacket. Part of him acknowledged that he did not deserve the happiness of being paired with a mate for eternity. At the same time, his path had changed too abruptly to be authentic.

Spurring these doubts was his suspicious nature. Consequently, he would not relax during the ceremonies, lest he forget that many Athanasians wished to dethrone him, rather than celebrate his union and elevation of power.

Another part of him longed for the partnership with Ruby to be genuine. Not only for the acquired advantage the union would yield, but also for the loneliness their marriage would dissolve. This side of him was emotional. And emotions made him abhorrently vulnerable.

Zagan closed his eyes, wondering if he could quiet all sides of his constitution.

"Am I interrupting, King?"

When he opened his eyes, Ruby stood before him, having traveled into the study. He gasped at her unparalleled beauty. An angel. Clutching his chair, he steadied himself.

"Feel free to interrupt me for the rest of eternity, Queen," he said, smiling. His stomach flitted like a cloud of bats. "Your beauty overshadows all infractions."

Vampires were naturally attractive to captivate their prey.

In his eyes, Ruby was beyond exquisite. On this occasion, she let her hair cascade over her bare shoulders. And draped around her neck was the diamond necklace he had left with her housemaid, to be presented to her upon waking. The necklace dangled a three-dimensional heart-shaped ruby.

Her gown was adorned with a full skirt. Starting at the hemline were clusters of bats in flight, flying toward her waistline, showcased with an ombré effect, from black at the bottom, to shades of gray, to white—disappearing into her gown's fabric. The bodice of her dress sparkled with diamonds, like the precious gems decorating her crown to represent stars.

She curtsied. "And *you* look very handsome in your white formals. The green bowtie and cummerbund match your eyes."

"Come," he said. "Let me show you a sight which has not been witnessed since The Rising."

Allowing his hand to linger on the small of her back, he guided her to the ledge overlooking the valley below. Citizens from Skotadi were making the trek to the Valley of Shade: some on foot, some on horseback, some in horse-drawn carriages. Most carrying glowing lanterns or flaming torches to light their journey.

"Wow," she said. "They're all coming for us?"

"Indeed, as decreed, save for the Queen of Light." He tightened his jaw. "How I will relish her diminished importance."

"Why won't she be there? I mean, she whispered to me before I blocked her. I was looking forward to meeting her in person. She's very beautiful."

"I received notice that her mare had taken ill," Zagan said, scowling. "As if she could not heal the beast and thought me a fool. The mare is an excuse. Liora wishes to avoid embarrassment over the coronation of another queen." He gently rubbed her back. "On to more pleasant subjects. Where is Gabriella?"

"Violette is escorting her to the venue."

"How are her spirits? For I imagine, expanding one's family can be disconcerting."

"She's remarkable." Ruby beamed. "Since our union benefits the planets by preventing war, she accepts it. Clay and I have taught her about sacrifice. And like she's told you, her Dad will always be her Dad. That won't change."

As she turned to face him straight on, his hand regrettably slipped from her waist. But then she clasped each of his hands in hers. His heart raced from her intimate touch.

"It helps," she added, "that I've promised to take her to visit Clay on every birthday. Hope you don't have a problem with that."

Thumps on the door interrupted their discussion. The knockers were Atea and Jasmine, pushing their cart.

He had not ordered divine wine, so he was not expecting them.

"Good mornight," Jasmine said. "Apologies for the intrusion, King. We bring you the traditional wedding tea, to be shared between you and the queen prior to departing."

"I had forgotten this custom," he said.

"What does the tea do?" Ruby asked.

"Since the celebration is long," Jasmine explained, "wedding tea provides energy and stamina. Endurance must not wane until after the...the consummation. And herbs like eleuthero and astragalus root are very effective toward this purpose. Please, indulge."

"Most thoughtful of you to remember," the king said. "Know my words are true when I admit I require no further stimulation. Eyes upon my bride and anticipation of our vows are all the arousal I thus need." He pointed to the cart. "Perhaps my mate will indulge?"

"Oh, no thank you," Ruby said. "I'm nervous as it is. The last thing I need is to get fidgety."

The two procurers curtsied and turned to exit.

"Before you go," Ruby called after them. "Will you attend the wedding? Familiar faces would ease my nerves."

Zagan answered for them. "They shall, as a traditional toast is required immediately following our vows."

"Oh, I didn't know that. But good." Ruby looked at Atea and Jasmine. "I'll see you there, then."

The procurers nodded and wheeled the cart over the threshold, closing the door behind them.

"About Gabriella," he said, referring back to Ruby's promise to her daughter. "When is her birth celebrated?"

"In eight months."

"Then we shall have other opportunities to discuss future travels." He held out his bent arm for her to hold. "For now, more immediate matters await us. Shall we?"

65

RUBY AND THE king arrived at the wedding venue well ahead of the ceremony. She was escorted to a private tent, heavily guarded, where she signed legal documents including a prenuptial agreement. She had to laugh. No doubt the king would've simply carbonized a mate whom he no longer desired or needed, but since he couldn't kill her outright, the paperwork sought to strip her of any rightful claim...to everything, including her crown. And if the king died unexpectedly, she was to be seized and placed on trial for his murder.

Did Zagan's immortal lawyers forget she was a traveler?

Trust was clearly a no-show at the Glissendorf wedding.

At least Zagan's behavior was no longer shocking.

Besides, she could carbonize any agreements. Including a wedding license. What court would enforce paper ashes?

When the master of ceremonies entered the tent, with Gabby and Violette in tow, they all sat at a table to review the sequence of the festivities. With each word, Ruby's anxiety skyrocketed. Every single sentence reverberated in her ears.

Her throat grew dry.

Although some of the future was beginning to be etched in stone, many surfaces were still blank. Too many possibilities continued to be viable. And like any hesitant bride, uncertainties made her leery.

Her thoughts were bombarded. *What if this? What if that?*

But her only choice was forward.

Grabbing her daughter and vanishing were not options.

Clay and humankind's survival and independence required that she and Gabby stay the course—despite the risks and sacrifices.

Church bells rang, signifying the ceremony was about to begin.

She embraced Gabby. *We can do this,* she whispered.

Her daughter nodded, giving a weary smile.

There were no bouquets to clutch. No wedding party to exchange nervous glances. Or her Dad to offer assurances while they walked down the aisle. No music to soothe shaky legs and a pounding heart. These marital traditions didn't exist on Athanasia.

Instead, Ruby and her daughter were led to a huge well-lit stage that overlooked the valley bathed in twilight. The king's guards were everywhere, armed to the teeth.

Holding lanterns or torches, masses of vampires had assembled over the landscape, as far as her eyes could see. In the distance, they resembled a carpet of twinkling dots.

The enormity of the gathering caused her knees to buckle.

A collective gasp wafted in the air when the citizens of each realm saw their soon-to-be queen for the first time.

Half the stage was adorned with an expansive dining table and 36-chairs, able to accommodate dignitaries from each realm. A gold chalice was at each place setting; Gabby's included a plate. At the head of the table, two throne-like chairs were positioned side-by-side.

The flower arrangements were breathtaking. Hydrangeas and peonies were clearly from Lampsi, night-scented orchids from The Shadowlands, and reeds and ferns from Skotadi.

The far half of the stage, the half where she was being led to, included a wooden arch decorated with similar flowers. Rose petals marked the walkway leading to Zagan and the chaplain.

As she neared, the king smiled, offering his hand. She clasped it.

Most brides felt butterflies.

Her stomach swarmed with bees.

She tried to push thoughts of Clay from her mind. Allowing herself to become overwhelmed with sadness and guilt would compromise her efforts. Because her first attempt to destroy Zagan was closing in.

So many moving parts were in play. Each one could fail. Each one could cause death for those whom she loved.

At least the vow exchange went quickly. Mostly because she had trouble paying attention. But her mind snapped into focus when Zagan revealed her wedding ring and slid it onto her trembling finger.

The design wasn't what she expected.

The ring boasted a ten-carat ruby, even larger than her pendant. The three-dimensional gemstone was cut and polished with brilliant facets that sparkled, raised on platinum prongs. And the band was ornamented all the way around with two rows of diamonds.

She reminded herself not to place hope in the gesture.

Zagan was a master of deception. Of manipulation.

When the ring was on her finger, he leaned toward her, his lips brushing her ear. "As you can see, *I* mined the largest star-ruby in Athanasia," he said. "Possessing the symbol of love has been my destiny, both as a gem and in the flesh."

"You can't possess someone else," she said. "Only the love in your heart truly belongs to you and can be freely shared."

Before he could respond, she presented his wedding band. His eyes widened. The thick platinum ring showcased a full row of sapphires all around one outer edge, an alternating pattern of a gray pearl and a heart-shaped ruby comprised the middle row, and citrines embellished the last row. Bats were etched on the inside of the band.

Zagan nodded and smiled, seemingly pleased with the symbolism of a unified Athanasia, similarly depicted on his crown.

When they kissed at the end of the vow exchange, she was also surprised that his lips stirred something inside her. Was the feeling regret? Although she had only known him for 25 days, they were the most intense days of her life.

The thing about intensity—whether good or bad—was that the emotions were deeply rooted. They burrowed into the soul and weren't easily discarded. Or forgotten.

The crowds cheered after their kiss. She and Zagan turned to face the masses. The king held her left hand and raised their arms together, causing those gathered to roar with approval.

Ruby wanted to cognitively eavesdrop into some of the vampires' minds, to decipher how they really felt about the Glissendorf union, but there was no time.

Icy nerves chilled Ruby's insides.

Zagan ushered her near the head of the table. They couldn't sit since the wedding toast had to be delivered standing, for all the crowd to hear. Gabby stood beside her.

A portable cart topped with a carafe of divine wine creaked and rattled over the stage, pushed by Atea. Jasmine walked beside her.

Atea wouldn't look at Ruby. Her eyes were cast downward.

Ruby made no attempts to whisper to her friend. She stayed focused on the stones and etchings in her mind.

In typical fashion, the procurers performed the testing ritual as Ruby and Zagan watched. Both of them had a stake in its outcome.

After Jasmine drank a sip, Atea clasped the knife and sliced the vampire's hand.

Jasmine recoiled from the incision, as if it hurt.

Blood oozed from the cut.

Looking at Atea, Jasmine formed trenches on her forehead. Her eyes narrowed.

"Mom?" Gabby asked, with worried eyes.

Say nothing, she whispered into her mind. *Read the stones.*

"Again," Jasmine pleaded. "Cut me again."

Shaking as she held the blade, Atea sliced her hand another time.

Both cuts remained open. Unhealed. Bleeding.

A hush swept across the valley.

Even Zagan looked shocked. Horrified.

66

Thursday, July 4, 2041
Valley of Shade: The Shadowlands, Athanasia

ZAGAN COULD NOT believe his eyes.

The surge of anger, betrayal, and emotional torment caused the fire inside his veins to intensify.

Trembling, Atea took a step away from her once-vampire associate. Most assuredly, the mayfly whom he had acquired had not forgotten the price that came with serving tainted blood.

"What is this?" he roared at Jasmine. "Do you attempt to poison your king and queen with mortality? At our union of matrimony?"

His heart pounded. Nails grew into daggers.

Incisors, to razor-sharp fangs.

The crowd cowered.

As a reflex, Zagan swept his hand to carbonize the traitorous procurer, but Jasmine failed to turn to ashes. Instead, she stood before him, bleeding from her hand. Pathetic and weak, as if she wished for her own destruction now that she had joined the inferior mayfly species.

Raising his hands and face toward the gray sky, he released a wretched, guttural growl. Frustration made his body shudder. Bulging veins could not be suppressed on his neck and face.

Making sense of the situation was crucial. For he understood he was under attack, yet he could not determine from which direction it came. Or by whom the battle was led.

The inability to carbonize had happened once before. When Ruby had given her mayfly spouse her blood, she had raised the protective shield of self-preservation. But why would Ruby share her blood with Jasmine? With a renegade?

Without intention, another likelihood flooded his thoughts.

One far crueler. And once again, the finger pointed toward Ruby.

"Did you not hand me all the berries you collected from The Tree of Awareness?" he asked his mate. "Was your offering deceptive? Part of a ruse to end my immortality during a wedding toast?"

"Stop," Ruby urged, while clasping his arm. "Stop and choose prudence over impulse, husband. Get a grip! Command yourself to think logically. To consider the facts."

The word *husband* penetrated his building rage. There was an affection, an intimacy to the title that was not inherent when she called him king. Or mate. *Husband* was her language.

Inhaling deeply, he locked eyes with her. Waiting. Hoping she could prove that she was innocent regarding the unfolding atrocity.

"I haven't shared my blood with Jasmine. Why would I?" Ruby asked, clearly gleaning his suspicions from his mind. "Instead, maybe she got her hands on the berries somehow. When the juice from The Tree of Awareness is concentrated in someone's blood, they can't be carbonized. The berries—the juice—can't be destroyed or sculpted into something else: that's fact.

"What doesn't make sense," Ruby continued, "is that the blood in our wedding carafe is safe. Pure. I can see this truth carved in stone. Why would a traitor go to the trouble of poisoning Jasmine and *not* the divine wine we're intending to drink?" She squeezed his arm to emphasize her point. "Rather than focusing on destroying the procurer, take this opportunity to drill into her mind, King. To shed light on this mystery."

He closed his eyes for a moment to slow his heartrate. To clear his mind from the chaos. To purge his anger.

Ruby's counsel sounded reasonable.

Knowing the truth would, indeed, be valuable.

The crowds began to murmur and shuffle, growing cautious and restless with the interruption and confusion. He ordered his guards to stand poised. Ready to use force on his order.

Silence returned. After all, Zagan *could* carbonize the entire gathering, save for Ruby, Gabby, and now Jasmine.

On the stage, beside the dining table, the king clutched Jasmine's arm and yanked her toward him. With eyes locking, he drilled into the depths of her memories, searching for answers.

Although parts of Jasmine's brain were meant to be hidden, blocked from discovery, he was a master at cognitive mining. He unraveled the glamours, restoring her thoughts into consciousness.

With memories released, he applied a truth glamour.

For questions posed, Jasmine voiced the horrid answers aloud.

At the center of every response: Titus.

Liora had whispered to the former henchman about Zagan's possession of the fruit, as well as the planned wedding between the king and Ruby. Both had been carved in stone.

Jasmine explained that Titus had stolen one berry from Zagan's secret chamber. The robbery occurred on the very night the king had placed the first two berries in his vault, the ones dropped by Ruby before she leapt over the cliff on Great Island. And since the king's henchman served at High Cliff and was also a whisperer, the Queen of Light had urged Titus to glamour Jasmine since she was the king's chosen procurer of blood.

Glamoured to be unaware of her traitorous actions, Jasmine had squeezed the berry juice into the wedding tea, in hopes that the king and queen would bypass the testing ritual, since the beverage was not blood. But when the tea was declined, she unexpectedly drank some herself in the kitchen, out of curiosity for the tea's energizing effects. Jasmine did not remember she had tainted the tea. Unbeknownst to her, she had turned mortal.

Jasmine was an unintended victim.

Thanks be to HIM, the assassination attempt on his life had failed.

"I shall destroy Liora once the curse is lifted." Zagan clenched his teeth and glared at Ruby. "But tell me this, *wife*. If you are a seer, why did you not *foresee* this ruse against me?"

"Against *us*," she corrected. "And truth is a complicated matter because it's everywhere. Truths are suspended in each nanosecond, in the minds of all beings. And they're constantly changing with every action and reaction. To retain sanity against the noise, I have to *choose* to press my mind toward a hunch, toward a question, to see if the answer has been carved.

"When it comes to the blood on that cart," Ruby continued, pointing to the full carafe, "I *did* seek the truth about its purity. But why would I have pressed my mind for answers about the wedding tea? We both declined the beverage, so there was no need."

The words Ruby spoke seemed absent fraud. But his trust in her had been thin to start, and now it had all but eroded.

He swept his hand. The filled carafe on the cart turned to ashes.

"Clearly, I had spoken the truth," she said, with irritation. "If the divine wine had been tainted, you couldn't have carbonized it. And now we have nothing to toast with. And a wedding toast, need I remind you, is a required component of our lawful union—a union which has *everything* to do with breaking the curse. A priority, I had thought."

Ruby already sounded like a nagging mate, and they had not even made it to the bedchamber.

Though in truth, he supposed her point had merit. Breaking the curse was of utmost importance. He should not lose sight of this fact. Ruby had warned him before of his tendency to sacrifice lofty goals for meager ones. To attend to inconsequential details while ignoring those with significance.

Turning toward two nearby guards, Zagan spoke in a low voice. "Take Jasmine into Gray Forest," he ordered one of the two. "When you are far enough for her screams to go unheard, rip her heart out. She will die indirectly, despite the juice in her veins."

To the other guard, the king commanded, "Bring Atea to me." He sculpted a new carafe. "Her blood will fill our cups, for a toast is in order. And our partaking of it shall not be further delayed."

Zagan wondered if Ruby would react to his order, but she remained stoic.

Atea attempted to flee.

Her legs must have forgotten she was surrounded by vampires.

As his human procurer squirmed and resisted capture, the guard held her wrist over the pitcher.

Zagan deeply sliced her wrist with his nail and the mayfly bled rapidly into the carafe.

When Atea's pupils hid behind her opened lids and her heart

sputtered, he ordered her to be removed from the stage. Atea would die, and he would not give her passing a second thought, although he had enjoyed her humor and tenacity.

A server poured the blood into the two chalices.

The crowds were unsettled again, for the masses were not privy to divine wine. They did not know that human blood represented fulfillment of yet another scripture: *And when truth is tasted once more, and lips are stained crimson, goodness shall be set free.*

Of course, goodness was the restoration of balance.

During the wedding celebration, he would address his kind and share the inspirational news. Human blood would eliminate hunger and allow animal populations to recover on all three planets. Without question, balance was created for vampires to govern.

First, Zagan had to survive.

Enemies were among him, suspected and unknown.

Nodding at Ruby as a cue, they raised their goblets in the air.

The crowds hushed.

"Glory to HIM!" the king roared.

"Glory to HIM!" the masses responded in unison.

"May our blessed union be ever pleasing to HIM and to each other," he finished.

He and Ruby lowered their chalices and faced each other. Her child remained standing near her side.

"It is customary that the bride drinks first," he said, dipping his head as a polite gesture, knowing he was lying through his teeth.

"Really?" she questioned. "The master of ceremonies said we were to drink at the same time. Together. Arms intertwined."

He raised his eyebrows. "Master Henry is mistaken. That particular toast does not occur until we bid the crowds goodbye at the celebration's end."

"I must've misunderstood," Ruby said. "But anyway, Atea's blood is safe to drink."

Was it? Should he believe her?

His heart palpitated as she raised her glass to her lips and drank. She lowered her chalice from her mouth, licking the blood from her upper lip. Without words, he reached for Ruby's left hand and she complied, resting her fingertips on his palm.

Zagan sculpted an incision on the top of her hand.

Blood trickled from the wound.

"Master Henry also failed to warn me of this tradition," she said.

"I believe Henry should be removed from position, for neglect of duties," he answered, while regarding the blood still oozing curiously from her wound. "Are you not *healing*, my queen?"

He detected an acceleration of her heartbeat, which regrettably was an organ he would seize from her chest if the delay in healing persisted. For then, she would surely rank as an enemy.

The union which had carried such promise was quickly unraveling.

"Why wouldn't I heal?" she countered, her incision beginning to mend. "Do you think I have a death sentence? That I'd lie about Atea's blood being safe and drink it anyway?" Ruby glowered. "Of course I wouldn't. Do you really think I'd want to be stuck here on Athanasia as a *mortal?* Unable to protect my daughter? Again, rely on logic, Zagan. I beg you."

Locking eyes with her, he regretted his doubt.

His utter lack of trust.

He wished his heart could quell the discord which resided within.

Surely, his actions would sour the rest of the celebration.

For being Earth-made and young, Ruby often seemed the wiser.

"Sincerest apologies are offered," the king said, bowing his head. "An untrusting heart does not correct itself easily. I suspected chicanery when none was present. Please, my Queen. Please forgive me for commencing our union in such a disgraceful manner."

She placed her healed hand on his cheek and caressed his skin with her thumb.

"I forgive you, Zagan Glissendorf. My king. My husband."

His heart was warmed by her kindness.

And so he drank.

67

Thursday, July 4, 2041
Valley of Shade: The Shadowlands, Athanasia

RUBY BRIEFLY CLOSED her eyes in relief.

At the same time, she fought back the fear that clumped in her throat and made swallowing impossible. Fear that made her body shake as if she hadn't eaten in a decade.

She wanted to drop to her knees, to hysterically cry, but she had to persevere. Gabby's safety depended on her.

Images of stones faded in her mind.

Uncertainty filled the void.

Her daughter tugged at her gown, gazing upwards, urging Ruby to go the distance.

Zagan's mouth was marked with a stain from Atea's blood. Ruby gently tried to wipe his lips clean. Her fingers trembled.

The crimson stain remained.

Pursed to speak, the king froze instead.

Commotion diverted everyone's attention.

Galloping down the hill in the distance, beyond the left side of the stage, were a legion of vampires on horseback. Curiosity marked the face of every head turned.

The rumble of hooves made the stage vibrate.

As the legion neared, Ruby could see the first two armor-clad vampires. They were mounted on stallions racing side-by-side, leading the cavalry and carrying a territorial flag representing their realm: one from Lampsi, one from The Shadowlands.

Zagan clenched his fists.

Riding behind the flagmen were Liora and Draven. Each wore a gold crown. No doubt the headpiece on Draven caused Zagan enormous distress. Not to mention confusion and rage.

The crowd looked frozen.

Wearing decorative gold armor, Draven dismounted his gray stallion and walked to Liora's white mare. He helped her dismount gracefully, despite her full gown made of gold satin and ornamented with sparkling diamonds.

The former henchman extended his arm to the Queen of Light. She placed her hand on his forearm.

The crowd didn't move, or whisper, or breathe as the pair walked onto the stage. No doubt, the vampire masses sensed the energy. Something monumental was happening.

"I see your mare has enjoyed swift recovery," Zagan sneered, glaring at Liora. "Yet you persist on harboring prisoners which are not yours to emancipate. And then you dress them like dolls to mock my authority." He turned to a garrison of guards. "Arrest them and all who rode with them. Or I shall carbonize every last one of you."

The garrison remained in place.

With clammy skin, Ruby worried she'd faint. She needed to focus.

Liora smiled and spoke softly. "Let us speak sensibly, Zagan. For our legion on horseback will be spared from any sleight of hand, as will your garrison. We've taken precautions.

"Hear my truth," the queen continued, "unless you wish to have the crowd witness, once again, your inability to carbonize. They do not love you, Zagan. Surely you know this. Your cruelty has brought this outcome to pass. And a weakened King of Darkness—one they no longer fear—will likely entice them into rebellion. They will tear you apart. Limb by limb."

"Speak quickly and to your point," he seethed, "or my mate and I shall sculpt restraints before ripping your hearts from your chests. Imagine the affirmation of power that act will have on our citizenry. For we are travelers and sculptors and you shall never be."

Clasping Gabby's hand, Ruby took a few steps back on the stage, providing a little distance from the escalating exchange.

Not to mention she wasn't feeling well.

Bile burned her throat.

Liora smiled at Draven before regaining eye contact with Zagan.

"As usual," the queen said, "distractions have prevented you from attending to details. Or surely you would not have overlooked the simple truth that you and Ruby were not the only coupling who could satisfy the sacred passage: *the King shall wed the Queen.*"

"Placing a crown on Draven's head makes him a fool, not a king," Zagan snarled, his nails growing to daggers.

"But surely," Liora said, "a coronation officiated by a sitting queen would legally bestow him with the position. Would it not?"

The king narrowed his eyes, as if digesting the queen's implication.

"Draven has been my true love since Creation," Liora continued. "Not only did I crown him prior to our matrimonial union in the Fields of Twilight, we also lawfully wed *before* you and Ruby, fulfilling all traditions, including consummation. Draven stands before you, before all our kind, as King of Swords and Shadows."

Ruby immediately pictured Neviah's tree tattoo which had been labeled: *The Blood of Three Kings.*

There were two kings now, if that even meant anything.

Before Zagan could respond to the queen, Liora took Draven's hand. Together, they raised their arms in unison while facing the crowd of onlookers.

"The king has wed the queen," Liora shouted. "Draven and I have broken the curse!"

The crowd erupted in cheers. Vampires from each realm threw their hats into the air. Others hugged and cried.

With his face turning red, Zagan staggered slightly on his feet.

A swarm of dust appeared.

Solange materialized on the stage.

Gasps filled the air.

The crowd had no clue there was another traveler.

Zagan trembled uncontrollably. His eyes wide with disbelief.

"This cannot be," he said. "You are a figment of my imagination. Has your likeness come to comfort me in my greatest hour of need, amid this coup?"

Solange approached him. "Dearest Zagan," she said. "I have come to set goodness free. The goodness suppressed within you. I seek, we all seek, to restore your soul." She glided her hand over his cheek. "Your imagination, I am not. My touch, my flesh…they are real."

"But I…" He took a deep breath. "But I carbonized you. Turned you to ashes in a fit of fear and rage. I relive this horror in my mind, watching you vanish before me. Not able to undo my heinous act and bring you back to me. Back into my arms."

"I am a traveler, Zagan," Solange said. "I kept this gift hidden to skirt repercussion from all who fear its power. But know this: near The Tree of Immortality, when you brought the curse into our world, I traveled to Liora to seek *help* for you, not to condemn you. For we were mates, to be coupled for eternity. My love was sincere. I would not have betrayed you."

Zagan's tears streamed down his cheeks.

"Fate allowed me to travel," Solange continued, *"before* you could extinguish me from existence with a sweep of your hand. It was dust you saw as I vanished, not ashes. Ever since, I have lived and served my queen in hiding. To remain safe from your discovery."

"Safe? Surely the truth was evident then, as it is now. That you have always been my one true love," Zagan said. "Awareness—most especially of evil—has been locked inside me, sealed shut once my immortality was reinstated on that grisly day. From then forward, my actions have been influenced in ways I often regret."

"Yet love is defined by actions, much more than words. I know this now, as Titus and I had become mates. He faced death by your hands to protect me, to protect our kind. Even to help you."

"Help me?" Zagan asked. "By attempting to dethrone me?"

"Wipe your tears," she said.

Zagan's fingers returned from his cheek with clear moisture.

"I am…*mortal?*" His lips quivered.

Whispers raced across the crowd.

He looked at Ruby. "Will you not save me, wife?"

Zagan's plea was desperate, an emotion she'd never witnessed from the king. His despair tore at her heartstrings.

Telling Gabby not to follow her, Ruby took small, careful steps and positioned herself next to Solange. Her wedding dress felt like it had been drenched in the river.

"Saving your soul," Ruby said, "is different than saving the body in which it dwells. And I *do* want your soul to be free from the evil you invited in. For your sake. For the sake of each planet."

Zagan placed his hand on her cheek, rubbing his warm thumb over her skin. "You have witnessed my attempts at goodness," he said. "Tell Solange. Tell them all. Please."

"It's true. I've seen you try," Ruby said, covering his hand on her cheek with hers. "But the evil inside you is way too strong. That's why you culled more humans after our agreement. Why you recently murdered on Earth and Athanasia. Truth is, if goodness could prevail within you, it would've over the last three mega-annum."

Zagan's eyes darted from hers to Solange's and from Liora's to Draven's. Perhaps he was beginning to understand that his survival wasn't a given.

"But as a mortal," he pleaded, "what harm could I cause?"

"The stones have revealed you'd regain your immortality."

"Tell me, Ruby," Zagan said. "What was your role in this ruse?"

Solange answered instead.

"The Tether rose to our cause," she said, "as the Sacred Scrolls had prophesied. Atea was the carrier of mortality, as she had ingested a berry given to her by Ruby."

"You both hate me that much?" he asked softly. "To orchestrate this deception and strip me of my immortality in front of my kind?"

"To the contrary," Solange countered. "We love you enough to set your goodness free, free from a corrupted vessel. *Truth,* as stated in the scriptures, is not human blood as you have fantasized. Rather, truth is mortality—which you have tasted once more. With mortality, every act, every thought, every word carries the weight of consequences. Sadly, as a uniquely gifted immortal, you have long neglected this truth.

"Do you not," Solange continued, "seek permanent rest from the malevolence poisoning your soul?"

"I will not deny that evil has made me weary. Has brought strife and discord within my own heart when I destroy or harm others."

"Then choose to become a victor over wickedness," Solange said. "Accept your sentence and rejoice in the forgiveness that awaits."

"Your offer promises hope," Zagan said, tears overflowing.

A breeze swept across the valley.

Not a breath was taken.

"Make it so, dearest Solange," he said.

Tears raced down Ruby's cheeks as she kept her eyes on his.

She had wanted so badly to save him from himself. But that victory could only have come from *within* himself.

With blurred speed, Solange's fingers pierced his chest—through his white tailcoat and shirt. When she withdrew her bloodied hand, the king's heart was clasped within her fingers.

Zagan slumped onto the stage floor.

Solange placed the heart into Ruby's opened palm.

Raising her hand, the crowd watched the heart beat one last time.

"Glory to HIM!" Ruby shouted, feeling perspiration bead on her forehead. "Zagan's goodness has been set free!"

"And glory to our Tether!" Liora echoed across the masses. "The scriptures have been fulfilled. Let balance be restored on all three planets. Harmony and peace shall flourish."

Ruby's body flushed with heat.

The crowd's jubilant response was muffled.

Sounding miles away.

Her knees buckled.

Zagan's heart slipped from her hand.

Gabby screamed from behind her.

Dropping onto the stage, Ruby landed by Zagan's crumpled body.

Darkness blinded her sight.

The last sensation she felt before being swallowed by nothingness was a prick of teeth puncturing her neck.

68

Sunday, July 7, 2041
Kaliméra Castle: Lampsi, Athanasia

RUBY SQUINTED, SLOWLY waking to sunlight streaming in through an open window in a bedroom. To her left, sheer white curtains twirled and touched from the breeze, like a bride and groom on their first wedding dance.

Finally, her pain had subsided. Her brain-fog was clearing.

Thoughts bolted to Gabby. Where was her daughter?

With her heartrate spiking, Ruby raised her back, throwing off the linens, prepared to leap from the bed. Her eyes darted around the room: assessing, processing.

Oxygen and adrenaline raced toward each muscle.

"Mom?" Gabby asked, sitting near a corner with a book in her hand. "Are you okay?"

"Thank God!" Ruby deeply inhaled. "You're here. Are you hurt?"

Gabby walked over to the bed and wrapped her arms around her. "Not hurt at all." Her daughter sat on the mattress edge and moved strands of hair from Ruby's face. "And Zagan is dead. They took his body to a tomb. His heart, too."

Ruby clasped her daughter's hand, running her thumb over the soft skin. "If you hadn't sculpted my hand to heal, once I was human, who knows what would've happened."

"My healing was slow," Gabby said. "I was scared."

"You were brave. I'm so proud of you. You read the stones and did what you needed to do. Your gifts are strong. Zagan's defeat

310

couldn't have happened without you, you know."

Tears trickled down her daughter's cheeks.

"Are your tears from sadness or relief?" asked Ruby.

"Mostly sadness. I mean, I sort of felt bad for King Zagan. Sometimes he tried to be nice. To be good. Didn't he?"

"Yes, deep inside I think he wanted to be good." She wiped the tears from Gabby's face. "But as an immortal who feared nothing, he mostly let evil guide his actions."

"Couldn't we have let him live as a mortal?"

"The stones revealed he would've recovered his immortality," Ruby said. "If he had lived, humans would've been culled for their blood. Which could've been you and Dad. And families everywhere, across the globe." She lifted herself higher against the headboard. "When you think of Zagan, think of his acceptance at the end. Once mortal, he took responsibility for his crimes and accepted his fate. He showed honor in that moment. And love for others."

Gabby nodded, but tears continued to fall.

"I don't understand why you didn't stay human," her daughter said. "Why you let Liora bite you with her venom, so you could be a vampire again. Why, Mom?"

"We're always looking for miracles, aren't we? Something outside of ourselves, bestowed from above to save the day. Well, sometimes I think God calls *us* to be the miracle. To use our gifts to help others. Being a vampire is how I'm supposed to help the world, because my gifts are strong when I'm immortal. And there's still a lot to do."

"But I'm human and I have gifts."

Ruby leaned forward and kissed her daughter's forehead. "You're a miracle, too. As a human, your gifts are powerful. And I have no doubt you'll be called to use them again, like you did on that wedding stage. Perhaps we'll both be needed at The Turning Point, when the animals choose their king."

The door opened.

Walking in, Atea held a goblet. Jasmine was beside her.

"Howdy, mate," Atea said, sounding cheery. "So glad you've decided to grace us with your smile. Fangs. Whatever."

With the smell of blood, Ruby hadn't realized her incisors had sculpted into points. She could barely control her thirst.

Ruby nearly guzzled all the blood in the chalice. "After giving a drop of my blood to each rider in the cavalry for Lampsi and The Shadowlands, as well as each soldier in Zagan's garrison, I was nearly emptied." She looked up at Atea and Jasmine. "Hunger aside, I can't tell you how great it is to see you both. To know you survived."

"Thanks to the kind guard," Atea said, "who decided to heal me, instead of draining me for lunch."

"I was bitten by my guard," Jasmine added. "His venom returned me to immortality. I woke a short time ago. And now here I am—a Skotadian in sunlight, since the curse has been broken."

"I need to thank you both." Ruby turned serious. "Atea: for giving a berry to Jasmine for the tea and for eating the other one when I whispered it was time. Most of all, for playing your role flawlessly, even when your wrist was sliced, and life was draining from you. You are audacious. Fearless. Words can't express my gratitude."

"No worries, mate. I'd do it all over again. For you."

"Jasmine," Ruby said. "Thank you for letting *me* glamour you with a tall-tale about Titus being a traitor and forcing you to spike the wedding tea. The cognitive trickery fooled Zagan, distracted him. And consuming the tainted tea placed you at even greater risk. Your courage was remarkable, and I'll never forget it."

Liora drifted into the room like an angel, dressed in a flowing white gown. Solange and Draven followed her.

"The Tether endures," said the Queen of Light, her brown skin shimmering. "My venom has served its purpose."

"Albeit after three days of painful transformation," Ruby said, smiling. "But thank you for turning me. For everything. Really."

"Rise and shine," Draven said, lovingly placing his hand on Liora's back. "We have much to do, such as returning humans to your planet. As king, I recommend we start with Atea." He winked. "She babbles on about reuniting with her mate. Which grows tiresome."

Ruby sculpted her standard black leather pants, jacket, and boots in place of her nightgown. Her hair was pulled into a ponytail.

"Then let's get started, friends," she said, rising from bed. "I'm longing for my husband and dogs. How about you, Gabby?"

Her daughter jumped up and down, clapping.

69

Friday, July 12, 2041
The Westin Annapolis: Annapolis, Maryland

CLAY SAT ON the couch in the living room of the hotel suite.

He had returned from New Zealand two days ago and was still shaking off jetlag. Thankfully for botanists and community ecologists around the world, his trip had been a success.

With help from a local guide, he boated to Great Island and trekked the trail that led to the exact spot where the one original-species of The Tree of Three Kings had stood less than two weeks earlier, before a 7.2 magnitude earthquake had destroyed it.

After planting the sprouted root, he erected fencing around the seedling to protect it from hungry rodents. His guide, named Harper Patel, promised to visit the site regularly, to ensure the critically endangered tree survived.

The adventure felt like one big mental-rewind.

Clay knew Ruby had glamoured him to feel puppies and rainbows every time he thought about being separated from his wife and daughter. But he was convinced she had tampered with much more than his emotions.

New Zealand, for example. Clay had clearly hiked on the same island, on the same trail, shortly before the natural disaster. How else could he have gotten a root from the rarest tree in the world? And Ruby had also known about the root. Obviously, she had glamoured him to forget the details about how he had gotten his hands on it.

No doubt there was something special about the tree, in addition to its uniqueness, that needed to be kept under wraps.

He couldn't remember what.

Harper admitted to having a déjà vu vibe herself.

Her wife Atea had taken a small group—a family Harper had thought, to Great Island on the very day of the earthquake. Not even the tourism department knew the names of the missing family. And as yet, no one had filed a missing person's report that remotely connected to New Zealand.

The Patel's Scarab boat had been found empty, anchored in the South East Bay. The dinghy was gone. Atea and the passengers were still missing, though Harper refused to give up hope.

Clay wouldn't be surprised if his confused reality intertwined with Harper's. Probably why Ruby had suggested he request *her* as his guide. At least they had made a good team and completed the task.

Once the seedling was planted, Clay returned to the States. Back to his very quiet hotel suite in Annapolis. In fact, the absence of his wife and daughter was unbearable. Glamour or no glamour.

Along with the perplexities associated with New Zealand and the tree root, he suspected Ruby had glamoured him to forget other key chunks of information. Like: why in the hell did his family go to Athanasia? To Skotadi of all places? And for how freaking long?

The hardest questions kept him tossing and turning every night. Were they okay? Did they need his help?

Today would be another day of trying to stay busy to move the hours along. If he didn't have projects, he might have ended up staring at a white wall in his hotel suite, hoping time would stop. Stop, until his family returned. Until he could breathe deeply again.

Prior to leaving for New Zealand, an excavator had cleared his and Ruby's Cedar Lane property of the rubble from the housefire. A contractor was also scheduled to lay their new home's foundation.

In an hour, he would meet with the project superintendent onsite to discuss framing. First, he'd swing by Margo and Tomas's house to pick up Mai and the puppy. The dogs would enjoy running and playing on their property's acreage while he took care of business.

He felt driven to finish rebuilding the house. But why? Without his family, the home would be too large for him and the pups.

Clay's smartwatch pinged.

Eyes was requesting to videoface.

"Want to display the videoface on the MV?" Justine asked.

"Sure. Thanks." Clay watched as the Secretary of Defense's image appeared on the screen.

"Hey. Sorry I missed the SWC meeting on Wednesday," Clay said. "I was flying back from New Zealand. Any news to share?"

"When the government's involved," Eyes said, raising his eyebrows, "there's always news. Unfortunately, it's never *all* good."

"Start with the good anyway. I could use some."

"Most of the victims who vanished in the cullings were just found, an hour ago, near the locations from where they disappeared: passengers from Flight 1733 in Wyoming, soccer fans from a bus in France, and spectators from a Canadian sports stadium. Even that tour guide from New Zealand was found by a lingering search party on Great Island. Everyone's healthy. The news is about to go public."

"Wow! That's awesome," Clay said, his heart pounding in his chest. "Did anyone see Ruby? Was she mentioned?"

"When we questioned them, every single one looked like a deer in headlights. No one knew anything," Eyes said. "We suspect Ruby's involvement, of course. Who else could be behind it? She probably glamoured the victims to forget, you know, to keep the existence of a vampire planet classified. Imagine the unrest that would ensue if the populace knew. But instead, the disappearance and return of the victims will be known as the greatest unsolved mystery in humankind's history." He rubbed his chin. "I take it you haven't heard from your wife yet?"

Clay shook his head. "So what's the bad news? I mean, besides the fact that Ruby hasn't returned or reached out to me? And that my brain's jumbled and confused."

"Here's some curious news to mix things up even more," Eyes said. "Apparently, the First Lady experienced a miraculous recovery. One-hundred-percent cancer free, according to the POTUS."

"Wait." Clay ran his fingers through his hair. "Ruby couldn't have been involved. She believed that curing Irene would interfere with what it means to be human. So how could the First Lady be cured?"

"Publicly, the White House Press Secretary is attributing her condition to the miracle of chemo. Between you and me, Irene didn't get chemo because her cancer was too far gone. I have my suspicions, though."

"Like what?" Clay said, already dreading the answer.

"For one thing, Emory Bradshaw was pardoned. That's the bad news, by the way." Eyes bit at his bottom lip, meaning he was angry and frustrated. "I went to talk to the dark-science weasel myself. Guess what? The bastard had already been released. His Russian troll Vladimir Volkov, as well. Released in the dead of night, When no one was looking."

"Are you fucking kidding me?"

"Not in the slightest," Eyes said, looking grim and disgusted. "I spoke to Warden Measures at the penitentiary. She claims she knew nothing about the releases. Said the POTUS and his decisions are above her paygrade. Besides, her hands are full investigating recent inmate crimes.

"Get this," Eyes continued, "there was a fire in the basement that almost forced an entire building evacuation. Firefighters found strange skeletons the size of large guinea pigs in what appears to have been a discreet laboratory. To boot, a prison guard named Lyle Owens is missing, as are two inmates: Dan Gregory and Kendrick Judd. Human bones have been discovered in a basement incinerator." He paused. "I'm curious: what page are you on?"

"On the page," Clay answered, "that says the warden's career is over. On the page that points to the mad scientist as Dr. Crazy, the one responsible for Irene Unger's bizarre recovery. The one guilty of the prison crimes. We both know how Em loves to love his human test-subjects...to death."

"Same page I'm on," Eyes said, nodding. "But we've got to tread carefully. Let's not forget the dangers of exposing a corrupt President. Been there, done that. Listen, if Ruby returns anytime soon, have her call me. Right away. Under no circumstances should she try and deal with this situation without backup she can trust. Seriously."

The page they were on had clearly been torn from a horror novel.

70

Friday, July 12, 2041
Cedar Lane: Annapolis, Maryland

RUBY COULD NOT contain her excitement as she and Gabby traveled to Cedar Lane to reunite with Clay and their dogs.

Zagan was defeated.

The planets would remain separate—no more cullings.

Her family would be safe. Together. Ready to resume life in Spencer fashion—albeit in an endearingly atypical and diverse style.

With Gabby's hand in hers, they materialized on the front lawn.

The day was sunny and hot, with a steady southeast breeze.

Where their house once stood, footings had been installed and gravel laid. A concrete truck with its rotating mixing drum was releasing its load, pouring their new home's slab foundation.

Ruby scented her husband and turned to look behind her.

Clay was talking to someone about a lumber delivery.

Wearing a hard hat, he glanced in their direction. He threw off his hat, dropped his clipboard, and ran toward them. Mai and Zoe bounded after him in a gallop.

All of them collided on the grass. Hugging, laughing, and crying. The dogs licked and wagged.

Home-sweet-home was found in the arms of those who held you. With those who claimed you in their pack.

After freeing Clay from his glamours, they huddled on the lawn, sitting crisscross and facing each other. Her husband had a lot of questions and she and Gabby did their best to answer them.

"But why didn't you stay human?" he asked. "You've been hoping for it since you were turned."

"I know the answer, Dad," Gabby said. "She wants to *be* a miracle, instead of expecting one."

"Do you remember why else?" Ruby asked her.

"There's still a lot of work to do on Earth, using Mom's gifts. Mine, too. Like making sure the animals recover."

"Anyway," Ruby said, "since you've planted the sprout of The Tree of Awareness on Great Island, the choice to become mortal will exist in the future, once the tree matures and bears fruit."

I hope you understand my decision, she whispered into Clay's mind.

"Some miracles are meant to be shared," he said, reaching out with his hand and touching her cheek.

She inched toward him and his breath touched her skin.

Butterflies took flight in her stomach.

Brushing her lips over his, she teased before kissing him and parting his lips.

They kissed deeply, forgetting their surroundings.

"Gross, Mom and Dad," Gabby squealed. "Get a hotel!"

Ruby winked at her husband. *Who am I to argue?* she whispered into his thoughts. *Tonight, at the Westin Annapolis.*

"You guys need some alone time," their daughter said, using air quotes for *alone.* "I'm going to play with the dogs."

Giggling, Gabby ran off with Mai and Zoe trailing her.

Ruby's smartwatch chimed with a vext from President Unger.

She had hoped for a little downtime before being called into service, but the POTUS sounded anxious. His message, urgent.

President Unger needed Ruby at the White House, ASAP.

The First Lady had been cured of cancer, but now Irene was having "an episode." An episode that had forced the POTUS to lock her in their bathroom. He was hoping for discretion in resolving the situation, preferring not to get the staff involved. Besides, he wanted Ruby's expert opinion on what was happening to his wife.

"I hadn't gotten to the news about Irene Unger yet," Clay said. "She may be cancer free, but the situation is over-the-top disturbing on way too many levels."

He shared what Eyes had reported in their earlier videoface.

"Eyes smells a skunk. Namely, the mad scientist," Clay added. "And he specifically told me that you should absolutely *not*, under any circumstances, get involved without backup. Which means you shouldn't go to the White House alone."

"Nonsense," she said. "After what Gabby and I have been through, I can handle 'an episode' with the First Lady in a White House bathroom. And who knows? My response to his summons may help mend fences between us."

"Then take me with you."

"I'll be quick in, quick out," she promised. "Besides, my immediate future is carved in stone. So it's all good."

"But I just got you back."

"This is why I chose to remain a vampire: to respond when there's a need or threat. To serve others more than myself. And that *doesn't* include putting you at risk."

She planted another kiss on his lips, reminding him there would be more to come that night.

"Please stay with Gabby," she said. "And in an hour, I'll return. Right here."

Her body swirled into dust.

As she traveled to the White House, her heart swelled with joy.

She was the happiest being in all the universe.

ૹ End of Book 2 ଓ

ACKNOWLEDGMENTS

I LOVED EVERY second of creating and writing THE TETHER, including working with an awesome team who supports my efforts.

First to readers of my debut, THE ONE AND ONLY: your enthusiasm for Ruby Spencer and her high-stakes efforts to save humankind keeps me energized and committed to improving my storytelling. Thank you for supporting my work.

Once again, my husband Rick listened word-for-word as I read my first draft of THE TETHER. He is my greatest cheerleader and my heart is grateful for him every single day.

I dedicated THE TETHER to my daughter Brooke who devours fantasy books as fast as I eat cheese puffs. As I created the world of Athanasia and the vampire "gifts" which affect the planet's society, she helped pinpoint areas to be strengthened. In addition, she is a masterful storyteller herself, and I truly appreciated her feedback.

My son Mitchell and daughter-in-law Stacey continually encourage me and appreciate my work. I'm extremely grateful.

My beta readers are fantastic—that's all caps FANTASTIC! As we journey together from one book to the next, their feedback keeps getting more insightful. My heartfelt gratitude is extended to the best of the best: Dena Baker, Deborah Faroe, Jed Faroe, Martha Mitchell, and Cheryl Tomlinson. Thank you for your impactful feedback.

As my proofreader, Charlene Sharpe was a wonderful addition to the team. I am so thankful for her expertise and awesomeness.

Once again, author and developmental editor Kerrie Flanagan was an integral member of my team. Kerrie pushes and challenges me to be the best writer and storyteller I can be. An all-around expert and professional, Kerrie is frank, encouraging, and kind. What better combination is there for a book mentor? With her guidance, THE TETHER has emerged into a stronger novel. She is AMAZING!

Thank you to *Damonza.com* for another intriguing cover. WOW!

To those who took the time to post a book review on Amazon, Goodreads, Barnes and Noble, and/or Kobo, you melt my heart. Your added efforts help with the success and visibility of my work. You are deeply, deeply appreciated!

WHAT IS NEXT…

RUBY SPENCER'S STORY CONTINUES
in the third installment
of The ELI Chronicles, to be released in 2020.

The
Turning Point

ಐ ೕ ಐ ೕ

For updates on
THE TURNING POINT
visit: https://juliaashbooks.wordpress.com

ABOUT THE AUTHOR

JULIA ASH is author of the dark-fantasy series: The ELI Chronicles. Her debut novel, THE ONE AND ONLY, was published in 2018. The second installment, THE TETHER, will be followed by a third, THE TURNING POINT, planned for release in 2020.

Ash lives with her husband Rick and two Brittany bird-dogs on Maryland's Eastern Shore.

For a complete biography, please visit her website. And please join her on social media.

Website:
https://juliaashbooks.wordpress.com

Facebook:
Facebook.com/JuliaAsh.Books

Twitter:
@Author_JuliaAsh

Instagram:
julia.ash.books

Goodreads:
Goodreads.com/julia_ash

Author Photograph by Sarah Murray Photography

Reviews

Please consider providing a star rating
(with or without a written review) of

The Tether
by Julia Ash

Vendors make it easy to give reviews
on the novel's detail page
(the online page where you purchased the book).

Authors appreciate reviews more than you know.

Thank you!

PRONUNCIATIONS

ATEA: **Ate**-*uh*

ATHANASIA: **Ath**-in-**ey**-zh*uh* (*Ath* rhymes with *math*)

DEPE: **D***eh*-pee

DRAVEN: **Dray**-vin

KALIMÉRA: **Kal**-lah-**mare**-*ah* (*Kal* rhymes with *gal*)

KAIKOMAKO: **Kay**-k*oh*-**may**-k*oh*

LAMPSI: **Lamp**-zee

LIORA: **Lee**-or-r*ah*

MEGA-ANNUM: M*eh*-**gan**-numm (*gan* rhymes with *ran*)

MAI: **My**

NEVIAH: **Niv**-vee-*ah* (*Niv* rhymes with *give*)

OZUL: Oh-**zoo**-ull (*ull* rhymes with *full*)

SOLANGE: **So**-lawn-j*uh*

SKOTADI: **Skoh**-tay-dee

TITUS: **Tie**-Tis

ZAGAN: **Zay**-gin (*gin* rhymes with *win*)